*The Private
Misadventures
of Nell Nobody*

The Private Misadventures of Nell Nobody

JENNIFER NEWBOLD

LUMINARE PRESS
WWW.LUMINAREPRESS.COM

Dedicated to all my heroes,
and to H.N., my North Star

Author's Note

Although members of the 69th Regiment of Foot did in fact serve as marines onboard HMS Agamemnon in the Mediterranean, the premise that there were riflemen in the regiment is fiction. The Experimental Rifle Corps, which used the more practical Baker rifle, was not formed until 1800.

Whilst unusual, it is possible to find documented evidence of women, disguised as men, serving in the armies and navies of the time. Although it was officially forbidden, it is likely that other soldiers or sailors knew the true gender of these individuals; if they were good at what they did and didn't create problems within the ranks, it may have been disregarded. Men with no sea experience at all were sometimes pressed when shortages of seamen became extreme, so a person with skill, even if he was of suspicious masculinity, may have been invaluable.

Although much of this story is based upon historical events, my interpretation of those events is my own invention. Many of the officers and others referred to in this work were actual people, and I hope that I have treated them fairly. Captain of Marines Raleigh Spencer, however, is entirely fictitious.

As is Captain Nelson's amanuensis.

'... I'll 'list as a rifleman and wear a cap of blue...'

'The Banks of the Nile'
— English Folk Song

Chapter One

My name was once Eleanor Buccleuch. My family called me Nell, but you must never call me that. To you, my name is Ned. Ned Buckley.

Nell Buccleuch is dead. I have buried her someplace I hope no one will ever think to look.

Someone is searching for me, you see. If I ever go back to England, it will be in a coffin.

After nearly two weeks of being bashed about by waves off the coast of Corsica, my mess and I disembark at St Fiorenzo on 7 February 1794. Jack Mackay has been violently seasick for so long that I wasn't sure he was going to live to see dry land.

We were never intended for marines, but there weren't enough of them in the Mediterranean, so here we are. We've been on the *Tartar* frigate since November. Back in England, we had been part of a rifle detachment.

The boat carrying us ashore wallows in the rough sea. I'd never expected to go to sea for any longer than it took to travel to Gibraltar. I don't know what the others expected. I never asked them.

Behind me, Mackay retches again. We have heard it so often that none of us really take any notice. It isn't as though there's anything we can do for him.

———————————

We bivouac on a nasty strip of beach, whilst the officers in charge try to decide what to do with us. Did they not have a plan in place before they dumped us here? They might have figured it out whilst we were being blown all the way to Elba; they had plenty of time.

I am soaked and frozen, and my messmates must be, too, but the relief of finally being off that damned ship overcomes any tendency to be sullen. That, and the anticipation of action. Tom Sharpe wipes his wet hair out of his eyes and grins at me.

Eventually the command overcomes their inertia, and we begin to inch forward. Ordnance, supplies, and canvas get offloaded and dragged into position, in preparation to attack the forts at St Fiorenzo. This is what the army does, and there is nothing particularly momentous about these preparations, but to me it feels almost like the advance of the Roman Legion. Not that, with approximately 1400 of us, we are anything even remotely approaching legion. Far from it.

This is my first siege. No; actually, this is my first real military engagement. My nerves and sinews feel as though there is a vibration coursing along them, not unlike the way the ground trembles when a group of horsemen thunder past. It is not anxiety, exactly; I know what that feels like. I think this is excitement. We are about to put the rifle and artillery drills of the past year to the test.

I read in one of my father's books that the great General Wolfe told his troops at the Plains of Abraham, '*The officers and men will remember what their country expects from them, and what a determined body of soldiers, inured to war, is capable of doing against five weak French battalions mingled with disorderly peasantry.'* I cannot say that I have any idea what it feels like to be 'inured to war,' but I am about to find out how I react under fire. If a bullet finds me, or a cannonball rips off my head, then, like Wolfe, I have nothing more to worry about.

––––––––––

The six of us in my mess form a rifle squad that gets sent ahead of the foot soldiers and artillery to cover their advance. It is not like fighting in close order; we do not advance in lines. We move as a loose unit, and we move fast. Under the command of Will Fowler, our acting corporal, we are practically autonomous.

To protect our artillery piece, not only do we have to try to take the French by surprise but draw their fire as well. It's a race from one position to the next.

We were trained to target their officers. I quickly learn that there is an element of demoralisation that affects the line regardless of who gets shot. If men are falling all around you, their rank ceases to be of much significance.

Will Fowler signals us to move. We sprint across uneven ground; my heart pounds to the rhythm of my feet. Behind us, I hear the line open a volley, and a field gun bellows. I am only remotely aware of all this. My only objective is getting to our next position.

Just as I am about to reach the stand of trees that is our goal, I see Billy Baxter hit the ground ahead of me. He flips over his own shoulder and lands on his back, and I have to dig in my heels to keep from running over him.

He rolls and gets back on his feet as I grab his rifle. Something whines past me.

'Go! GO!' Baxter shouts. The French have sighted us.

He can't run. He tries to put weight on his leg and staggers.

It is only about twenty yards to the trees. I shove his rifle at him and drop to one knee. 'You go—I'll cover you!'

I see the man who fired at us. He is reloading his musket as quickly as he can. He withdraws the rammer and sockets it smoothly home.

I sight down the length of my gun. As the French soldier brings his Charleville to his shoulder, my finger tightens on the trigger. The Frenchman takes aim, and I fire.

I saw his eyes. He knew that I had him; I was just a split second ahead of him. The barrel of his gun jerks skyward as his body spins away, a bullet in his left shoulder.

I run like mad.

Billy Baxter did not get shot. 'My foot landed in a bloody hole,' he tells Fowler.

Jack Mackay and Tom Sharpe are firing from a shallow rise in front of us as the gun crews advance. Bertram is reloading at the edge of the copse.

'You stay here and harass them from the trees,' Fowler tells Billy. 'We'll collect you on our way back. Buckley, you're with Bert. Good shooting.'

The guns are established and dug in for the night. The army has managed to push the French back a few hundred yards towards St Fiorenzo.

'D'you think you've killed any of them?' Jack asks, as we sit near the cooking fire in the darkness. The days are not that bad, but it gets cold at night. I am glad of my wool blanket.

'I've not really thought about it,' I tell him. 'I know that I've hit some of them. Does the idea bother you?'

'I'm not sure.' He pulls his blanket closer around his shoulders. 'It's war. We shoot at them; they shoot at us. Some of us are bound to die, so it stands to reason that some of them will die, too...'

'Yes,' I say.

We let the subject drop.

It has been twelve days. I record in my journal, *'Today marks the fall of St Fiorenzo. One of the French frigates in the harbour is burning, and the navy has taken the other into its fleet. The French are fleeing into the hills. We have done it!'* Twelve days that passed in a blur of powder and smoke. I saw some men wounded, but no one killed, and my mess survived unscathed, apart from Baxter's turned ankle. We're set to pursue the French over the hills towards Bastia, propelled by the momentum of victory.

It doesn't exactly work that way. On 23 February, we reach the summit, and there we halt. We wait, whilst the officers confer. And then, inexplicably, we are told to retreat. We return to St Fiorenzo to sit on our hands for the next three weeks.

We're finishing our evening meal when the officers appear. The sun is sinking, and the mosquitos are starting to buzz. Billy Baxter slaps at one on the back of his hand and his palm comes away smeared with his own blood. 'Shit,' he says in disgust.

The two officers are looking at our mess and talking between them. I recognise Captain Clark. I haven't seen him since Gibraltar. Our mess went to the *Tartar*, but Captain Clark was on the *Agamemnon*. He is talking to a man who I realise, with a start, is Lieutenant Colonel Villettes.

Tom Sharpe pokes me with his elbow and nods in their direction. 'They 'as lookin' at you, Neddy.'

'No, they weren't,' I retort, but my gut clenches. What would these officers want with me, unless someone has guessed my secret?

For the first eight weeks after I joined the 69th, I said very little. I drilled, and mustered, and followed orders. And I observed.

I had no sisters. I have one brother, and we were very close until he was sent away to school. I learnt a great deal of unladylike things from, and alongside, Arthur. We remained close even after his marriage, until our world began to come apart at the seams.

I remember riding from Surrey to Brighton with Arthur when we were both in our teens. I was riding astride, in breeches, and had a borrowed saddle that did not fit me. When we stopped for the night, Arthur observed with amusement, 'Nell, you walk like a man!'

'You try riding with that horrible saddle tomorrow,' I snapped. But remembering that experience reminded me how to walk 'like a man.'

I cannot say how successful I have been at becoming a chameleon, but I have seen no indication that any of my messmates suspect me. That does not mean that someone else does not.

'I think they are, Ned,' says Jack Mackay softly. He is the quietest of us all, except for Bertram, who rarely says anything at all, so he doesn't count. Jack's eyelashes are long and pretty, and if I were still who I used to be, they would make me jealous.

Captain Clark strides towards our fire. We all jump to attention. 'Edmund Buckley.'

'Sir.' I try to keep my voice steady. It wants to waver like marsh grass in a breeze.

'Come with us, Buckley.'

My messmates don't dare look apprehensive, but I can feel it. Each one of them is wound as tight as a watch spring. I clench my jaw and step forward.

Captain Clark looks at my companions. 'Relax, men. He will come back to you on his own feet.'

Meaning they do not intend to beat me... or drum me out of the army. He leads me away from the others.

Colonel Villettes greets me with, 'Captain Clark tells me you write a fair hand.'

'Yessir.' I try to remember when Captain Clark had seen anything that I had written.

'And you are trained with artillery.'

'I was on an artillery crew until they reassigned me to a rifle unit, sir.'

'You've been on HMS *Tartar.*'

'Yessir.'

'There is someone we want you to meet.'

Captain Clark and Colonel Villettes lead me down to the bay. There is another clutch of officers standing on the mole, all red coats except for one. I recognise Lieutenant Colonel Moore and General D'Aubant, among others. Clark isn't taking me *there,* is he? He is.

The other man is obviously a naval captain. His dark blue coat sports gold lace that gleams in the setting sun, and his fair hair creates a glowing nimbus around his face where it emerges from under his hat. He and the others are having an animated discussion, but the navy man is more animated than the rest. There's an energy about him that fairly vibrates, compared to the army officers. The other thing that sets him

9

apart is how much smaller he is than the army men. He can't be very much taller than I am, and he is as slender as a reed.

Clark and Villettes march me straight for this group of officers. My heart wants to climb into my throat.

One of the army officers gestures in our direction with his chin, and the navy captain turns around.

Villettes steers me into this knot of men and addresses the captain. 'Captain Nelson, this is Edmund Buckley. We think he will serve you well.'

I feel like a suspect horse being offered at auction. Everyone is inspecting me critically.

Captain Nelson has a startlingly boyish face, with a long nose and a rounded, narrow chin. With the sun behind him, his hair is almost as bright as the lace on his coat. His lively blue eyes meet mine, and I sense a quick mind behind them.

'Mr Buckley,' he says. His voice is rather thin, and higher than I expected. There's a hint of a drawl in the way he says 'mister'. He indicates that I should come with him with a jerk of his head. 'Walk with me.' Without looking to see if I am following, he stalks off in the direction of the town. I glance at Clark and Villettes, then hurry to catch up.

He slows his pace a little when I reach him. He looks over at me. 'Edmund Buckley.'

'Ned, sir.'

'Do you not like "Edmund"?'

'No one ever calls me that, sir.'

'Well, I do not intend to call you that, either. I shall call you Mr Buckley.'

'Yessir.' He could call me Guy Fawkes if he wanted to. I'm not going to argue with him.

'My first name is Horatio. But I am not inviting you to call me that. I am only called that by my family.'

'Nosir. I mean, yessir.'

'Those gentlemen,' he says, referring to the officers on the mole, 'think that I need a liaison to handle communications between themselves and me. I agreed because we are going to be at Bastia, and most of them intend to stay in St Fiorenzo. I will need you to bring dispatches and so forth to them here in St Fiorenzo, because I am going to be too busy to come here myself.' He stops walking and looks me up and down. 'Have you seen action, Mr Buckley?'

'I fought in the siege of St Fiorenzo, sir. As a rifleman, although I trained with an artillery company initially.'

'Perfect,' says Captain Nelson. 'I don't expect this will take very long, perhaps no longer than it took to take St Fiorenzo. Then you should be free to return to your rifle company.'

'Very good, sir.' We're a squad, not a company. Not even a unit. But it isn't my place to correct him, and I'm sure he doesn't care.

'Go back to your camp and get your kit. Bring it back here, then you will come with me on *Agamemnon*.'

***

I hurry back to camp. The sun is low; it's going to be dark soon.

Most of my mess has scattered, but Jack Mackay is still there by the fire, carving a little horse with his knife. Jack carves beautiful wooden animals. He gave me a lion rampant when we first joined the *Tartar*. That was before the sea got so rough that some days he could hardly sit up without vomiting. He looks up with questioning eyes.

'They're attaching me to some sea captain,' I tell him, 'to act as his secretary, sort of. "Liaison", they're calling me. But it sounds like I'm to be a dispatch runner.'

Jack shudders. 'You're going back to sea?'

'Only around Cape Corse. As far as Bastia. It sounds like the rest of you will be following any day.'

He blanches.

'Oh, Jacky. Don't worry,' I say softly. 'It can't be as bad as before, and even if it was, it's a short voyage.'

'I think that the sea will kill me, Ned.'

'Nonsense. You made it all the way from England. And that wasn't so bad. It was just a rough patch on the way here to Corsica. Buck up, Mackay.' I punch him gently on the shoulder.

'Easy for you to say, Buckley.' But he punches me back.

I grab my kit out of our tent and prepare to make my way back down to the harbour. Mackay sits by the fire with his knife again, but his face is long.

'Jack, tell the others where I've gone.'

'I will, Ned.'

'See you soon.' He lifts a hand as I shoulder my rifle and head back to the bay and my new assignment.

There's a barge waiting, and I take my place in the stern with Captain Nelson whilst his coxswain commands the sailors with the oars. A wind from the ocean ruffles the captain's hair, and thankfully blows the blasted mosquitos away as the barge takes us out into the bay. HMS *Agamemnon* rides at anchor about a third of a mile out.

Captain Nelson doesn't speak as the oars flash and dip. I sit silently beside him and mentally compare him with Captain Fremantle.

Fremantle is a bluff, sturdy man; good-natured, but a hard disciplinarian with his seamen. Although it is hardly an uncommon punishment in the army, I'd not seen a man flogged before I shipped on *Tartar*. Now, I've seen my share.

He also has strong opinions. I'd heard some things when I was posted as sentry outside his cabin, things that I know far better than to repeat. I have never met Lord Hood, but I have a pretty comprehensive picture of him thanks to Captain Fremantle. It isn't entirely complimentary.

In contrast, Captain Nelson is slight, quiet, and brisk. His hair, I see, is not the gold I had thought it in the light of the setting sun, but more the colour of beach sand where it meets the ocean. He looks impossibly young for a post-captain. I try to assess his age; even accounting for his rank, he can't be very much more than twenty-five, maybe twenty-eight.

Captain Nelson addresses me. I thought he did not intend to speak in front of his barge crew, but apparently he was just waiting until we were away from the shore and my superiors.

'We have been blockading Bastia since the army arrived in St Fiorenzo,' he tells me. 'We've been successful in severely disrupting their supply lines, and there are growing shortages of food and munitions. The French soldiers that flooded the town after St Fiorenzo fell are compounding the problems. I am told that morale is poor and getting worse.

'I expected the army to attack from the ridge after we took St Fiorenzo, but nothing happened, and we lost our advantage.' He glances at me, as if waiting for an explanation.

'I expected it too, sir. We couldn't figure out why they marched us up there and then told us to turn around and go back to St Fiorenzo,' I volunteer, then wonder if I ought to have spoken.

'I could not initially myself,' he admits, 'but now I'm getting a better picture of how your command's minds work.' There is a dry tone to his voice that surprises me. I did not expect this officer to be candid with me. I'm a nobody.

He looks at me again and says perceptively, 'I told them that if I was going to accept their proposal to work with a liaison, I needed someone with intelligence. They told me that they couldn't spare any subalterns, and I said that I was not going to let them saddle me with some clodhopper who needed constant direction. I expect you to use your mind and be discreet.'

'Yessir.'

'It will be more difficult now, since the French have managed to reinforce the heights, but with good cooperation between the army and navy, it can be done; I am sure of it. I need you to help foster that cooperation, because some of your commanders are not inclined to be agreeable.'

How am I to do that? I wonder. I wouldn't presume to speak to these officers, and they would not condescend to speak to me. I have managed to keep my head down for almost a year; this is going to make that much more challenging.

'Just be respectful, Mr Buckley, and be perceptive,' he says. 'I am counting on you to gauge their responsiveness.'

Onboard *Agamemnon*, Captain Nelson turns me over to the Sergeant of Marines, a rat-faced man with crooked teeth. 'Assign Mr Buckley a hammock for a few days,' he says. 'When we go ashore at Bastia, he will not need it any longer.'

'Sir.' The sergeant acknowledges this order. He turns to me. 'Come with me, lad.'

'Come to my cabin tomorrow at six bells of the morning watch, Mr Buckley,' Captain Nelson tells me, as the sergeant starts to lead me away.

'Yessir.' I salute him briefly and follow the Sergeant of Marines down the companionway to the lower gun deck.

'You pretty much got your choice where to sling it,' he informs me, pointing; 'So long as it's here, or here.' He gives me a smile as crooked as his teeth. 'What has the captain to do with you, anyways?'

'I think I'm his new errand boy,' I say. 'Captain Clark and Colonel Villettes assigned me to him.'

'Oy. That's strange. Why you?'

'I wish I knew,' I mutter.

Chapter Two

As ordered, in the morning I present myself at Captain Nelson's quarters at six bells. The sentry at the door isn't allowed to react, but I can feel the man studying me. He stands aside to let me pass.

I am not sure what I expected, but it wasn't this. The captain's dining table is laid for breakfast, and there are a half a dozen men in the room. Captain Nelson springs up from his chair and says briskly, 'Mr Buckley. Thank you for joining us.'

'I… I'm sorry, sir, if I am late.' I stand frozen by the door.

'You are not late. I asked these gentlemen to come a little beforehand.' He takes my shoulder and steers me into the room. 'Introductions, gentlemen.' He indicates the men seated around the table, starting with the man on his right.

'Midshipman Withers, our schoolmaster, and my clerk.' A young man of about twenty-five or six nods to me. 'Frank Lepee, coxswain, and my steward. Mr Lepee and I go back to my time in the Leeward Islands. Lieutenant Andrews. I knew his family in St. Omer, in France. Midshipman Hoste; a Norfolk man, like myself.' A very young man with a round face gives me a broad smile. 'And my son-in-law, Midshipman Nisbet.' This boy looks even younger. 'This is Master John Wilson.' The master is the oldest man in the room, probably older than the captain, although surely Captain Nelson is older than he looks. 'And this, gentlemen, is Mr Buckley, my new secretary.'

He says it proudly. *Secretary.* Probably a highly glorified term for what he will call upon me to do. He directs me to the vacant seat on his left. 'Have a seat, Mr Buckley.'

I take the proffered chair, the only red coat in a sea of blue. I hope that I am not the same colour as my coat.

Servants uncover the dishes. There is coffee and soft bread, butter, bacon, fish, and pickle. There is stewed fruit. And Canary wine. This is the first time I have seen an officer's table, and I am astonished.

Captain Nelson says a prayer of thanksgiving for the food, then asks a blessing upon it. The other men wait for the captain to begin, then everyone falls to their meal with gusto.

The conversation around the table is casual, with every man talking to his tablemates between bites. Captain Nelson doesn't say much. 'Have more of this bacon, before it is gone,' he says to me in an undertone. 'It is excellent.'

The master, on my left, speaks kindly to me. 'Don't be uncomfortable, son. You'll get used to it. Don't mind the colour of the coats.'

'Thank you, sir,' I whisper. I am afraid to raise my voice.

It is a strange circumstance. In my former life, I was the hostess at table, and my husband's guests were at least as distinguished as these men, dining on delicacies and multiple courses. But since I ran away, my dining companions have been the most common of folk. I keep my mouth shut and concentrate on my manners, covertly watching how the other men behave. If anyone wonders why Captain Nelson chose a common soldier as his 'secretary', they are too correct to ask.

After the breakfast is over, everyone rises to go about his duty. I hover uncertainly by the door until Captain Nelson motions to me. 'Come to my cabin, Mr Buckley.'

Above, I hear the boatswain pipe 'all hands.' Captain Nelson wears a satisfied expression. 'Ah, good. The wind is favourable this morning. We're weighing.' He opens the door that connects his small dining room to the great cabin.

The room is fairly sparse, with a table and some straight-backed chairs, a couple of trunks, and his berth above a locker on one side. He directs me to the table. There is a coal-fired brazier, which startles me. In addition to the favourable wind, there is rain this morning, and the air is damp and slightly chilly. Captain Nelson takes the chair closest to the brazier and rubs his hands together. 'I feel the damp and cold profoundly,' he explains. 'This is one benefit of being the captain.' I nod solemnly.

'I wanted you to become acquainted with those men, and they with you. You will undoubtedly have interactions with them. So, Mr Buckley. I need to be honest with you about our situation.'

'Sir?' I thought he had been remarkably frank yesterday evening.

'It took me the work of the devil to convince your masters to undertake this siege. Lord Hood insists that we attempt this land assault, but General Dundas and Colonel Moore have convinced themselves that it will fail. General D'Aubant is even worse than Dundas, refusing to commit men or materiel. Fortunately, Colonels Villettes and Wemyss agree with me, and Captain Clark supports me as well.'

'You said last night that you believe it can be done, sir.'

'I did; and I do. But the army is not inclined to be help-ful. I am hopeful that if my dispatches are delivered by one of their own, hand-picked by Captain Clark and Colonel Villettes, it will facilitate cooperation. They are not likely to want to respond to me directly. Your presence will necessitate that they address me sooner rather than later.' He searches my face, finds the doubt there.

'Have confidence, Mr Buckley. Confidence works wonders.'

It takes just over two days to round Cape Corse. We lose our wind for a while during the afternoon of the first day, then again that evening, but between we make good time. Captain Nelson is proud of *Agamemnon*. 'She's a remarkably good sailer,' he tells me. 'She can make ten knots before the wind.'

Three days later, north of Bastia, we are at work on the first ridge planned for a battery, making it ready for the guns.

The fleet arrives on 3 April.

I pause and set my paperwork aside to ascend the hillside, observing. The British fleet, spread out along the Bastia coast, is magnificent.

HMS *Victory* flies a flag of truce, and as we watch from the heights, a boat pulls out. Whatever parley occurs in the town is quickly determined. The boat returns, the white flag is hauled down, and a red one is run up the mainmast in its place. Bastia has refused to surrender. Captain Nelson's plan is about to be tested.

I find my messmates on the evening of 4 April. I have to take a certain amount of ribbing from Sharpe and Baxter. Bertram is as taciturn as usual, and Jack Mackay just looks fagged. But everyone wants to hear about my assignment to Captain Nelson.

'Why th' devil did they choose you, Ned Buckley?' asks Fowler, our *de facto* corporal.

'I don't know, Will. I think because they couldn't come up with a better candidate.'

Jack Mackay and I are the least senior in the mess, so we always sleep on the end of the tent near the entrance. Fowler, the most senior man, gets the spot at the back of the tent where no one getting up for a piss in the middle of the night will step on him. Fowler never gets up in the night. He must have a bladder like a horse.

Jack and I usually take turns being the man next to the tent pole and the door flaps. If it rains or blows, that man almost always gets damp or cold, and is the most likely to get stepped on. I offer to take the pole tonight. In addition to being the most junior, I'm also the smallest in the mess, so there's less of me to step on.

'How are you, Jacky?' I whisper when Baxter's snoring is shaking the tent walls.

'I'm alright, Ned,' he says tiredly. 'I only puked once this time.'

'See? You're getting used to it.'

He sighs. 'I'll never get used to it,' he says.

Captain Nelson has been maintaining the blockade of Bastia offshore since we returned on 22 March, but on 3 April he had come ashore and personally supervised the off-loading of men, stores, and equipment during the hours of darkness with Colonel Villettes. I'd left him the previous night, springing between loads of ordnance, counting and conferring and muttering to himself. 'I'm going to need you in the morning, Mr Buckley,' he'd told me as he sent me off. 'Get some sleep and come to me at dawn. I expect to be up on the ridge.'

Building the batteries is gruelling, backbreaking work. The sea-service gun carriages with their little wooden trucks are next to impossible to manoeuvre on land, but somehow the sailors manage it. The redoubts are constructed of sandbags and wooden casks, and each has to be filled with earth and sand. The sailors haul endless barrels of powder and tons of shot and shells up to the ridge, and gun platforms are installed behind the breastworks. My duties are primarily in the camp behind the batteries, whilst Captain Nelson seems to be everywhere.

I am in the medical tent, inventorying medical supplies with a surgeon's mate, when the sailor comes in, his left hand cradled in the crook of his right arm. All the bones in his hand are crushed.

'Gun slipped,' he says to the surgeon, between clenched teeth. 'Big twenty-four-pound bastard.'

The surgeon drugs him insensible with opium and manipulates the bones in the hand, but it's hopeless. The sight of that flaccid, swollen, lumpy hand, like a glove filled with mud, makes me queasy. The mate is wrapping it in strips of linen when Captain Nelson bounds into the surgical tent.

The surgeon shrugs his shoulders and shakes his head. 'Nothing I can do,' he says. 'When he comes out of the opium enough that he's not likely to choke on his own vomit, I'll have to amputate it.'

Captain Nelson has been unflappable in the face of setbacks and shortages, but now his expression turns black. 'Do what you must,' he says, then motions to me with a quick jerk of his head. I follow him to the wall tent where he is meant to sleep, but I have yet to see him do so. His blanket roll is still rolled up against one wall.

He sweeps his hat off and throws it on the ground, then kicks it savagely. 'Damn D'Aubant!' he snarls. 'If he could be bothered to supply just a few field carriages...' He stomps around the perimeter of the tent whilst I stand mute in the middle. Finally, he sinks down on a wooden sea chest and runs both hands through his hair. It sticks out like stuffing from a straw man. He looks at me and sighs heavily.

'It's a damned waste, Mr Buckley.'

'Yessir; it is.' *Oh, is it ever. That man has lost his hand.*

He lifts himself off the sea chest and opens the lid, extracting a bottle and a small footed glass. He pours a generous amount of amber liquid into the glass and gulps it down, coughs, and pours a smaller measure, which he offers to me. 'Brandy,' he says hoarsely.

I take the glass and hesitate. In my father's house, ladies didn't drink brandy except medicinally, and then barely more than a thimbleful. I have never swallowed this much brandy at one go in my life. I lift the glass and swallow it the way I have just seen him do.

My throat burns and my eyes are blinded momentarily with tears. 'Hnngh...' I gasp. I wipe my eyes on my sleeve and see him regarding me with an amused expression. 'I'm not much of a drinker, I'm afraid, sir,' I try to say. My voice sounds like my vocal cords are paralysed.

'Neither am I, Mr Buckley,' he confides. 'Once in a while, though, I find it necessary.' He picks up a pitcher from the ground beside the chest and refills the glass with water, then hands it back to me. After I swallow the water he takes the glass, pours himself a measure, and drinks it down.

'Now I am no longer likely to take off the head of the next man I meet.'

I cannot imagine Captain Nelson verbally savaging anyone. It is the first time I have seen the merest hint of the stress he must be under.

He puts the bottle and glass back into the chest and picks up his hat, thumping the dust from it and pounding it back into shape. 'Come, Mr Buckley. Back to work.'

In the afternoon, I am in the midst of checking a list of powder and shot when the sound of an explosion launches me to my feet. It is followed by a barrage of shells and shot from the French redoubt. Drums beat a frantic tattoo as men scatter, and I shove my lists into my waistcoat as I grab my Ferguson and cartridge box.

Our battery isn't ready to respond, but I slip into place behind the sandbags next to Bertram, who is already firing down on the French gun crews. We are not in a particularly good position to hit any of them, but we can make them nervous, at any rate.

A rifle shot pings off the dolphin of a French cannon, and the man with the linstock jumps and yelps. Bertram mutters, 'Take that, you frog-eating swine.' Bert so rarely says anything at all that I feel almost privileged to be party to this declaration.

I discover that although it isn't easy to target their gunners from this position, by hitting their redoubt just right I can throw up bits of earthworks that blind and cut, and make the loading and firing of their guns more difficult. If I can't take them out, at least I can slow them down.

The bombardment lasts for what feels like a long time. Bert runs out of cartridges first, and I divide up my remaining ones with him, but we're both out of ammunition before the barrage stops.

The French fire high. They don't damage our battery, but they tear up some of our tents in the camp behind.

When the firing stops and we take roll, everyone is accounted for. Later I find Captain Nelson standing outside his tent, talking to Colonel Villettes. There's a streak of dirt across his cheek and his hat is missing. Colonel Villettes walks away, and Captain Nelson turns towards me. 'Not a man injured!' he exclaims. 'By the grace of Almighty God!'

Two days later, we are ready. On the morning of 11 April, Lord Hood again sends a messenger under a flag of truce. We wait, silently, as the boat returns to the flagship; then we see the red flag ascend to the top of the main royal. A roar goes up from our batteries. The colours are raised above Nelson's tent to cheers, and our guns begin to pound the French positions.

It isn't all glorious. In the afternoon, one of the British frigates catches fire, having been hit by red-hot shot from a French tower. She burns to the waterline, the other ships powerless to help her. I see one of her officers talking to Nelson that evening. The man is burned and bandaged, but he has chosen to come to the batteries and fight. Captain Nelson touches the man's shoulder gently in a gesture of solidarity and friendship.

The following day, 12 April, I'm waiting for Captain Nelson to return from reconnoitring the ridge on which he hopes to put another battery. He expects me to write up his report and take one copy to the army command in St Fiorenzo, while he himself communicates with Lord Hood. Five men went up the ridge. Only four come back, and only three are walking. Lieutenant Duncan is carrying another soldier, assisted by Colonel Villettes. Nelson is covered in blood. So is the soldier in Lieutenant Duncan's arms. As they get nearer, I see that the unconscious soldier is Captain Clark. I race towards the group.

Captain Nelson clambers down to meet me. 'Are you hurt, sir?!' I exclaim.

'I am not. Run; alert the surgeons. Captain Clark is badly wounded.'

I run.

Cannon shot tore off Captain Clark's arm, and the Corsican partisan leader was killed when the ball ploughed into the midst of their group. I am horrified when I see the mutilated remains of Captain Clark's shoulder. It is only a glimpse, but it will remain with me forever. I stagger off down the hillside behind the surgeon's tent and am sick behind a scrubby bush.

When I make my way to Captain Nelson's tent, I find him sitting on the ground with his back against his trunk. He has cleaned his face, but not very thoroughly. His hair is stiff in places with Captain Clark's blood. Underneath the gore, his face looks pale.

I swallow. 'Sir?'

He looks up. 'Mr Buckley. Sit down, sir.'

I sink to the ground opposite him. He reaches behind him and retrieves the brandy bottle from the lid of the trunk. 'Do you need a glass?' he asks.

'Nosir.'

He uncorks the bottle and takes a swallow directly from its mouth, then holds it out to me.

I do the same. This time the burn of the brandy down my throat and into my belly is a welcome sensation. *Oh, God. Papa would kill me.*

Captain Nelson takes another drink from the bottle and offers it to me again, but when I shake my head, he re-corks it. 'Takes away the sour taste of the vomit,' he supplies.

'I am sorry, sir. You should not have had to see me do that.'

'I didn't. I was occupied elsewhere.'

'Oh.'

'Do you want to write up this report now?' he asks.

'If that's what you wish, Captain. But perhaps you want to wash and change first, sir?'

He looks down at his clothes. 'Do you know, I think we can write up the report tomorrow.'

When I join my mess for supper, they have all heard about what happened up on the ridge. Even Tom Sharpe is subdued. They give me the best piece of the pork, but I have no appetite. I let Billy have it.

It starts to rain after supper. I am on the end tonight, but the bit of rain that gets past the tent flaps doesn't bother me. I wish it could wash away the blood from my memory.

I feel the tears well up as Billy snores. Tom farts in his sleep. Salt pork and beans don't agree with him, but it's the rest of us who suffer for it.

This is the first time I have seen a man mangled so horribly; and someone whom I know, as well. I cry silently, trying to keep my horror and grief private, but the tears won't stop coming. I'm shaking with the effort of trying to suppress them. Beside me, Jack shifts, then reaches over and puts a hand on my shoulder. He doesn't say a word, just lets me cry.

Chapter Three

I n the morning, I write up Captain Nelson's report. He is brisk and business-like, and says nothing about the accident except to note that the Corsican chief was killed and Captain Clark gravely wounded. He survived the night, Captain Nelson reports.

I take the report over the back of the hills to St Fiorenzo. If the French outposts were not there, the route would be far shorter and less dangerous. I scramble down a ravine, sliding part-way unintentionally on the seat of my breeches, and remember Captain Nelson swearing, 'Damn D'Aubant!' I'm inclined to agree. I discover that the scree has made a deep scratch in the case of my compass, and the word that comes to mind once earned my brother a smack across the mouth.

By the time I get to St Fiorenzo, it is evening. I go to D'Aubant's headquarters, but the adjutant says that he is at supper. The man is eating his own supper, a piece of roast chicken and potato dumplings. It makes my mouth water. I ask if General D'Aubant will be back this evening, and the adjutant says he doubts it.

I leave the house that the officers have commandeered and go looking for the camp QM. He also is eating his supper, although it doesn't look as appealing as the adjutant's. He invites me to share it, though, and I accept gratefully. Trail rations will keep you alive, but that's about all.

The QM lets me sleep on the floor in his office for the night. He has a cot in the room behind.

Once, I slept on a straw mattress in the summer, and feathers in the winter. At the change of every season, the housekeeper oversaw the turning out of the mattresses; washing the feathers in the spring, seeing that the summer ticks were filled with fresh, fragrant straw. We had fine sheets, feather pillows, and soft woollen blankets.

In the last two years I have learnt to sleep wherever I lie. In the barracks we had wooden cots, and at sea, hammocks. Now we have a stout wool blanket, and the ground. The ground is actually preferable to the stone floor of the QM's office... no matter how I lie, the stones make my bones ache.

In the morning, I present myself again at the commander's office and give the report to the adjutant, who takes it in to General D'Aubant. I wait, standing alone in the outer room for nearly an hour, while D'Aubant composes a reply, which is delivered to me, sealed, by the adjutant.

I know this man is an officer, although his rank isn't apparent, and he outranks me. But his supercilious attitude gets under my skin. I do much the same job for Captain Nelson, and more, instead of sitting on my backside outside someone's office all day. I take the letter, salute the adjutant, and leave to make my way back over the hills to camp. So much for the idea that the command in St Fiorenzo will be pleased to receive me. I have been here twice now, and I haven't seen one of them.

The trip to St Fiorenzo and back takes essentially two days. I get back to camp in the late afternoon. I don't see Captain Nelson, and he isn't in the battery. I feel trepidation about approaching the surgeon's tent, but I tell myself to stop being a girl.

The surgeon's tent is quiet. There is a man having a cut in his calf dressed, but no other activity is evident. I set my jaw and look into the infirmary tent, half expecting but dreading to find Captain Clark's bed empty.

He is there, looking barely alive, but alive just the same. The surgeon's mate looks up and sees my red coat, and says, 'It's alright if you want to talk to him. I don't know if he'll hear you, but he'll know someone's there, just the same.'

I approach the cot. The whole right side of the captain's torso is bandaged, but there's an appalling amount of it missing. The place where his arm used to be is just empty space. I kneel next to the bed and pick up Captain Clark's left hand.

'Erm… hello, sir… it's Edmund Buckley. Ned. I mean… Private Buckley. I…' I swallow. 'I just wanted to say thank you for recommending me to Captain Nelson, sir. He's a good man. I like working for him.'

Captain Clark doesn't move at all. His chest rises and falls, but except for that he might be made of wax. I hold his limp hand and squeeze the fingers, trying to think of something else to say.

'I'm very sorry that this happened, Captain. I don't know you at all, but I think… I think you are a good man, too.'

I press my lips together hard to keep them from quivering. I put the captain's hand back down on the bed and nod to the surgeon's mate before walking out of the tent.

The surgeon sees me emerge. 'Is he going to live?' I ask.

'God knows, son.'

'What happened to the man with the crushed hand?'

'We amputated it. Sent him back to his ship. The ship's surgeon will look after the dressing; he'll have a better chance of fighting infection in the sick berth.' He gives me a searching look. 'This the first time you've seen what war can do to a man's body, soldier?'

I feel ashamed. 'Yessir.'

'Everybody has to have a first time. Don't let it eat at you. I hate to say it, but you'll begin to get used to it.'

I walk slowly back to Captain Nelson's tent. He still isn't there, but I see the engineer, Lieutenant De Butts. He tells me that Captain Nelson began building new batteries down by the shore yesterday, and that he is probably there. Lieutenant De Butts leads me on a sheltered but tortuous route down to the new batteries.

Nelson sees me arrive with the lieutenant and waves me over. 'Mr Buckley, you're back! Did you get a reply?'

'I did, sir, but it's sealed. I didn't see the general, only his adjutant.'

'Bah. That does not sound promising,' he muses. 'Hold on to it, I shall read it when I get back to camp.'

He gestures at the work going on around us. 'I intend to get five guns and a few mortars in here to fire on the tower at Toga,' he tells me animatedly. 'They will pay for burning Captain Serocold's ship!'

He walks with me back up the track to camp. 'I went to see Captain Clark this afternoon,' I tell him.

'I saw him this morning,' he says. 'Is he still hanging on?'

'Yessir. The surgeon says he cannot tell whether he'll recover, though. He didn't seem to know I was there when I talked to him.'

'Sometimes, when a man is so gravely wounded, he retreats into a place where we can't reach him,' Captain Nelson says quietly. 'I saw it in the hospital at Port Royal in Jamaica, when I was there during the American rebellion.'

'Did the injured man come back from… wherever he'd gone?'

'Not that time,' Nelson replies.

Outside his tent, he reads the letter from D'Aubant and his face closes. He crushes the letter in his fist. 'How can he keep denying us assistance…?!' he exclaims. 'I begin to think they *want* us to *fail!* These are the most unreasonable excuses I have ever heard!'

He looks like a thundercloud. 'Damn their eyes. We will win this fight one way or another, and we'll do it without them if we have to.' He smooths out the letter and folds it inside his coat. 'I am mindful that you have just walked all the way to St Fiorenzo and back, Mr Buckley. I release you for the evening.'

I'm on the inside tonight, which puts me between Jack and Tom. At least we didn't have beans for supper tonight. It hardly matters either way. I'm asleep almost as soon as I roll myself into my blanket.

———

Work continues on the shore batteries. Captain Clark doesn't die. He opens his eyes on the fourth day after the accident. Captain Nelson comes back from the surgeon's tent at noon with a rare smile on his face. 'He is awake, Mr Buckley!' he announces. If he continues to improve, the captain tells me, plans will be made to send him to Gibraltar and from there, home.

When not with Captain Nelson, I take my turn sniping at the French from the batteries and the rocks on the hills. The Corsican partisans are crack shots. They're rough, wild-looking men, and I can't understand them when they speak, but they seem to respect my skill with the Ferguson.

Sometimes the French fire musket shot back at us, but they haven't even come close to hitting any of us yet.

Captain Nelson has divided his gun crews into two shifts, and the guns work day and night. Bert and Billy are working on the night shift, so there's more room in the tent at night. I'm still the closest to the door, but now we don't have to sleep belly to bum anymore.

On 19 April, I am taking stock of a shipment of munitions from Naples that was dragged into camp this morning. The sailors all complain about the quality of the Neapolitan ordnance, but we have to use everything we can get. Nelson says that it doesn't matter what we hit the French with, as long as we keep hitting them.

I hear a shout and look up to see Captain Fremantle come into camp from the track to the shore batteries. Captain Nelson is with him, but he looks shaken. Both of them are a little dirty and dishevelled, and when they come abreast of me, I can see that the back of Captain Nelson's coat is black with blood.

'Mr Buckley,' says Captain Fremantle, 'will you see Captain Nelson to the surgeon?'

'I don't need assistance,' Captain Nelson says.

'Humour me, Horatio,' Captain Fremantle replies.

I walk with Captain Nelson to the surgeon's tent. 'What happened, sir?' I ask, a little anxiously.

'We took a shortcut,' Nelson answers. 'It was a little too exposed.' He laughs shakily. 'Fremantle vowed he will never take the shortcut again.'

The surgeon and his mate help Captain Nelson out of his coat. There is a slice, made by a flying fragment of rock, through the wool of the coat, through his waistcoat and his shirt, and into the flesh of his back. It is an ugly cut, but not dangerous. 'I have ruined another coat,' Nelson observes ruefully.

The wound having been cleaned, treated, and dressed, Captain Nelson has to walk back through the camp to his tent bare-chested, with a blanket over his narrow shoulders. I carry his bloody coat, shirt, and waistcoat. It generates a lot of attention.

He reassures everyone that he is fine; nothing serious, nothing to worry about. He goes into the tent, dresses in fresh clothes, then re-emerges and goes back to work. In the evening, though, he looks tired and admits to feeling a little feverish. He actually retreats to his tent to sleep, and I lie awake for part of the night, vaguely worried. But in the morning, apart from moving a little stiffly, he looks the same as ever and bounds around with his usual energy again.

Dawn on 21 April witnesses the opening of the shore batteries. I am there with Captain Nelson as the big guns begin to roar. His eyes are alight as he shouts encouragement to the sailors manning the guns. I feel a sense of exhilaration when the first shots hit home. This is British might!

Lord Hood and Captain Nelson thought that Bastia would fall to us in about the same amount of time that it took to take St Fiorenzo. They were wrong. It has been almost a month, and the French still show no sign of surrendering.

'I don't understand it,' Captain Nelson mutters. 'What are they eating, dust?' A ship made it through the blockade last week. It was only a single ship, but it resupplied the town for a few more days.

Captain Nelson immediately began building new batteries on the ridge where Captain Clark was injured as soon as the seaside batteries began to operate. Getting the guns up there is the hardest job yet, and to complicate things, the site is exposed to fire from Camp Cabanelle.

The fag is beginning to tell on us all. Captain Nelson has lost little of his characteristic energy, but his spirits have suffered. He mutters about the lack of support from St Fiorenzo and the increasing sense of futility, even as our guns bellow day and night. 'For all our effort, we cannot do what an infantry assault from the heights would have done,' he complains. Another trip to St Fiorenzo has yielded nothing but the thinning of the soles of my boots. April turns to May, and the assault continues.

At night there is very little banter amongst the men in my mess. Bertram rarely says anything anyway, but now the rest of us are nearly as taciturn. Jack Mackay sits silently by the fire carving his latest wooden figure, and even Tom Sharpe's attempts to rouse us are merely irritating. 'Give it a rest, Tom,' Fowler mutters. Billy Baxter and Bert Bertram go off to cover their gun crews, and eventually Fowler and Sharpe crawl into the tent to sleep.

Jack and I are always the last into the tent. It makes no sense to go in before the other men, because they would have to step over us to get to their sleeping spots. Jack puts away his knife and carving. Tonight, he has finished a bird of prey, its wings outspread and talons extended. 'What do you intend to do with them?' I ask.

'Dunno,' he says. He has already given one to each of the men in the mess.

As the weather has got warm, we have taken to sleeping on top of our blankets, rather than in them. We use our folded coats as pillows. They smell like sweat, dirt, and powder. Some soldiers choose to sleep outside the tents, but the canvas keeps the worst of the mosquitos away.

Fowler sleeps flat on his back, and Sharpe sleeps sprawled on his stomach. Mackay and I tend to sleep back-to-back on our sides, except when Tom has one of his attacks of wind. Then we all sleep facing away from him. Not that it helps, really.

Sleeplessness is never a problem. Everyone can sleep at the drop of a hat, except perhaps for Captain Nelson. Sometimes when I join him in the morning, I am certain that he hasn't been to bed the night before.

I come awake abruptly in the middle of the night. Moonlight illuminates the tent walls.

When Billy Baxter is here, the only thing you can hear are his snores. We would not hear a shell explode if it burst right over our heads. Now that Billy is covering nights, it's a lot quieter. I know the sound of the breathing of each of my messmates.

Jack is snoring in strange, short inhalations that sound almost like panting. He has rolled over against me, and his knee is pressing against my bottom. *Is he ill?* 'Are you alright, Jacky?' I whisper.

He makes an odd whimpering sound in his sleep. With a sudden sense of panicked horror, I realise that what is pressing against me is not Jack's knee.

I try to edge away, but I am up against the tent pole. Jack moans and presses against me more urgently. I try to turn to face him. 'Jack,' I whisper in a strangled voice. His eyes flutter behind closed lids.

I cannot risk waking the others. Even though he's clearly dreaming, any hint of buggery is enough to get Jack whipped at the very least; and I don't really know Will or Tom well enough to know how they would react. I lie there, fighting the urge to flee.

Jack's body tenses from head to foot, and he groans. I bite my tongue to keep from crying out. I can feel his cock jump against my hip as he climaxes. The tension drains from his body with his seed, and he gives a snuffling sigh and collapses onto his back.

I can't stay any longer. I jump up and am out the door of the tent before I know what I'm doing.

I try to keep myself from running or sobbing. I stumble to the near edge of the camp and sink down against one of the rock walls, trembling.

I have heard men pleasuring themselves regularly during the time I've been in the army. I know what it sounds like, and I can tell when they release. Not that I don't have direct experience. That's the problem.

Kind, gentle Jacky would never hurt me. I'm sure he's not inclined *that way*. He carries a drawing that he made of a pretty girl with laughing eyes. He's a talented artist. *Annie*. When he comes home, he intends to ask her to be his wife.

Wife. I shudder. What my *husband* did to me, and let others do, is something that I have tried to bury in a place in my mind where it will never resurface. I have not had courses in two years because of what my hus-band, *who stood beside me in front of God and a bishop of the Church of England, and swore to love, honour, and comfort me,* did to me. I lost my infant son, who never drew breath, because of what my *husband* did to me. I lost three more pregnancies before the babies were even babies. Then he let his best friend into my bedchamber and locked the door.

I struggle against the bile that rises in my throat at this memory. I am panting almost the way Jack did, and that doesn't help. I stare at my boots and will myself not to vomit.

'Mr Buckley.'

Oh, no.

I look up, seeing Captain Nelson picking his way down from the path that leads to the ridge batteries. 'What are you doing out here during the middle watch?'

'I couldn't sleep, sir.' I'm relieved to find that my voice sounds normal.

He sinks down beside me against the rock. 'I am well acquainted with the experience,' he says. He looks searchingly at me in the moonlight. 'Are you unwell?'

'One of my tent-mates is subject to attacks of wind. It's... nauseating.'

'Another of the benefits of being a captain,' he murmurs, with only a trace of humour. 'You are welcome to sleep in my tent tonight. I am not using it at the moment.'

'Oh, no sir, Captain; I couldn't do that! Although I thank you very kindly,' I add.

'You very well could,' he replies, 'but do as you like.' He picks himself up off the ground with a groan. 'I will see you in a few hours, regardless of where you sleep.'

He nods and walks off in the direction of the camp. I sit there for a moment longer, then rise and brush off the seat of my breeches. I realise, in that instant, that I left the tent without my coat, and I have been sitting here talking to him in my small-clothes. He didn't comment. My face burns with embarrassment. One doesn't appear before an officer improperly dressed.

I make my way back to our cooking fire and sit on one of the stones that Fowler dragged over to serve as seats. It is my turn to make breakfast tomorrow—*today*. We pooled together and bought suet and molasses this week, and I told them I will make hoecakes. I lie down in the flattened grass next to the fire pit and sleep for an hour until the sky begins to lighten, before the drums beat reveille.

I have the fire started, and the skillet heated, and am mixing the batter when Jack approaches from the tents, slightly before reveille. He sinks down on a rock and holds his head with both hands.

'You alright, Jacky?' I ask cautiously.

He looks up. His face is as open as ever, but there are dark shadows under his eyes. 'I'm alright, Ned,' he says. 'I just slept badly. I had a dirty dream, and now the front of my breeches is all stiff with spunk. I just put them on two days ago,' he adds, 'and I haven't been able to wash the other pair yet.' He smiles crookedly. 'The worst part is, I can't remember what I dreamt. I hope at least that I enjoyed it.'

'Hand me your cup.' He passes his tin cup to me, and I fill it with 'coffee.' There's some coffee in it, but it is cut so heavily with burnt biscuit and God-knows-what-else that it's sort of a joke to call it that. Thankfully, my hand doesn't shake.

'I couldn't sleep myself,' I tell him. 'I went out for a walk and forgot to take my coat, so of course I met Captain Nelson.'

'Does *he* ever sleep, Ned?' Jack asks.

'I don't know. He doesn't sleep much, I don't think.'

The rest of our mess arrives a little after reveille. Billy and Bert come down from the hills. Billy has been having trouble with his eyes, and he squints in the morning light. He refuses to go to the surgeon. A rifleman who can't see won't be a rifleman for long.

Everyone enjoys the fried cakes and molasses, and Tom tells me effusively that I'm the best cook of all of them. I know he'd like to get out of his turn cooking, but this time, he seems sincere.

Chapter Four

On 12 May, *Agamemnon* captures a boat trying to escape from Bastia with sick and wounded men. The captives say that there are upwards of five hundred casualties in the town, and that morale is dismal. The French commander, Lacombe St Michel, deserted the town—and his men—two weeks ago.

Still, the French shot continues to batter us. But Captain Nelson and his guns keep inching closer.

We have not been without losses of our own. By the end of April, Nelson's dispatch to Lord Hood and the army command in St Fiorello lists twenty-six British casualties. *Still*, I think, *twenty-six to their five hundred has to mean something.*

Despite throwing everything he can at Camp Cabanelle, it refuses to fall. Its walls crumble, but intelligence says that the eight hundred defenders in the camp are unbroken. Captain Nelson cannot get the guns close enough to make a breach in the walls of Bastia's citadel. And General D'Aubant still refuses to attack the heights. The latest communication from St Fiorenzo declares that 'with the whole of our forces we are unequal to the taking of Bastia.'

Captain Nelson slumps with his head in his hands. His dinner sits untouched.

'Sir,' I venture, 'Lieutenant Andrews.' The young lieutenant who I met so many weeks ago on *Agamemnon* looks dirty and tired, but there is something positive in his face. He has been manning the guns on the ridge above the Cabanelle.

Captain Nelson looks up, his dejected expression brightening. Andrews makes a gesture of respect and begins his report. The big 24-pound gun and the carronades that Nelson had dragged up to another part of the ridge high above the citadel four days ago are working on the Cabanelle to great effect. Captain Nelson leaps up and trots off towards the ridge to observe for himself.

———

On the morning of 18 May, I am in the ridge battery with Jack Mackay and some of the Corsicans when the unthinkable happens.

Jack has fallen back to refill his cartridge box when the grape shot comes from out of nowhere. We all hit the dirt, and I hear Jack scream.

I scramble back to where the munitions boxes sit, protected from direct shot. Jack must have been on his way back when the shot hit. He is crumpled in a heap, blood pouring from a wounded leg. One of the Corsicans appears beside me and grabs Jack under the arms, pulling him out of the battery.

One of the other soldiers, a man who I don't know, downs his musket and runs for a tourniquet, but I can see already that there's no place to apply it. The wound is in Jack's groin. The blood just keeps pumping from his body. I take him in my arms.

'Hold on, Jacky. Help is coming,' I tell him.

'Oh, shit... Ned. ...It hurts.'

'Yes, I know.' I take his hand and squeeze it tightly. 'Can you feel my hand, Jacky?'

'I… yes.'

'Good.' He is already horribly pale. 'Squeeze my hand. Keep squeezing my hand.'

'Ned.'

'I'm listening, Jack.'

'You've been my best friend.'

'I'm still your best friend.'

His voice is growing weaker. 'Write to Annie. You'll do it properly.'

'You'll write to you herself, Jacky. Tell her you're coming home,' I say.

He tries to smile. 'I love you, Neddy. I'm… not going home.'

'I'm sure you will.'

His eyelids flutter; those long, pretty eyelashes. He opens his eyes again. And smiles.

'I'll never be seasick again, Ned.'

They were the last words he ever spoke.

———————

After supper the rest of the mess and I divide up Jack's possessions. We each put some money in his purse for his family, a few shillings and pence for each of his things. Jack already gave each one of us one of his carved animals, so we decide to send the rest home to his family.

Tom Sharpe buys Jack's knife. 'Mebbe I'll learn t' carve the way 'e did,' he mutters softly. Each of them stows Jack's things in their own packs, then fades away into the gathering dusk to deal with their emotions in their own way, leaving me with the purse and the carvings and his drawing of Annie.

There is also a cheap journal bound between two pieces of rough leather, with drawings in it of other people; probably his family. There is a distinct likeness between Jack and the older man; this must be Jack's father. These drawings stayed in the pages of his journal, but he carried Annie in his coat.

I look at the little animals. Here is the horse, and the falcon, the last thing he carved. There is an English retriever, and a red fox, and a Barbary ape. These tiny wooden creatures cut through the numbness that has protected me since they took Jack's body away. I hold them in my hands and weep.

I don't hear Captain Nelson come up beside me. He puts his hand on my shoulder and says, 'Mr Buckley.'

'Sir.' I cannot look at him, not with my face all wet with tears. But looking at the carvings makes the tears flow afresh.

He takes them from me and holds them up, one by one. 'Remarkable. He was very talented,' he says gently.

I have no idea how he learnt that Jack was dead. 'Someone must write to his family,' I say. 'Captain Clark was our officer ashore, I guess… I don't know who will do it now. Jack asked me to write to his… his fiancée. But I don't know where she lives, nor even her last name.'

'I will find it out. If you write to the lady, I shall include it with the letter to his family.'

'Thank you, sir.'

'It is permissible to cry, Mr Buckley.'

'I… I'd rather not cry, Captain.'

'Walk with me, Mr Buckley.'

I follow him from our kitchen fire, carrying Jack's purse and journal, the drawing of Annie tucked inside. Captain Nelson wraps the little carvings in his handkerchief and puts them in his waistcoat.

'Tell me something about this man.'

'He… he was one of the best shots in our mess, sir. He was quiet, and kind. I never heard him say a bad word to anybody. Jack and I were the most junior men in our mess. I guess I was closer to him than to anyone else in our company.'

'And he to you?'

'I suppose so, sir.'

'What else?'

'He was artistic. He could draw as well as carve.' I open the journal and show Nelson the drawings of Jack's family, and Annie.

'Is this his lady?' he asks.

'Yessir.'

'Look. This drawing is of you.'

He shows me a page of sketches, one of several that Jack obviously made around the cooking fire one evening. There are quickly executed portraits of each of us. My throat aches with grief.

'Keep talking, Mr Buckley. If I'm to write to this man's family, I wish to know something about him.'

'You, sir...?'

'It is unconventional, I realise. But I can do it as easily as any other officer. Continue.'

'Erm... he couldn't sing at all. He was generous and would share anything he had. And he was terribly, horribly seasick.'

'And they assigned this man to be a marine?' Captain Nelson says.

'They didn't know. I would be surprised if they cared. The last thing he said to me was that he'd never be seasick again.' I smile sadly.

'You were with him when he died.'

'Yessir. I was holding him. He died in my arms.' I'm surprised that I can say this without my voice breaking, but it doesn't.

We have reached Captain Nelson's tent. He takes the purse and the journal from me and puts them together with the wooden animals. 'I shall make sure that these things get to his family.' I am astonished to see tears standing in his eyes. 'You have been a good and loyal friend.'

'Sir...'

'I am very tired, Mr Buckley. I am more susceptible to emotion when I am tired.'

'Yessir.'

'Would you like me to pray with you for his soul?'

I haven't prayed since the day Richard locked me in my chamber with his friend Dudley. I have attended divine service because it is required, but I have not prayed. Captain Nelson is offering to pray with me for Jacky. I nod silently. I will do it for Jack.

Captain Nelson goes into his tent and returns with the Book of Common Prayer. 'I shall read the first three pieces of scripture, and the committal. If you think it will suffice.'

'Yes, Captain. Thank you, sir.'

We stand together in the evening light outside Captain Nelson's tent. He begins to read in a low voice.

'I am the resurrection and the life, saith the Lord: he that believeth in me, though he were dead, yet shall he live: and whosoever liveth and believeth in me shall never die.

'I know that my Redeemer liveth, and that he shall stand at the latter day upon the earth. And though after my skin worms destroy this body, yet in my flesh shall I see God: whom I shall see for myself, and mine eyes shall behold, and not another.

'We brought nothing into this world, and it is certain we can carry nothing out. The Lord gave, and the Lord hath taken away; blessed be the name of the Lord.'

He pauses and turns the pages in the prayer book. He clears his throat gently and reads:

> *'Man that is born of a woman hath but a short time to live, and is full of misery. He cometh up, and is cut down, like a flower; he fleeth as it were a shadow, and never continueth in one stay.*
>
> *In the midst of life we are in death: of whom may we seek for succour, but of thee, O Lord, who for our sins art justly displeased?*
>
> *Yet, O Lord God most holy, O Lord most mighty, O holy and most merciful Saviour, deliver us not into the bitter pains of eternal death.*
>
> *Thou knowest, Lord, the secrets of our hearts; shut not thy merciful ears to our prayer; but spare us, Lord most holy, O God most mighty, O holy and merciful Saviour, thou most worthy Judge eternal, suffer us not, at our last hour, for any pains of death, to fall from thee.*
>
> *Forasmuch as it hath pleased Almighty God of his great mercy to take unto himself the soul of John Mackay, our dear brother here departed: we therefore commit his body to the ground; earth to earth, ashes to ashes, dust to dust; in sure and certain hope of the Resurrection to eternal life, through our Lord Jesus Christ; who shall change our vile body, that it may be like unto his glorious body, according to the mighty working, whereby he is able to subdue all things to himself.'*

He goes on, and suddenly I am saying with him the words that I have been unable to speak for years.

*'Our Father which art in heaven, Hallowed be thy
Name, Thy kingdom come, Thy will be done, in earth
as it is in heaven. Give us this day our daily bread; And
forgive us our trespasses, As we forgive them that trespass
against us; And lead us not into temptation, But deliver
us from evil. Amen.'*

I am crying again, not only for Jack, but for my stillborn
son and the babies that I never held in my arms; for the
children I will never have; for my mother, and my father;
and for Nell Buccleuch, who is just as dead. I open my eyes
and see Fowler and Bertram standing a little apart, and I see
tears on their faces, too.

Captain Nelson is not crying. He closes the prayer book
and rests a hand lightly on my shoulder.

'Be comforted, Mr Buckley.'

'Yessir,' I whisper.

Unknown to us, whilst we have been dealing with the melancholy aftermath of death, wheels have been turning on board
Lord Hood's flagship.

In the morning, shortly before noon, I walk back up
to the ridge batteries with Captain Nelson. I stand in the
spot where Jack died, and I feel nothing more than the dull
ache that I have felt since praying with Captain Nelson
the night before.

Nelson is conferring with the man who took Lieutenant
Andrews' place after the lieutenant was wounded. Nelson sent
him to Leghorn to heal. It seemed to wound Captain Nelson
emotionally to have the young officer hurt. It didn't occur to
me yesterday that when Captain Nelson had tears in his eyes,

it might have had as much to do with Lieutenant Andrews as it did with Jack.

I kneel in the place where Jack and I fired from yesterday and look vacantly out over the sea, which sparkles dispassionately in the late-morning sun.

Movement from one of the ships catches my eye. I look towards *Victory*, and my eyes widen as I see the white flag ascending the mainmast. 'Captain!' I shout.

Nelson turns, and I point out at the ship. 'It's a truce!' I exclaim. He dashes to crouch beside me, and all the men on the battery stop in their tracks and gaze out to sea. The guns fall silent in our batteries and in the French defences, and everyone seems to hold his breath.

All throughout the afternoon, we watch boats pass between the ships and the town. It seems as if nobody eats, or drinks, or leaves his position all afternoon, as we wait to learn the result of what is happening in Bastia.

Then suddenly the French officers are leaving the Cabanelle. Nelson, Villettes, and Lord Hood meet them and clasp hands, signifying informal agreement. It has been forty-five days, but the siege of Bastia is finally over. The town has surrendered.

The formal capitulation occurs on 22 May, and two days later 4,500 French and Corsicans ground their muskets on the mole and board the transport ships. Captain Nelson is ecstatic. 'Four-thousand five-hundred men, surrendering to less than a thousand English seamen and soldiers!' he crows. 'And your masters told us it could not be done,' he goads me gleefully.

'I'm very satisfied that they were wrong, sir,' I say properly, but I can't help sharing the grin he flashes at me.

I am helping him prepare his dispatches. Although clearly exhausted, he cannot keep from pacing animatedly around his cabin on *Agamemnon*. Earlier it had given him immense pleasure to thank all the men who had served on shore, on behalf of Lord Hood.

'Expenditures: twenty-thousand shot and shells. It matters not how many of each; I don't know how it breaks down. I'm sure that you can find that information for me if you care to. One thousand barrels of powder. Casualties: sixty men.'

He sits down at the table for only a moment before he is up and moving again. 'Break that out by those killed and wounded from each ship, and by regiment and company for the soldiers.' He stops short. 'Unless you would like me to do that,' he offers.

'No, sir, I don't mind,' I say. 'I have already written his name into the log.' We both know who we are speaking about; there is no need to say more.

'Good, Mr Buckley.' He pauses thoughtfully for a brief second, then resumes: 'Now, we acquired eighty artillery pieces, and *La Flêche* corvette from the French. And the town, of course! The town of Bastia! A negligible amount of powder, though. Lord Hood intends to move on Calvi next, and we are going to require more powder—a lot more powder. I don't have the final figures on the supplies taken…' He continues to pace back and forth between the table and the window as I scribble down his words.

The following day, though, Captain Nelson's exuberance has vanished. He slumps in his chair, a dull look in his eyes. In his hand is a copy of Lord Hood's public dispatch.

'*... command and direction of the seamen in landing the guns, mortars and stores...*' he reads to me. 'He makes it sound as if I did nothing but what the commander of any store ship could do!'

A servant comes into the cabin with a tray of tea. He puts the tray down on the table where I am sitting, then pours a cup for Captain Nelson and leaves it at the captain's elbow before leaving the cabin again.

Nelson picks up the cup of tea and looks at it, then sets it back on the table. '... can't seem to remember that I take milk in my tea,' he mutters.

I present the pitcher of milk to Captain Nelson. He pours a splash into his cup and gives it back wordlessly.

'Tell me, Mr Buckley, what does this mean to you? *"Captain Hunt was on shore in the command of the batteries from the hour the troops landed to the surrender of the town"*.'

I am bemused. 'Did Lord Hood confuse you with someone else, or could he not remember your name? Who is this Captain Hunt?'

Nelson takes a swallow of his tea. 'Bless you, Mr Buckley.' He rubs his brow as if his head aches. 'Captain Hunt was at Bastia in the very beginning, and rarely after that. If he was ever in any of the batteries, I am not aware of it. I think that he was already elsewhere before the first battery was even being built. I cannot tell you truthfully of any service he performed during the siege.'

I thought that Colonel Moore and General D'Aubant's behaviour had been reprehensible, but at least I can discern their motive, even if I condemn it. This betrayal of Captain Nelson by Lord Hood is inexplicable. 'Why would he write something so patently false, sir?'

'Interest, Mr Buckley. Patronage. Lord Hood has some personal reason to promote Captain Hunt, and it does not matter what it is.' He tries to sound nonchalant, but I have never seen him look so hurt.

'If I may say so, sir, that is terribly unfair. Did Captain Hunt tell Lord Hood that it was he who did all the things that *you* did?'

'You may say so, Mr Buckley, but only to me. As for what Captain Hunt told Lord Hood, it hardly makes a difference. What will be remembered is what Lord Hood wrote in his dispatch.'

'All the men who fought with you here know that it was you, not Captain Hunt, sir.'

Captain Nelson's lip twitches. 'Perhaps that will stand me in good stead when Fremantle or Serocold becomes an admiral.' He takes another swallow of tea and says, 'Captain Hunt has been sent back to England with Lord Hood's dispatches. So, when we take Calvi, no one will be able to say that Hunt played any role at all.'

His slow smile is charming.

Chapter Five

T he army sends a new commander-in-chief, recalling D'Aubant. Hs name is Lieutenant General Charles Stuart, and he is young, handsome, and every bit as energetic as Captain Nelson. He has also pledged the full support of the army for the siege of Calvi. Nelson frets about our lack of powder, but he is busy loading ships for the Calvi campaign, and his spirits are buoyant again.

On 7 June, I am wakened from my temporary berth on *Agamemnon* by an unusual amount of activity. It is not yet dawn, but all around me, men are stowing hammocks and grabbing kit and pounding up the companionways. I roll out of my hammock, yank it down and roll it up on itself.

'What's happening?' I ask the soldier to my right.

'We're getting off. The fleet is going after the Frogs— they've come out of Toulon.'

I gain the deck to find crates of materiel, just loaded over the course of the last few days, being off-loaded again. I stow my hammock in the hammock-rail and lend a shoulder to a barrel being fitted into a sling. The sailor I'm assisting smiles a gap-toothed grin when the barrel is lifted from the deck. 'Thankee for th' hand, younker,' he says, and moves on to the next crate.

The boats are fully loaded and cast off by the time the sun rises, and I have not yet found my commanding officer.

Sergeant Preston says to me, 'I dunno, lad. I seen him all over the place, but I can't tell you where 'e is now. You want t' stay on board, ye might get t' see action against the French!'

I usually mess with the servants when I'm on board unless I'm invited to eat with Captain Nelson. This morning, though, breakfast is scotch coffee and a piece of biscuit and hard cheese eaten on the fly. The minute the last empty boat has returned, *Agamemnon* is pressing on sail to catch up to the rest of the fleet. I have never seen the anchor weighed so fast.

I don't see Nelson until we are bearing up to follow the main fleet, when I get a glimpse of him on the quarterdeck. He is striding rapidly from the fore to the aft end and back again, gesturing with both arms, his first lieutenant and Mr Withers keeping pace. I feel about as useful as a pig with a parasol, and stay out of the way.

Captain Nelson does not find me until four bells of the afternoon watch. Leaving the quarterdeck, he catches sight of me where I stand speaking to one of the regular marines. If we *are* about to see action, I want to know my role, and I am ready to fight from anywhere they'll have me.

'Mr Buckley! Come here, sir!'

I immediately drop the negotiation and respond to his summons.

'You are on board,' he observes when I reach him.

'Sir, I didn't know your pleasure. I decided it was safer to stay aboard and risk being superfluous than to disembark and leave you short if you wanted me. I hope I did right, Captain.'

'Excellent. Come dine with me, Mr Buckley.'

'Dine' is a relative term this afternoon. He is joined at the table only by First Lieutenant Hinton and the master, in addition to me. There is fish soup and cold meat, an austere meal in contrast to the usual fare at his table. Nelson eats little. He

is businesslike, but there is a feverish glint in his eye, and he can barely contain his need to be on deck again. 'I pray we may meet this fleet,' he mutters repeatedly.

I do not believe he eats much, or sleeps at all, until we locate the French in Golfe Jouan on 10 June. They are hugging the shore, and we all wait again, on tenterhooks, while Lord Hood weighs the logistics of an engagement. Captain Nelson comes back from the flagship deflated. The admiral has ordered him back to Corsica to complete his task of loading the men and materiel for Calvi. Whatever happens here, Captain Nelson and his *Agamemnon* will not be a part of it. He retreats into his quarters, and I do not see him again for twenty-four hours.

By 12 June, the fleet of army transports, store ships, and victuallers is underway to Mortella Bay at St Fiorenzo. It has been an impressive undertaking, and Captain Nelson has done well. But I sense that his treatment in Lord Hood's Bastia dispatch and subsequent dismissal at Golfe Juan is still smarting. Nelson is looking to Calvi with eager anticipation.

He is losing a staunch ally in Colonel Villettes, who has been appointed acting governor for Bastia. But he expects good things from General Stuart. The new commander-in-chief shares Nelson's philosophy. He is also the first man I've ever seen whose energy is greater than that of Captain Nelson. The one time I saw them together, I watched Stuart run roughshod over him; and the two of them *agree* with one another. Captain Nelson introduced me, but I don't believe Stuart saw me, nor registered a word that Captain Nelson spoke about me. The man clearly knows his own worth; it apparently exceeds everyone else's.

General Stuart encourages Nelson not to wait for Lord Hood's return. Hood expects Nelson to remain at Bastia until he, Hood, returns with the fleet. Throwing in his lot with General Stuart, Captain Nelson is escorting the army's ships around Cape Corse before Hood is anywhere near Corsica again. I cannot help thinking that Lord Hood will not be greatly pleased.

Nelson and Stuart have spent hours over Captain Nelson's table, drawing up plans. General Stuart surveyed the land while the fleet was at sea chasing the French, and he has an audacious strategy. Captain Nelson sketches it for me one night as the convoy of ships sails towards the west coast of Corsica.

'Calvi is heavily defended from the sea, and any concerted attack from that quarter would not only expend precious stores, but it puts our ships and seamen at risk. However, the town is virtually unprotected from the inland side, except by mountains. We are going to bring the guns up from the other side of the mountains and erect our batteries above the town. The mountains are challenging, but they are not insurmountable. We will completely wrong-foot them!'

Nelson proved at Bastia that his guns can go practically anywhere. The French have yet to learn that lesson.

The challenges begin almost immediately. The only place to land the men and equipment is the mouth of a ravine, a shallow and rocky place with little beach. The ships are not able to anchor and have to keep a mile out from the shore, and the swell is fast and treacherous, endangering the boats as they attempt to make landfall.

The ravine itself seems impossibly steep, but it is the only way up.

It takes only two days to get the men and munitions from the ships to the rough camp established on the beach. The weather is miserable, and the surf heavy, but Captain Nelson is moving fast. Speed is crucial, he says, so that the French do not have the chance to reinforce those mountain ridges the way they did at Bastia.

It is his complement of sailors who lug those guns up the ravine, then along approximately two more miles of punishing terrain to a staging area at a mountaintop shrine. My respect for these men grows daily. They seem to have little resentment to interfere with the execution of their jobs, and they work like dray horses. Their loyalty to Captain Nelson is unbelievable.

He himself is everywhere. He is on the beach, and in the surf, and on the hillside. The skies open up and make the mountain even more treacherous, but he is there, making sure that the guns keep advancing as lightning splits the skies and thunder rumbles. His clothes have been soaked through for days, but he seems neither to notice nor care.

The other soldiers and I follow the sailors up the mountain. I have found my mess again, and we are all wet, bruised, scraped, and miserable. My hands are torn from the sharp rocks and scrub of the ravine. There will be no cooking fires, and no shelter, until we reach the position where the batteries are to be established. The first night we sleep back-to-back in the lee of an outcropping of stone. Billy Baxter rubs his irritated eyes and grumbles, but he, like all of us, knows that it is pointless. At one point he says to me, 'It's a good thing Mackay didn't have to make that trip by sea. He'd be dead now if he wasn't already.'

I am tired and sore, and thinking of Jack makes tears mingle with the rain on my face. Life is short, and full of misery… at least Jack is free of it.

The summer has been hot; even in Surrey, by mid-afternoon the house is unbearably warm. The child—our first child—will be born within weeks, according to the London accoucheur Richard found after he got impatient with our local doctor. Even the baby in my womb grows listless in the heat, and only becomes active again at night, when it interrupts my sleep.

The heat makes Richard irritable. He complained that tonight's supper was poorly prepared, then grew annoyed when I did not eat much of it. The wine he has consumed with his meal has not helped his disposition.

'I went out of my way to find a nice cut of mutton for you, and you do not eat.'

'I apologise, my dear. I appreciate your effort, but I have no stomach for it.'

My husband regards my burgeoning belly and I recognise the look that comes into his eyes.

'Well, if you don't care to eat, then perhaps I can distract you with a different activity,' he says suggestively.

The bigger I have become with child, the more desirable Richard finds me. Our doctor told him he must stop as I approach my time. I have a disloyal suspicion that this is why Richard found the London specialist.

I try to smile at him. 'I do not think so tonight,' I say, as sweetly as I can. My back is aching, and my limbs are heavy. I cannot even contemplate the activity that Richard is proposing.

His expression grows sullen. 'Don't be ungrateful, Nell.'

'I am not ungrateful, Richard. But I feel rather unwell tonight. And you do remember what Dr Calhoun advised, do you not?'

'I told you I wanted to hear no more about that old fraud. Dr Blanchard has not said anything of the sort, and he is your doctor now.'

Perhaps it is the relentless heat, or the discomfort of my swollen belly, or the burning sensation in my chest and throat after meals, as if the food cannot get past the baby. Whatever the reason, I reply hotly, 'That is very well. But I tell you that I do not care to go to your bed tonight. You will please excuse me.' I lay my serviette on the table and push back my chair.

I am opening the door of dining room when I hear Richard throw down his serviette and shove his own chair back from the table.

I continue through the door and into the hallway to the stairs. If he will only allow me to get to my bedchamber, I can turn the key on him tonight and apologise to him in the morning, when we are both in a better temper.

Behind me, the door to the dining room slams open as I prepare to mount the stairs. 'Come back here, Nell, now!' Richard shouts.

I ignore him and try to hurry up the steep stairs to the first floor, but as ungainly as I am, I am not fast enough. I hear his feet cross the hall, and I am nearly at the top of the stair when he catches up with me. He grabs the back of my gown and pulls me down onto the stairs.

'You will never turn your back on me!' he growls. He is undoing his breeches. 'I intend to have that which is my right.'

'Richard—no! If you don't care whether you hurt me, think of the child!' I try to fight him off, but my efforts are useless; they only inflame him further.

Richard yanks up the skirts of my gown and takes me on the third step of the stair below the first-floor landing. As his thrusts force my back painfully into the bullnose of the step above, I realise that I hate the man I married.

At dawn, I search out Captain Nelson to see if he has a job for me. Lately he has greeted me and told me that he will have more work for me as soon as we make camp, and I have returned to my mess to wrestle with crates and guns.

This morning he and General Stuart are having an animated discussion. 'It isn't working,' General Stuart insists. 'Without the carriage, the gun is useless, and it took half a day to get it up here. Throw out the blocks and tackles. Get enough men on each gun and they can *carry* it up the hill.'

'My men are already breaking their backs,' Captain Nelson says. I think he is working to control his temper. 'I understand what you are advocating, but…'

'Just try it, Captain,' General Stuart says, cutting him off.

The soldiers are working alongside the sailors now, hauling guns and supplies. It seems as though it's all we do, endlessly, day in and day out.

Tom Sharpe and I are struggling with a howitzer. It isn't a big gun, but neither of us are big people. We finally manage to manhandle it into position, and Tom flops onto the ground and says, 'I en't movin' for five whole minutes. I don' care *who* shouts at me.'

'When the sergeant told me they wanted me for a rifleman, he said I'd have an easy time of it, because "*riflemen don't have to haul things, chick*",' I tell Tom. 'He was talking about bloody cannon.'

He groans and presses a fist into his gut. 'M' bowels is all wrong,' he complains. 'I en't been able t' shit for days.'

'Go to the surgeon,' I tell him. 'He can set you right.'

'Wher' *is* th' bugger?' he says. 'Can't nobody tell me.'

'He's in the base camp; I just don't yet know exactly where. But whoever the duty officer is will be able to tell you.'

Tom picks himself up off the ground. 'I'm goin' to go find that sergeant an' tell him I got to see the surgeon before m' guts bust.'

I'm fairly certain that Tom's walking right into a great big clyster. But if he's miserable enough, I don't think he'll mind too much.

————————————

The base camp is back by the shrine of the Madonna, but there are smaller outposts of tents in redoubts behind the batteries. Because as riflemen our primary job is to harass the enemy and protect our gunners, my mess sleeps in one of the redoubts. As do Captain Nelson and General Stuart.

Captain Nelson has retained me as his amanuensis. I was afraid that now, with General Stuart right here in camp, the captain would no longer have any need of me. I have come to appreciate our working relationship deeply, and every day my respect and admiration for him grows. Without the work I do for him, I think the monotonous slog and repetition might drive me mad.

He sets me to keeping the records, receiving his communications, and writing out copies of his dispatches. I maintain a log of the requests received for supplies and keep track of the expenditures. He uses me to run between the redoubts and the base camp. Doing these things for someone else might be tedious and unpleasant, but Nelson's unbounded enthusiasm and ceaseless activity make even unpleasantness tolerable. When he is tired, he can be irritable, but his bad-temperedness is rarely directed at me.

But despite the novelty of the initial cordial relationship between the army and the navy, things are starting to break down again. The weather continues to be filthy, and the ships have not been able to stay, as they are threatened daily with being swept ashore by the heavy seas. General Stuart accuses the navy of failing to support the army, in an unjust turnaround of the roles at Bastia, and in a tense conversation with Captain Nelson, he threatens to quit.

The general rails at Nelson about the disruption in the supply of materiel and demands to know where the ships have gone. Captain Nelson tries to explain to him about lee shores, but Stuart doesn't want to hear it. I am seated outside Captain Nelson's tent in the redoubt keeping the letter book, and I can hear Stuart's voice getting louder and more strident. Captain Nelson's voice is not loud, and I have never heard him get into a shouting match with anyone yet, but I can hear the impatience behind his measured tone. General Stuart demands more men and supplies; Captain Nelson tells him that we are pleading for every barrel of powder we are able to get.

I know that Captain Nelson has great admiration for the general; he has told me so. He thinks that Stuart is visionary, and an excellent judge of terrain. From my perspective, General Stuart may be an excellent judge of terrain, but his vision appears to be blinkered. And I am beginning to suspect the man might be unbalanced. I have some experience with that, unfortunately.

Once again, Captain Nelson is in a position of having to intercede diplomatically between the army and the navy in the persons of General Stuart and Lord Hood, and neither one of the two likes the other.

Chapter Six

In early July, the captain and the general launch an ambitious plan to build a battery to attack the Mozzello fort, audaciously close. Delays disrupt the first attempt, and General Stuart is in a fury. He aborts the action.

'We go again tomorrow night,' Captain Nelson tells me.

The following night goes more according to plan, but at dawn Captain Nelson has only one of the guns in place when the sun rises. The French appear flabbergasted, but quickly turn their fire on the battery. Captain Nelson does not retreat, remaining in the battery under the weight of their assault while the remaining guns are installed. As soon as all his guns are in place, Nelson opens the full fire of the battery on the French. He is triumphant, but the high is followed by a devastating low.

A number of valiant British men are killed or brutally wounded when the French open fire, as they coolly persevere to complete the battery under a furious rain of shot and shells. In the evening, back in the redoubt, two exhausted and battered naval officers stand conversing outside the captain's tent. I see Captain Nelson lay a hand consolingly on the other's shoulder. Captain Hallowell returns the gesture, then turns and walks dispiritedly away.

'We lost some excellent and able men today,' Captain Nelson tells me quietly. 'Captain Serocold departed this world this morning. Captain Hollowell tells me he was peaceful when he died. It was in as green and placid a valley as one could wish.'

'Would you like me to pray with you for him, Captain?' I will never forget his kindness in the wake of Jack Mackay's death.

'No; thank you for offering, Mr Buckley. I shall pray for him later. Right now, there are other things I must attend to.'

The obvious threat imposed by this battery, and its exposed location, make it the enemy's most important target. Daily the French bombard it, killing and wounding our men and dismounting our guns. And every night we restore it, Captain Nelson finding new guns somewhere to replace the disabled ones.

The regular army continues to gain ground. Tom Sharpe and Bert Bertram are assigned to cover their advance. Will Fowler, Billy Baxter, and I are amongst the snipers in the batteries. That is, when Captain Nelson can spare me. He is leaving more and more clerical responsibility in my hands.

In the morning I present myself at Captain Nelson's tent after muster as usual. I am always punctual; it is expected, but it is also a token of my respect. Often he is busy with some other business, and sometimes he isn't there at all, but he always acknowledges me graciously; I appreciate that, regardless of how long I must wait for him.

This morning, the flaps of his tent are closed, and he is nowhere to be seen.

One of the seamen from *Agamemnon* walks by and sees me standing there. ''Ere, you're Cap'n Nelson's lad, an't ye?'

'I am. Have you seen him?'

'Not this morning, no. Bless 'im; you tell 'im we're fightin' for *'im*.'

'I shall, sir.'

I toe the dirt with my boot and wait.

The sun is climbing, and the guns, which are never silent, are barking on the ridge. I count the time between firings. The seamen are keeping up a good rhythm. I'm embarrassed by this conflict between the services that nearly scuttled the Bastia initiative, and now threatens this one. Soldiers and sailors may have different cultures, but we serve the same King, and these egotistical tantrums give the French a break that they don't deserve. When I joined the 69th Regiment, I never thought for an instant that I'd end up a marine, and it has given me a new, deep respect for the navy. Certainly, our artillery crews are not as crack as their gun crews, not even on a good day.

It is beginning to get hot.

Behind me I hear a cough. I look around, but there is no one there.

The cough comes again; someone clearing his throat, then an indistinct murmur. 'Sir...? Captain?'

'Mr Buckley.' Captain Nelson's voice from inside the tent. I am confused. *Why does he not come out? He must have heard me talking to the sailor earlier...*

'Mr Buckley, will you come in, please?'

I push the tent flap aside and stick my head into his wall tent.

'All the way in, please.'

I enter the tent and stand against the opening.

He is lying on a ground-cloth wrapped in his blankets, his coat suspended from a hook on the rear pole. Despite the size of the tent, there is very little in here. He hasn't a cot, nor a chair. There is a trunk, a chamber pot, and a portable writing desk. For a time, we had a little table where one could stand and write, but one day it vanished. All my efforts could not discover where it went. His stockings, breeches and waistcoat are folded on top of the trunk.

'Sir? Are you unwell?'

'Aye; it's my old complaint. Do not worry, it is not contagious.'

'I... I wasn't worried, sir. Do you need me to find a surgeon?'

'No. There is not a damned thing they can do for me. There's Peruvian Bark in that trunk. Would you find it and bring it to me?'

I pick up his clothes from on top of the trunk. I look around, but there isn't anyplace else to put them.

'Just set them on the ground. They can hardly get any dirtier,' he says.

I lift the lid of the trunk and find a box of medicines underneath a spare shirt and some stockings. There are multiple bottles inside, and I lift each one until I find the one labelled 'Tincture of Peruvian Bark.' I lift it out of the box.

'Pour some water from that pitcher there into a glass and bring it, and that bottle, to me.'

I do as he instructs.

Captain Nelson pushes himself up to sitting, still swathed in his blankets. He unstoppers the bottle and lifts it to his eye. He tips an amount into the glass, but his hand is shaking and the bottle clinks against the glass. Muttering under his breath, he holds the bottle up to eye level again. 'It will do,' he says, but he's not addressing me. He drinks the contents of the glass down with a grimace. He is shivering badly.

'That is likely to make me a bit sick to my stomach,' he tells me. 'But it will allow me to do my duty.'

'Is it intermittent fever, sir?'

'It is. Which type remains to be seen. I hope it is quartan, rather than tertian. That would afford me an extra day of remission.'

'How can I help, Captain?'

'Do as you always do. I may need to rely on you a bit more than usual, but in general, your duties need not change.'

'Yessir.'

'Thank you, Mr Buckley. At the moment, I need you to serve as valet. Will you bring me my shaving things?'

I go back to the trunk. I feel strange pawing through his possessions. I find the case containing his razor, and his shaving soap and brush, and hand them to him. Then I return for the basin and mirror.

I pour water from the pitcher into his shaving basin and pick up the mirror to bring it to him, but I make the mistake of glancing into it.

Once I had curves, and soft ringlets of curls. On my wedding day, my hair was teased into a cloud of curls and crowned with silk blossoms, and my gown had an overskirt of lace. Now I look at myself in his shaving mirror, and I see a stranger looking solemnly back at me.

My cheeks, once rounded and rosy, are hollow, and my cheekbones are sharp. Beardless *(because of course I cannot grow a beard)*; but one would hardly know because of the grime on my face. My red coat is stained with dirt and bleached across the shoulders by the sun, and my waistcoat and breeches, once white, are grey with sweat and dust and stained with blood where I knelt in the puddle leaking from Jack Mackay's body. My shorn hair would be lank but for the sand and dust, which makes it stand out stiffly. I have not untied my queue, nor properly dressed my hair, since I lost my comb when I skidded and fell on the mountain last week and the contents of my pack spilled out. I am suddenly ashamed for him to see me like this.

'What's keeping you?' he asks tersely, and I hastily pick up the mirror and his shaving bowl and bring them to him.

'My apologies, sir. I just caught a glimpse of myself in the glass, and I fear I am hardly fit to be in your company.'

'Hmph.' He exhales through his nose. 'You are no worse than the rest of us.'

I hold the mirror as he lathers soap on his cheek and picks up the razor. He draws the blade up his face, but his hand isn't steady and the blade stutters. Blood wells into the soap on his cheekbone.

'Oh! —Captain, sir; you have drawn blood. Would you allow me to shave you?'

He touches the cut with his fingertips and looks at the blood on them. 'There's some styrax in my kit.'

I open the box he indicates and locate the little bottle. When I bring it to him, he says, 'Finish shaving me, if you will, and then I will apply it.'

I don't know why I offered to do this; it was impulsive. I don't have experience shaving anybody. But he accepted my offer without hesitation, and now I will just have to fake my way through it. I take the blade from him.

'I am going to kneel behind you, Captain, and you must rest your head on my breast, as we have no chair.' I look apprehensively at the sharp blade. God help me. If I cut him, it will be the end of me.

He leans upon me, and I arrange the towel around his throat and pick up the razor.

I have watched men do this countless times; and I have pretended to do it myself, but rarely, and only to further my deception. I know how to hone my razor, but I hardly need to. The blade has nothing to dull it.

I hold his head steady and his skin taut with my left hand, drawing the razor carefully up his cheek. I'm thankful that he cannot see my face, or his confidence in me would be completely lost. I'm wincing each time I stroke the blade across his skin.

On top of my anxiety about the blade, there is nothing but the blanket around his shoulders between myself and his shirt. I can feel the heat of his body against mine, and it is unnerving. I have not been this close to a man in undress since Richard… *I will not think about that.* I have to lift the razor when the ague causes him to shudder, so the blade will not skip.

Somehow, after what seems like an interminable age, I manage to shave him. I wipe the remaining soap from his face and throat with the towel, and hand him the bottle of styrax. I pick up the mirror and hold it so that he can use it to anoint the cut with balsam.

He examines my work. 'It will do,' he tells me, kindly. 'Tell me, have you ever shaved a man before?'

'Nosir,' I say, shamefaced. 'I rarely have to shave myself.'

'I'm glad you did not tell me that before you shaved me. Nevertheless, I doubt I could have done much better today. At least *you* didn't cut me.' He groans softly. 'I must get up and dress. Wait for me outside and I shall join you shortly.'

I exit his tent and stand outside, waiting as he instructed. I hear him make water in the pot and I feel my cheeks redden. *Zounds, what is wrong with you, Ned? You see men make water in front of you all the time.*

I am sitting by the trail side, eating my piece of bis-cuit and cold bacon, when I hear water splattering in

*the dirt to my right. I jump up, disgusted, and Sharpe
laughs and tucks himself back into his breeches.*

'Damn your eyes, Tom! That isn't funny!'

*'Sure i' t'was, Neddy. Ye sprung up in t'air like it were
a bullet 'stead of a stream o' piss!'*

*'I'd rather take a bullet than let your piss touch me,
Sharpe,' Fowler says, his mouth full of biscuit.*

*'Neddy en't ne'er pissed in front of us, ye noticed,
Fowler? 'Is sensibilities is too delicate.'*

'I was raised to a higher standard than you, Tom.'

*'Yeh, right orfficer-material you are. More likely
'is pizzle is so small ye can't see it without a spyglass,'
he says to Fowler.*

*Fowler slings the rest of his biscuit into the scrub
and stands up, brushing dirt from the seat of his
breeches. 'He's got a point, Tom Sharpe. You got the
manners of a delinquent schoolboy. Remember you're
a British soldier, not a drayman.' He picks up his
pack and jerks his head up the trail. 'C'mon, gents.
Time to go.'*

Distracted by this memory, I don't hear Captain Nelson
emerge from his tent until he clears his throat behind me.

'I'm sorry, sir. I was thinking.'

'What about?' he asks, but I don't think he's interested.
He's merely being polite.

'Nothing important.' I look at him.

His waistcoat and breeches are nearly as stained with sweat
and rain as mine, but his blue coat with its gold lace, despite
the hard use it gets, still looks very fine. However, this morning he looks exhausted, and the cut on his cheek stands out
angrily against the uncharacteristic pallor of his skin.

'We're back in the forward battery this morning,' he tells me. He shivers and passes his hand across his forehead, as if he's trying to wipe away a spiderweb.

'Do you want me to go on your behalf, Captain? I can report back to you.'

'I know you can, Mr Buckley. But I need the activity. It will help dispel the ague.'

'Yessir.'

We start on the trek to the forward battery. Captain Nelson is usually as animated as a grasshopper, but he doesn't spring today. He trudges. I have no trouble keeping up with him today.

'How old are you, Mr Buckley?' he asks as we climb the hillside.

'I am twenty, sir.'

'Are you indeed. I would have thought you not much more than seventeen.'

'I know I give people that impression, sir.' He doesn't reply. 'The sergeant, he says he doesn't know how I ever got into the army. He said if he had been at the house of rendezvous, he would have sent me back to my mother.'

'Do you write to your mother, Mr Buckley? Josiah needs to be constantly reminded to write to his mother.'

'My mother is dead, sir.'

'Ah, so is mine,' he says quietly.

I feel bad for deceiving him. My mother *is* dead, as is my father. Had either of them still been alive, I should not have ended up married to Richard Buccleuch. But I am thirty years old, not twenty. And my deception is the only thing keeping *me* alive.

Captain Nelson speaks to every man on the battery and watches them serve their guns. As he engages with his men, his weariness seems to fall away. The men, in response, work faster and more efficiently. They will do anything for him.

The gun captains bark their orders, but their crews hardly need to hear them. They know this drill the way they know how to breathe. General Stuart insisted that each crew have an army artillerist as gun captain, and it was awkward for the sailors at first, but they've adapted.

Normally Captain Nelson would spend a greater portion of the day here on the ridge, but today it appears he doesn't intend to stay. As we are preparing to leave the battery, a shell comes arcing over the sandbags at one of the carronades. The carronade's crew scatter as it thumps into the hill behind us, and we hit the ground as sharp fragments of rock fly.

I pick myself up, my heart pounding so hard I think my ears may burst. I expect to hear Jack's scream, but it doesn't come. The men of the gun crew are rising slowly, all except the man on the gun lock. The other guns bellow in affronted fury as this gun crew tends to their wounded man.

I recognise him; he is not a soldier. This is one of *Tartar's* gun crews, and this sailor is young; only nineteen or twenty. He can play the fife, and dances like St. Elmo's fire. He does not appear injured, but he is unconscious. One of the men who have been moving powder and ball for the guns picks him up and prepares to carry him down to the base camp.

Captain Nelson appears beside me. His coat is dirty, and he has lost his hat, but he is unharmed. I look at the silent gun, down a man.

'Captain, I can take up the quill and linstock. With your permission, sir.'

'They will send another man,' he says.

'Yessir, but I can take his place until another comes.'

Nelson looks at the carronade's crew. 'Mr Buckley has offered to take up position on the gun lock until another man can get here.' He looks at the rest of the men. 'Will you have him?'

I try to stand as tall as my five feet, three inches will allow. I am not unfamiliar to these men, but I am not one of them. I represent the discipline some sailors resent mightily.

'Ge' in here, lad!' cries the sponger.

I pick up the discarded quill, powder horn, linstock, and canister of slow-match, and scamper to join the gun crew.

Our rhythm is not as smooth as it was before. Whilst I have done this with army artillery, naval gun crews work at a far faster pace. But I begin to pick up their cadence. Unstop the touch hole. Prick the cartridge. Prime the pan. Bruise the priming. Secure the powder. Stop the touch hole. The other men sponge, load, ram, aim. Unstop the touch hole. Fire!

I don't know how many times we fire before another man comes to take my place. The men don't acknowledge my leaving, nor my replacement. They just keep on serving the gun.

I leave the battery to make my way back down into the redoubt camp. I presume Captain Nelson has already returned to camp; but there he is, sitting on an outcropping of rock.

'Sir?'

He has regained his hat, although it now needs a good brushing. One of his stockings is ripped, and there is a scrape on his calf. He stands and waits for me to join him.

'Excellent work, Mr Buckley,' he says quietly.

'Thank you, sir.' My heart glows.

'They scored no other hits, those filthy French curs.'

'It appears to have been a lucky shot, sir.'

'May I write a letter to your father, Mr Buckley? He would be proud.'

'My father is dead too, sir.'

'I am sorry. I am sure he would still be proud of you.'

'Thank you, sir.' *But my father, if he knew, would be appalled by the things that have happened to me.*

We have come most of the way back down the hillside when he stops and bends forward, an arm clapped around his belly. His face has gone grey under his sunburn.

'Captain? Sir!'

'It is only a cramp, Mr Buckley.' His voice is strained.

I look around for a place where he can sit down, but there's nothing but the steep slope and scree. I stand by uselessly while he grimaces, breathing shallowly. After a minute or two, he straightens, slowly.

'Are you alright now, sir?'

'Aye. More or less. I'm never sure if that is to do with the fever or the bark, but it comes on and goes off again fairly quickly.' He moves stiffly a few paces down the track, then gripes again.

'Sir, please; let me help.'

'Thank you, Mr Buckley, but there isn't anything you can do.' He lowers himself stiffly to the ground and sits in the dirt of the track, his knees drawn up against his chest, forehead resting on his knees. I kneel in the dirt beside him. We are in a declivity between two higher parts of the hillside, and can't be seen from either above or below, so no one is going to come to his assistance. His entire body appears clenched with pain.

I unsling my canteen and offer it to him. He holds up a hand in a 'wait' gesture. I kneel there, stupidly holding the canteen, and wait.

Eventually his body begins to unclench; his rigid muscles to soften. He gestures for the canteen, and sips the warm, stale water gingerly. He holds the canteen and waits, as if to see if the water is going to stay down, before taking another swallow. Finally, he hands me my canteen again and watches me sling it back over my shoulder.

'Give me a hand up.'

I take his hand and he uses me to lever himself to standing again. He continues down the track as if nothing had happened.

————————

When we reach the redoubt on the windward side of the mountain, Nelson sends me to check on the wounded gunner and report back to him. I thread my way through what passes for company streets, to the surgeon's tent on the edge of the base camp.

As at Bastia, the surgeon's tent is actually two tents, one his sleeping place and surgery and the other with cots for men who can't be sent back to their mess. These are practically the only cots in camp. Most of us sleep on the ground.

The wounded sailor is the only man in the surgery today. He has been laid on a cot, his eyes closed. Graham, the surgeon, is making notes on a page already covered with heavy, black spiderwebs of ink. He looks up and sees me. 'Can I help you, Private?'

'Sir, Captain Nelson sent me to find out about this man's injuries.'

'Ah. Well, you can tell Captain Nelson that the only injury this man seems to have is a great lump on his head. But he hasn't regained consciousness, and his eyes don't dilate properly in response to light.'

'What is to be done for him?'

The surgeon shakes his head. 'All I can do is observe him. If he does not improve, it may be necessary to trephine him.'

I shudder. The idea of cutting a hole in this lively young man's skull is horrifying. But so is the possibility that he may never be lively again. 'Can you tell me his name, so I can tell the captain?'

'His name is James Franklin. Able seaman from the *Tartar*.'

They call him Jemmy. 'Does Captain Fremantle know yet?'

'I doubt it. I'm not aware of where *Tartar* is at the moment.'

I thank Mr Graham and make my way back to Captain Nelson's tent.

The flap is tied open, and Nelson is seated on the ground inside, writing in a leather-covered book. His tent is partially shaded by a stunted tree, but it is still very warm inside. Nevertheless, he has a blanket around his shoulders, and he shivers as he bids me enter. I attempt to pretend that I do not notice, since that appears to be what he wants.

'Mr Graham says that the seaman's name is James Franklin, of *Tartar*, sir. He has no visible injuries other than a lump on the head, but he is still unconscious, and his pupils are not responding to light. Mr Graham says that if he doesn't show any improvement, he may have to be trephined.'

Captain Nelson's face is melancholy. He lays down his pen and motions to the writing box. 'Get some writing paper and another quill. I need you to write to Lord Hood, and I'm going to tell you what to write.'

'Captain Fremantle doesn't know yet,' I volunteer.

'I shall make sure to inform him.' He brushes his hair off his brow with his left hand, and I see that the smallest finger is swollen and discoloured. The skin looks tight and shiny, and strains against his wedding band.

'What happened to your hand?!' I exclaim.

'I struck it against something when the mortar hit. The finger is bruised, but I can still move it, so I believe it will recover.'

'Can you get your ring off? Otherwise, it will act like a tourniquet and cut off the blood flow to your finger.'

He tries to move the ring and winces.

'Have you any sweet oil?' I ask.

'No, but there is a bottle of opodeldoch liniment in my trunk. Perhaps that would work.'

Once again I find myself rifling Captain Nelson's trunk. I shift his personal linen and feel my face grow hot. *A lady has no business in a gentleman's trunk.*

Yes, *but I'm* not *a lady; I'm* Ned, I remind myself. I have been Ned successfully for almost two years. In the army. At sea. There's no call to get all silly about his linen.

I bring the bottle of soap liniment to him and apply some to the swollen finger, working it underneath his ring as best I can. I ease the ring towards his knuckle, and he flinches, inadvertently jerking his hand. The ring pops over the knuckle and slips out of my hand, flying into the dirt and scruff and matted grass at the edge of the tent wall.

'Ah…!' he gasps.

'I'm sorry!' I yelp.

'Find my ring,' he says, with a strained laugh. 'My finger will survive, I think. I cannot lose my ring.'

I search until I find the ring and return it to him. He looks at the ring, then at his finger, which is regaining a more natural colour. There is a contracted band of flesh around his finger where the ring used to be. 'Put it in my chest,' he tells me, 'until I can wear it again. Tie it into the corner of one of my handkerchiefs, so that I can find it.'

Once more to the trunk; once more amongst his linen.

I tie the ring into a corner of one of his handkerchiefs and return the bottle of opodeldoch to the medicine chest.

I write as he dictates, then re-copy the letter in a fair hand. He seals it with a wafer and tells me, 'Have your mid-day meal, then take that letter to Lord Hood. Stay there tonight and return to me tomorrow. Oh, before you go, Mr Buckley…'

Nelson sets aside the blanket and retrieves his towel and wash bowl. He pours water into the wash bowl and dips one end of the towel in it, then wipes the wet towel across my cheek. He shows me the towel. It is black with powder and smoke. 'You had best wash your face.'

I am mortified. It must show, because he responds with one of his rare smiles. 'Use my shaving mirror and this towel.'

'I can't get your towel all filthy…'

'I have other towels,' he says. 'When was the last time you dressed your hair?'

I look at my feet. A British soldier is supposed to honour his uniform by maintaining his appearance. 'I lost my comb last week on the mountain. I nearly lost my father's watch. I was so relieved to find *it* that I did not realise I had lost the comb.'

'How did that happen?'

'I missed my footing and started sliding down the trail. My pack came open and some of my things fell out,' I say to my boots.

'Mr Buckley. Look at me, please.' I raise my eyes. 'We are fortunate that we didn't lose you, rather than just your comb. Wash your face, and I shall fix your hair.'

'Oh, no sir! I cannot ask you to do that!'

'It is not a request, Mr Buckley. It is an order,' he says dryly.

I scrub my face with his towel. When all the dirt and smoke are removed, my face glows pink in Captain Nelson's shaving mirror.

He sits on his trunk and has me kneel whilst he undoes my queue and combs the snarls and grit from my hair. He plaits my hair into a tail again and wraps the ribbon into a queue once more. 'You have skin like a girl's,' he says quietly. 'It is fairer than my fourteen-year-old son-in-law's.'

I feel myself blush scarlet.

'I am sorry; I have embarrassed you.' He puts down the comb and runs his hand over his brow. 'I apologise. I am not myself today. You look presentable again. Get on your way, and I shall expect you tomorrow.'

I pick up the letter. He remains sitting on the trunk. Another chill seizes him, and he shivers.

'Sir, will you be alright?'

'Today is the ague. Tomorrow will be the fever. Then I shall get some respite. I am used to it, Mr Buckley.'

'Yessir.' I salute him quickly and take my leave.

I find my mess and take my share of dinner. Fowler sits beside me with his bowl. Now that there is no need to hide our activity from the French, we have fires again and cooked food. Will Fowler rarely initiates a conversation, but today he says, 'What's it like, working for the captain?' This is the first time he's asked about Captain Nelson since Jack's abbreviated burial service.

'He's a good man. His sailors love him. He... he makes you feel as if he cares about you, about what happens to you.'

I'm not about to tell Fowler about Captain Nelson dressing my hair. For some reason that feels wrong, too unlike an officer. I try to think of another example. 'This morning, up on the ridge, a shell got over the earthworks; it injured a man from one of the gun crews. When we got back to camp,

Captain Nelson sent me to find out how the man was. It was a man from the *Tartar*, not one of his "Agamemnons".'

Fowler works a tough piece of gristle with his jaw, then fishes the meat out of his mouth and throws it in the fire. 'What is this, mule?'

I shrug.

'I'm glad Colonel Villettes assigned you to him. Keep you safe. You're too pretty, Ned. Some o' these buggers wouldn't think twice about getting their hands on you. This way I don't have to worry about you s' much.'

I turn red, then white. 'I'll shoot dead the bastard who lays a hand on me.'

'I don't doubt it. But you wouldn't get the chance 'til arfter. You ought t' get a knife.'

He picks himself up off the ground and tosses a handful of grit into his bowl, rubbing it around to get rid of the remaining grease, then stumps off in the direction of the latrines.

A knife. I need to get a comb, first.

I refill my canteen and cartridge box, and pick up my pack, blanket roll, and Ferguson. I'm proud of the Ferguson. I joined the army with my father's old fowling piece, and they thought me a good enough shot to give me the rifle. It weighs less than a musket, making it easier to handle for someone small like me. It is also the first breech-loading firelock I have ever used; it increases the rate of fire compared to a regular rifle, because I don't have to use a rammer. As long as it doesn't foul, that is.

Our mess is experimental. Somebody said that we're the only rifle squad in the Mediterranean. I don't know if that's true, but I know that there aren't a lot of these guns. They were last used in the American Rebellion.

It was hard to give up my father's fowler, but I had no one to leave it with. *I'm sorry, Papa.*

Men are starting to fall sick. It's worse amongst the soldiers than the sailors, but the sun and the heat and the endless fag up and down these mountains are taking a toll. I saw intermittent fever in Gibraltar last year. *Malaria,* they call it. So far, Captain Nelson seems to be the only man with those particular symptoms, but it doesn't matter where the fever comes from. It mows men down like grass.

I pick my way down the mountain towards the beach camp, where the supplies are off-loaded from the ships. This beach is less treacherous than the one at Port Agro, but still the ships have to anchor far off the land. Captain Nelson has written orders to have men row me out to the flagship. I have never been on *Victory* before. Captain Nelson usually goes alone.

I am more disturbed by what Fowler said than I want to admit to myself. As soon as I get back from the flagship, I intend to rub dirt all over my face again. It won't be hard. The sun makes men sweat rivers.

I uncork my canteen and take a mouthful of water. It's stale when we draw it from the butts, and it only gets worse in the canteens. But it keeps us alive, so nobody is going to complain.

The commanding officer at the beach camp today is Colonel Moore. He is a sturdy, good-looking man, but he has worn a sour expression since March. It only got worse after the fall of Bastia. It's as if he begrudges the navy any success at all.

Moore looks me over before taking Nelson's letter. 'You were one of Villette's men, weren't you?' From his tone, I suspect Moore doesn't like Colonel Villettes any more than he likes Captain Nelson.

'Yessir,' I respond. I know that as a naval post-captain, Nelson outranks him, which probably doesn't help.

Colonel Moore opens the orders from Captain Nelson and his acerbic expression intensifies. 'Oh, yes. You're that lad.' He looks at me as if I'm some sort of traitor. I may owe the army my obedience, but I rather resent this attitude.

I swallow my indignation. Ned Buckley doesn't have any progressive ideas; he just follows orders.

Moore takes up a quill and scribbles on the reverse of Captain Nelson's letter. 'Take it down to the cutter,' he says brusquely. He peers at me again.

'How old are you, Private?'

'Twenty, sir,' I respond, precisely as I am expected to.

'Would have taken you for sixteen,' he mutters. 'Don't know how you got into the army.'

'I am a rifleman, sir,' I volunteer. This is risky, because he didn't ask.

'I can see that,' he says. 'Regardless. You look like a child. Maybe Villettes knew what he was doing when he assigned you to that busybody, Nelson. You're dismissed, soldier.'

Smarting, I leave his tent and make my way to the beach, where sailors wait to row me the mile out to where *Victory* is anchored. I will have to wait aboard the ship for the next boat going back to the beach. Captain Nelson expects me tomorrow, but he can only request that they return me directly.

The sea is choppy, and my nerves are tense. I don't get seasick easily, but the two things combine to make me feel distinctly queasy. I decide to ignore it. Sailors are accustomed to seeing landsmen puke over the side, but I don't intend to give them the satisfaction.

Victory rides the chop out beyond sight of the shore. Two frigates, *Meleager* and *Lowestoff*, and 64-gun *Agamemnon* sit in attendance, within easy distance of each other.

The sea-state makes the leap for the boarding ladder more precarious than usual. My Ferguson in its sling whacks me sharply as I mount the ladder and clamber up the side.

On board, I hand Nelson's other letter to the officer of the watch and stand at attention while he reads it. He tells me to wait as he goes below.

An older marine whom I recognise from Gibraltar gives me a brief nod. He outranks me. Everyone outranks me. I nod stiffly in return. All around me, the business of maintaining a one-hundred-gun ship of the line goes on, as I stand there without any business to keep me from feeling foolish.

After an eternity, the lieutenant returns and bids me follow him down the companionway to the upper gun deck and into the stern of the ship. The marine at the door of the admiral's cabin stands stiffly at attention as I'm admitted to the cabin, then the door shuts behind me and I am standing alone in front of Admiral Lord Hood.

Lord Hood used to come ashore at Bastia frequently, but I never saw him. I was usually employed someplace else at the time.

I never expected to be face to face with him. His craggy, hook-nosed features make Colonel Moore's disgruntled expression look benign. He looks up from the letter I carefully transcribed this morning and snaps, 'More powder. More shot. What the devil do they think this is, an armoury?'

I know I'm not supposed to answer this, so I stay silent.

'Who are you, anyway? Why is Nelson sending me some ratty little soldier instead of coming himself?'

Ratty little soldier. I try not to let this shot rattle me. But I'm thankful that Captain Nelson made me wash my face and tidy my hair before coming here.

'My name is Buckley, my Lord. I was assigned to act as Captain Nelson's liaison to the army. He intended to come himself, but he is unwell today.'

'Thinks he's the only one who's unwell?' Lord Hood growls.

'Nosir. I don't believe he does.'

'Why does Captain Nelson need a liaison to the army?'

I think I can be candid here. 'I believe it was because Colonel Moore and General D'Aubant didn't want to deal with the captain directly, my Lord.'

Hood stares at me, then mutters, 'Sounds about right.' He tosses Nelson's letter on his desk. 'You speak well, boy. I presume this is your penmanship, as well?' He gestures at the discarded letter.

'Yessir.'

'Yes, *my Lord*,' Hood corrects me.

'Yes, my Lord,' I repeat stoically.

'Nelson thinks that this General Stuart is more cooperative than that fool D'Aubant.'

If he's trying to get a rise out of me, it isn't going to work. I know General D'Aubant is a fool.

Lord Hood picks up the letter again. 'However, General Stuart demands more ordnance. Where am I supposed to get it, tell me?' He rattles the letter.

I stay silent. He is the commander-in-chief of the Mediterranean fleet; it's his job to find it. I know from working with Captain Nelson that it was Hood's decision to besiege Calvi, even though Nelson was with him all the way. I also know, from mutterings by Moore, D'Aubant, and Stuart, that Lord Hood lost us Toulon last year. I keep my expression wooden.

Hood drops the letter on his desk again and mops his face with a silk handkerchief. His complexion is sallow. 'You are obviously educated, and you appear to have good breeding. Why are you only a private soldier, Buckley?'

'My father could not afford to buy me a commission, si—my Lord.'

'Too bad. You can tell Captain Nelson that I have received his request and will act on it as soon as I am able.' He picks up a pen and a sheet of paper and scrawls on it, then brandishes it at me. 'Take this and tell the officer of the watch that you're to go ashore.'

I take the proffered paper. I had expected to be here until it was convenient for a boat to take me back. His Lordship appears to want me off his ship. 'Thank you, my Lord.'

He waves a hand imperiously, dismissing me. I make a quick bow at the door, and an even quicker escape.

A storm is blowing up as we regain the cove. We have to get out of the boat and drag it through the heavy surf to beach it. By the time I make it to the command tent, the rain is coming down in sheets.

Moore is not there, and I speak to a captain I do not know. He directs me to a supply tent and tells me that I can sleep there tonight until the storm abates.

The supply tent contains crates of I know not what. I lay my Ferguson on top of one of the crates and remove the rag I stuffed in the muzzle, then use it to dry the rifle. I rub the barrel, and the lock and loading mechanism, with sweet oil from my pack. My clothes are soaked with seawater from the waist down, and rain from the waist up, but at least it isn't cold. The air is like a wet towel.

I climb up on another of the crates and open my blanket roll. I'm grateful that only the outermost part of it is wet. I pull it around myself and use my pack for a pillow. Lightning cracks overhead, and thunder argues as vehemently as the guns in the batteries above. Still, sleeping alone is a luxury, even in a supply tent that smells faintly like spoilt meat. It takes me no time at all to fall asleep.

Chapter Seven

I am back in the hillside camp by dawn, and I am surprised
to find Captain Nelson making his way back from the
battery. His clothes are soaking wet. He is as surprised to
see me as I am to see him.

'We're getting closer, Mr Buckley.' He motions for me
to follow him to his tent. 'I did not expect to see you back
here so soon.'

'I think Lord Hood wanted to get rid of me, sir.'

He unties the tent flaps and tells me to come inside. He
sinks down on his trunk and cradles his head in his hands
as if it is fragile. 'Did Lord Hood send a response?' he asks,
looking up.

'He said to tell you he would act on your request as soon
as he was able.'

'Did he give you any idea when that might be?'

'Nosir.'

He sighs. 'I'm not surprised.'

'Are you feeling better, sir?'

'No, Mr Buckley; regrettably I am not. I was on the batteries trying to protect our powder last night. The lightning
strikes were too close for comfort. Had the magazines gone
up, it might have ended our assault right then. We shifted
the barrels down the hillside and then back again once the

weather improved. We were able to get the guns working again as soon as the storm ended, so I consider it worth my effort. But I fear I shall pay for it.'

'I understand the necessity, sir, but could General Stuart not have done it as easily?'

'Did you think he was not there, Mr Buckley?'

'Oh.'

He sits up and looks at me. 'I need to change into dry clothes, Mr Buckley, and so do you, it appears. Go do so, and get some breakfast, then come back here.'

'Yessir, Captain.'

The Corsican sun is blazing again when I lay my damp shirt, breeches, and waistcoat on the scrub near the tent I share with my mess. I have only one spare shirt, and one pair of trousers. I also have three pairs of spare stockings and three pairs of drawers. I sewed a secret pocket into the front of each pair of drawers and stuffed it with rolled rags to make my breeches look correct. Most of the men don't wear drawers, I've learnt. They think I'm uppity. Let them.

My coat is still damp on the outside, but the lining is mostly dry. The wool broadcloth keeps the rain out, unless you have to stand in it for hours. Even wet, it will keep you warm. Not that keeping warm is a problem in the Mediter-ranean in July.

Breakfast is a bowl of gritty porridge, prepared by Tom Sharpe. Billy Baxter produces a lump of hard brown sugar and chips off bits, which he sells us for a ha'penny. He's making out like a highwayman, but it improves the porridge.

There were originally six of us in our mess until Jack Mackay was killed at Bastia. It feels as if we lost more than one man when Jack died, but perhaps it is only something in me that died that day. Now it's me, Will Fowler, Billy Baxter, Tom Sharpe, and Bert Bertram. Nobody knows what Bert's real first name is. Tom got to teasing him one day and Bert offered to beat him to a pulp. He'd likely have done it, too. Tom may be foolish at times, but he's wise enough to know when to back off, at least where Bert's concerned.

When I return to Captain Nelson's tent, the flaps are still closed. I listen carefully, before calling softly, 'Captain? Sir, it's Buckley.'

'Come in, Mr Buckley,' he says in a low voice. I push aside the flap and enter.

He is sitting on his folded blankets in his small-clothes. His coat is still wet, and it lies limply on the lid of the trunk. Someone has made him an egg and coffee. There are also some cooked greens, tangy with vinegar. Fresh greens! Who knows what they are, but it hardly matters. They're fresh, and they're green. The smell of it all makes my mouth water.

He sees me looking at his breakfast. 'You may have it,' he tells me.

'No, sir; you need to eat.'

'I would not keep it down. You eat it.'

'Can I get you something else, Captain?'

He shakes his head. 'I don't want anything. Cook is done for the morning, at any rate.'

I take up his plate. I have to remind myself to eat like a civilised human being, and not like a ravenous animal. Or a starving soldier.

He sips at a glass of water and watches me eating. 'You are thinner than I am,' he remarks. 'Not many people are thinner than I am.'

'I know I'm small, sir. But the army has made me strong.'
I take a slurp of his coffee. *Real coffee*. It is barely warm any longer, but it's heavenly.

'You're little more than a boy,' he says. 'Don't be offended,' he adds, when I look up. 'They said the same of me when I was your age.'

'Colonel Moore called me a child yesterday.'

'Colonel Moore is an ass.' My eyes widen. 'Don't repeat that,' he tells me dryly. 'I should hold my tongue.'

'I won't repeat it, sir.' I mop up the remaining egg yolk with the rest of the greens. 'It was nicer than what Lord Hood called me, though.'

'What did he say?'

'He called me a *"ratty little soldier"*.'

'Lord Hood is a good man and a very fine admiral, but he sometimes lacks the ability to get along with people,' Nelson says tiredly.

I set aside the plate. 'I'll wash this up, Captain, and then you can put me to work.'

'I appreciate you washing my dishes, Mr Buckley. But we won't do any work this morning, I think. I need to sleep for a while.'

'Let me take care of your coat, too, sir.'

'See what you can do with it, Mr Buckley.'

I take his dishes to the kitchen fire and scrub them with hot water and soft soap, then dry them with my handkerchief. It's a clean one; I just took it out of my pack this morning. Unfortunately, it's my last clean one.

I hope when we take Calvi there'll be clean water for washing. In February and March, we had rain almost all the time, and there were streams flowing down the mountains. Now, despite last night's storm, there's not a lot of fresh water up here. The rain runs off the rocks down into the ravines and vanishes.

I return to his tent with the dishes. 'Sir?' I call softly, and wait for a response. I don't get one.

I part the tent flap a crack and look in. Captain Nelson is asleep on top of his blankets. It is uncomfortably warm in the tent, and his face looks flushed. He can't sleep in here like this. He'll roast.

I leave the dishes on the trunk next to his coat, then tie back the tent flaps on either end of the tent. A hot breeze creeps through, but at least the air is moving. It should help.

Picking up his coat, I take it outside. There is a straggly little shrub next to the tent, and I turn the captain's coat inside out and lay it over the branches. If the lining dries completely, the outside can continue to dry overnight. Then I plant myself outside the entrance to his tent like a sentry. I take my journal and a pencil out of my waistcoat and start to write.

After an hour, I have completed a very long journal entry, and I am attempting to draw Jack Mackay. I do not have the skill he had. I can put lines together into a reasonable depiction of an object, but I am dreadful at trying to draw from memory and my drawing remains flat and lifeless.

Captain Nelson emerges from his tent and sits cross-legged in the dust beside me. He peers at the drawing.

'You need to use pressure and the density of your line to create dimension,' he says. 'Let me show you.'

I offer him my pencil and watch as he creates areas of shadow and light on the figure's shoulder. He makes the throat recede under the chin. It obscures details of the neck stock, but it gives a roundness and depth to the throat. He picks out the plane of the cheek with shadow, the way it angles towards the jaw, and follows the contour towards the ear. He gives me back my pencil and journal. 'Well, you get the idea.'

The figure still doesn't look particularly like Jack, but it does look more like an actual person, rather than an ordnance survey map. 'That's very well-done, sir. Thank you,' I say admiringly.

My praise doesn't have any effect on him. 'I used to draw, on occasion. Rarely anymore.'

He still looks unwell, and his lids droop uncharacteristically, but he appears improved since his nap. 'How do you feel, sir?'

'I think that I am a little better. I need to make myself eat something.'

'What would you like, sir?'

'What I would like, and what I can get, are different things,' he observes. 'I must find out what the cook has that I can tolerate. I shall do it myself, Mr Buckley. I appreciate your offer, but you do not know my constitution.'

The next day Captain Nelson is himself again, and I see little of him. He is in the batteries, and examining the ridge where the next battery will go. He is in the base camp arguing with General Stuart's subordinates. He is advocating for barrels to build new fortifications, and for the rock and soil needed to fill them. At supper, he reads the messages that have arrived during the day while he eats.

He expects a return of the ague fit the following day, but it holds off. Buoyed by this development, he seems to throw himself into his work with even greater energy and enthusiasm. My messmates come back in the evening and practically fall asleep in their suppers; I do not know how Captain Nelson sustains his level of activity. The only person who can match him for tirelessness is General Stuart; and the more I see of *him*, the more convinced I am that the man is mad.

Some hours after sunrise on 12 July, I am proofing the statistics in one of Captain Nelson's reports. He told me last night that he would spend the night in his most forward battery and would likely not come back into camp until mid-day; he informed me of what he needed me to do in his absence. In the base camp, they are just changing the picquets, but in the redoubts, we have been at work since dawn.

Someone shouts my name. I look up to see one man supporting another coming towards me. The supported man is stumbling, his head bound up in a blood-soaked cloth. I throw the ledger and Captain Nelson's report into his tent and run to meet this pair, because the bloody man is Captain Nelson.

'Run to the surgeon's mate; tell him that we're on our way,' the uninjured man says. I have no idea who he is, but he is tenderly guiding Captain Nelson, whose right eye is obscured by the bandage. I don't wait for an explanation. I am off like a shot.

The stranger accompanies the captain to the surgeon's mate, then leaves us. The mate is Mr Jefferson, from *Agamemnon,* and he speaks quietly and reassuringly as he removes the bloody bandage from Captain Nelson's head. It appears to be a sailor's neckcloth.

'Wounds to the head bleed very freely,' he says soothingly. 'It is probably not as bad as it looks.'

The captain's eye is a shocking mess. Lacerated flesh at the outer corner begins to well fresh blood as the mate examines the wound. Part of Captain Nelson's right eyebrow appears to be missing.

'I believe I can fix this up so that you will have hardly a scar, Captain. But I doubt you will be able to see out of this eye for a while, so you won't be too bothered when I bandage it.'

'As long as the bandage doesn't interfere with my work, you may bandage my whole head, as far as I'm concerned,' Captain Nelson says. His voice is thin with pain.

Mr Jefferson works efficiently and methodically. He has to cut away some of the flesh that is the most badly torn. 'Best not to leave it to invite infection,' he says quietly.

Once the wound is clean, the mate packs it with lint and winds a linen bandage around Captain Nelson's head, over his eye several times, and back around his head. He secures the bandage with pins. 'Go back to your tent and rest, Captain. Too much activity may put pressure on your eye and make the wound begin to bleed again.'

'For how long must I do this?' Nelson asks.

'Let me look at it tomorrow. We'll make a determination then.'

Captain Nelson lets me take his arm and guide him back to his tent.

'What happened, sir?'

'Shot hit a sandbag. I reacted too slowly,' he says tersely. He has been stoic throughout all of Mr Jefferson's ministrations, but his teeth are clenched, and his voice strained.

'There is nothing wrong with my left eye, but I cannot seem to see properly,' he complains. 'The perimeters of things are indistinct.'

'Would you prefer to go to the base camp, sir? Perhaps you would be more comfortable on one of the cots in the hospital.'

'I will be fine in my own tent, Mr Buckley,' he tells me. 'I don't want to walk all the way to the base camp. In addition to the pain of the wound, I have a violent headache.'

Before he will allow himself to sleep, he dictates a letter turning command over to Captain Hollowell for the day and assuring the men in the battery that he is alright. He allows me to make a pallet for him from his blankets and fold some clothes into a makeshift pillow.

I do not understand why Captain Nelson has never asked for a cot. Most of the army officers sleep on cots, particularly those in the base camp. I've seen them being off-loaded, and I can even tell you how many there are in the redoubts. But as far as I can tell, the naval officers seem to sleep like common soldiers. Perhaps they are simply Nelson's men, and they are following Nelson's lead. He sleeps for a time, but later in the day he writes personally to Lord Hood.

I have now seen first-hand how effective targeting the breastworks can be. I am not sure how I feel about it.

In the morning, Mr Jefferson examines the wound and tells Captain Nelson that he may return to limited duty. By now, I could tell him that 'limited' means nothing to Horatio Nelson. Despite having only one working eye, and still suffering a headache, nevertheless Captain Nelson is back on the battery, sporting his impressive bandage, after breakfast.

Chapter Eight

By the third week of July, Captain Nelson has twenty-five guns mounted along the ridge, battering the defences of Calvi. It has been a fag like no other, and it has come at a personal cost, but Nelson appears to be satisfied.

We have neutralised the Mozzello and the Fountain batteries. When the Mozzello fell to our troops, they found that Nelson's guns had so effectively destroyed the fortress that they were able to take it easily. Every day we inch closer to Calvi and victory. I just hope that our combined forces can hold out until then.

The captain's malarial fits seemed to have remitted after the first episode, but before his wounded eye has a chance to heal completely, they return. Men are falling ill at an alarming rate. Captain Nelson has sent more than two dozen men back to *Agamemnon,* too sick to work. Another seventy of his 'Agamemnons' are unwell, but not so badly that they cannot continue. Nelson himself seems to hold on, even though every new day seems to give me something else to worry about.

Illness does not spare his officers. Five of them are down with fever; and if his concern for them does not distract him, still, every evening he asks for a report on their condition.

The fever is also affecting the army officers. Colonel Wemyss is gone, recalled due to ill health. Even General Stuart is not well. If we lose many more officers, there will be none to take their places.

Captain Nelson continues to fag along. In addition to what he has done since we arrived, I fear that he is trying to do more; taking up the reins where some of his officers have had to put them down. He has had to make more trips to the flagship recently, as well. Lord Hood is maintaining position off the western coast aboard the *Victory and* seems to require reports daily. Yet when Nelson returns, he rarely has anything positive to show for it. Lord Hood, who is also unwell, broadsides Captain Nelson about requests for shot, or casks, or men, or practically anything else. Ironically, powder is no longer in short supply, but there is frequently a delay in getting it to the guns.

Captain Nelson stands in the centre of his tent, listening to General Stuart rail. Despite their mutual respect and the cordial relationship that they have maintained, General Stuart nevertheless sometimes takes a tone with Nelson that Nelson bears stoically. Tonight, he is berating Nelson for his latest lack of success in getting the ordnance that Stuart demands.

'*My dear sir*, I begin to believe that Lord Hood has stores that he is refusing to release! I do not trust him, and I believe that you tell him too much of our intentions,' he says accusingly. 'Indiscretion will sink us, Captain. Hood will use what you tell him to undo all of our work; mark me!'

'I admit that the admiral is often a difficult man to work with, General,' Captain Nelson returns patiently, but with less than his usual spirit. 'But he would not sabotage our campaign without a comprehensive plan of his own. We may disagree about strategies, but I believe that Lord Hood will not impose his plans behind our backs.'

'I fear that is *exactly* what he will do, sir!'

Stuart looks ill. His staff have had to beg him to go to bed, and he resists them. It does not improve his temperament.

'I hope to have better news tomorrow, Captain.' He turns on his heel and stalks out of the tent.

Captain Nelson looks at me. Stuart has yet to acknowledge my presence. I believe that to the general I am such a nonentity that he does not even see me. One of Richard's friends once lived in the West Indies and had black house slaves. He spoke of them as if they were not people. I begin to see what that might have been like.

'I shall not ask you to record any of that,' he tells me. He rubs his brow and winces when his hand encounters the wounded flesh of his eyebrow. He has no need of a bandage any longer, but the healing wound is still tender and angry looking.

His eye has lost its bloody aspect, but the pupil remains unnaturally dilated, and his sight has not returned. For a while he entertained the notion that his vision was getting better, saying he was beginning to be able to distinguish light from dark. But he has not spoken of any improvement recently, and the bright spark that always animates his eyes is swallowed up by the pupil of the injured eye.

'I should like to make an excuse for him,' Captain Nelson continues, referring to Stuart. 'He is unwell.'

'Yes,' I concur. 'But you are far from well yourself, if you will permit me to say so, Captain.'

'I am well enough, considering,' he says.

I think about what he told General Stuart. Captain Nelson does not think that Lord Hood would use such information to his own advantage. But given what he did to Captain Nelson after Bastia, I cannot help wondering if, in this case, General Stuart might not be correct.

In the morning, the cold fit is upon him again. On the ridge, it is like standing in a cooking-fire, and it is an oven in Captain Nelson's tent, yet he perspires and shivers at the same time.

'I cannot think clearly this morning,' he tells me.

Lord Hood has demanded his presence on *Victory* again today, but Captain Nelson begs a deferral. 'Help me to set it down,' he requests of me, 'and I shall write it in my own hand before I send it.

'*Today is my ague day*,' he writes. '*I hope this active scene will keep off the fit. It has shook me a great deal, but I have been used to them, and don't mind them much.*'

I wish I thought this statement were true. He completes the letter and seals it, leaving it for me to take down to the beach, and drags himself up the ridge to the batteries once more.

This is the day that Tom Sharpe doesn't come back.

Tom had always been the one who would try to raise our spirits when the weather was foul, or the food was bad, or the fag was long. He was uneducated and spoke in the most awful dialect I had ever heard. I am not even sure what region it was; it was just a mixture of dropped consonants and tortured vowels. We didn't always appreciate his jokes, but he wasn't mean, and officers liked him; he was an excellent rifleman.

He was good-looking, and women liked him, too. I remember more than once in Gibraltar when he didn't come back before curfew and showed up in the morning wearing a satisfied smile. 'Don' tell no-b'dy, Neddy,' he'd entreat. As if any of us would. We all covered for him whenever he disappeared. 'The señoritas, they don't care that he talks like a waggoner,' Jack said once. 'They can't understand him anyway.'

He didn't drink liquor, and if he was crude, he was also loyal. I don't think we realised how much we appreciated Tom until he wasn't there anymore.

The fever had been dogging him, too.

He tried to laugh it off, but he had started looking faded and insubstantial. He'd stopped eating his full share of meals. 'M' gut can't 'andle it,' he told Fowler. Come evening, he didn't have the energy to play jokes on us.

He left in the morning, and he just didn't come back.

Will Fowler is cooking today, and he has boiled a piece of pork until it's almost soft enough to eat without having to chew each bite all night. Then he threw pease in the pot and boiled them, too, so the flavour of the pork seasons the pease. One just has to be careful eating pease. Often there's gravel in it, and no matter how hard you try, you can't always sort it all out.

There are also some greens cooked into the pease. Fowler always finds something green when he cooks. I don't know what kind of leaves they are, but he hasn't ever made us sick. He says we have to eat fresh greens, or our teeth will all get loose. The prospect of that is horrifying to me.

We're all here, except for Tom. The unit he has been supporting is in camp; I have seen them. It occurs to me that maybe Tom finally went to sick call this morning. Not that they can do much for the men who go to sick call. There are so many men sick that I cannot imagine that the surgeons and surgeons' mates can do anything more than pat them on the head and give them a drink of water.

Fowler serves out the pork and pease and sets aside Tom's portion. We're all so tired that nobody talks. The heat saps your energy almost as fast as the work.

A man walks up to our cooking fire. He is as grey as a ghost.

'You the men from the rifle unit?' We nod. 'Thomas Sharpe one of your number?'

Fowler speaks. 'He is. Do you know *where* he is?'

'He's dead. Just laid down on the ground this morning and died.'

I put my bowl down slowly. Bert Bertram gets up abruptly and walks away. Billy Baxter rests his arms on his elbows and looks at the dirt between his boots. Fowler addresses the man.

'Begging your pardon, but who are you?'

'Fergus Allison. I'm the sergeant for the Captain's Company, 50th Regiment of Foot. Now I've found you, I have his rifle and cartridge box. I'll make sure it gets to you.'

'Obliged, sir,' Fowler says. 'Can you tell us where Tom's body is?'

'I imagine they buried it with the others who died today. I wasn't on the burial detail.'

'Have you had supper, sergeant?'

'I'm on my way there now.'

'Well, if you care to eat with us, we have a spare portion,' Fowler says.

Bert doesn't come back to the tent tonight. Will, Billy, and I lay in the darkness. I can tell by their breathing that neither one of them is asleep, either.

This is not the way Tom was supposed to go. He was supposed to die fighting, like a soldier is meant to do, with his rifle on his shoulder. *'He just laid down on the ground and died.'*

Finally, exhaustion takes over, and I don't open my eyes again until the sun rises.

After breakfast, we perform the necessary business of dispos-
ing of Tom's things. Billy volunteers to take Tom's rifle, pack,
and cartridge box to Sergeant Grimes.

Tom didn't own much. Apart from the necessities like
his spare small-clothes, eating utensils, and blanket, and the
tools to maintain his rifle, there's only Jack Mackay's knife,
and a piece of deadfall wood that Tom had been trying to
shape into a roe deer. He didn't get very far before he sliced
his thumb with the knife and couldn't try again until the cut
healed. 'N' worse'n a flint cut,' he'd said; but I'd bandaged it
up, and it was a whole lot deeper than that.

There's also a folded paper tucked into his razor case. I
open it gently, because the folds are worn and fragile.

'Dere Tom
   I hop the Army treets you well and you finds Onor
and Glory. Da allus sed you was the ~~brite~~ bright un.
Yr bro
Francis'

The hand is unpractised and child-like, and there are places
where the quill caught the page and left a blot of ink.

I begin to re-fold the letter and see some faded writing
on the back. It is in pencil, and the letters are wobbly. A, b,
C, D, e… Tom had practiced writing his alphabet on the
back of the letter.

I give the letter to Fowler. 'It should go to his family.'

Fowler looks at the page. 'He *was* clever,' he says. 'The
officers didn't know that he was practically illiterate.'

There isn't much to send back to his family. Bert Bertram
ties Tom's purse, and the razor case with the letter inside it,
into one of Tom's handkerchiefs and gives it to Billy to turn

over with the rifle. Before we report to muster, Fowler takes me aside and hands me Jack's knife. He doesn't say anything, but he doesn't need to.

The heat is already uncomfortable when I arrive at Captain Nelson's tent. He himself is seated on a canvas camp stool, studying a diagram. This stool is a new acquisition. I had nothing to do with procuring it, so I don't know how he got it.

He is completely dressed, save for his coat. Given his 'ague day' yesterday, this seems to me a good sign. But when he raises his head to look at me, my optimism fails.

'I have been up to the ridge' he says, 'and I have here General Stuart's plans for the next assault.' But his voice is lacklustre, and his eyes are dull. 'It cannot fail,' he continues. I have been with Captain Nelson long enough now to know that these initiatives fire his enthusiasm; today, however, the fire is almost out.

'Sir,' I venture, 'have you had breakfast?'

'Have I? Oh, yes; I have.' He presses a fist to his breast and coughs dryly. 'Too much dust,' he says.

I pour some water from his pitcher into a glass and give it to him. He sets aside the pages in his hand and sips the water cautiously. The fever is rough on his stomach, in addition to sapping his strength.

'I don't know how much we will be able to accomplish today, Mr Buckley,' he says quietly. 'My head is splitting, and all my bones ache. If it does not improve, I may have to go to *Agamemnon* for the night. I am nearly out of the bark, and perhaps a night's rest in my cot will set me up again.'

He looks as if he should go to the field hospital, not to *Agamemnon*.

Captain Nelson picks up one of the pages again. 'This is a list of the guns that General Stuart wishes to deploy next, and the positions where he wants to establish them.'

I look at the list. General Stuart is demanding thirty-five pieces of artillery, to be repositioned in new batteries even closer to the town.

Upon capturing the Mozzello, General Stuart offered terms. Our guns have stood silent for a few days, but the French declined his offer. When the guns speak again, Calvi is in for a battering like they have not yet seen.

'I need to determine which guns we will take from which positions, and plan how to get them to these new batteries. I have here the general's latest requests for materiel, as well.'

Requests. General Stuart doesn't 'request'. He demands, and if his demands are not met, woe betide the man who conveys that message.

I take the proffered page. Lord Hood is likely to unleash another verbal broadside when he sees this, and at the moment, Captain Nelson looks as if a tops'l breeze could blow him over. 'All this…?'

'I confess that I'm a bit puzzled by this request, since the stores in the Mozzello are beginning to look like Woolwich Arsenal,' he says, rubbing his eyes with thumb and forefinger. 'It is not my intention to question it, however.'

He drinks a little more water and says, 'Get me the list of which guns are currently in which positions… I think I know, but I don't trust my memory today.'

I open the log. 'Starting with the twenty-fours,' Captain Nelson begins, then stops. 'One moment,' he tells me.

He gets up from his seat and walks to the chamber pot in the corner of the tent, where he is quietly sick. He wipes his mouth with his handkerchief and returns to the camp stool.

'Apologies, Mr Buckley.' He sits down shakily.

'Let me take care of that for you, Captain,' I say quietly. I know that when one is already ill, the smell of vomit is unbearable. I go to retrieve the chamber pot and see that Captain Nelson's stomach had contained only water.

'You said that you had breakfast, sir.'

'I did. I disposed of that outside the battery this morning.'

'Oh, sir.'

I take the chamber pot and empty it in the latrines outside of the redoubt, then rinse it in a ladleful of wash water from the cooking fire. When I return, Captain Nelson is studying the diagram once more.

I return the pot to its corner and resume my place. Captain Nelson does not look up, but says, 'Do not worry about me, Mr Buckley. I am like a reed. The wind may knock down mighty oaks, but the reed bends and springs up again.'

'Yessir.'

Something unintentional in the tone of this word makes him look at me. 'You do not believe me, Mr Buckley?'

'I believe you know yourself, sir.' When he continues to look intently at me, I sigh. I had not intended to tell him.

'One of the men in my mess died yesterday, sir. He went off in the morning and never came back. The sergeant said that he just laid down and died. He had had the fever, sir, but he said it wasn't anything. He refused to go to the field hospital.'

Captain Nelson is silent for a moment, then he says, 'We will decide which guns to take from which batteries, and then I will be pleased to rest for a while.'

He keeps his word. He sleeps through the mid-day meal, but it doesn't seem to help. When he sits looking at General Stuart's map of the terrain, sketching a plan for moving his guns, he has to support his head in his left hand while he writes with the other.

What worries me, amongst other things, is that despite the debilitating heat, he doesn't perspire very much. The sweat is pouring off me, and he has given me permission to remove my coat. Most of the officers and soldiers work without coats now. Otherwise, even if a man didn't have the fever, the sun would strike him down. The sailors haven't worn jackets since Bastia.

He has been conscientious about taking regular sips of water and he hasn't vomited any more of it up again, but it's like pouring water on sand.

He receives other messages throughout the day, which he reads and sets aside. 'We will address those later,' he says, in response to my questioning look.

When the plan has been developed to his satisfaction, he says to me, 'Write that up in a legible fashion,' and lies down again on his pallet. After the injury to his eye, I may have used nefarious means to secure a palliasse for him. Getting the straw to put in it was even more difficult than obtaining the palliasse. I imagine he suspects that I requisitioned these things by representing that the request came from him, but he hasn't confronted me about it. I knew he wouldn't ask for them himself.

The sun is sinking, and I've finished transcribing, but I am reluctant to leave him. I can't put Tom Sharpe out of my mind. *'He just laid down and died.'*

I step outside the tent and take a walk down to the base camp. I'm tempted to speak to the surgeons' mates at the field hospital, but I don't know the right questions to ask, and I'm fairly certain that Captain Nelson wouldn't appreciate it. I'm about to start back to the redoubt when two young army officers pass me, and I hear one of them say Captain Nelson's name.

The other man makes a scornful noise. 'I don't know how the man ever became a captain,' he says, 'but things must work differently in the navy. He would never have made even a subaltern in the army. He is not a gentleman, neither in appearance nor demeanour.'

My face burns for Captain Nelson. It's true that his speech is not refined like these officers' speech, and he doesn't hold himself completely aloof from his men, as though he breathed more rarefied air than they. But in his courtesy and consideration of other people, he is more a gentleman than these men, or even General Stuart, will ever be. He fights alongside his sailors and takes the same risks that they take.

The scornful officer has a point, although he may not realise it. Things *do* work differently in the navy. In my limited sea experience, I have seen two 'young gentlemen' whose attitudes are similar to that of these army officers, yet there are plenty of naval men who have worked their way from ordinary seaman to warrant officer, and some who have even made the leap to lieutenant. I know whose company I prefer. Through my marriage, I have known enough men who were 'gentlemen' by birth only.

When I get back to the redoubt, I stand outside the captain's tent and say softly, 'Captain Nelson, sir? It's Buckley.' No sound issues from the tent. 'Captain?' I call a second time but receive no reply.

Apprehension swirls around me on the hot breeze. I push aside the tent flap and stick my head inside. I had debated leaving one flap tied open when I left, to keep the air circulating, but I was considering his privacy. It's stifling inside, and I am suddenly worried that I made the wrong choice.

Captain Nelson is lying on his pallet, and he looks terribly still. I kneel next to him and am relieved to see that he is breathing quietly. His hand lies limply on the straw mattress, and I take it up gently. I can feel the pulse beating in his wrist. I know nothing about how to read a pulse, other than if it is too fast or too slow, it indicates that someone is ill. Captain Nelson's feels awfully fast to me, but I haven't any idea how fast is normal for him. His skin is hot and dry, and I didn't think it possible that anyone could feel dry in this heat.

I leave the tent again and find the cook. He is not the captain's regular steward; the officers here are sharing one man. But he knows that Captain Nelson didn't eat at mid day, and I presume that he knows what Captain Nelson can or cannot eat.

'It don't do to feed a man with a fever,' he tells me.

I know this. 'He has to take some nourishment,' I say, 'or he won't have the strength to keep going.'

'Lemme boil some milk, and mebbe he'll be able to drink that. Mek sure he don't drink more'n few sips at a time, though. Oftentime, it curdles in the belly, but if 'tis boiled right, it sits better.'

I'm not entirely sure about this, since even water didn't sit well with the captain this morning. I was thinking of something closer to a clear soup. But I thank the cook and go back to Captain Nelson's tent.

I call again before entering, and this time he answers me.

'May I come in, sir?'

'Aye, Mr Buckley; come in.'

He is lying on his side, supporting himself on one arm. His shirt is soaked with perspiration.

'This is the end of the fever day, thank God. I shall not need to go back to my ship after all.'

'Cook is boiling some milk for you,' I say, kneeling next to the palliasse. 'I wasn't sure it was quite the thing, given that this morning—'

'I think that I can stomach it again,' he says. 'I might even be able to eat some bread soaked in it, if you'll tell him so.'

I leave him and go back to the cook, who smiles knowingly and plops a bit of biscuit in the milk. 'I'll mix a bit o' sugar into it, too. He'p restore his energy.'

The milk is body temperature, almost the same temperature as the air. The bread absorbs some of the milk and softens, but the whole thing looks unappealing to me. Appealing or not, Captain Nelson eats it slowly, and it stays down. He looks much restored. I guess Cook was right.

Chapter Nine

On 28 July, with the new batteries ready to go, General Stuart tries to negotiate terms with the French again. It looks as though we might be approaching the end. The following day, however, a ship carrying supplies for Calvi evades the blockade, and the French reject Stuart's offer.

At this point, General Stuart and Captain Nelson release the full fury of the new batteries on Calvi. At night on 30 July, I stand in the far battery and watch the town burn. The French defensive fire has slackened, Captain Nelson's artillery having dismounted a number of the French guns before night fell. It appears that there is not an undamaged building left in Calvi.

Two days later, it is over. On 1 August, Calvi surrenders.

The white flag is something of an anti-climax. The French demand nine days before they relinquish the town to the British. Nine days during which we wait and do nothing. Captain Nelson is restless, and Lord Hood is impossible. General Stuart refused to involve Lord Hood in the negotiations for capitulation and he is offended, which makes him even more difficult than usual.

'He's not well,' Nelson says, his own exhaustion clearly apparent. His right eye is still painful, and he confesses to me that it appears he may not regain his sight in that eye; when the fleet physician examined it, he told Captain Nelson that it seems unlikely.

He derives some pleasure from the spoils, particularly in the acquisition of two French frigates. He tells me he had fought them, off Sardinia, last fall, and it is very satisfying to take them into the British fleet. He sends one of his favourite lieutenants to take command of them.

Hood has departed in a huff, leaving Captain Nelson to deal with the logistics of arranging multiple transport ships for both British allies and French troops, and with the redistribution of ordnance and stores amongst the warships. Once again, he is everywhere, unable to be still, and works until late at night, falling into bed for a few hours before rising and attacking the mountain of tasks again.

I am back aboard *Agamemnon,* and I rarely see my messmates. With Tom's death, our mess had begun to break up. I would not have thought of Tom as the anchor that held us fast, but without him, we have gone adrift. When the redoubt where we camped is disassembled, I see Will Fowler and Billy Baxter for what turns out to be the last time.

Bert Bertram has deserted to the Corsicans, Billy tells me in an undertone. In what was probably the longest speech Bert had ever made, he told Will and Billy that he was going to marry the sister of one of the partisan sharpshooters we had worked alongside, then he melted into the hills. Will says a patrol found his coat and kit in a ravine south of the Fountain battery. He apparently took his rifle with him. The army could court-martial him for theft as well as desertion, but they'd have to find him first. And frankly, they have other things to think about. I wonder idly where he met the Corsican's sister.

Captain Nelson tells me that he has arranged for my permanent transfer to *Agamemnon* as a marine. 'You may refuse it, if you like,' he says, 'but I have come to rely on your clerical assistance. I shall not have as much work for you, since I no longer need a "liaison" to the army.' He says this with a certain amount of irony. In the end, I was no more a liaison to the army command than Tom Sharpe was. 'But you know how to shoot a rifle, and you know your way around a gun. And I anticipate that I will still be able to employ your secretarial skill. It will be unnecessary for you to keep any logs, or maintain any inventories, but if you would continue to manage my correspondence, it would help a great deal. I am afraid that I cannot pay you anything beyond your regular wages as a marine, but I will try to compensate you by other means.'

So as the transports leave the bay, and endless guns and barrels of powder and crates of shot are hauled down out of the hills and redistributed, I find myself slinging a hammock with a new mess.

Illness is still rampant. As the work of withdrawing from Corsica goes on, more and more sailors and marines are sent back to the ships, too sick to work. The fluxes are more easily corrected, but the fevers get their claws into a man and refuse to let go.

Captain Nelson's feverishness continues, but its severity has mercifully lessened somewhat. Every third day, however, he has to conserve his energy as the fever threatens to drain it. These are the days when he relies upon me most. 'I need your organisation today,' he tells me one morning.

When the dispatches go out this time, Nelson is once more disappointed. He has been passed over again. While other, less industrious men received direct praise, Captain Nelson is mentioned only vaguely, or peripherally. In a scene that seems eerily familiar, I sit in his cabin as he reads the official dispatches. I don't believe that either General Stuart or Lord Hood intended to slight him deliberately. But I cannot understand how what I saw and what they reported could have diverged so strongly. 'Never mind,' he says. 'I shall get my accolades, if I have to write them myself.'

On 20 August, one of Captain Nelson's fever days, he receives a message informing him of the death from fever of Lieutenant James Moutray, the officer he had sent to take command of the two French frigates, at Calvi. His injured eye is painful today, and he has been using me to read to him and write drafts of his letters. When I read this message aloud to him, the light in his uninjured eye seems to dim. The expression on his face is melancholy and gentle.

'I knew his mother, years ago in the Leeward Islands. She was a lady of great accomplishment, and he was every bit her son.' His eyes are unfocused, his thoughts far away for a moment. Then he passes a hand over his eyes and says to me, 'Begin a new letter. "My dearest Mrs Moutray…"'

When we finally depart Corsica, I stand in the mizzen top watching the land recede. We are leaving the island that claimed Jack Mackay and Tom Sharpe, Captain Serocold, and Lieutenant Moutray; as well as over one hundred others of our British soldiers and seamen, resting peacefully in its now quiet valleys. Below, in the sick berth and in their own hammocks, another one hundred and fifty men lie sick. Corsica is free from French rule, but it is a melancholy sort of victory. We'd expected to bear up for Gibraltar, but poor *Agamemnon* is in such bad shape that she can't make it that far.

'I'd thought to be able to release you at Gibraltar,' Captain Nelson tells me, 'but we must make for Leghorn. I hope it will not be a hardship to remain with us a while longer. Once *Agamemnon* is patched up, I expect us to be ordered home. I shall be able to return you to Gibraltar at that point.'

The marine whose hammock is slung closest to mine has been unable to rise for several days. His name is Fierson. He has a thin face and sad eyes. His best mate, who I know only as Joe, looks after him devotedly. He sponges his friend's face and helps him drink. He tries unsuccessfully to get Fierson to eat a bowl of sago.

'He ourt ter be in th' sick berth,' Joe says to anyone who will listen, but all the cots in the sick berth are already full.

One evening, I come down and find that Fierson's hammock is gone. Joe sits on a shot box, his hands dangling from his knees, his gaze on the floor. I put my hand on his shoulder, and Joe squeezes my hand for a second and then shoves it away. He doesn't know me. At this point, he doesn't want to.

In the morning, Fierson's body is committed to the sea, along with those of two seamen. The chaplain is among those who are not well, so Captain Nelson reads the same burial sentences that he said for Jack Mackay, apart from the bit about commending their bodies to the deep rather than the earth; then each of the bodies, shrouded in their hammocks and weighted with shot, is tipped into the sea.

In his cabin, Captain Nelson sighs deeply. 'It is a duty I'd gladly forgo,' he says, 'but for the honour of the departed.'

'You preside very well, sir,' I console him.

'My father is a clergyman,' he says neutrally.

'Our vicar at home was not a good presider,' I tell him. 'He raced through the liturgy as though he could not wait to get it over with. And he mumbled, so he might well have been speaking in Latin, for no one could understand him. I prefer to listen to you.'

'The sacraments are effective regardless of how well or poorly they are administered,' Captain Nelson says, 'but thank you, Mr Buckley.' He lays the palm of his hand over his injured eye and winces. 'I am so dreadfully tired.'

'Is your eye any better, Captain?'

'It is a little painful today, Mr Buckley; yesterday was better. But for all useful purposes, it appears to be blind. No matter,' he continues. 'I can see perfectly well with the other one.'

'What else can I do to assist you today, sir?'

'Nothing more, I think. I shall record this in my log and then I must write to my wife. With luck, I hope to see her again by the end of the year.'

Lord Hood urges Nelson to take command of a seventy-four-gun ship and leave the *Agamemnon*. I read the letter to him whilst he reclines in his berth, holding a compress over his right eye. I try not to allow any hint of apprehensiveness to creep into my voice. If Captain Nelson takes another ship, I will very likely be stranded in Leghorn until another captain is appointed, and then I shall be at the mercy of that captain's will. Despite the work being done on her, *Agamemnon* is so worn out by hard service that she will be paid off when she returns home; although no one can predict when she will be in a fit condition to sail as far as England.

He is silent for a few minutes, then he says quietly, 'I must decline. I cannot leave this loyal ship's company, who with me have seen such difficult service.' He sits up and looks at me. 'Besides that, I hope to sail *Agamemnon* home to England. I need a rest almost as badly as she does. Afterwards, when she is refitted, and I am restored, we both can return to the Mediterranean in fighting form.'

The Admiralty has granted Lord Hood permission to go home, and Captain Nelson hopes to take him. He envisions himself, the admiral, and *Agamemnon* returning gloriously to the Mediterranean in the spring. In the meanwhile, he takes two of his 'young gentlemen' to the spa at Pisa. All three of them return looking markedly improved.

Joe, whose name turns out to be George Augustus Josephs, waylays me one day after drill. 'I ourt ter say thank you for your kindness,' he says quietly. 'You're a good lad, Buckley.' He doesn't wait for me to reply, but walks quickly away.

The marines get a new officer. He is Captain of Marines Raleigh Spencer, and my initial impression is that those two army officers whom I overheard at the base camp at Calvi would approve of him; he is very proper and aloof.

He reviews us at muster, quietly calling the sergeant's attention to infractions: some legitimate, but one or two others strike me as unwarranted. I suppose that is why he is the Captain of Marines, and I am not. But he orders one man reprimanded for poor posture who hurt his back last week when he missed his footing on the ratlines. For a day or two, this man couldn't stand completely upright and was excused from muster. But although Spencer listens when Sergeant Preston informs him of this, he doesn't rescind the punishment.

When we are dismissed, I am walking away to return my rifle to its rack in the gunner's storeroom when Spencer steps in front of me. 'One minute, Private,' he says.

I stand at attention while he looks me over from head to foot. 'Are you even old enough to be a marine?' he says. His tone reminds me of Lieutenant Colonel Moore.

'Yessir; I am, sir.'

He reaches for my Ferguson. I have no choice but to let him take it.

'This is not a sea service musket.'

'Nosir, it is not.'

'What are you doing with this gun?'

'I am a rifleman, sir,' I say, staring straight ahead. *Does he think I stole it?*

'Are you indeed.' He thrusts the Ferguson back at me and I have to grab it before it ends up on the deck. Fergusons are fragile, and their stocks are liable to crack if they're roughly used.

'You are dismissed, *rifleman.*'

'Sir.'

He walks away. There is just a hint of a swagger in his step. I fear that trouble may have just found me.

Chapter Ten

The closing months of the year are trying for Captain Nelson, essentially laid up in Leghorn. He chafes under the inactivity of an extended stay in port. Except for one fruitless diplomatic trip to Genoa, when I stood at attention with the other marines as Captain Nelson, resplendent in full dress uniform, disembarked for a meeting with the doge, his duties have extended no farther than overseeing repairs and the replenishment of stores.

This is not without significant difficulties. Stores are so scarce that ships are reusing canvas and cable which ought to be condemned, but there is nothing with which to replace them.

Nelson's frustration stems largely from the fact that the French fleet is getting stronger, and the French army is menacing Italy, and Admiral Hotham, with his decaying ships and lack of stores and shortage of men, is reluctant to try to do anything other than keep the French in port.

'Even with the state of our ships, we would still be superior to the French fleet in a fight,' Captain Nelson grumbles irritably.

He has found lodgings in Leghorn and spends a good amount of time there. Although he attends *Agamemnon* daily, he spends most nights ashore, and occasionally he appears during the forenoon watch looking as if he has had very little sleep the night before. One of the other marines came back from leave ashore and said that Captain Nelson spends his evenings with a 'companion.' I have heard that she is his landlady, but I have heard other theories as well. One says that she is an opera singer. Another, that she is a high-class prostitute. I don't know why any of it should bother me at all... but it does.

Today he is lying sprawled on the mattress in his berth while I read to him the letters that require his attention. This is one of the days when he looks as if he had been out all night; his eyes are red and tired. He yawns.

'Would you prefer me to go, and let you rest, sir? I can return at your pleasure, if you—'

'No; I'm sorry, Mr Buckley. Let us finish with work, and then perhaps I will nap for a short time. I was entertaining some other officers last night: first with a dinner, then we attended an opera performance, and we did not part ways until quite late.' He sits up and swings his legs over the side of his berth. 'I would like your opinion of something.'

He reaches into his waistcoat and pulls out a slim package wrapped in paper. He opens the paper to display a miniature portrait, painted in oils on some sort of card. 'I had it done for my dear wife, but I don't think it a particularly good likeness. Nor does Josiah—that is, Midshipman Nisbet. What do you think?'

I think that the one of me, that my brother had commissioned for my wedding day, is superior; and I think that my bastard husband did not deserve it.

Where did *that* come from? I shove Nell back down into the dark recesses of my former life and examine the miniature.

The artist has captured the captain's features individually, but they don't quite combine into a cohesive whole—rather like my aborted drawing of Jack Mackay. He has made Captain Nelson's lips a little too thin, and the manner in which he has rendered the captain's injured eye makes him appear wall-eyed. The pupil of Captain Nelson's right eye does not dilate and contract like the other, but the eye moves largely in tandem with its partner. The artist's treatment of the captain's coat is perfunctory.

'I am afraid I would be inclined to agree, Captain. It resembles you, but the artist didn't get it quite correct. You are much more interesting looking.'

He considers this. '*Interesting* looking...?'

'Well... yes. This man is pleasant-looking enough, but not very interesting. The artist has not captured your character. The spark in your eyes is missing. And I think... he has made your nose a bit too round.'

Nelson studies the miniature. 'I think you are right about my nose. But what of my character is lacking?'

'If you told me that this man was Captain Nelson, who took Bastia and Calvi from the French, I would not believe it. There's no fire in him. This man looks like a... clergyman. Someone who stays at home and... cultivates roses.'

'I think you just described my father.' He looks bemused.

'I'm sure she will love it, sir,' I reassure him. 'Even if it only resembles you a little.'

Richard holds another miniature, painted on ivory; one that he had commissioned of our first child. He is inconsolable, and I do not have the energy or the heart to try. It is a death portrait. The tiny boy who was delivered weeks too soon was blue and lifeless when they drew him from my womb. The nurse gave him to me to hold before they took him away, and my heart broke when I looked at his little face. He was beautiful, and perfect, and dead. The life that I had carried inside myself for so long was just... gone.

'We can have another,' Richard tells me. I look away. Another child is another child, but it is not a replacement for this child. There can be no replacement for this child.

Richard thought that the miniature would be a comfort for me, he says. It is a beautiful painting, the ivory emphasising the transparency of my son's perfect skin. But I cannot look at it. I'm not sure how he ever thought I could.

'Put it away,' I whisper to him. 'One day I will cherish it. But now it is too painful.'

I have encountered no further difficulties with Captain Spencer, but that does not mean I have not encountered him. I can feel his eyes on me every day at muster. I do not dare look his way. Wandering eyes will get a man called out, and God forbid I should make eye contact with the man. While he is always cool and correct and speaks in the undertones of a gentleman when talking to the other officers, there is something predatory about him. He makes me feel like a rabbit. I do not like him.

In preparation for Christmas, Captain Nelson purchases gifts for people at home and arranges for bequests to be distributed from his agent in London. He directs £200 to be sent to his father's parish in Norfolk, to be spent on blankets and warm clothing for the poor. I know that he frets about the money of his own that he expended in Corsica, for which he has yet

do you use "Joe" instead of "George"?' I ask Joe.
t i'nt just George, is it? It's George-Augustus.'
t realised that the two names contained a hyphen.
rents had grand idears,' he mutters.

---

ghorn again on 24 February; and Captain Nelson
his cabin. He still looks most unwell.
nd the sickest men to hospital,' he tells me. 'They
sfer tickets. I need you to go to the surgeon and
they are.'
ptain.'
know,' he says tiredly. 'But I have been very low.'
is burning, and his cabin is warm and dry,
to be cold. He sits hunched in his chair near

u now, sir?' I venture.
g, Mr Buckley, but only just. I have requested
e to try and get myself back up again.'
ou shall, sir.'
good reason, Mr Buckley.'

'good reason' arrives just two weeks later.
to be on the way to try to retake Corsica.
antic activity, *Agamemnon* puts to sea with
rteen ships.
till under-strength, and Captain Nelson
recovered himself, but his internal fires
ore. Gone is the listlessness that had
him like a fog. He is intent, focused,

to see any hint of reimbursement, yet he spends nearly as much on these gifts.

'It is not as if I can use the money here, Mr Buckley. I have all that I need.'

All that he needs, except for cable and canvas, spars and pitch… the shortages of these things hang over the fleet like a storm cloud.

The fleet puts to sea on 21 December for St Fiorenzo. We are nearly three weeks at sea; three weeks of heavy seas and violent storms. It is unclear to me why we undertook this cruise. We see no enemy ships. Whilst I might think that it is craven of the French to cower in Toulon, even so, they are not being bashed about, soaked, and sea-sickened as we are.

Captain Nelson hosts a belated Christmas dinner ashore in St Fiorenzo for *Agamemnon*'s officers and the captains of some of the other ships that also languish here. When I encounter him the following day, he looks a little… out of kelter.

'This sitting in port will be the death of me, Mr Buckley,' he groans. 'I am stagnating, and trying to drown my frustration in good cheer only makes me repentant the following day.'

I decant a drop of ether from the bottle in his medicine chest into his palm, and he claps his hand to his forehead and holds it there.

'I fear I have been remiss,' he says after a minute or two. 'I neglected to ask you if there was anything I could do for you, in observance of Christmas.'

No one has offered or asked me such a question in two years. Apart from the requisite divine service and some extra rations, the observance of Christmas has been almost nonexistent.

'Thank you, Captain,' I say softly, 'but there is nothing that I need.'

He seems disappointed. 'I should have liked to have given you something, but I didn't know what you might like.'

I try to think. 'Perhaps a book, sir. Of whatever you would like.'

'But what do you like to read, Mr Buckley?'

'If it is something that interests you, sir, I know it will interest me.'

I do not see him the following day because he is sitting a court-martial, but when I go to sort his mail, there is a package on his desk with my name on it. I undo the string and paper, and inside is a volume of *Henry V*, by William Shakespeare. The edges of the binding are worn. When I open the book, *Horatio Nelson* is written across the top of the flyleaf.

On 7 February we put to sea again, and spend another seventeen miserable days cruising. If possible, the weather is even worse than before. Men are falling sick again.

We cannot drill, which adds to the tedium of the marines' days. But it means that I do not have to see Captain Spencer, who when he last inspected us walked between the ranks and stood behind me for longer than necessary, breathing in my ear. It was all I could do not to shudder.

Captain Nelson is not well, and he has not requested my assistance for several days. During the last time I spent working with him, he was pale and feverish, and crampy with a flux. I did my best to work quickly and efficiently as he lay curled in his cot, giving me direction, but eventually he told me,

'That will be all, Mr Buckley. I
Andrews, now his first lieuter
the captain's physical duties, a
on deck very little. When I h

I should not be surprised
seems to sicken almost one
in my mess, and two of th
from Captain Nelson's co
throughout the other shi

I suppose I should n
geon and his mate are d
Captain Nelson has an
of ease in the quarter-
walk, stiff-legged and
in all likelihood they
available. Men who
through their watch
until they have to

George Augu
meal, what there
Bennett, had to
dehydrated that
us could provid
work, but he
going to go t
replaced Fier
his presence
stay long. T
I've been h

Joe is
his relatic
Jack Mac

'Why
'Well,
I hadn'
'My pa

We reach Le
calls me into
'I must se
will need trar
discover who
'Yessir, Ca
'I ought to
The brazie
but he appears
the brazier.
'How are yo
'I am survivir
leave to go asho
'I hope that y
'All I need is

Captain Nelson's
The French appear
In a single day of fr
a British fleet of fo
Agamemnon is s
does not look fully
are stoked once m
seemed to surroun
and collected.

This looks as though it might be our first fleet action. Captain Spencer reviews our ranks. As he passes behind me, he stops. My gut clenches, and it has nothing to do with any flux. He twitches the tail of my coat.

'What is this, Private Buckley?'

'Sir.'

'The lining of your coat tail is torn, sir.'

'What...?' I say, startled, then bite my tongue.

'I did not invite you to address me, Private.' His voice never rises; it stays menacingly soft.

Oh, but you did, sir. You asked me a direct question. Regardless, my coat lining was not torn this morning. I can't say any of this, so I stay silent.

'You will repair it, Private, and then you will stand a double watch tomorrow.'

I don't speak, and he moves on. But before he does, he brushes his hand against my bum. I clench my jaw so hard that I think my teeth will crack.

When I go below and remove my coat, I discover that the lining of my coat tail is not torn; it has been cut with a knife, an L-shaped rent in the fabric that hangs down below the hem. I feel a dangerous rage build inside me.

There is no evidence that it was he who cut your coat. Be careful.

As I try to repair my coat lining, I realise that the rage has less to do with my coat, than with where his hand had lingered before he walked away.

Thanks to my exchange with Captain of Marines Spencer, I am beginning the first of my two consecutive watches at noon the following day, 10 March, when the French fleet finally comes into view. Admiral Hotham makes the signal for a general chase, and Captain Nelson has *Agamemnon* off like a shot in pursuit of the fleeing French. As he passes me on deck, he says, 'Hah, Mr Buckley—now we shall give the French fleet a taste of true English valour!' before he goes below.

It doesn't happen that way. Half-way through the first dog watch, it appears that the French have got a favourable wind and are gaining distance. As the sun is setting, Admiral Hotham calls off the chase.

The consequence of a double watch is that one only gets four hours off duty before the next watch comes around. I am back on duty at the beginning of the middle watch. It will be four o'clock in the morning before the watch ends, and I will get no more sleep tonight. I cannot complain; the sailors always do four hours on, four hours off, and not all marines stand watch daily. Our watches serve only to guard the stores and the officers.

At two bells, I am surprised to see Captain Nelson on the quarterdeck. He seems calm, composed, and alert.

'Good morning, Mr Buckley,' he says, quietly coming upon me in the starlight.

'Good morning, sir.'

'Perhaps it will be today, God willing.' He stands silently for a minute, then asks me, 'Are you prepared, Mr Buckley?'

'I believe so, sir.'

'The sooner it comes, the better,' he says. 'I shall not sleep until we engage them.' He lays a hand on my shoulder, then returns to pacing the quarterdeck.

It does not come today, however. We cannot get close enough. The wind is uncooperative, and any breeze we catch soon deserts us. We go to our suppers with a sense of a frustration.

'You ever fourght aboard ship, Buckley?' Joe asks.

'You ever fought *anywhere*, Buckley?' Simon Greeley echoes.

I throw a piece of particularly weevily biscuit at him. 'No, never, Simon. I spent all summer on Corsica enjoying the scenery. No,' I continue, addressing Joe and pointedly ignoring Simon, 'I haven't fought aboard ship before.'

'Ah, well… it i'nt that different from fighting on land. 'Scept how th' ship rolls when th' guns fire,' he says.

'They'll likely put you in the fighting tops,' says Tom Scully. 'You're small and quick, and good with that rifle of yours.' He has recovered from the flux, although he's thinner than he was when he joined us. Francis Bennett, who was sent to hospital when we got back to Leghorn, hasn't re-joined the ship yet.

'Won't matter that he's quick,' says Simon. 'There's no place to run.'

'Ah, stop being an arsehole, Greeley,' Joe tells him.

Matthew Tinsdale, a tall, lean, muscular man who never says very much, volunteers, 'If they put you in the tops, Ned, I'll be up there with you. They've assigned me a volley gun.'

I've seen these monsters. They have a short stock and seven muzzle-loaded barrels. One has to be strong to handle them, because they kick like a horse. I think they were designed to be used by sailors, but sailors don't like them. Sailors aren't dumb. I'm not sure that Tinsdale likes them much either, but we don't get to say, 'Actually, sir, I'd rather not.'

I lie in my hammock, listening to the sounds of men sleeping, and think of Captain Nelson, who will not sleep until the battle is over.

Chapter Eleven

Sometime in the early hours of the morning, the wind
dies. When the light gathers, we are becalmed and dis-
persed into two loose groups. Then, to the windward,
we see the French fleet.

Our group of only six ships is vulnerable. We are closest
to the French, and easy prey for an attack.

We wait uneasily for the drum beat to quarters. Captain
Nelson sends to HMS *Princess Royal* with a pledge of support,
but he requests reinforcements if she has any men who can be
spared. Under-manned as she is, *Agamemnon* is at a disadvantage.

The French ships get closer. They can cut us off from
the rest of the fleet, and Admiral Hotham's ships will not
be able to assist us.

We watch silently. Something about the French fleet is off.
Twice they attempt to form a line of sail, and twice they fail to
achieve it. They are within three miles of Admiral Hotham's
division when they abort their attack. The admiral forms a
line of battle, but the wind thwarts us again. When darkness
falls, the two fleets are at a standoff.

Captain Nelson calls me to his cabin, but he isn't looking
for secretarial assistance. He paces energetically in the lantern
light, waving his hands. Two nights without sleep seem to
have affected him not at all.

'They are not professional!' he exclaims. 'Did you see the way they sailed? They were uncoordinated—they have very little control!' He turns on his heel and addresses me with an index finger in the air. 'If they sail in so undisciplined a fashion, then I am sure their gunnery is just as poor. I am more convinced than ever that we can take them! If we can only entice them to fight…!'

His supper sits untouched on the table. 'Sir,' I suggest, 'perhaps you should take a moment and eat something.'

'I cannot eat. If I can just get in close with them—!'

Lieutenant Andrews appears at the cabin door, followed by John Wilson, the master, then a moment later by the second lieutenant and the gunner. Captain Nelson waves them in.

'Gentlemen, I hope you have had your suppers—thank you for coming. I have observations I would like to make, and I would like to solicit your opinions and advice. Please have a seat.'

I vacate my chair and pick up the captain's plate. 'I'll leave this on your dining table, sir…?'

'Fine, fine.' I do not think he's really hearing me; all of his attention is focused on the issue at hand. 'Good night, Mr Buckley. Thank you.' He resumes his pacing as he addresses the officers, and I slip from the cabin and retire to my hammock.

Daylight finds us twelve miles to leeward of the French, who could easily overtake us, having the wind in their favour. But instead of making any effort to engage, they run. I can see the agitation in Captain Nelson's posture as he traverses the deck, never still. When Admiral Hotham signals for the general chase, his energy is uncontainable. He practically bounds about the quarterdeck as the seamen brace the yards for optimal speed. *Agamemnon* is soon out in front of the fleet.

She is the fastest ship of the line in the Mediterranean. Her crew has spent two years perfecting their performance in engagements off the Corsican coast, and they can make her fly. This is truly a chase, and it is thrilling. In a short time, she has closed the distance by half.

Men clear the decks for engagement: partitions, bulk-heads, and furnishings swiftly stowed, fires extinguished, decks and rigging and sails wetted, and sand strewn on the decks. We have practiced this drill until it is like breathing. The tension and anticipation ratchet up; this time, it is no drill.

Barely two hours into the chase, the unexpected occurs. I am astonished when two of the French ships collide, and the main and fore topmasts of one of the two crack and come down, with all their rigging and canvas, on her leeward side. 'Well, I will be damned,' says a man standing behind me.

The British lion scents blood. Captain Fremantle's frigate *Inconstant*, of thirty-six guns, darts in to engage her. *Inconstant* is like a wren worrying a hawk. She has to be outgunned by about forty guns, and huge guns at that, but the French ship's starboard broadside is disabled by the wreckage of her masts. All of *Agamemnon*'s complement seems to catch their breath as little *Inconstant* fires her broadside into the vast ship, then comes about to fire her second broadside.

'That's *Ça Ira*,' says the man to my left. 'She's carrying at least seventy-four guns, maybe more.'

'Eighty,' corrects his companion authoritatively.

Men cheer as Captain Fremantle unleashes his second broadside, but the crew on the French ship has almost cleared the debris of her damaged masts. The British fleet is coming up fast, but the line-of-battle ships are still out of range.

Inconstant bravely comes in for a third attack and fires one more broadside into *Ça Ira,* but this time the big two-decker is able to bring her guns to bear. *Ça Ira* savages the frigate, and Captain Fremantle falls back.

My heart has been in my throat during this contest, but as the wounded *Inconstant* bows out, she is passed by *Agamemnon. Agamemnon's* men cheer *Inconstant* with a mighty roar, then the drums beat to quarters. It is Captain Nelson's turn.

We are far in advance of the rest of our fleet, and we are going in unsupported.

Silence falls as each man waits with coiled sinews at his station, listening for the order when they will spring into action.

As Scully had predicted, I am in the foretop. Big Matthew Tinsdale is there too, with the vicious volley gun. I was not originally chosen for the fighting tops, but *Agamemnon* is as short of marines as she is of seamen.

In scarcely an hour from the time that *Inconstant* first engaged the big French ship, we are within range of her guns. Nor is she alone any longer.

Agamemnon advances on *Ça Ira.* The French ship has only her stern chasers to fight with from this position, but she puts them to use. The first fire from her guns sends balls whistling through our sails, splintering spars and pulling down rigging. I cannot help shouting when an explosion of splinters from the topmast comes flying through our position on the fore fighting top, but miraculously no one is impaled by them. Captain Nelson resolutely reserves fire.

After a few more shots from *Ça Ira*'s stern guns, it is apparent that she's trying to disable our masts. Although a good number of them punch holes in our canvas, more of them go sailing between the rigs to land harmlessly in the ocean. Still, we endure nearly half an hour under her fire, our guns remaining silent.

Then Captain Nelson orders the sails braced a-shiver, and as her bow falls off, *Agamemnon*'s broadside comes to bear.

Our guns begin to roar in quick succession. There is not a gun crew in the Mediterranean that can fire as expertly as *Agamemnon*'s seamen. They are fast, and they are deadly accurate. They double-shot the guns, so that each round sends two balls hurtling into the stern and quarter of *Ça Ira*. *Agamemnon*'s guns may be smaller than those on the French eighty-gun ship, but her gun crews are professionals, and her position is lethal. Each shot sends balls and debris hurtling the length of the French ship, disabling guns and cutting down men.

With each broadside to her stern, *Agamemnon* creeps ever closer to *Ça Ira*. With each broadside, we in the tops get closer to being within musket range. I believe I could make a shot already with my rifle, but I hold my fire with the rest.

Agamemnon is within range of two other French ships, one of them the massive one-hundred-twenty-gun *Sans-Culotte*. But neither of these ships come to *Ça Ira*'s assistance. They seem to watch impassively as *Agamemnon* wreaks devastation upon her. Towed by a frigate, her masts in ruins, *Ça Ira* cannot bring any of her guns to bear except her stern chasers.

Two hours into the fight, the French seem to realise that they have to change tactics. The frigate towing *Ça Ira* brings her head around, and *Ça Ira* follows with her. Our next pass will be broadside to broadside, at close distance.

I aim my rifle and intend to make every shot count. As the guns roar from both ships, *Agamemnon* rolls like mad; trying to aim this way is a challenge I have never encountered before. To add to it, the French are still firing high. It tears apart our rigging and shreds our sails, but *Agamemnon*'s hull remains undamaged. I cannot stop myself from flinching every time a ball hurtles through the rigging, though: we are exposed up here in a way that I have never been in combat on land.

There is a furious noise over my right shoulder as Tinsdale fires the volley gun. He has the mast at his back, or the gun might have knocked him back into the topmast shrouds. I have no idea whether its seven barrels managed to hit any-thing, but they are still smoking slightly as Tinsdale begins the process of reloading.

Captain Nelson fires our after guns at *Ça Ira* and turns *Agamemnon* to make another pass. Remarkably, our guns fire almost continuously as their crews serve them rapidly and efficiently. We are at optimal rifle range, but I cannot get off an effective shot; the roll of the ship impedes my aim every time.

On our lee bow, *Sans-Culotte* and several other French ships are poised to pass us to the leeward, and to remain would be foolhardy. Captain Nelson has no choice but to leave off action. After almost three hours of battle, Admiral Hotham recalls *Agamemnon*. The French fleet collects their frigate with the battered *Ça Ira* in tow as they make their retreat. Not a single one of the other British ships of the line engaged *Ça Ira*. The day belongs to Fremantle and Nelson.

We make our way down from the fighting tops to the deck. My arms are shaking with fatigue, and my legs with the aftermath of engagement. Normally I have no trouble with the ratlines, but twice on the way down I almost miss my footing. It would be ironic to survive my first sea battle only to fall into the ocean and drown.

Captain Nelson is no longer on the quarterdeck, but as I make my way to the gunner's store to secure my rifle, one of his servants finds me.

'Captain asks that you come to his quarters directly,' he says breathlessly.

Directly: as in, 'right now'. *Why?* I secure my Ferguson in its rack and proceed to the great cabin, without stopping to check how presentable my appearance might or might not be.

The bulkhead walls and the windows of the captain's cabin have already been restored, and the furnishings are in process of being returned. Above, the carpenters have already begun repairs, and men will work through the night to restore *Agamemnon*'s damaged rigging. Hardly anything hit her hull.

The captain is jubilant. He is not usually an effusive person, but now he beams with pride and excitement.

'Mr Buckley! Do you know what we just did?! We are making history! We took on that French giant and beat her soundly!' He cannot contain his energy, sitting down and then springing up again, stalking around the cabin, arms gesturing.

'I gambled that she would fire high and without skill, and I was right! And my poor brave fellows—they did it all themselves, without another ship to aid them!

'Did you see Captain Fremantle go in there right under her guns...? Bold work, Mr Buckley!'

He spins around with the biggest grin I have ever seen him wear. A sailor walks into the cabin carrying the captain's table, but he doesn't even seem to notice. His mind is racing on to other things.

'Had we had the support of other ships, we could have gone after that monster first-rate of theirs—*Sans-Culotte*—and I wager we'd have beaten her, too!'

He stops pacing and looks at me. 'I have to contain myself. There are things we must do next.' But even as he seats himself at the newly restored table, he reminds me of a small boy trying not to fidget in church.

'I want you to go to the surgeon right now and get a list of the wounded. I shall order a small celebration for the men this evening at supper; it will be short, but it is absolutely necessary! They must know the depth of my appreciation for what they have done today. I shall dine in the wardroom with my officers tonight. I am hosting this meal, and I would like you to be there, as well.'

'But sir—'

'It is official business, Mr Buckley. I shall give you an opportunity this afternoon to square things with your mess.'

'Thank you, sir.' There is no use trying to dissuade him; he will get what he wants. I am no stranger to the officers of the wardroom, but I do not feel that I belong there.

I go below to the cockpit in the orlop. There is only one wounded man there now, but there are also three bodies. The surgeon gives me the bill.

'Four wounded; three dead. Here are their names.' He passes me a sheet of paper, with the casualties' names written on it. Their names will go into his log, and into the captain's log, as well.

In over two-and-a-half hours of fighting, seven casualties; and at a distance toward the end of less than fifty yards. Surely that is unusual...? In the height of the battle, I had had no awareness of men falling wounded; I simply accepted that some of us would.

When I return to Captain Nelson's cabin, it is completely restored. The cabin door is standing open, and I walk in to find him alone, on his knees in prayer. I back up and wait outside the doorway until he rises.

'I'm sorry, sir; I didn't mean to intrude on your private devotions.'

'I was thanking the One who sustains us for our success today. It is neither particularly private nor personal. Is that the list from the surgeon?'

I hand him the paper. 'Poor souls,' he says quietly, reading the names. He retrieves his logbook; taking up his quill, he writes the names solemnly in the book.

'How was your battle, Mr Buckley?'

'I found it hard to aim properly with the ship rolling as she did, sir. I don't believe I was terribly efficient.'

'The next time it will be easier.'

'Yessir.'

'We may have another chance at them tomorrow.' He yawns. 'I think I shall actually be able to sleep tonight.'

He indicates the pen and inkwell. 'My right eye in particular is badly irritated from the smoke. You will please scribe for me for a bit; then you will be free until supper. Let me know when you are ready.'

I take up the pen. 'Begin, sir.'

———

My mess survived uninjured except for Matthew Tinsdale, who has a massive purple bruise on his shoulder. 'Round of shot flew by me just as I was aiming. It broke my concentration and made me jerk my finger on the trigger. Damn near broke my shoulder, too, when it fired.'

'You're lucky you didn't go right out of the top,' Scully says.

'I'd be happy to let someone else try her out,' Tinsdale says of the volley gun. Nobody feels inclined to take him up on the offer.

Dinner in the wardroom is a mix of celebration, strategy, and reportage. It starts with a celebratory air, moves on to reporting and strategizing, and ends with celebration again. I watch the officers. These men are professionals: good at their jobs, emotionally strong, and mentally resilient. I remember Wolfe's phrase, 'inured to war.' If I wasn't sure what that looked like a year ago, I know now.

The drink flows, and the celebration gets a little boisterous toward its end, but there are still watches to stand and preparations to make. Captain Nelson fully expects that the fleet will have another go at the French in the morning. The group breaks up just before the middle watch.

'Mr Buckley, please walk up to the quarterdeck with me, if you would,' the captain requests.

He did not drink a great deal, but he is slightly unsteady and uses my arm as a guide. Of course; he has hardly eaten or slept since we sighted the French fleet. I'm surprised that he's still standing.

I wish him good night and he says quietly, 'Good night, Mr Buckley. I expect great things to happen tomorrow. Be ready.'

'Yessir.'

He goes into his cabin and shuts the door. I stand on deck in the starlight for a moment before retrieving my hammock from the rails.

After everything I have been through with him in this past year, I have come to respect, and admire, and even have affection for Captain Nelson. This makes me uneasy in a way I can't entirely explain, but after Jack Mackay's death, I told myself that I would not get attached to anyone ever again.

I suspect that Captain Nelson is not the only person who slept soundly, but by first light, no one is sleeping. The French fleet is still out there, and we are ready for it. The morning is hazy, with light rain and equally light winds, but they have already been spotted. And if Captain Nelson's reaction is typical, then the British captains are confident of a fight.

The French are missing two of their ships, one of them the massive *Sans-Culotte* that Captain Nelson was so warm to take on last night. I wonder if they have noticed.

Ça Ira has not restored her topmasts and is now being towed by a seventy-four, *Censeur.* The two ships are lagging the rest of their fleet by over a mile, and have fallen to leeward, where they are fighting the light winds. Admiral Hotham closes in like a wolf on an injured sheep.

Just after seven o'clock, the British line interposes itself between the two stragglers and the rest of the French fleet. Our two leading ships, HMS *Captain* and HMS *Bedford,* draw the fire of the two beleaguered French ships, and it is a terrible thing to watch.

Either the French have revised their tactics, or *Agamemnon* was incredibly lucky the day before. They are still firing high, but their aim is accurate. Before long, both *Captain* and *Bedford* have been disabled; *Captain* is completely dismasted.

Behind our two lamed seventy-fours follow *Illustrious, Courageux,* and the ninety-gun *Princess Royal,* followed in turn by our valiant little sixty-four, *Agamemnon.*

We engage the two big Frenchmen, but on our weather side, the rest of the French fleet has caught a wind and is approaching. I imagine that all of us above decks have one eye on the two ships to starboard, and the other on the rest of the fleet bearing down from the windward.

'Reckon they'll try to get between us and these two,' a veteran sailor comments. 'If they do, it's going to get warm for us.'

I refrain from commenting that to me it seems pretty warm already. I am learning how to adjust my aim to the roll of the ship, but I still haven't managed to do any real damage with my rifle. On land, that would be a point of embarrassment for me, but in this situation I can only focus on the motion of loading, aiming, firing. The lock mechanism and barrel grow hot with repeated firing. I pray that she doesn't jam.

I am sighting down the barrel and about to take the shot when a piece of metal comes flying. Just as I release the trigger, the projectile comes within inches of my head; I hit the deck of the fighting top hard as I throw myself out of the way.

I lie on the boards for a moment, discerning whether all of me is still in one piece. I feel numb and shaken by the impact of my body with the deck of the top. Nothing hurts, and there is no blood, so I figure I am still functional; but when I pick up the Ferguson, I find that it is not.

The stock is badly cracked at the wrist. This is the gun's weak point, and one that I have been very careful to protect. It can perhaps be repaired with a plate, but it will never be strong. And now I have no weapon.

'My rifle is disabled!' I shout at Matthew Tinsdale. 'I'm going down for another gun!'

I sling my rifle over my shoulder and ease myself over the edge of the top into the windward shrouds. And then I get an eyeful that I wasn't expecting.

Instead of interposing themselves between us and *Ça Ira* and *Censeur,* the van of the French line has come up on our windward side, and our seventy-fours are now beginning to engage the French on both sides. I'm not sure whether this is good or bad. The officers would say that depends on the state of the French gunnery, and Captain Nelson has been right so far; but we all saw what *Ça Ira* and *Censeur* did to *Captain* and *Bedford* this morning.

I clamber down the shrouds to the deck and am met immediately by one of the younger midshipmen. 'Captain wants to see you on the quarterdeck!' he bawls over the discharge of guns.

How the devil did he see me? Alright, he has a spyglass, but surely it was just by chance.

Instead of going for anther gun, I follow the young man to the quarterdeck.

'Are you wounded?' Captain Nelson asks in a fairly normal voice, considering the noise surrounding us.

'Nosir; but my rifle is. Her stock is cracked. I was on my way to try and get another gun.'

'Stay here just now. Things are about to get very warm.'

There is that phrase again, the same one that the old sailor had used. Presumably it means that all hell is about to break loose.

That would not be an inaccurate description. We are battling *Ça Ira* again, and even damaged as she is, the big French ship still fights like a tiger. Her companion *Censeur* resists furiously as well. On our windward side we are also hurling broadsides at the rest of the French fleet, but they have not got close enough for the shot to be very effective.

A shot splinters part of the mizzenmast, barely missing Captain Nelson and Lieutenant Andrews. The captain ducks, but the splinters fly widely, one of them striking Mr Wilson, the master. Wilson has always been kind to me; I rush to his side as he crumples on the deck.

'It's not bad, son,' he says, but the blood is running out from between his fingers.

'Let me take you to the surgeon,' I implore him. I put an arm under his shoulder, and we make our way painfully down the companion ladder.

The guns fire in rapid succession, and the smoke on the gun decks is thick and stinking. The noise is like nothing I have ever heard before. All these guns in this enclosed space; their incessant roar is physically painful. There is no way the gun crews can hear their captains. They have to use the physical memory of their limbs and rely on the rhythm of their mates working in concert.

The orlop deck is another level of hell. Although not currently crowded with injured men, it is hot, and dark, and reeks with the metallic odour of blood. The noise from the guns penetrates here as well, as does the shaking of the ship's frame as the guns leap and buck against their breeching ropes. The surgeon has a man on the table, his face contorted in agony. I turn my face away from the harrowing sight.

'Just leave me here, lad,' Mr Wilson tells me. 'They'll get to me in a short time, and there's no need for you to stay. I'll be fine.'

Back on deck, the smoke is becoming almost as bad as it is below. It is difficult to make out the enemy ships to the leeward; but on the larboard side, the rest of the French fleet is retreating from the conflict, leaving its two trapped ships to their fate.

By eleven o'clock it is almost over. Both *Ça Ira* and *Censeur* strike their colours, but the smoke is so thick that

Courageux cannot see it and continues to fire on *Ça Ira* until Admiral Goodall signals her to stop.

Illustrious and *Courageux* can claim the honours today, but they are both so badly mauled that they have no boats to take possession of the prizes. Vice Admiral Goodall asks Nelson to take possession, and he proudly dispatches Lieutenant Andrews and prize crews to the two French ships. *Agamemnon* takes *Censeur* in tow.

Agamemnon did not escape unscathed, and once again her carpenters have much work ahead of them. But compared to *Captain, Bedford, Illustrious,* and *Courageux,* she is in good condition.

I never made it back into the tops, nor did I manage to get another gun. I hope that escaped the notice of Captain Spencer. I do not care to have any more confrontations with him.

Before leaving the quarterdeck, Captain Nelson says to me, 'Get me the butcher's bill, and the gunner's report when it is ready, and come to my cabin at'— he peers at his pocket watch — 'three bells. Thank you, Mr Buckley.'

I descend once more to the cockpit, where the surgeon is cleaning his instruments. The loblolly boy is mopping up blood. Mercifully, this time there are no corpses.

'Seven casualties,' the mate says, handing me the list. I scan it quickly. Again, Providence has protected us. Seven casualties, and no deaths.

Men are hard at work restoring the ship as I climb back up to the sunlight. The decks are in the process of being washed. The galley fire is lit again, and there will be a hot meal for dinner. The stench of smoke clings to everything, and men are still coughing from hours spent inhaling it on the gun decks.

When I arrive at the captain's cabin at three bells, he is deep in discussion with Lieutenant Andrews, who has returned from *Ça Ira* looking grim. Captain Nelson looks up and addresses me.

'Give me another hour please, Mr Buckley.'

'Yessir,' I reply, leaving the cabin.

I go in search of my mess. Most of them have finished cleaning their guns and Joe is shirtless, scrubbing water over his head and chest. It looks as if Simon Greeley has simply poured the water over himself; he has removed his coat and waistcoat, and his shirt is wet and clinging to his torso.

I will find a more private place to wash and change later.

Matthew Tinsdale hails me. 'You never came back up, Ned. I didn't think about it at the time, but after it was over, I wondered if you'd been wounded. What happened to your rifle?'

'The stock cracked when I threw myself out of the way of a piece of something... I don't know what. Langrage, maybe. It must have hit the deck pretty hard; I know I did.'

'Did you not get another gun?'

'No. The captain saw me climb down the shrouds and sent for me.'

'Spencer?' Tom Scully mutters. His eyes narrow. 'I don't like that cove.'

'No; Captain Nelson. I didn't see Spencer.'

'He was on the poop,' Joe says. 'With me.'

'Poor you,' Greeley says under his breath.

This is interesting. None of the men seem to like Captain Spencer. I wonder what he has done to *them*.

When I ask Joe, he says quietly, 'It i'nt what he's done so much as how he treats us. Captain Clark made us feel he respected us. Captain Spencer treats us contemptuous-like.'

I have not told any of them about my encounters with Captain Spencer, and I don't intend to. But if he treats us all contemptuously, then maybe he hasn't singled me out. Then I think about his hand brushing my bottom, and I'm not convinced.

When I return to Captain Nelson's quarters an hour later, I hear no voices in the cabin. The sentry tells me that the captain is expecting me. I tap on the door before entering.

The captain's wash basin contains cooling soapy water, and a damp towel lies crumpled beside it. His coat is folded over the back of a chair. Captain Nelson himself is asleep on his berth, damp hair spread out across the pillow.

Having watched him command from the quarterdeck and seen the amount of energy he expended, and the way he maintained that level of energy through taking possession of the prizes and assessing the damage to his ship, I think, *He has to be exhausted.* I lay the reports on the table. I know that there is much work still to be done, but there are enough hours left in the day. I pick up the pen.

> *'Sir, I came as you requested, but I did not want to wake you. Send for me when you are ready. I hope I have done right.*
> *Buckley'*

I turn to leave, but I feel as though I should do something for him; his hair is wet, and he is asleep on top of the bedclothes. He could catch a chill like this; I am mindful of his susceptibility to cold.

He turns on his side and draws his knees up without waking. I look around the cabin, but I don't see anything like a blanket, and I don't feel that I can open his trunk or locker to look for one without his permission. I pick up his coat from the back of the chair and lay it over him.

In sleep, he looks almost like a boy. The unflagging energy and fierce determination are gone, and it softens his features and erases the lines that the recurring pain from his injured eye has drawn on his face these past months. Again I feel an affection for this man, and I put the feeling aside reluctantly. When we get to Gibraltar, I will be reunited with the remainder of my squad, and it is unlikely that I will ever see Captain Nelson again. I do not want to miss him when he is gone.

Chapter Twelve

As it turns out, Captain Nelson doesn't send for me again that day, and on the following day, he goes to the flagship to speak to Admiral Hotham. I am not sitting idle waiting for him; we have taken some of the injured Frenchmen aboard from *Ça Ira*, and it is the marines' duty to guard them.

They hardly appear to need any guarding. I have never seen such a miserable set of wastrels in my life. Even the beggars in London are more presentable than these men, and most of them appear to be grateful for even the smallest humane gesture. Some of them are so pathetic that they probably wouldn't have the strength to revolt if there were twice as many of them as there are of us.

None of them appear to speak English, and my French is fairly rudimentary, but they are not a gregarious group. They don't even speak amongst themselves. I can't imagine what has happened to these men that has broken their spirits, as well as their bodies.

Captain Nelson tells me.

'When Lieutenant Andrews went to take possession of the French ships, the scene was beyond belief—between them there must have been two thousand men on board, comprising both the ships' crews and the invasion army, and there were perhaps eight hundred of them dead and wounded. Their officers are the worst band of villains he has ever seen, and more than half the men are not seamen at all; just pitiful bodies pressed into the service by the National Convention.

'I had the *privilege* to speak to one of these French "gentlemen" on the *Britannia,*' he says, with barely concealed sarcasm. 'What I learnt merely confirmed my opinion: we should be pursuing the rest of their fleet. We have the skill and discipline that they lack, and we could take their entire fleet with ease!'

I admire his determination, but when I consider the state of our four seventy-fours, I'm not sure 'with ease' is a completely accurate assessment. But he is ploughing ahead:

'Their leadership behaved most shamefully in leaving these two valiant ships to fight unassisted. They ran, rather than engage us! And we have seen the inadequacy of their seamanship and gunnery! At times, it appears that they were merely taking shots at random! They have no stomach for a fight. And yet we will not go after them.' He throws himself into his chair. 'I am frustrated, Mr Buckley.'

His frustration is not relieved in the following days, and his spirits sink lower. Poor brave *Illustrious*, completely dismasted in battle, is driven ashore in a storm and lost. Days become weeks, and the fleet does nothing more than cruise between St Fiorenzo and Leghorn, with an occasional diversion to the waters near Minorca.

Captain Nelson requests that I come to write for him when his eye is painful, but he largely sits alone in his cabin, scribbling personal letters to friends and to his wife. 'All I do is record the monotonous business of the ship, and monitor inventories,' he complains to me. He has received word that Admiral Hood will not be returning to the Mediterranean, which makes him lower than ever. 'This Admiralty Board does not care for us,' he tells me. 'They will make our job here more and more difficult, and without a good commander to manage our fleet.'

One respite comes in June, with reinforcements to the fleet. Thomas Troubridge, the captain of HMS *Culloden,* is a friend from Captain Nelson's time in the East Indies, when both of them were youths. Nelson is buoyed once more, both by the presence of his friend and by the additional ships. 'Now, surely we will take on the French fleet!' he declares confidently. But Admiral Hotham is now the one who appears to have no stomach for the fight. We continue to cruise off Minorca without a French ship in sight.

June wears on towards July.

I am finishing the first watch and gratefully looking forward to my hammock. This day has seemed a particularly weary one. I had managed to avoid the attention of Captain Spencer for a time, but being one of the smallest of the marines, I am always front and centre when we drill. I do not understand why the man appears to dislike me so, but he seems to be determined to intimidate me.

I slot my mended rifle back into its position in the marines' rack before climbing the companion ladder to trudge down the upper gun deck, towards the rear companionway that will take me to my berth. It is just past midnight, and apart from those on the middle watch, everyone is asleep.

Everyone except the one who speaks to me out of the darkness.

'Good evening, Private Buckley.'

I tense. 'Sir.'

Captain Spencer materialises out of the shadows, very close to me. I can smell brandy on his breath. *Trouble, trouble, trouble,* beats the accelerated tattoo of my heart.

'Would you care to join me for a nightcap, Buckley?'

I swallow. 'No; thank you very kindly, sir.' My voice sounds thin. This can only mean one thing, and it's very, very bad. I take a step back and find myself up against the rail of the companion ladder.

Captain Spencer takes advantage of this. He braces an arm against the ladder, effectively preventing me from escaping up it. 'I insist,' he says quietly, narrowing his eyes. There is a slight slurring of his consonants.

'You are... a cock-tease, Buckley,' he continues. The way he says my name makes it sound obscene.

Oh, God.

'You have the face of an angel, and the body of a boy.'

The gun deck is deserted but for him and me.

'I admire your pretty, tight little arse. It must be as soft as a girl's.'

My breath is coming so fast now that I feel light-headed. His own breathing begins match mine. He grabs my chin with his large hand and presses his mouth on mine, and I feel his other hand between my legs.

The tension in me snaps like a faulty mainspring, and I kick out hard, connecting with his knee. As he recoils, I bolt up the companionway towards the quarterdeck and the presence of other men.

I did not kick him hard enough. He is close behind me, and in front of the captain's cabin, he manages to grab my queue.

Pain shoots through my scalp like fire and knocks me to the ground. Captain Spencer is on me in a flash, and straddles my hips, wrenching me around to face him, fury and lust blazing in his eyes. I can feel his arousal against my belly. I try to get out from underneath him, but he is too strong. My mind snaps back to Richard and the stairs of our home in Surrey, and for a moment I am helpless again.

'You will pay for that,' Captain Spencer snarls, but even in his passion his voice is low and cold. He is fumbling with his breeches' buttons.

Surely not here?! I can see the marine guarding Captain Nelson's door; his face is white and shocked. Spencer rises on his knees and rips at the buttons of my front fall. I hear fabric tear, and one of my buttons lands on the deck planks and rolls away.

My secret is about to be laid bare on the quarterdeck, in front of my commanding officer's door. Why is everyone so silent? In desperation, I buck and contract my knee against his back, and manage to reach my boot.

Jack Mackay's knife flashes in my fist, and I slash out blindly, opening a line of blood down the side of Spencer's face. He cries out and falls back.

'Arrest this man!' he orders the sentry, blood welling through his fingers as he presses them against the wound.

'What is going on here?'

I scramble to my knees and see Captain Nelson standing in the doorway to his quarters. He is wearing a banyan over his small-clothes, and a nightcap, and if he is bewildered by this scene, it doesn't show.

I realise what he is seeing. I am kneeling on the deck, my clothes disordered, with a knife in my hand, and my officer is sitting on his backside, bleeding. The sentry appears to be paralysed. The man on the ship's wheel, the officer of the watch, a shocked midshipman: all stand in frozen disbelief.

'I will take custody of this man,' Captain Nelson says to the sentry. 'Attend to your officer.'

The sentry mumbles a response and helps Captain Spencer to his feet, then leads him away, back down the companion-way toward the surgeon's cabin.

'Come with me, Mr Buckley.'

I follow the captain into his cabin. 'Please explain what I just saw,' he commands me, sinking into a chair. He has a heavy summer cold, and his consonants are muddy.

I am shaking so hard that it is difficult to speak. 'I... I'm going to be sick, Captain,' I manage.

He rises and puts an arm around my shoulders and guides me to his quarter-gallery, then closes the door to give me privacy.

When I emerge, he motions to a seat at the table where he has poured a glass of water. He watches me drink with a troubled look on his face.

'I am so sorry, sir,' I say miserably.

'Just tell me what happened,' he says quietly.

After that time with Richard, I wept for hours, days... I don't have any tears now. Just fear, and shock, and anger. And shame.

'He told me to come to his cabin, sir. He called me a... a... *cock-tease*. And he made an obscene observation about my... my bottom.' I cannot look at Captain Nelson.

'So you took a knife to him, Mr Buckley?'

'He put his hand between my legs, sir,' I whisper.

He sighs. 'Oh, lad.' He extracts a handkerchief from his sleeve and blows his nose. 'There will be an inquiry,' he says, folding the handkerchief and putting it away. 'Captain Spencer will ask for a court-martial, I imagine.'

'I know, sir,' I mumble.

'I must keep you in custody until the trial.'

I nod desolately.

'You will stay here in my cabin tonight, until I determine what to do with you.'

'Yessir.'

'I had heard murmurings about Captain Spencer,' he says softly. 'I am disturbed that we shall have to confront them following this incident. Perhaps he will consider that and will not call for a trial.'

For the rest of the night, I lie on a blanket listening to Captain Nelson's congested breathing, my scalp still burning and the bones in my neck aching. My life is ending.

The captain rises early, at the beginning of the morning watch. I am aware of him kneeling silently in prayer for a few moments, then he dresses in the dark and leaves the cabin without a word. He might be able to tell that I am awake, but if so, he doesn't acknowledge me.

I fold my blanket neatly, and stand looking out the stern lights at the faint phosphorescence that follows the ship. Normally I find this phenomenon beautiful and mysterious, but it doesn't lift my spirits now. I don't go out onto the gallery. I'm afraid I would be tempted to throw myself overboard.

I panicked. I should not have panicked. I reacted instead of reasoning. They will flog me, at the very least; they might sentence me to hang. I think I would prefer the latter. They will know the truth if they remove my shirt for the cat. If they decide to send me back to Richard, I *will* throw myself overboard.

I feel myself trembling again. First Richard, then Dudley, and finally Roger.

'Do you know why my name is Roger?' he leered.

That night, when the household was asleep, I took all the money I had secreted away, plus whatever more I could find in the house; my mother's dressmaking shears; and my father's fowler and watch, and walked all night to Kingston-upon-Thames. In the morning, I hid the fowler and the scissors in a hay shed whilst I went to the rag fair and bought second-hand a boy's shirt, waistcoat, coat, and breeches. I bought a pair of boots at the shoemaker, and a cocked hat and ribbon for 'my nephew.'

I took them all back to the hay shed, and when the sun went down, I dressed in the boys' clothing. Thank God that Richard was careless with his money; he had not noticed that I had been skimming from the household accounts. I still had a good deal left over. I secured it in the pocket of my waistcoat, because I had forgotten to buy a purse.

Richard was undoubtedly livid when he discovered that I was gone. More so, I imagine, when he discovered I took the household money with me.

When it grew late and the town was quiet, I walked to the river, where I sat on the bridge and cut my hair, letting the shorn locks fall into the water. Then I tied my women's clothes and undergarments around a stone with the string from my packages, and I hurled the whole thing as far as I could into the Thames.

If I was so calm and deliberate when I left my husband, why had I reacted the way I did with Captain Spencer?

Four successive pregnancies had claimed all my soft curves and made my face angular and my limbs thin. My breasts, never large to begin with, had shrunk to nearly nothing. After the last miscarriage, my womb wasted, and I no longer had courses. Richard's London accoucheur examined me and told Richard that I was barren.

When Richard learned that I could no longer bear children for him, he was furious, as if it were my fault. He told me that I was now his wife in name only; and that, being his property, he could do with me as he wished. One of the things he wished was that I should 'entertain' his friends. When Dudley left my room, he said scornfully to me, 'I thought you were pretty once, Nell, but look at you now.'

Why couldn't Captain Spencer have found me as unattractive as my husband and his friends had done?

'You're too pretty, Ned,' Will Fowler had said.

I am still staring out the windows at the grey, gathering dawn, when Captain Nelson returns. I hear him cough behind me before I realise that he is there. As nervous as I am, that gentle cough makes me start and whirl around to face him.

He lights a candle and uses it to illuminate the lanterns. His uniform coat now sports gold epaulettes that gleam in the warm light, a recent addition that lends him a graver, more authoritative air.

The ship's bell strikes twice. It is five o'clock.

'Come and sit down, Mr Buckley,' he says quietly.

I sit at the table and make myself meet his eyes.

He looks weary. Maybe it is his cold, or the early hour, but I'm afraid it has more to do with the repercussions of last night.

'Captain Spencer says that you solicited him.'

My mouth falls open. Even though I might have expected this, it hits me like the slap of a wet hand. 'That's not true!' I protest.

'I am inclined to believe you, Mr Buckley, although I probably should not tell you that. However, that is the accusation against you. Captain Spencer claims that you have been trying to capture his attention ever since he came on board. He intends to tell the court that you were attempting to seduce him but tried to flee when he denounced you.'

I try to swallow, but I can't. There is something obstructing my throat.

'Captain Spencer admits that he was intoxicated, but says it made him momentarily weak to your advances,' Nelson continues soberly. 'He claims that he was trying to apprehend you to arrest you.' He speaks unemotionally, but it is apparent that he finds this distasteful.

When I am able to speak, I say, 'Sir, they will hang me.'

He doesn't reply.

'Oh, sir; how could anyone believe that I would be such a fool as to solicit an officer...?!'

'It comes down to how convincing Captain Spencer is in his testimony, Mr Buckley.'

'Let them charge me with assaulting an officer, or mutiny— I would rather kill myself, sir, than stand trial for buggery!' I jump up from my chair, but there is nowhere to escape.

Captain Nelson rises and grabs both my hands. 'Do not talk like that!' He shakes me sharply. 'I shall advocate for you,' he says more gently, 'but you must trust me, and cooperate.'

'Yessir,' I whisper.

He releases me and says very softly, 'What is of greater concern to me, Mr Buckley, is the irrefutable evidence that you assaulted an officer with a weapon.'

I sink down into my chair and bury my head in my hands. Realisation hits me like a broadside: 'Article Twenty-One. I have killed myself already, sir.'

'*Why* did you pull a *knife* on him?' Captain Nelson asks me.

'I was afraid of what he intended to do to me,' I say in a defeated voice.

'He touched you inappropriately.'

'He kissed me forcefully and thrust his hand between my legs!' I cannot help the anger that this memory rekindles in me. 'He tore my breeches! What he said to me makes it clear what his intentions were!'

'He claims he did not. He says you misinterpreted his intent. He also says that your breeches tore whilst he was struggling to subdue you.' He clears his throat. 'Mr Buckley, I fail to understand what would possess Captain Spencer to attempt such a thing in view of other members of this ship's crew.'

My mind flashes to Spencer's face as he loomed over me on the quarterdeck, that snarl on his lips, the insane light in his eyes. *Possess*, indeed. 'He is mad, sir.' My fingers start to tremble and dance on the tabletop. I put my hands in my lap and trap them between my knees. 'He is completely mad.'

'I do not know if the board will view your case in the same way,' he says quietly. 'He is some sort of a cousin to the First Lord of the Admiralty.'

'Ah—! Lord, have mercy…' I feel as though I am caught in an anchor cable, being dragged beneath the waves. 'What is to become of me, Captain?'

'I'm afraid I am at a loss to say at the current time,' he replies, not unkindly. 'I shall see what I can do, and believe me, I shall do all that I can.'

He rubs his brow as if his head aches. 'I have seen that you have courage. Do not let it fail you.'

Captain Nelson goes to his locker and gets out the medicine chest.

'You are going to have to stay here for the time being, whilst we figure out what's to be done with you,' he says. 'I do not intend to put you in irons. Also, I question whether you will do yourself some harm if left unattended.'

'I know what I said a moment ago, sir, but I don't think my will is strong enough to do away with myself,' I say, chastened. 'A part of me believes that self-murder will damn me forever.'

He doesn't reply, but removes a bottle from the chest and unstoppers it. I can smell the sal volatile from where

I'm sitting. He inhales deeply of the vapour and sneezes several times.

'My head is so heavy today that I can hardly hold it up,' he says thickly. 'After we breakfast, I may have to take a short nap.' He blows his nose vigorously. 'All the same, Mr Buckley,' he continues, 'I prefer to keep you where I know that you are safe. Both from yourself, and from anyone else.'

I had not thought of this. If something happens to me, Captain Spencer will not need to recount what happened last night, even if he is confident that he will be vindicated. *Would he resort to such a thing?* Having seen the irrational rage in his eyes when he straddled me, I think there is a distinct possibility.

The captain re-stoppers the bottle of sal volatile and says to me, 'I must ask you to give me your knife.'

My knife. I had not thought about the knife since I fought off Captain Spencer. I don't even remember what I did with it.

I reach into my boot and feel the handle against my fingers. When I pull it out, I see a dried line of blood on my stocking. I hand the knife to Captain Nelson without a word.

'I hope I shall be able to give it back to you at some point,' he says.

He puts the knife away in his locker with his medicine chest and leaves the cabin again. I hear him speak to the sentry at the door.

'Mr Buckley is under arrest and is not to leave my cabin.'

The marine replies affirmatively. I wonder if he is one of our number who knows me well.

I don't feel any remorse for Captain Spencer. If I am to hang, I wish that I had killed him first.

Chapter Thirteen

I do not see Captain Nelson again until the servant is laying
the table for his breakfast. It appears that he doesn't intend
to have any guests at his table this morning.

The captain is accompanied by George-Augustus Josephs,
who has my pack and blanket.

Joe hands me my possessions and mutters, 'We don't
believe it none, Ned,' before he leaves the cabin. It's only one
sentence, but it encourages me a little.

Captain Nelson has considerately included me in his
morning meal. It is austere compared to the first breakfast I
ate at his table. Still, there is cold beef, an egg for each of us,
bread and butter, a Spanish orange, and coffee. Against the
food that ratings get, these are delicacies. But they may as
well be made of chalk. I cannot eat them.

Nelson does not eat much, either. He drinks his coffee and
has a bit of egg with a piece of bread, but much of the food
goes untouched. He peels the orange and offers half to me.

'No; thank you kindly, Captain.'

He continues to hold out the orange as he looks at the
food on the table. 'Seems a shame to waste it, Mr Buckley.'

'Ordinarily I would not, sir. 'Tis more than a shame; my
father would have said it was a sin.'

'Mine would too. Unfortunately, I cannot taste it today.'

'You cannot taste it, and I cannot swallow it,' I observe quietly. 'Will no one eat it, sir? Have the orange, at least. It is said to be helpful for easing a cold.'

'It will be eaten, Mr Buckley; I don't care to see it wasted.'

It seems we have nothing to talk about, apart from the incident that got me here; and neither one of us wants to speak of that, so the meal proceeds largely in silence. I am glad to see Captain Nelson finish the orange, then wonder with some surprise why I cared at all.

The same servant has removed the remainder of the meal before the captain speaks again.

'My officers and I have decided to confine you here in my cabin until we reach port and there is a suitable place ashore for you. I have requested that the carpenter make a screen to partition a corner of the cabin, and you will have a palliasse that you may unroll at night and roll up in the morning.'

I am momentarily stunned by this generosity. Ordinarily a man would be chained to a knee in the forward part of the upper gun deck, guarded around the clock, and allowed to move only to use the heads. 'I am deeply obliged to you, Captain; I do not think I am likely ever to be able to repay this debt. I am mindful of your privacy, sir. Will it not inconvenience you greatly...?'

'Have you ever known me to be inconvenienced, Mr Buckley?'

'You have never said so, sir.'

'Well, if I am, I shall be sure to tell you so.' He sneezes twice. 'Later today, I intend to speak to the people who were present on the quarterdeck last night. But first, I am going back to bed for an hour. I have a thumping headache.' He rises and shrugs off his coat. 'I apologise that you have no space of your own, but that will be remedied by this afternoon.'

I turn away as he unbuttons his waistcoat. When we were first married, Richard used to undress down to his shirt before he bedded me, but after a while he often did not bother to do anything more than open his breeches. Still, the intimacy of a man removing his clothing, alone in my presence, makes me tense involuntarily. 'That's very generous, sir, considering that I don't normally have a space of my own,' I say to the quarter-gallery wall.

I don't think he notices. 'I sometimes forget that you are not accustomed to such things. You have the manners of a gentleman. I tend to think of you the way I think of my midshipmen.'

'Had I been a gentleman, sir, I would not be in this position,' I observe sadly.

He sits on the edge of his berth and removes his shoes. 'It is a distasteful business, Mr Buckley.' He sneezes again and groans softly. 'Oh, how wretched I feel today. Do not despair,' he orders, as he reclines on his pillow, a hand over his eyes. 'I have limited interest, but I shall not hesitate to use it on your behalf.'

Do not. Do not throw it away and jeopardise your career for me. You would be insane to oppose the First Lord of the Admiralty if Captain Spencer appeals to him. As desperately as I want to find a way out of this, I don't want this kind and generous man to suffer because of it. I have known too few kind men, of late.

My father was a kind man, with an easy laugh and a humorous glint in his eye. He had liberal ideas and educated me alongside my brother until Arthur was old enough to go away to school. He taught us both to ride and shoot, and he delighted in the fact that I could shoot as well as Arthur. When he died, he bequeathed me his old fowling piece and his pocket watch.

I open my pack and take the watch out of the soft cloth bag that I stitched to protect it after I left my *(my husband's)* home. I cradle the watch in my palm and feel tears slip from underneath my closed eyelids.

He died too young, our father. It was an influenza, the doctor told us. Papa was strong and only forty-eight; he wasn't supposed to die. But he did die. He went to sleep after breakfast one morning and never woke again.

Our mother had been gone for ten years by then, along with the brother who had lived for only a few days, and suddenly we were orphans. Arthur was twenty-five and I was twenty-two. He was engaged to marry a good young woman, but I had no suitors. Under the terms of our father's will, Arthur became the administrator of my inheritance until I turned twenty-five or married, whichever occurred first.

It was a generous inheritance. Father was a successful silk merchant, and Mother had been a prestigious mantua-maker before their marriage. He always told people that there had been a lot of unhappy gentlewomen in London when Mama agreed to marry him.

He left the house in Surrey to me, and the house in Marylebone to Arthur. Arthur inherited Papa's business, and he divided his other assets between the two of us. Had I remained a spinster all my life, I would still have been well-provided for. But then came Richard.

Richard was the son of one of my father's business associates. He was Arthur's age, and had been to good schools, although not the same ones my brother had attended. He was pleasant looking, well-spoken, had gentle manners, and dressed well. He told us he was a junior barrister, although that wasn't completely true. He was a barrister's *clerk*, but he *intended* to be a barrister, so if he was putting the cart before the horse a little, where was the harm in that?

He also had depraved appetites, but how could we have known?

Captain Nelson stirs and coughs. I hastily wipe the tears off my face with my sleeve, but he only turns on his side with a sigh.

I return the watch to its pouch and slip it back into my pack. I feel fortunate that I still have it. Theft is punishable by flogging, but that doesn't mean that some people don't still feel compelled to do it.

My fingers encounter Jack Mackay's carved lion, folded in a handkerchief. I don't take it out of the pack because I'm afraid that the sight of it would make the tears flow again. Instead, I take *Henry V* from the bottom of my pack.

When we were young and our father was teaching Arthur and me, he and Mother, Arthur, and I, used to read Shakespeare aloud together, and Papa would explain it to us. As we got older, he would make us explain it to him.

I open the book. Instead of feeling sorry for myself, I should read it. Before today I seldom had enough time, or enough light, or enough quiet. Suddenly I have these things in abundance.

The first verses bring back to me the sound of my father's voice as he read them aloud. For a minute or two I think the misery of it will defeat me, but I fight back the despair and begin again. As I read and hear my father's voice in my memory, it is as if he is standing behind me; strong and handsome, the way I remember him when I was six or seven, encouraging me with his hand on my shoulder.

'*That's right, Nell; my brave, lovely girl. Daughter, you make me proud of you. What wonderful things you are going to do someday!*'

I hope you are still proud of me, Papa. You told me to make my life my own. I had to take it back from Richard, and I must defend it now. I know this is not what you dreamed for me, but don't be dismayed. I have survived this far, and I have at least one friend who will help me.

I am halfway through Act I when Captain Nelson gets up. He comes to the table, rubbing his eyes. 'Is that the book I gave you?'

'It is. It's hard to feel defeated when reading *Henry V*.'

'Exactly.' He coughs and clears his throat.

'Do you feel any better, sir?'

'A little, I think. It will have to suffice. There is work to do.'

'Do you want my assistance?' I ask, setting the book aside.

'I wish I could employ you in it. No, Mr Buckley; I must conduct an inquiry. As I anticipated, Captain Spencer has demanded a court-martial; I must conclude whether the incident merits one.' He rises from his chair and slips on his waistcoat. 'It is the way the thing is done,' he says, his long fingers deftly working the buttons. 'I must conduct the inquiry before a court-martial can be called. If I was to find that the accusation is baseless, I could decline to refer it on to the commander-in-chief. That isn't going to happen in this instance, I am sorry to say. I may, however, find evidence that you were not the instigator of the incident, and that will help your defence.'

Some of my newly recovered confidence falters. 'He approached me on the upper gun deck, sir. It was deserted, else I would have shouted,' I say, very softly.

He is preparing to put on his coat, but he stops and lays it down again. 'I think I shall change my plan a little. My throat is rather irritated; I shall call for some tea. Then I want you to tell me exactly what happened last night.'

He speaks gently, but it is underlaid with firm authority. I will do this, or he will know why not. He has always been relaxed and almost affectionate in the manner of his instructions to me, but I would do well to remember that his authority exceeds that of everyone on this vessel.

I will have to recount it eventually anyhow.

He has not shaved this morning, and light from the gallery windows catches the faint stubble on his jaw and makes it look like fine beach sand dusting his face. He goes to the door and speaks quietly to someone in the lobby, where his daily servants wait when they are on duty.

My body has tensed like a bowstring in anticipation of this retelling. I try to will myself to relax, but it isn't working. It is as if my muscles have stopped responding to my reason.

Captain Nelson goes into the quarter-gallery, and I have an irrational urge to bolt. *There is a sentry on duty at the door,* I remind myself. And it would not help my case at all if I tried to run. At any rate, there is no place to run; one can only go over the side.

Oh, Papa; help me.

I hear Captain Nelson blow his nose energetically, and somehow this homely noise calms me a little. He may represent the sword hanging over my head, but he blows his nose just like anyone else.

A servant comes in with a tray and sets it on the table. It is the boy who can't remember how the captain takes his tea. He sets up the table and pours the tea into two cups, then exits the cabin just as Captain Nelson emerges from the quarter-gallery.

The captain retrieves a familiar bottle from a mahogany box and brings it to the table. He sits, looks at his tea, and murmurs something as he adds milk. 'I know his father,' he tells me. 'He's a good lad, but I can't determine whether he is simply forgetful, or completely empty-headed.' He pours a tot of brandy into each of our cups without asking me whether I want any.

I take a sip of the hot tea. It, and the mellow warmth of the added brandy, seem to melt the knot in my belly a little, although my hand still trembles and rattles the cup against the saucer.

Captain Nelson sets his teacup down. 'There is no point in putting this off. I want you to tell me everything that happened between you and Captain Spencer, leaving nothing out, even if it appears that the revealing of it might hurt your defence.' He goes to his locker and retrieves his portable writing desk with pen and ink and paper.

I stare at the tabletop. I have to take two deep breaths before I can manage to say anything. 'I am not sure where to start, sir.'

'Start at the beginning, Mr Buckley.'

'It might take a while, sir...'

'It will take as long as it takes. Please begin.'

So, I begin at the beginning. I tell him about the first time Captain Spencer called me aside and questioned my competency as a marine and a rifleman. I tell him about when Spencer lingered behind me at inspection, breathing in my ear, and about the incident with my coat-tail lining. All this is difficult enough, because my emotions waver between shame and anger. But when I get to the point where I have to begin talking about last night, I freeze up again. I stammer and drop my head into my hands.

Captain Nelson pours more tea into our cups and says gently, 'Breathe, lad. Pause and drink your tea. We'll continue in a minute.'

I do as he tells me and try to compose myself. '*Buck up, Ned,*' I hear Jack Mackay admonish me.

Easy for you to say, I retort mentally.

I put down my teacup and begin again.

'I was walking on the upper gun deck, sir, after putting my rifle away in its rack. My berth is below aft, but I chose that deck because there are no hammocks.'

He nods. 'What time was this, Mr Buckley?'

'The first watch had just ended, so it must have been a little after midnight, sir.'

He makes a note and says, 'Continue.'

'I was almost at the aftermost companionway when he spoke to me.'

'Just to be clear, Mr Buckley, by "he" do you mean Captain Spencer?'

'Yessir.'

'What did Captain Spencer say to you?'

'He bade me good evening.'

I stop, and Captain Nelson prompts me again. 'What happened when he bade you good evening? Did you respond?'

'I did, Captain. I acknowledged him; I think I just said, "Sir."'

'Did you wish him good evening in return?'

'Nosir, I didn't.'

'What happened next?'

'He asked me if I would come to his cabin and share a drink with him. He came up very close to me.'

'What did he say, to the best of your recollection?'

'Erm… he said, "Would you like to come to my cabin for a nightcap?" I thanked him very kindly but said I would not.'

'Go on.' Captain Nelson does not look up from his notes.

'I suppose he had already been drinking, because I could smell the liquor on his breath. It was brandy, I think, or whisky. At any rate, it didn't smell sour like wine, or ale. He said to me, "I insist", and he slurred the word a bit.'

I pause to allow Captain Nelson to finish writing. I take another swallow of tea and clatter the cup in the saucer.

He comes to the end of the sentence and waits for me to continue.

'He, ah… he moved closer to me, and I tried to back away from him; but I couldn't go anywhere, because the companion ladder was behind me. He put his arm on the rail of the ladder so that I could not get past him to go up.'

I can smell Captain Spencer's breath again in my memory. It does not smell sour, as I had observed to Captain Nelson, but there is something foul underneath the smell of the brandy. My heart stutters.

'What did you do when he put his arm on the rail of the companion ladder?'

'I didn't do anything, Captain. I was afraid of him.'

He puts down his pen and suppresses a sneeze. He motions to me with his hand to continue.

I have to clasp my hands together and clutch them tightly to keep them from shaking. I lower my head and close my eyes before I go on, because I can't bear to see his face when I say this.

'He… he said to me, "You are a cock-tease, Buckley". He said I had the face of an angel and the body of a boy.' I swallow. 'Then he said he liked my… he said, "I admire your pretty, tight arse".'

I hear Captain Nelson sigh. I risk opening my eyes and I can see that he is scrubbing his face with both hands. He leans one elbow on the table and rubs his brow with thumb and forefingers. 'And then what happened, Mr Buckley?' he asks softly.

I wrap my arms tightly around my middle, as if this will keep me from flying apart. 'He grabbed my chin with the hand that was on the rail and held my head still while he kissed me, and he thrust his other hand between my legs,' I choke.

I do not shatter into pieces like a bulwark struck by a cannonball. But I cannot keep from shivering, and Captain Nelson says gently, 'Would you like to pause for a minute?'

'Nosir.' I am surprised at myself, but I want it to be over with. 'I think I lost my head then. I kicked him in the knee and tried to get up the companionway to the quarterdeck, but he was right behind me. He caught me by my hair and pulled me down to the deck, and he sat on my hips. He told me I would pay for it; and he was trying to open his breeches with one hand, whilst he pawed at mine with the other. He tore off my left button.'

This is all coming out in a rush, like vomiting up a meal of spoilt meat. 'I was sure he was going to rape me, sir. I could feel his erect member up against my belly when he sat on me. I fought and tried to get away, but he was stronger...' I realise that I am twisting my fingers together in my lap like a girl, and I force myself to stop.

'I got the knife out of my boot somehow. I didn't think about where I was cutting him; I just slashed at him. If I had planned it, sir, I would have stuck it in his groin.'

Jack, in my arms, the blood pumping out of his body from the wound in his groin. I am shaking uncontrollably now. 'I would have killed him, sir, if I'd remembered I was going to hang anyway.'

'I shall not write that last statement down,' Captain Nelson says in a low voice. 'Oh, lad.'

He puts down the pen and stands beside my chair, then lays his hand lightly on my shoulder, where my father's hand used to rest when he praised me. I am powerless to stop the tears that spill down my cheeks.

Captain Nelson bends and puts his arm around my shoulders then. I bury my face in my hands and sob in a way that I had never done as a child, not even when my mother died.

'I am aware that there are men who do these things, Mr Buckley,' he says quietly. 'I am sorry that you had to learn of it in this way.'

'I was not unaware of it, sir,' I whisper roughly. 'I am all too familiar with it. Another man did it to me once.'

I can feel him stiffen. 'Merciful God,' he mutters.

Richard, tucking himself back into his breeches: 'Do not snivel. Since you cannot provide me with a child, it doesn't matter where you receive me, Nell.'

Remembering Richard makes me clench my fists in anger. It stops my tears like a dam across a stream.

Captain Nelson produces two of the little footed glasses and pours brandy directly into them, then gives one to me. He also gives me a clean handkerchief. 'Dry your face, and drink that down,' he instructs me. He swallows his own brandy. There is an expression on his face that I have never seen before. I think it is revulsion.

'Oh, please tell me that you believe me,' I say miserably.

'I believe you, lad,' he says, as I drink my brandy as instructed. 'After all, we have been alone together countless times in the past year, and you have never tried to seduce me. And I flatter myself that I am at least as attractive as Captain Spencer.'

Chapter Fourteen

Captain Nelson leaves to go speak to potential witnesses from the quarterdeck. Apart from the marine sentry, whose name I do not know, I cannot remember specifically who was present, but the officer of the watch will.

The servant comes in to remove the tea tray, and then I am alone.

The captain bade me use his washstand to wash my face, and he told me to keep his handkerchief. 'I have enough others, and if I do not, I can get more,' he says. The handkerchief is embroidered with an ornate '*HN*' in the corner.

I examine my face in Captain Nelson's shaving mirror. The mirror I use when I pretend to shave is cracked and the silvering is flaking off, so I rarely look at myself in it.

The face that peers back at me doesn't look like a girl's, but it doesn't look like a man's face, either.

I have my father's long face and thin nose, and my mother's large eyes and narrow chin. 'She's just like a little elf,' our nursemaid used to say when I was small.

Richard thought differently, at least at the end when he had turned bitter and mean. 'You have a face like a horse,' he told me at supper one night, in front of the boy who did the serving. He had attended a dinner at his club with some 'men of business,' and had returned half-drunk and irritable. I hoped that he would continue to drink until he fell into a stupor, and then I would not have to see him anymore that night.

Today I do not see an angel, an elf, or a horse in Captain Nelson's shaving mirror. I do not know this person. He is not someone I recognise.

At the bottom of my pack, tied into one of my old torn stockings, is the other thing I took with me when I left. I get it now and tip it out of the toe of the stocking.

It is the miniature of me that Arthur had commissioned as a gift for Richard when we married. One day I shall send it back to Arthur, just so that he will know that I am still alive. Every time I consider doing it, though, something in me warns, *too soon*. Richard wants me back; I *belong* to him. No matter where I posted this: from Gibraltar, Madrid, or Lisbon; Naples, Leghorn, or St Fiorenzo… Richard would find me.

I take the miniature back to Captain Nelson's shaving mirror and compare it to the face in the mirror.

We have the same cheekbones, the same eyes, the same shape of the chin. But the girl's face is soft and rosy, her lips are pink, and her eyes sparkle with the same frank humour that used to grace our father's eyes. She wears a slight smile, and curls crown her forehead.

The face in the mirror is thinner and harder. His eyes do not sparkle, and his skin is roughened and burnt by the wind and the sun. He does not smile, and his hair is coarse and sun-bleached.

I do not hear Captain Nelson come back into the cabin. The door is fixed open, so he did not need to turn the latch. I see him behind me in the mirror, and I start, and whirl around.

'I'm sorry,' he says. 'I did not intend to startle you.'

'I … you didn't, sir,' I reply, but my voice squeaks.

'What were you looking at?' I must hesitate, because he says, 'It's fine if you don't want to show me.'

I open my hand and give him the miniature. I have already determined that it looks nothing like me anymore. That girl is dead and gone.

He gazes at the miniature. 'It is very fine,' he says. 'This girl, she must be your sister.'

'Yessir.'

He actually smiles. 'You could be twins.'

'We were both born on the same day, sir, but she died with our parents.'

'I am very sorry, Mr Buckley.'

I don't like to lie to him. I had hoped that Nell *was* dead and buried in the depths of my former life, but she just won't stay there.

He picks up his quill, the inkwell, and the sheaf of paper he had been taking notes upon, and puts them into his writing box. 'I intend to pursue this inquiry until dinnertime, then we shall dine with my son-in-law, Lieutenant Andrews, and Mr Withers.'

'Sir, please do not feel compelled to include me… I am already imposing too much upon you.'

'I do not want to hear it, Mr Buckley. If I do not want your attendance at a meal, I shall tell you so, otherwise I expect you to eat with me.' His voice is stern.

'Yessir.'

'Good. If you tire of Prince Hal, you may borrow anything else in my library.'

'Thank you, sir.' But he is already out the door; he just waves a hand over his shoulder in acknowledgment.

Dinner is an ordinary affair. The men talk as if one of us had not been accused of something vile and shameful. They include me in their conversation, and ask for my opinion, and ignore the event of the night before.

Captain Nelson's stepson, Josiah Nisbet, is seated beside me. He is in an awkward phase; now as tall as I, but still with the mannerisms of a child at times. At other times he is almost worldly. He repeats a slightly off-colour joke that he heard in Naples at the home of some diplomat or other, and Captain Nelson frowns, but doesn't reprove him in front of the others, apart from murmuring, 'Josiah,' in a cautionary tone. The boy blushes and swallows the rest of his claret in a gulp.

When dinner is over the other men go back to work, and the servants clear the table. Captain Nelson addresses me.

'The carpenter's mate will come this afternoon to install the screen that will allow you a more private place to sleep. Do not protest, Mr Buckley; it is for my privacy as much as yours. I shall work here in the dining room while they are working in the cabin.'

'Is there anything I can do for you, sir? I dislike being idle. It makes me feel... useless.' I have felt worse than useless since Captain Spencer cornered me; I feel humiliated and disposable. But I doubt that Captain Nelson cares to know that. I have been made to feel like this before, and I survived.

'You are still very useful; but I cannot employ you at anything pertaining to the inquiry. I expect you to continue everything else you have been doing for me, just as before.'

'Thank you, sir.'

He coughs and rubs his brow with three fingers. 'If only my head would clear a little. I can scarcely breathe through my poor nose.'

'May I get you anything for it, sir?'

'If you would. Bring me the bottles of sal volatile and camphor from my medicine chest. Also, a clean handkerchief. Thank you, Mr Buckley.' He hands me the key to his locker.

I open the locker underneath his berth and lift out the medicine chest. My knife is sitting there in the locker, carelessly placed on a shelf. He is apparently not at all worried about it, nor about giving me access to it. I select the two bottles he requested and set the chest back in the locker, then turn the key again.

I carry these things to Captain Nelson and set them on the table. He is resting his head on his hand, his eyes closed. He doesn't open them, just says, 'Next please get my writing box and bring it here to me.'

He unstoppers the bottle of sal volatile as I return to his cabin to retrieve his writing desk. It makes him sneeze repeatedly, and I wait discreetly until the fit is finished. I personally don't care for sal volatile for relieving congestion; I find that it seems to make one's nose run rather more than less, but it does tend to open a blocked nose. It also has a tendency to incapacitate a person for a minute whilst it does so. I imagine that he might not wish me to witness that.

'Perhaps that will help,' he says hoarsely. He dampens the clean handkerchief with camphor. 'You may take these bottles back, Mr Buckley; thank you.' He sneezes violently one last time. 'If this cold does not ease soon, I fear I may be confined to bed.'

'I hope not, sir.'

'As do I, Mr Buckley, as do I.' He opens the writing box and removes pen, ink, and paper, and goes back to work, holding the camphor-treated handkerchief against his nose with his left hand.

The screen that the carpenter's mate installs is a piece of canvas lashed to a frame and tied off to eyebolts in the ceiling and the forward bulkhead. It is rather less substantial than a tent, having only one side, but it separates out a space large enough for a pallet from the rest of the cabin. There is room enough for my pack and my bed, and it is a luxury. Anyone going into the quarter-gallery can look right into the space, but that doesn't bother me at all.

The captain is back and forth between the cabin and the quarterdeck for the rest of the day. There is no mail, and the only letters he writes are personal ones, so I am not required. I rummage in my pack for my housewife and spend part of the afternoon replacing the button that Captain Spencer tore from my breeches and repairing the buttonhole. I have to use one of the buttons from my knee; it is smaller than the button I lost, but it stays in the buttonhole. At least my fall isn't half undone anymore. It restores some of my sense of dignity.

At the supper hour, Captain Nelson returns to the cabin with a bit of cloth under his arm. He lays it on the table. It is a short blue jacket, like the ones the sailors wear when they go ashore.

'Since you are relieved of duty pending the results of this inquiry, you should not wear your marine's coat. I hope you might find this comfortable.'

'It is certainly cleaner, sir.' My coat reflects the hard usage it has seen since Corsica, and it is a wonder that Captain Spencer didn't punish me for its sun-bleached fabric and blood-stained hem. Not that there is much I can do about either of those things. There is nothing in the marines' store that is small enough to fit me. I shrug the coat off my shoulders and put on the jacket. It is not fitted like a soldier's coat, or like the coats worn by naval officers. It is looser, boxier, and easy to move in. I feel undressed and suddenly shy.

Captain Nelson doesn't seem to notice my discomfiture. 'Has no one brought the palliasse?' he says, with a touch of irritation.

'Nosir.'

He goes to the door and speaks to one of his servants, and the young man scurries off. 'If that does not get results, I shall go to the purser myself,' he says, sinking into a chair. He still sounds badly congested. 'I hope you have not been terribly bored today, Mr Buckley.'

'I don't believe I ought to complain about that, sir, since I should have been far more bored sitting in irons in the fo'c's'le.'

'Given what I have learnt today, I think I prefer to have you here.'

He doesn't elaborate on this statement, leaving me to wonder what it was that he has learnt, and from whom.

'I hope you're feeling better, sir…?'

'Not perceivably. I believe I shall go to bed directly after supper. You need not worry about the lanterns; leave them lit if you like. It will not disturb me.'

'Yessir. Thank you, sir.'

'What have you done whilst I have been neglecting you?'

'You have not been neglecting me, sir.'

'Don't dispute me, Mr Buckley; just answer the question,' he says tiredly.

'I read the first act of *Henry V;* I wrote an entry in my journal; I walked one hundred times around the cabin,' I recite dutifully.

'Have you done any more drawing since Calvi?' he asks.

'Nosir.'

'You should. It is a useful skill to have. All midshipmen should learn to draw; land features in particular.'

I forebear to point out that I am not a midshipman.

'You have obviously been classically educated, to a degree. You should learn navigation. Do you know your knots?'

'Nosir.' I have no idea where this is heading. Captain Nelson seems to think that I have a future in the Royal Navy, although I can't imagine why.

He rises and goes to a shelf, pulling down a small volume. 'Here is something else to read.'

The book is *The Seaman's Vade-Mecum and Definitive War by Sea.*

'Thank you, sir,' I say, trying not to sound puzzled.

There is a rap on the cabin door. When given permission to enter, a boy comes in carrying a rolled-up mattress. 'Put it behind the screen there,' the captain tells him, and the child does as he is instructed, makes a gesture of respect to Nelson, and leaves.

Some of the ship's boys and warrant officers' servants are little more than twelve, a few possibly even younger. Most of them are orphans sponsored by the Marine Society. I think of these boys and predatory men like Captain Spencer and shudder. '*You have the body of a boy.*'

On the heels of the child, the captain's steward and a servant come in carrying trays containing our supper. When they set the food on the table, I am sure that they have given me the captain's meal. I have bread and meat and soup, and Captain Nelson has... soup.

'No, this is what I intended,' he assures me, and he doesn't even drink all of it.

When he retires to bed, I extinguish the lantern near his berth and retreat to my pallet behind the screen with *The*

Seaman's Vade-Mecum. I unroll the palliasse and find that
they have given me a pillow. A pillow! If I am to die, at least
I will have enjoyed my sleeping accommodations until that
point. I curl on my side with the book and try to make out
the print in the lantern light.

'You will ruin your eyes, Mr Buckley; get a candle.' Captain Nelson pauses outside the quarter-gallery. 'There is one
on the table.' He closes the door to the quarter-gallery, and
I obediently get up and light the candle. On the way back
to bed he says, 'That's better,' and climbs back into his berth
before I can thank him for the pillow.

The captain feels no better in the morning.

I was aware that he had slept poorly. He has developed a
chesty cough that must have interrupted his sleep repeatedly,
because I woke more than once hearing it. He habitually rises
before the sun, but today he remains in bed. I lie on my pallet
as the daylight strengthens and listen, but I cannot tell if he
is sleeping or awake. Finally, I get up, roll up my mattress,
and peer out from behind the screen.

'Captain, sir?' I ask quietly.

'I am awake, Mr Buckley.'

'Do you need anything, sir?'

'Please bring me my writing box, if you would.'

I locate the writing box and bring it to his berth. It is an
ingenious thing that contains ink, paper, quills, sealing wax,
and wafers; when opened it creates a sloped writing surface.
He sits up with a groan and takes it from me.

'I am very unwell this morning. I shall write to Lieutenant
Andrews, if you will give a message to one of the servants to
deliver to him.'

'Yessir, of course. Will you have breakfast?'

'I will take tea and toast, but I have no appetite for anything more.'

He writes a few lines on a page and seals it with a wafer. Sitting there in his berth, in his shirt and nightcap, he looks impossibly young once again. *How old is Captain Nelson?* I wonder.

Writing Lieutenant Andrews' name on the front, he gives the message to me. He closes the writing box and asks me to take it away.

It is undeniably a particularly severe cold, and he undoubtably feels unwell, but I have seen Captain Nelson work through malarial fevers and violent fits of ague without taking to his bed. I experience a sharp pang of worry when I remember the influenza that took my father.

'Are you feverish, Captain? Shall I ask the surgeon to come and see you?'

'I perceive I have a slight fever, but I don't believe I need to see the surgeon. Not just yet, anyway. I have hope that a day of rest will set me up again.'

I take the letter to one of the servants in the lobby. 'Captain Nelson wants you to take that to Lieutenant Andrews,' I tell the youngster. He looks at me suspiciously.

'Why does he not tell me himself?' he asks.

'He is not well this morning and intends to rest in bed.'

The boy hesitates. 'Go on,' I hiss. 'I haven't taken a knife to him; I give you my word. He requests tea and toast this morning, but nothing more. Perhaps you could see to that?'

'I'll speak to the steward, sir,' the boy says, a little more respectfully, but I'm not convinced he believes me. Dressed as I am, I would appear to have no more authority than he does.

Mr Lepee, the captain's steward, apparently doesn't believe me either, because he comes to verify the request.

'What is the good of having someone to convey my messages if I have to confirm them myself?' Captain Nelson grumbles. 'Yes, that is all I want. You might ask Mr Buckley what he wants.'

'May I have an egg and an orange with my tea?' I try not to mumble. Nell knew how to speak to servants graciously. Ned has forgotten.

The captain gets up to use the quarter-gallery and to shave. I pick up *The Seaman's Vade-Mecum* again, but I am so lost in beckets and braces, bights and bitts, that I can't remember one thing from another. I try to visualise each thing and where I have seen it on the ship, but I fear I would make an abysmal seaman.

'Draw it,' Captain Nelson says to me. 'Take ink and paper and draw it out if you are having trouble putting it all together.' He has donned his banyan but looks as if he would just as soon go back to bed.

'How did you know that I couldn't put it all together?' I ask.

'By the look on your face,' he says. 'Do you think that I have not seen that look before?' He coughs heavily and presses his fist to his breast, as if it pains him.

'Is there anything I can do for you, sir?'

He waves a hand dismissively. 'I will take some Friar's Balsam with breakfast. Do not worry about me, Mr Buckley. I don't require you to nurse me.'

'I should confess, sir, that although I am naturally concerned about your health for your sake, I fear I am also thinking of my own interest,' I say quietly. 'If you are too unwell and have to leave the station, then I have lost my only advocate.'

'It is only a cold, Mr Buckley. I feel dreadful, but I don't anticipate having to go home. It is not as bad as that.'

I must not look convinced, because he says gently, 'Do not fear, lad. I said that I would see this through, and I shall. Why should you not believe me?'

'I'm afraid I have lost faith in such things, sir.'

He rests his head on his hand. 'Do we need to talk about faith, Mr Buckley?' Like the vicar when I was a child, listening to my catechism.

'I am not speaking of my faith in God, Captain. Only my faith in men. And I do not doubt your word, sir, but I have learnt that Providence is not always kind.'

He studies me. 'I have never asked you how you ended up in His Majesty's army. You are not the typical foot soldier, you know. Was it illness took your family, lad?'

'Yessir. It was the influenza. We thought it was only a cold, but it was not. It took... took them all.' *Forgive me for deceiving you yet again, sir. They are half-truths, but a half-truth is still a lie.* I hope he will not continue down this path, because I do not know what I would say. I had never intended to tell this story to anyone.

A rap on the door signals that our breakfast is here, and I jump up before the conversation can get any more uncomfortable.

I peel the orange as I watch Captain Nelson pour Friar's Balsam on a lump of sugar. It is a gentler remedy than syrup of squills, for example, but it tastes appalling. He swallows it with a grimace and takes a sip of tea.

'Sir, will you have part of my egg?' He starts to decline, but I add, 'Please.'

'Very well. If it will make your mind easier, then I shall eat part of your egg,' he says resignedly.

I get him to agree to eat half of the orange, too.

'I expect Lieutenant Andrews at six bells,' he informs me. 'I think I shall lie down for a few minutes until he arrives. Do not mind me; go on with your studies.' He slips out of his banyan and lays it on his trunk. 'If you'd like, I could arrange with Mr Wilson to give you lessons in navigation.'

'That's very kind of you, sir, but let me see how I get on by myself before you engage Mr Wilson.' I think of myself sitting with the midshipmen at lessons and cringe, even though at least one of them is as old as I am.

'When the lieutenant arrives, please admit him,' Captain Nelson says, drawing up his coverlet and closing his eyes.

I return to the table and pick up the pen. I am attempting to draw out a sail and all its lines when six bells sounds. I think I have confused the clew-lines and sheets.

I set the quill on the table and open the door for Lieutenant Andrews.

'Good morning, sir. The captain appears to be dozing, but he was expecting you; I'll tell him you are here. Would you care to sit?'

The lieutenant takes a chair and examines my drawing. I feel embarrassment creeping in a blush over my face. 'Please excuse it, sir. It's my first attempt.'

He looks amused but says nothing.

I rouse Captain Nelson gently. 'Sir, Lieutenant Andrews is here.'

He blinks blearily at me. 'I did not think I would fall asleep. Here, set the pillow up behind me,' he tells me hoarsely. 'Forgive me for not getting up, Andrews,' he says to the lieutenant.

Lieutenant Andrews rises and comes to stand by the captain's berth. 'How are you feeling, sir?'

'I am miserable,' Captain Nelson replies frankly, 'but I hope that a day of rest will restore me. I am turning the routine command over to you for the day, with every expectation that it will be routine. However,' he continues, 'should we unexpectedly encounter the French fleet, I shall be back on deck, even if I require Mr Buckley to hold me up.'

Lieutenant Andrews smiles. 'I have no doubt, sir.'

The two officers talk for a few more minutes while I try to correct my drawing, but my mind isn't entirely on the task. I have just gained another insight into the captain.

Despite how efficiently Captain Nelson commands his ship, I know that simply running the ship is not what inspires him. If an enemy engagement were imminent, he would suddenly forget that he had a violent cold. He would run up the rigging himself if the situation called it. Suddenly I am not as worried.

As he leaves, Lieutenant Andrews says to me, 'Your drawing isn't all that bad, honestly. Keep at it.'

I glance at Captain Nelson, but he has closed his eyes again. If I am to ignore him, it appears he intends to ignore me, too.

I try again to read through the running rigging for the mizzen topsail, but the lines get all tangled in my mind. I pick up the book and stand up, thinking that if I look at the sail, I could pick out the specific lines, before I remember that I have been arrested and cannot leave this cabin. I sit back down slowly. I am being treated like a gentleman prisoner, but I am a prisoner just the same.

Leaving the rigging of sails, I flip through the pages of the book. There is a section describing the companies of each rated ship, from commander to ordinary seaman, and how many of each are allocated to first-rates, second-rates, and so on. I read that all captains are allowed a clerk, but only flag officers get secretaries.

Someone taps on the door of the cabin, and I glance at the captain again, but he doesn't stir. I go to the door and open it.

'Good day, Mr Buckley.' Mr Withers, Captain Nelson's clerk, schoolmaster, and now also a midshipman, holds a stack of reports. 'I have the weekly audits from the counter-books for the captain.'

'I think he is asleep, Mr Withers,' I tell him. 'Shall I see if he wants to speak to you?'

Withers shakes his head. 'No, don't wake him. If he has questions, have him send for me. Tell him I found no irregularities.'

'Do you ever?' I ask him in a low voice.

'Not yet,' he replies with a smile.

I take the reports from him and put them on the captain's table. He withdraws, latching the door behind him.

Returning to the book, I open it at random. '*Of Courts-Martial*' says the heading at the top of the page. I have never been present at a court-martial.

'*The said Court to be assembled in the Forenoon, and in the most publick Place of the Ship, where all, who will, may be present; and The Captains of all His Majesty's Ships in Company (which take post) have a Right to assist there.*'

It does not detail much, except that anyone and everyone can attend, and that testimony will be heard in front of all of them and judged by all the post-captains on station. That in itself is enough to make my stomach heave. I push back my chair and escape quickly to the stern-gallery.

I grip the rail and close my eyes. I shall have to stand in front of the entire ship's company —*possibly before men from the entire fleet!* —and listen to Captain Spencer slander me and accuse me of his own vile crime. I shall be required to recount my story to the Judge Advocate knowing that every person present will be judging whether Captain Spencer or I am telling the truth.

He is a Captain of Marines and cousin to the First Lord of the Admiralty. I am an illegitimate, orphaned private. Who will they be more likely to believe?

The day is squally, and a spatter of rain blows into the gallery, but it cannot wash away the taint that seems to cling to me.

And that is not the worst, because the evidence that I used a knife on an officer is irrefutable. I cannot do this!

I must have spoken aloud, because Nelson's voice beside me says, 'What can you not do?'

I open my eyes. He is standing a little behind me, to avoid the worst of the rain.

'Why are you standing in the rain?' he asks. 'Come inside.'

I follow him mutely back into the cabin. All my will is suddenly gone.

He takes a seat at the table and indicates that I should sit with him. 'What has happened to upset you?'

I cannot answer, because I don't know what to say. I'm afraid he will not understand.

He sighs irritably. 'I believe I have asked you three questions now, and you have not answered a single one of them.'

'I am sorry, sir.'

'Well, will you please tell me what is wrong?' He coughs into his handkerchief. 'I cannot go back to bed until you do.'

I touch the cover of *The Seaman's Vade-Mecum*. 'I read the page about courts-martial,' I say quietly. 'Captain, I can't... I shall never be able to look anyone in the eye again once I have been publicly accused of soliciting an unclean act in front of the entire fleet. I'm afraid that I will faint, or panic, or...'

He picks up my hand from the table and grips it tightly. 'You will do none of those things, because you did not do what he is accusing you of. It will have to be recounted, however, because it describes the circumstance under which you cut him with a knife.'

I shudder and he squeezes my hand firmly. 'Do not give in to fear. You are stronger than that.'

'I think I could do anything but this, sir.'

'You can do this, too.' He releases my hand. 'It may not be as bad as you fear. I have yet to complete my inquiry, but you may have a stronger defence than you think.'

He presses his fingers against his temple. 'I got out of bed to take something for my headache, but the door was standing open, and I had go find out why. Now that I've retrieved you from out in the rain, do you think you could get it for me if I go back to bed?'

'Yessir. …Thank you, sir.'

He waves away my gratitude. 'Do not make me lock the gallery door. I do not want to wake up to find that you decided to go for a swim.'

'Nosir; I don't intend to do that.'

I make up the medicine he requests.

'What else have you read in that book?' he asks me, giving me back the glass.

'I read that only flag officers are allowed secretaries,' I tell him.

'You are not recorded in the muster-book as anything other than a marine. You are paid only as a marine. I placed you in this position, so I can call you anything I like,' he says defensively.

'You said something like that on the day I met you, sir.'

'Did I?'

'You asked me why I didn't use "Edmund". I told you that no one calls me that, and you said you would not call me that, either.'

'My father's name is Edmund, and my younger brother was named Edmund, although we called him "Mun", God rest him. I remember; I told you I would call you Mr Buckley. It is only appropriate.'

'I thought at the time that you could call me Guy Fawkes if you wanted to; it wasn't my place to contradict you. I am sorry about your brother, sir.'

'Thank you. It was six years ago, poor fellow.' He reclines against his pillow. 'Is there anything else that I should address, or may I close my eyes again, Mr Fawkes?'

'Mr Withers brought the weekly audits, sir. He said to tell you he found no irregularities.'

'He will need to record the official tallies. If you would, write a message to him and tell him he may come whenever it is convenient; it will not bother me. If he prefers to work in my dining room, he is welcome; or he may take the books to his cabin.'

'Yessir, Captain.'

'You could also ask the servant to bring me some tea. The hotter the better. My head is so heavy today that even my teeth ache.'

'I'll do so right away, sir.'

'Thank you,' he murmurs, closing his eyes.

Chapter Fifteen

His cold is not only heavy, it is stubborn, and Captain Nelson spends two miserable days in bed. On the morning we reach St Fiorenzo, he is up, but subdued. His head is getting better, but the cough and the pain in his breast show no signs of easing.

I am subdued, too. Now that we are in port, I expect to be transferred to a much less comfortable location; and the mechanics of the court-martial will begin to grind into action.

Captain Nelson sips his coffee. He eats very little when he is unwell, and his breakfast plate reflects it. I have no appetite either, but for quite a different reason. Lately we have returned a lot of food to the galley uneaten. Mr Lepee must do something with it; I have no idea what.

'I know you are worried,' the captain says. He is hoarse from coughing. 'Cheer up, Mr Buckley. I am not ready to refer this to Admiral Hotham yet. I have not yet finished the inquiry. I intend to keep you on board until I do.'

'Thank you, sir.'

He nods at my plate. 'Eat your breakfast,' he says, as if I am his stepson.

'I shall, if you will eat some of yours, sir.'

He acts affronted, but there is no sting in his rebuke. 'I had not intended this to be a negotiation,' he grumbles, but he eats some of his egg. We have not had beef at breakfast recently; he says it is too heavy for his digestion when he is not well. I personally have no preference at all. Everything tastes like sawdust to me.

We receive mail after breakfast. Amongst the letters is the notice of a court-martial aboard *Princess Royal* for an army lieutenant of the *Diadem* sixty-four, who refused to submit to the authority of the navy aboard its ships. As one of the senior captains on station, Captain Nelson is expected to participate, although illness will excuse him. I am stoic as I read the notice to him.

He is quiet for a moment, contemplating. 'Tell them I will sit on the Board,' he tells me, then is interrupted by an episode of coughing.

I would not normally question him. I am aware that we have become more familiar with one another recently, particularly since we have been sharing quarters, but I think it is hardly appropriate to suggest that he reconsider. He looks decidedly more wan than I would like, however. 'Are you quite sure, Captain?'

'The reason for my decision is twofold, Mr Buckley,' he croaks, refolding his handkerchief. 'To begin with, I believe it will assist my recovery, however tedious the proceedings might be. In addition, if I am employed on this court-martial, it will delay my completing the inquiry into Captain Spencer's accusation. And my most recent orders indicate that we may not be in St Fiorenzo for long.'

'I see, sir. Thank you, sir.'

He has not discussed the progress of the inquiry with me; there is every reason why he should not. But he says, 'I have good reason to believe that I have not heard all there is to hear from everyone who ought to testify. What else does the mail contain?'

'The rest appear to be personal letters, Captain.'

'Then I shall read them later. The court-martial is in two days; today I shall catch up on some of the duties I have neglected while I was unwell. You are at leisure for a while, Mr Buckley.'

At leisure to do what? I am half-tempted to ask if I might walk on the poop under guard, but the thought of people watching an armed marine follow me around me makes me cringe. Mindful of his admonition that I should practice drawing, I take my journal and a pencil onto the stern-gallery and try to sketch the landscape surrounding the port. At sea, there is no landscape to draw. I don't know how useful developing this skill will be; if things go badly for me, I am unlikely ever to draw anything again. But I find that there is a certain amount of serenity in putting pencil to paper.

I was taught drawing and watercolour when I was growing up; all young ladies were expected to do such things as part of their education in becoming an accomplished gentlewoman. But while my drawings and paintings were not particularly bad, I never had much interest in them. I was a more accomplished needlewoman; but truth to tell, I enjoyed riding and shooting with my father far more than drawing and painting *or* needlework.

When our mother died, Arthur came home from school briefly. He had not been there when she was brought to bed; he was sent for when it became clear that she was dying. He never saw the baby brother who preceded her in death by only a day.

But I was there, and I had held the tiny little boy whose skin was so transparent, whose lips and eyelids and fingers were pale and bluish.

I had heard Arthur weeping in the night. I wanted to comfort him, but I couldn't. I couldn't even cry; it was as if something had taken all my emotions and dammed them up where I could not access them.

Arthur and I took our guns out into the orchard the following day. Arthur had a beautiful rifle that had been a present from our father on Arthur's fifteenth birthday. I had my father's fowler; it was too unconventional, even for my father, to buy a twelve-year-old girl her own gun. The fowler was long, and I was short, but fierce determination made me able to shoot it. After a while, it became too heavy for me, but I had learnt to shoot it accurately by resting it on a wall or fence. I was pleased with myself, because Arthur couldn't do that. He always complained that it threw off his aim.

He set up a target in one of the apple trees and took the first shot. We were meant to take turns.

When it was my turn, I took my shot. Then I reloaded and took another. I loaded and fired until my arms shook, and the target splintered; until I couldn't lift the fowler anymore.

Arthur stood there with his mouth agape when I threw the gun, and myself, on the ground and folded myself over my knees. I still couldn't cry, but something had broken the dam, and what flowed out was anger; anger that what should have been a cause for celebration had instead left us bereft and desolate. Arthur sat beside me. 'Oh, Nell,' he whispered. We sat and clutched one another in the orchard until our old nurse came to look for us.

I realise that there are tears on my face now. That tiny, fragile little soul, our lost brother; so much like my own son, who never drew breath at all.

I wipe the tears away angrily. God forbid that anyone should look through the stern lights and see me crying. If I am sentenced to hang, at least I shall be reunited with my mother and my father; with my child; with Jack Mackay and Tom Sharpe.

I close my journal and put away my pencil. The drawing is unfinished, but maybe I will go back to it later. Maybe.

Frank Lepee, the captain's steward and coxswain, is seated at the table with one of Captain Nelson's coats. It seems that many of us fill more than one role on *Agamemnon*.

He has a needle and thread and is scowling at the coat. He looks up as I come in from the stern-gallery.

'Mr Buckley,' he acknowledges.

'Mr Lepee,' I return. 'What is wrong with that coat?'

'Tore the tail, somehow. He doesn't even know how he did it. Caught it on something, I imagine.'

I look at the damage. Caught it on his sword, it looks like. It's a tricky repair, and it's clearly frustrating Mr Lepee.

'Would you like me to try to fix it?' I ask him.

He looks relieved. 'Do you think you can? I've got plenty of other work to be getting on with. I've still got to finish washing his linen today before the mid-day meal.'

'I'll work on it.'

Not only is the coat torn, but the lining is torn as well. I will have to open up the lining and work from the inside of the coat to re-join and reinforce the broadcloth where it is damaged. The shalloon lining will be more difficult to fix; it should have a new section of cloth pieced into it. This is not something that I expect the purser to have, but maybe he can get it somewhere.

When Captain Nelson returns to the cabin, I have re-joined the cut edges of the broadcloth and am stitching a patch made from a bit of coarse flannel to the wrong side of the cloth. It will be covered by the lining once I have repaired that, so no one will see the patch.

'Are you doing Frank's work for him?' Captain Nelson asks, taking a seat at the table.

'I think this repair was exceeding his patience.'

He watches me work. 'Another skill I did not realise you possessed, Mr Buckley. Are you a tailor as well?'

'My mother was a mantua-maker.' I tie off the thread. 'This will serve well enough, Captain, but it will need a new piece of shalloon to finish the repair.'

'I'm sorry, what? "Shalloon"?'

'That is what this lining fabric is called.'

'Write it down, and I shall see if Mr Fellowes can obtain some.'

I set the coat aside. The captain looks exhausted. He is grey-faced, and the forenoon watch has only just ended. The ratings will be having their mid-day meal; since being confined here, I have shared Captain Nelson's mealtimes instead. Our dinner will not be for another two hours or so.

'Are you alright?' I ask.

'Well enough. I am still trying to recover my energy. I think I may doze for a while before dinner, and afterwards I will read my letters.' He doesn't appear to have the energy to move, though.

'Is this what I think it is, sir?' I indicate the length of marline and a slim leather-covered book that he has laid on the table.

'Aye, if what you think it is involves learning seaman's knots.'

I begin to say, 'I appreciate your efforts to keep my mind occupied...', but he starts to cough, and I don't finish the thought.

When the cough subsides, he presses a fist in the middle of his breast and massages it briefly. He catches me watching him.

'I remember a matron at school looking at me that way when I was in the infirmary with the measles.'

I sigh. 'You must know that I worry about you, sir.'

'You have my deep appreciation; but don't worry, Mr Buckley. I am deceptively difficult to kill.'

On the day after the court-martial, Captain Nelson is preparing *Agamemnon* to return to sea. His energy and spirits are returning, even if his chest complaint is still lingering. In the evening we depart for Genoa with two frigates, a sloop, and a cutter, to support the Austrian army on the Riviera.

'You may relax, Mr Buckley; as long as we are actively engaged, it will delay the necessity of referring Captain Spencer's demand to Admiral Hotham.'

Captain Nelson reclines in his chair in the lantern light as the ship sails northwards. He is visibly tired, but has shaken off the lethargy of his cold, and tonight his manner is relaxed, rather than exhausted.

'I am relieved, sir; but I regret that it means that I have to continue to impose upon your generosity. I am uncomfortably aware that you get no respite from me.'

'I do not consider you an imposition; and if I had wanted respite, I might just have spent three nights ashore in St Fiorenzo. But perhaps *you* are weary of *me*. Would you prefer to be confined somewhere else?'

'No, sir! I am not tired of your company at all! I am merely sensible that you cannot get away from me,' I say unhappily.

He yawns. 'I assure you, Mr Buckley, that I have no particular desire to get away from you.' There is a tap on the cabin door, and he raises his voice. 'Who is there?'

'It is Andrews, sir.'

'Enter, by all means, Lieutenant,' he calls.

Lieutenant Andrews comes into the cabin followed by the largest, blackest man I have ever seen. In the dimness of the cabin he seems almost to disappear, apart from his eyes and his clothes.

'This is Seaman Washington, Captain,' the lieutenant says.

'Come in, Washington. You are a difficult man to find. Did you not hear that I wanted to speak to you?'

'I did, sah; but I was leery of talking to you 'bout it.' Seaman Washington's teeth flash white in the lantern light when he speaks. I retreat into the shadows. I suspect that this conversation should not include me.

'Have a seat, please.' Captain Nelson lights a candle and places it on the table. 'You are an Able Seaman, Washington?'

'Aye, sah. I joined His Majesty's navy in Port Royal some five year ago. Before dat, I served on a merchant vessel out of Bermuda.' It is a soft voice for such a big man, laced with the cadence of the West Indies.

'You are a free man.' I get the impression that Captain Nelson already knows the answer to these questions, so I am not sure why he is asking them.

'Aye, sah. I bought my freedom when I got to be twenty-one years. My mastah, he taught me to read and figure.'

'I owe my life to a free black woman in Jamaica,' Captain Nelson tells him, 'who nursed me when I was beyond the medical skill of the Royal Navy. But that was almost fifteen years ago. I do not know if she is still there.' The captain's tiredness seems to have disappeared.

I file this information away. If he was in Jamaica fifteen years ago with the Royal Navy, then he is certainly older than twenty-six, unless he was an exceedingly young officer's servant.

'You know why I asked you to come and speak to me, do you, Seaman Washington?'

'Aye, sah; I do.'

'So tell me what you saw.'

Seaman Washington is silent for several moments. 'I was not supposed to be where I was, Captain, sah,' he says finally.

'We will set that aside for now,' Captain Nelson says quietly.

'Yessah. On de night we are speaking of, I was on de aft part of de upper gun deck, between de two larboard guns fo'ard of de aft companionway.'

'Why were you there?'

'I was intendin' to sleep on watch, Captain.'

The captain doesn't bat an eye. He clasps one hand on top of the other and rests his chin on them. 'Go on, Washington.'

'I gone to de orlop looking to rest my eyes somewhere quiet, but I seen de boy marine on duty outside de gunner's storeroom, sah, so I gone up to de gun deck where dere wasn't anyone around.'

'What time was this?'

The big sailor speaks quietly but frankly. 'Would have been de last hour of de fust watch, Captain.' He is respectful, but not diffident.

I can't breathe. I realise what Captain Nelson is asking this man about. I sit frozen just beyond the lantern light as the captain clears his throat before asking his next question.

'And were you asleep?'

'Not s'much dat I didn't hear someone coming down de deck. I backed all de way up 'gainst de bulwark and de gun carriage; and I put my head down, so dey wouldn't see me.'

'Did you see who was walking on the deck?'

'Not right at fust, sah. But I heard de voices.'

'Could you hear them clearly?'

Washington nods. 'T'was quiet on de gun deck, Captain, so I could hear dem clear.'

'Tell me what you heard.'

'I heard de marine captain say good eve'n to someone.'

'Do you know who he was talking to, Seaman Washington?'

'Aye, sah. He was talking to dat boy marine I seen on duty outside de storeroom.'

Captain Nelson taps his lower lip with the knuckle of his first finger. 'Did he say the marine's name?'

'Aye, sah; he called him Private Buckley.'

I squeeze my eyes shut. Would it be easier to hear this if I could become invisible?

'Did he say anything else, Seaman Washington?'

'De marine captain, he as'd de boy to come to his room and drink wit' him.'

'And did you hear Private Buckley's response?'

'He said "no t'ank you" to de captain.'

Over near the door, Lieutenant Andrews shifts his weight from his right foot to his left.

'What happened next, Washington?' Captain Nelson asks softly.

'I heard a shuffling and a hissing sound. I crept fo'ard to de end of de gun carriage and sneaked a look around de muzzle. De marine captain, he had de boy up 'gainst de companion ladder and was real close to him.'

'Go on,' the captain prompts, very quietly.

The sailor frowns. 'If I say, Captain, what happened next, I'm 'fraid of what gonna happen to me if dat man, he find out.'

Captain Nelson folds his hands. 'Whatever you tell me tonight is sealed until the court-martial. There can be no way that the man will find out until the trial. And if necessary, I will ensure that you are protected.'

Washington listens solemnly. 'And you got to court-martial me for sleeping on duty, sah?'

'You know that neglect of duty is a violation of the Articles of War,' the captain says flatly. 'I should not need to recite it to you, as I know that you have heard it countless times, that under Article 26 they call for *"death, or such other punishment as a court-martial shall think fit to impose, and as the circumstances of the case shall require"*. But you are not the man whose actions are currently under investigation, Seaman Washington. I cannot guarantee that you will not stand trial, but I think a case might be made that the circumstances require some leniency. Apart from this instance, you have a good record. You must recognise, however, that I cannot promise you any particular outcome.'

Silence descends. Captain Nelson waits. Lieutenant Andrews stands as still as an effigy by the door. Finally, Seaman Washington nods.

'Seems fair, Captain. I know what I done and I know it ain't lawful, but I want you to know I ain't made a habit of it, neither.'

'Very good, Washington. Shall we proceed?'

'Yessah. De marine captain, he had de boy up 'gainst de companion ladder, and he was very close to him. Den he said somet'ing mighty indecent.' The man sounds disgusted.

'Who did, Washington? The captain or the private?'

'De captain, sah.'

'Can you recall what he said?'

'To de best of my recollection, Captain, he called de private a *cock-tease*, and made a comment about de boy's arse. He said it was pretty, and he imagined it was tight and soft like a girl's.'

I dare not move or even lift my eyes to look at the two officers. My face burns with humiliation all over again.

'Did you see what happened then?' Captain Nelson asks softly.

'Most of it, sah. I seen de marine captain grab de boy marine by de chin and press his mout' on de boy's, and de boy try to get away from 'im. I seen where de captain put his ot'er hand, too. Den the boy marine, he done kick de captain in de leg and run up de companion ladder to de quarterdeck. De captain run after him.

'Dat's all I seen, sah. At dat point, I gone up on de quarterdeck fo' a minute, but nobody seen me because dey was all looking at de captain fighting wit' de boy on de deck. So I gone below, sah.'

Captain Nelson steeples his hands under his nose. He closes his eyes and seems to think for a moment, then he says quietly, 'Ned, will you come here, please?'

I am not sure my frozen muscles will move, but somehow I manage to stand up and walk into the lantern light.

The captain puts a hand on my shoulder and turns me to face the big sailor.

'Is this one of the men you saw?'

'Aye, sah. He's dressed like a servant now, but dat's de boy marine, de one de captain called Private Buckley.'

'Thank you, Ned. You may go now,' Captain Nelson tells me softly.

I walk woodenly to my pallet behind the screen and lie on it, staring at the ceiling as Captain Nelson addresses the seaman again.

'You said that you can read and figure, Seaman Washington. Can you write, too?'

'Yessah. I ain't no Thomas Paine, but I can write just fine.'

'I would like you to take this pen, ink, and paper into the other room and write out your statement as you told it to me. Lieutenant Andrews and I will witness your signature.'

'Yessah. T'ank you, sah.'

I hear the cabin door open and latch again. Captain Nelson coughs. Then he says, 'Mr Buckley.'

'Sir.'

'May I speak to you?'

'Yessir.' I push myself up reluctantly, but Captain Nelson comes to the foot of the screen.

'Don't rise; I shall come to you,' he says, and lowers himself down to sit on the end of the palliasse. He scrubs his face wearily with both hands.

'That is the testimony I was waiting for. It is not without significant problems, however.'

I sit silently against the bulkhead, staring at the floor. 'I can see that, sir,' I say finally.

'There are two reasons why the board might take a dim view of Seaman Washington's statement. First, because he was violating one of the Articles of War when he witnessed the assault by Captain Spencer. Second, because he is a black man, free or not. It depends upon who sits on the board, whether that second fact will be an issue. It is in your favour that he does not have a history of disciplinary problems. He has only been flogged once, for fighting, and the other man was clearly the instigator and received more lashes.'

He sighs. In the dim light from the lantern, he looks impossibly young, and more exhausted than ever.

'I also flatter myself that I am not completely without interest of my own, where Lord Spencer is concerned. At least, not yet.'

'Sir... do not sacrifice your good standing with the First Lord for my sake.'

'If, given the evidence I have collected, Lord Spencer prefers to take the side of his relation... well, there will be other First Lords.'

I am dismayed by this statement. 'Captain, I am aware that I have not shown much spirit, nor inclination to fight for myself. This has shaken me very much. But I would prefer to fail on the basis of my own insufficient defence, rather than allow you to damage your future on my behalf.'

He affects not to hear me. 'Seaman Washington was mistaken that his presence on the quarterdeck went unremarked. It was how I knew to look for him. But I did not want to coerce his testimony from him; he had to give it of his own free will.' He rubs his eyes with his right hand. The injured eye looks irritated, and the eyelid droops slightly. I have noticed that it often does when he is tired.

'However, Captain Spencer is likely to claim that Washington gave it in expectation of leniency in regard to his own possible trial,' he continues. 'The circumstances will come out; he would be asked why he was skulking between guns at midnight if he does not confess the reason up front. I would simply deal with the infraction myself, was that not the case. Despite what he has confessed to, I don't care to punish a man for giving testimony that harms himself. But I cannot be perceived to show any partiality. This whole thing is a damnable mess, and not one that I bargained for.'

He gives me a very slight, troubled smile, meant to be reassuring. 'We are not in safe harbour yet, Mr Buckley, but I believe we are getting closer.'

Eight bells sound outside the cabin doors. It is midnight, and the watches are changing over from the first to the middle watch. The same time of night when Captain Spencer set all of this in motion.

Lieutenant Andrews taps on the door and opens it. 'Captain? I have his statement, sir, if you will come and witness Seaman Washington's signature.'

'I will be there in a moment,' Captain Nelson tells him. He picks himself up from the end of the palliasse. 'How very fagged I am. Go to sleep,' he says to me, 'we can do no more tonight.'

'Thank you, sir,' I murmur. 'Good night, sir.'

'Good night,' he says, as he leaves the cabin, latching the door behind him.

Chapter Sixteen

We do not speak of this latest development on the following day. I did not hear Captain Nelson return to the cabin last night, nor leave this morning, but I heard him cough in the middle of the night, so I know he must have slept.

The daily business is routine, but the captain is happy to have a goal and it is reflected in his mood. I think that he anticipates another initiative similar to those on Corsica, and the expectation has raised his spirits again. If the pain in his chest is still troubling him, he doesn't mention it.

On the morning of our second day of sailing, Nelson receives word that the French fleet is out again. He thanks the officer of the watch and doesn't interrupt the letter he is writing, but I can tell that his pulse is quickening. He has barely finished writing when the message comes that the *Ariadne* frigate has spotted large ships to the northwest. He is immediately on the quarterdeck, without a word to me.

Mr Lepee lays the mid-day meal on the table, but Captain Nelson does not arrive to eat it. I wait, tying and re-tying a bowline knot until my fingers can do it practically on their own. Not that I ever expect to use the silly knot. The steward comes back, raises his eyebrows, and leaves again.

When the captain finally does come to eat, the soup is cold; as are the other dishes, but he does not seem to care. I do not believe he is tasting the food.

'What appeared initially to be a merchant fleet, which I thought might provide us with a nice prize if they were French, is rather their main battle fleet,' he informs me as he bolts his dinner. 'There are at least fifteen of them, and two of their frigates have been taking our measure. However, at the same time, I am taking theirs, so we shall see.'

We do not see anything for the rest of the day, however. The lookouts report that the French fleet comprises seventeen ships of the line, plus six frigates. I know Captain Nelson well enough to be certain that he would not shrink from taking on two frigates, or a single ship of the line, but if the entire fleet takes an interest in him, there is no way he can fight. Given the way the French fleet has behaved in the past, though, it is possible that we will not be of interest to them.

That would be a fine thing, but it isn't going to happen. Undoubtedly the French recognise *Agamemnon* as the ship that pummelled *Ça Ira* and ultimately caused them to lose her. After a largely sleepless night on our part, in the morning we are approached by four large ships flying Spanish colours.

Captain Nelson has no illusions. He signals to our cruisers to flee, and brings *Agamemnon's* head around to sail for St Fiorenzo again. If he can get there and get the British fleet out before the French catch up, there is a good chance we can engage them effectively. But they take up the chase, and we cannot manage to lose them.

Agamemnon is indeed a good sailer, as Captain Nelson had informed me on the day that I met him. For twenty-four hours, she leads the French on at a furious pace. I cannot participate, and have to sit in the cabin, waiting anxiously for any information that comes my way. Mr Lepee, Mr Withers, and Midshipman Hoste all feed me titbits when they have business in the captain's cabin, but the most comprehensive information comes from Captain Nelson.

He comes to the cabin to eat, or to catch a brief nap, but he never stays for long. It is as though he cannot be confined for more than an hour before he must be back on the quarterdeck for his own peace of mind. Whereas when we are on the larboard tack, I can see the French fleet from the stern-gallery, and it gives me no peace of mind whatsoever. Still, Captain Nelson keeps out in front of them, and they gain no distance.

That is, until the morning when the wind dies. We are so close to St Fiorenzo, but we can get no closer. What breeze there is benefits the French fleet, bringing them ever nearer. I stand on the stern-gallery with my heart in my throat.

I hear the signal to clear for action, and Captain Nelson comes into the cabin shortly thereafter.

'We are going to have to defend ourselves,' he says grimly. 'I have to hope that we can hold out long enough for Hotham to realise what is happening and come to our assistance.'

He is composed and speaks with conviction. But I sense an undertone of fatalism that is not like Captain Nelson at all.

'I am sorry, Mr Buckley, but in a moment they will come to clear the cabin. Mr King will escort you to the boatswain's store. I believe you will be safe there.'

There is nothing I can say. I understand the necessity of this, much as I dread being locked in the boatswain's store-room. Before Mr King leads me below decks, I reach for the captain's hand.

'Good luck, sir. God bless you.'

'You as well, Mr Buckley,' he says quietly.

Mr King unlocks the storeroom reluctantly. 'I'm sorry, lad; I don't believe you belong down here. Seems to me you have as much right to fight as any of the rest of us. But the captain says that he wants you to stay alive to clear your name. He always thinks long term, does Captain Nelson.'

At least there is a lantern and some ventilation in the storeroom. When the fighting starts, I will have to douse the lantern, so it cannot set fire to the stores should we be hit. Come the night, it will be black as pitch, but I doubt I'll still be here come nightfall. I cannot say where I might be, but I doubt it will be here.

I sit on a coil of cable. I can hear tompions being drawn, bare feet pounding on boards. They will be wetting the decks, sails, and rigging, and strewing sand under foot. The armourer will make ready to distribute muskets, pistols, cutlasses, and boarding pikes. Every man at his quarters. And then the silence descends, as we wait, dead in the water.

I close my eyes and picture Captain Nelson on the quarterdeck. Will he be able to summon that ferocity that inspires his men to do things that they might not do otherwise? I have never yet heard him raise his voice in anger at another man, but in the engagement with *Ça Ira,* I'd heard him bellow commands in a voice that Neptune himself would envy. I had been amazed he'd had any voice left to speak with that night.

God protect him, I find myself praying.

I am slightly surprised at myself. Captain Nelson is not normally fatalistic, and neither, once, was I. Richard changed that. Since leaving him, I have often thought that the only way to keep going was to resign myself to fate. And yet, now I am praying for the captain's protection, and I find that I mean it.

Suddenly I feel the ship begin to heel, and at first, I am sure I am mistaken. But no, *Agamemnon* is moving. *She's moving!*

I have no sense of direction down here, nor any of speed. But it feels as though she's flying, after that dreadful calm.

After an interminable time, I hear our guns fire; but they're signal guns. Nelson has brought *Agamemnon* within hearing distance of the British fleet.

I don't know how long I sit in the storeroom before I hear the key turn in the lock. I jump up as bosun's mate opens the door.

'Seems they might 'ave forgot ye, lad,' he says, 'but I guess the captain remembered afore too long. He said he didn't mean for ye to stay down here all night.'

I am not allowed to pass through the ship unaccompanied, but they might have put me in shackles, and I'm grateful that they did not.

It is early evening, and as we climb up out of the orlop, the shadows indicate that the sun is skimming the horizon. The mate leads me up to the fo'c's'le and along the gangway to the quarterdeck. I can see feverish activity on all the British ships in port, while *Agamemnon* hovers anxiously in the bay.

The sentry allows us entry and as the mate opens the door to the captain's cabin he says, 'Sir, 'ere's your prisoner, safe and sound.' The way he says 'prisoner' makes it sound like a jest.

Captain Nelson is standing at the stern lights, and he turns to thank the bosun's mate. 'Apologies, Mr Buckley,' he says, as the mate leaves, 'I hadn't intended to leave you in the storeroom, but I have been distracted.'

'I understand, sir.'

'I hope it wasn't too disagreeable.'

It was. But there is absolutely no point in saying so. I know why he made the decision.

'What happened, sir? Did the French leave off the chase…?'

'No, they did not. Providence sent us a wind just as they were coming into range. We were expecting they would test their range at any moment when the wind returned. We were able to escape through the shallows, where they could not follow.'

He is teetering between exhaustion and indignation. 'The British fleet is putting to sea, but the villains have fled; as soon as they realised that our ships were mobilised, they ran. Blackguards—they are neither seamen nor officers!' he says with disgust.

'We are pursuing *them* this time, and God grant that we catch them. Cowards! Their entire fleet will chase a single ship, but they run from a fair fight!'

He refuses to eat or rest until he sees the entire British fleet set sail in hot pursuit. It is in the early hours of the middle watch, and except for the men on deck, the ship is quiet. I am not sleeping, because Captain Nelson is not.

He comes in from the quarterdeck and says, 'Come with me, Mr Buckley.' He leads me up to the poop and says quietly, 'Look at them. As fine a fleet as ever graced the sea.'

Twenty-three ships of the line, with attendant frigates, spread out in the moonlight. HMS *Britannia, Victory,* and *Princess Royal,* bearing the admirals' flags, proudly shepherd the two-decked seventy-fours. It is a majestic sight, astonishingly moving. British colours fly boldly above every vessel. I am speechless.

'Impressive, is it not?' the captain says softly.

'It's breath-taking,' I murmur. 'No wonder the French ran.'

Little *Agamemnon* is amongst the first and foremost. She is the smallest of all the sail of the line, but she has the heart and soul of a first-rate.

It takes us four days to locate the French fleet again. I don't believe that Captain Nelson has slept for more than a few hours at a time in the past week. He has barely eaten. I don't know how he sustains himself, but he is so intent that he cannot rest.

I have tried to keep pace with him, if only to bear him up. But I cannot do it. For one thing, trapped as I am in the cabin, I cannot generate physical energy with exercise the way he does. Little food and lack of sleep have begun to make me feel physically ill.

He was up before daybreak again, and I know he did not go to bed before the beginning of the middle watch. Even when he makes himself lie down, I am not sure that he sleeps.

Daylight has begun to filter through the stern lights, and I have risen, washed, dressed, and rolled up my palliasse when he returns to the cabin. 'We've found them!' he announces excitedly.

I rise from my seat at the table, but standing too quickly makes me light-headed. My vision starts to go dark at the periphery, and I have to grab the back of the chair to keep myself from falling.

In a flash, Captain Nelson catches me. He sets me on the floor and crouches beside me. 'Put your head down, lad. Breathe, Mr Buckley.'

'I'm alright, sir,' I mumble. 'I just stood up too fast.'

'I have been remiss,' he mutters. 'Look at you; you're worn to a shadow.'

'With respect, sir, look who's talking,' I retort.

'You must not try to keep up with me. This is my nature; I cannot help it. But you are not like me. You need to eat and sleep, or you will make yourself ill.'

He is hardly exempt in that regard, but I find I lack the energy to say so.

He helps me up from the floor. 'I cannot stay, but I shall be back. Lie down in my berth until breakfast.'

'I am fine, sir,' I insist irritably.

'That is an order, Mr Buckley,' he says, equally impatient.

'Yessir.'

He stands resolutely, watching until I climb into his berth. Then he removes my shoes and pushes me gently down on the pillow.

My mind flashes to another man pushing me down on a bed; but that man was not gentle. I involuntarily try to rise again.

'Do not argue with me, Mr Buckley,' Captain Nelson says firmly.

The tension runs out of my body at his voice. He is not Richard. Richard is thousands of miles away.

'Nosir. I don't mean to, sir.'

'Good.' His voice softens. 'I shall be back for breakfast. It will be brief and meagre, but we shall eat it together.'

He turns and is gone in a flash.

I close my eyes. I am uncomfortable lying on his bed. His pillow smells faintly of the lavender water that he combs through his hair between washings. I think that I cannot sleep here. But it's the last thing I think until he shakes my shoulder gently to come to breakfast.

Breakfast is indeed meagre and perfunctory. It is served in the captain's dining room and attended by some of the junior officers, but none of us engage in conversation. They eat quickly and leave.

Captain Nelson and I watch one another covertly, each of us trying to ensure that the other is eating. I attempt to eat what I think is a reasonable amount, but the captain is distracted and restless, and again, barely eats anything at all.

When we are the only two left at the table, I say reproachfully, 'Sir, you didn't even make an effort.'

He looks down at his plate, the food still sitting on it. 'No, I suppose I did not. I shall make up for it when the battle is over.'

The signal lieutenant sticks his head into the dining room. 'Sir, Admiral Hotham is signalling for us to take our position... again. Sir.'

Captain Nelson tosses his serviette onto his plate and rises. 'I will be right there.' He pauses at the door.

'Mr Buckley, when we clear for battle, I apologise that you will have to return to the boatswain's storeroom. I wish it were not so.' His voice is regretful. Then he is gone.

I retreat to his cabin and try to occupy myself with a book, but I cannot keep my mind on it. What made me think that I could read, in light of the impending battle? I watch the sea through the stern lights, the book lying open and unread on the table, my mind a maelstrom of disordered thoughts.

The captain reappears unexpectedly an hour later, accompanied by Lieutenant Andrews.

'He wastes valuable time!' Nelson cries impatiently. 'Had he immediately changed tacks, we might have cut them off. I have half a mind to break from the line and go after them myself.'

'Supported, that might work, Captain, but to go in alone would be madness.' If the captain seems to have forgotten the tense chase that we endured only days ago, the lieutenant has not.

'I am certain that *Culloden* would go with us,' Captain Nelson says, but some of the urgency in his voice has been diffused.

'With respect, sir, perhaps it is a chance worth taking, but I do not care to assume your command while a court tries to determine whether your actions constitute contempt for your senior officer.' Lieutenant Andrews' voice is deferential, but underlaid with practicality.

Captain Nelson takes a deep breath and blows it out in frustration.

'Perhaps they will still turn and engage us, Captain.'

'I very much doubt it. The only way they will fight is if we force them to.'

The two officers leave the cabin again, neither one of them having apparently registered my presence.

It is yet another hour, at the start of the forenoon watch, before Admiral Hotham signals a general chase; and *Agamemnon* is like a hound that has been unleashed. She, and her captain, are in their element.

The winds are again not in our favour. Despite being in the forefront of the fleet, *Agamemnon,* along with five others of the fastest, most well-commanded ships, has only been able to catch up with the French rear. As the decks are cleared, I am escorted back to the storeroom in the orlop. I do not see Captain Nelson. He has put me completely from his mind.

It is Mr Withers who has been given the duty of turning the key on me today. His open, pleasant face can't conceal his discomfort. 'It's alright, Mr Withers', I say quietly. 'I understand the necessity.'

He shakes his head. 'I hope this ends soon, Mr Buckley.' He is not referring to the encroaching engagement.

I can hear the crew shouting encouragement to the first ships to engage, and soon the guns begin to speak. Before long *Agamemnon*'s guns add their voices, and the orlop deck resounds with the roar of the guns above. I douse the lantern, and darkness closes around me.

I have never been afraid of darkness, nor particularly of small spaces, but the two combine to make me uneasy. I know that there is no less air in this space than there was when the lantern was lit, but it feels as though every blast from the guns sucks a little more air from the storeroom. I ground myself securely on the coiled cable and close my eyes.

If I say, Surely the darkness shall cover me; even the night shall be light about me.

Yea, the darkness hideth not from thee; but the night shineth as the day: the darkness and the light are both alike to thee.

The ship shudders in a way different than that from the report of her guns. She is receiving fire on her bow. I keep my eyes shut and breathe. I picture Captain Nelson on his quarterdeck, roaring like his ship's guns, his eyes blazing.

… he shall give his angels charge over thee: to keep thee in all thy ways.

They shall bear thee in their hands: that thou hurt not thy foot against a stone.

Thou shalt go upon the lion and adder: the young lion and the dragon shalt thou tread under thy feet.

Because he hath set his love upon me, therefore will I deliver him: I shall set him up, because he hath known my Name.

Another blow rocks *Agamemnon*'s bow, but her guns do not even stutter. My eyes fly open. It is still so dark that I am not sure whether my eyes are open or closed, but something has changed. I smell the sea. I hear water rushing. Then I feel it, running across the decking at my feet. My breath catches in my breast.

Oh, great God…

They will be working the pumps, and the carpenters will attend to the damage. It is very difficult to sink a wooden warship. The French guns are so poorly manned that they are unlikely to hit us again; it was luck that they managed to hit us at all.

I do not want to die down here in the dark.

I cannot see to move anywhere, and the coil of cable grows wet beneath me, but the water continues to run through into the hold and does not rise in the storeroom; at least, not as far as I can tell. I cannot tell where it is coming in, but I can hear it running and pooling.

Have mercy upon me, O God, after thy great goodness: according to the multitude of thy mercies do away mine offences.

Wash me thoroughly from my wickedness: and cleanse me from my sin.

For I acknowledge my faults: and my sin is ever before me.

Against thee only have I sinned and done this evil in thy sight: that thou mightest be justified in thy saying, and clear when thou art judged.

Behold, I was shapen in wickedness —

A ferocious explosion rocks the ship, and I hear a shriek—I leap up from the cable and feel blindly around me, searching with my hands. Was it *Agamemnon*'s magazine? Are we going to go to the bottom at any minute? Who cried out in that horrible way?

It takes me only seconds to realise that *Agamemnon* is not sinking, at least, not yet; that she is not moving, and that the person who cried out was me.

I sink back down and feel the seawater running over the floor, but to my hands it seems no deeper. I am shaking from head to foot. I force myself to be still and listen.

Know that I am God.

Two years ago I would have cried, *Where have you been?! Why have you forsaken me? I have no need of you now...*

I did not expect to become reacquainted with God on a

mountainside in Corsica, or in the captain's cabin of *Agamemnon*, or here, in this dark place, with seawater coming in.

Nelson, it was you who reclaimed me.

In thee, O Lord, have I put my trust: let me never be put to confusion, deliver me in thy righteousness.

Bow down thine ear to me: make haste to deliver me.

And be thou my strong rock, and house of defence: that thou mayest save me.

For thou art my strong rock, and my castle: be thou also my guide, and lead me for thy Name's sake.

I did not know that I remembered these psalms; I had grown up with them, and in my misery, I had cast them away.

Father in Heaven, take me back. Before I drown and am cast forever into the dark.

I get down on my knees in the water running over the boards and bow my head on the coil of rope.

If I die here, I will not have to stand trial.

I will regret not having seen Captain Nelson again.

I am not afraid to die. I am only afraid of the process of dying. I do not want to drown.

Agamemnon's guns stopped firing some time ago. I hear boats coming alongside, and men shouting. Have we been taken? Which ship exploded?

Captain Nelson would never strike his colours. So either we have not been taken, or Captain Nelson is dead.

I do not know how long I kneel there in the dark, with the cold seawater running across the deck and pooling against my calves. I am not aware of whether I am praying; I barely register the ship beginning to move again. I might even be asleep. I cannot tell.

When the door to the storeroom opens, the dim light of the orlop deck feels blinding. I blink and see Captain

Spencer standing in the doorway, a murderous scowl on his face, and I scramble on my hands and heels to back out of the light, to escape...

"Ere, Private, what's got into you?'

It is not Captain Spencer. It is Sergeant Preston, with Mr King. I think I may collapse.

'I... I'm sorry, sir. For a moment I thought you were a Frenchman,' I stammer.

'Do I *look* like a Frenchman?' he asks. 'Come wi' me; Mr King 'ere needs to see how much damage the water's done, and Captain Nelson is waiting to reclaim you.'

I have trouble getting to my feet. My legs are cold and leaden and feel as though they have forgotten how to hold me up. The sergeant takes my arm. 'Are you ill, lad?'

'My legs are numb. It's alright, sir; I can walk.'

He leads me out of the orlop. The sun is still high, and its light is brutal after the complete darkness of the store-room. I'm afraid of being a spectacle, but no one is paying any mind to me at all. The business of restoring the ship commands all their attention.

'Which ship exploded, sir?'

'A Frenchie, *Alcide*. She'd struck her colours, but she caught fire. We've taken about a dozen of her men aboard, but we lost more of 'em than we saved.

'The wind failed us again. It becalmed us, and we couldn't close with the French fleet. Then, just as it picked up and we were almost in range again, the admiral signalled to leave off action. Captain Nelson was that mad, I can tell you.'

'Is he alright, sergeant?'

'Oy, why wouldn't he be?'

'I don't know. Sitting there in the dark, I got to thinking all kinds of ridiculous nonsense.'

''Spect it'd do that to anyone. But you seem to 'ave come through it a' right.'

He returns me to the door to the captain's quarters and leaves me there. I look at the sentry, but he doesn't look back, so I open the door and go in.

Captain Nelson is seated at the table with his back to me and doesn't register my presence immediately, but when I latch the door, he looks over his shoulder. He is on his feet in an instant.

'Mr Buckley—you look shocked. And you are all wet! What happened, lad?!'

'A shot that hit the hull, sir... the room was in total darkness, so I couldn't see where the water was coming from, but I'm afraid that Mr King's stores are wet.

'I couldn't tell what was happening, sir. I heard the explosion. For a moment I wondered if it was *Agamemnon*. Then everything went quiet. I thought we must have struck; and if we'd struck, I knew that you were dead.' My voice cracks embarrassingly.

He has been standing with his hands on my shoulders, but when I say this, he clasps me to him and holds me tightly. 'Bless you, Mr Buckley, that you should be afraid for me.'

His arms are thin and strong. I have not allowed a man to touch me in this way for years, but my body is too tired to react in alarm. I think I could almost sleep, standing here with my head on his breast.

He lets me go. 'We are both worn out,' he observes. 'Change into dry clothes and go to sleep. I cannot take myself to my own bed yet, but I shall before too long. I shall wake you for supper, but I'll not expect you to eat it if you don't care to.'

He goes back to his work, and I retreat behind my screen and change into my spare shirt and trousers. My waistcoat and the blue sailor's jacket are not soaking, but the waistcoat is damp, and the hem of the jacket is wet. I hang the wet clothes and the jacket over the top of the screen and lie down on my palliasse. I am asleep almost before I close my eyes.

Chapter Seventeen

I n port at St Fiorenzo, Captain Nelson slumps in his chair
and massages his chest. He looks ragged.

Mr Reynolds, the surgeon, finishes his examination.
'I could blister you, but I don't believe it would help any.
The best I can tell you, sir, is that you need rest. If you was
to apply to the admiral for time ashore, I would endorse it.'

'I'll consider it, Mr Reynolds.'

The surgeon packs up his instruments and leaves. Captain
Nelson coughs.

The heavy congestion has disappeared with his cold, but
the cough remains, along with the pain in his chest. The
surgeon required him to remove his coat and waistcoat and
open his shirt; now he sits in his banyan without coat, waistcoat, or stock, the throat button of his shirt undone. Not
long ago, being alone in a room with a man in this state of
undress would set my heart racing in panic, but I trust the
captain. In addition, he hardly looks as if he has the strength
today to subdue a child.

'My brother Mun died of a consumption,' he tells me
gloomily. 'I suppose that one day I shall follow him.'

'Don't say that, sir.'

'We Nelsons have never been blessed with strong constitu-
tions,' he asserts. 'What have we in the way of mail, Mr Buckley?'

'These appear to be personal letters, sir.'

'I suppose it cannot kill me any faster to read some letters.' His face brightens a little. 'Ah—it appears that my father has sent the newspapers.'

We have been back in St Fiorenzo for less than a day. Repairs are in progress on *Agamemnon;* despite my alarming experience in the bosun's store, she was not badly damaged. Most of the French shot hit her sails and rigging, as usual. The captain plans to resume the interrupted mission to the Riviera as soon as *Agamemnon* is restored.

Captain Nelson had warm water for washing this morning, and after he had bathed his face and torso, and washed his hair, he ordered more warm water to be brought for me. If he has noticed how infrequently I 'shave', he hasn't remarked about it. Not since that day in Corsica, almost a year ago.

I looked at my face in his shaving mirror and was shocked. What has happened to me?

My face is pale, and the colour appears to have drained from my hair. I look bleached, apart from the shadows around my eyes. Is this the result of having been assaulted and accused by Captain Spencer, confined, and confronted with the prospect of drowning in a dark room? Whatever the reason, no one from my former life would recognise me now if I walked into their sitting room.

I finished *Henry V* days ago, and I have moved on to Captain Nelson's copy of *The Life and Opinions of Tristram Shandy, Gentleman.* My father had a copy in his library, but I was not allowed to read it. Having read Tristram Shandy's account of the circumstances of his conception and birth, I now know why. *Tristram Shandy*, however, causes me to forget that I have been badly used, or that I am worried about what may happen when the captain runs out of excuses for keeping me here.

'Hah,' says Captain Nelson, and then, 'Ha-ha!' I look up from the book.

He is sitting back in his chair with a satisfied look on his face. He swings around and awards me one of his rare smiles.

'I have been promoted to Colonel of Marines of the Chatham Division. I have been receiving an additional salary since 6 June. But that is not the best part—I now have a solution to a difficult problem!' He takes up his pen and scribbles something on a sheet of paper, then seals it. Jumping up, he takes the message to Mr Withers, who is working on the books in the lobby. I do not hear what he tells him.

'Help me get dressed,' he orders, shucking off his banyan. 'And put on your marine's coat.'

I do as instructed, fastening his neck stock for him, and helping him into his coat as he buttons his waistcoat. Then, to my surprise, he girds on his sword.

I am trading the sailor's short jacket for my marine's coat when there is a rap on the door. Captain Nelson has barely voiced permission to enter before the door opens and Captain Spencer walks into the room.

I have not seen him since that horrible night. He stares at me coldly. I look woodenly back.

There is a thin, healing wound that starts at his left temple, skips over the hollow of his eye, and continues over the cheekbone towards his nose. It cannot have been particularly deep, because it appears that the surgeon did not need to suture it. But he will wear a scar for the rest of his life.

Good. Let him think of me every time he looks in the mirror.

'Captain Nelson,' he says, his voice cold, soft, and correct as ever. 'I hope your health is improved.' It is a courtesy only; it does not sound sincere.

'It is only so-so,' Captain Nelson replies mildly, 'but it will suffice.'

'Have you called me here finally to discuss my request for justice?' Captain Spencer doesn't look at me, but he emphasises 'justice' ever so slightly.

'I have.' Captain Nelson does not invite Spencer to take a seat. Captain Nelson remains standing, as do I. I don't think I could move now if I saw a cannonball coming directly at me.

'It has taken me some time to complete the necessary inquiry into your request for a court-martial,' Captain Nelson begins. 'In addition to the obvious French interference, some witnesses were reluctant to give a statement. But I now have everything I need.'

He coughs to clear his throat. 'Captain Spencer, I am not referring your request for a court-martial on to Admiral Hotham.'

Spencer's eyes narrow. 'I do not understand, Captain. If you are protecting your—'

Captain Nelson cuts him off. His voice is suddenly as cold as Captain Spencer's. 'I believe it is in your best interest, Captain Spencer. And be careful what you say. I am your superior officer, not only as the captain of this ship, but also as a colonel of marines.'

Captain Spencer's face freezes. He removes any trace of expression from it.

'I have testimony from a man who saw the incident on the upper gun deck, and who heard clearly what passed between you and Private Buckley. I also have three independent witnesses whose statements attest that your behaviour on the quarterdeck comprised execrations, drunkenness, uncleanness, and corruption of good manners.

'To prevent all this from being made public at a court-martial, I suggest that you withdraw your petition. I also suggest that you request a transfer to another ship. If you decline to do the latter, then I shall request that you be reassigned. I need not give a reason, but I can if it is necessary. You will remove your belongings and go ashore with speed, sir.'

Captain Spencer's face does not change, but a nerve in his neck beats visibly against his tightened jaw. I have seen that hard look in his eyes before. It is thwarted rage.

'That will be all, Captain Spencer. You are dismissed, sir.'

Captain Spencer turns with icy control and leaves the cabin. He closes the door with a click.

I do not know if I have breathed at all since Captain Nelson informed Captain Spencer that he had denied his demand. My brain seems to be having trouble processing information.

My locked knees give way, and I crumple.

Captain Nelson is beside me in a flash. I have not fainted; I am still conscious of my surroundings, but it is as though I have been plunged back into the disorienting darkness of the bosun's storeroom.

His deft fingers unfasten my stock and undo the throat button of my shirt. I sit on the floor of the cabin, supporting myself with my arm, my breath coming in gulps.

'You are alright, Mr Buckley.' He crouches on one knee, his sword in its scabbard, the symbol of his authority, resting on the floor in front of me. It is a command, not a reassurance, and it does the trick.

When my breathing returns to something resembling normalcy, I ask him, 'Is that it, sir? Is it over?'

'I hope so, Mr Buckley,' he says.

We return to the Riviera, and I return to my mess. The marines all know of Captain Spencer's departure and my release from custody, but no one is talking about it, which suits me fine. I would be happy to forget about the entire episode. Apart from the strengthening of the ties of loyalty that bind me to Captain Nelson, that is… and I am conflicted about that.

The captain is energised by his promotion and the independence he enjoys in command of his little squadron of two frigates, a brig, and a cutter, plus any other ships that come temporarily into his sphere of operations. But he is frustrated by Admiralty red tape and harrowing diplomatic affairs, and his health is not improving. I suggested that he return to the spa where he took his midshipmen last year, after we came to Leghorn from Corsica, but he is too busy to hear of it.

Captain Nelson still employs me for a few hours a day to help him untangle the administrative and diplomatic snarls surrounding his attempts to keep supplies from reaching the French army. Genoa is supposed to be neutral, but Nelson suspects subterfuge to supply the French everywhere, and I doubt that he is wrong. The French army is entrenched in Genoa, and even as Nelson's squadron attempts to cut off their supplies by sea, they are now being supplied by Genoese traders on land. So much for neutrality; the Genoese government is afraid of the French and makes no effort to stop this abuse. Captain Nelson's squadron is endlessly examining 'neutrals' for the proper passes, and suspicious papers abound.

He also has taken a 'guest' aboard. His pretty friend, Signora Correglia, now shares his cabin. 'Only temporarily,' he says. But unlike me when I shared his quarters, Signora Correglia does not have her own sleeping arrangements.

Adelaide Correglia apparently speaks no English, and Captain Nelson speaks no Italian. They appear to communicate in French, although the captain's French is worse than mine. Still, she seems to understand him. She is solicitous of his cough and pours his tea with a warm, lovely smile. She doesn't forget the milk. She pets his arm or his cheek, and he glows like a schoolboy in the throes of a first infatuation.

These little displays of affection make me slightly uncomfortable, and more than a little sad. The ring that I searched for last summer in the dusty grass of Corsica still adorns his last finger; the ring itself was found, but somewhere since then, its symbolism has been lost.

Don't be idealistic, Ned. You know men are faithless creatures at heart.

He frequently hosts other captains at his table when their ships are on the Riviera, and I have seen Captain Fremantle and Captain Troubridge several times. I am no longer invited to dine with him, but I expected no differently.

Captain Nelson apparently negotiated an agreement with Seaman Washington. He receives two dozen lashes for neglect of duty. I don't like to watch the floggings under any circumstances, but this one is particularly unpleasant. Signora Correglia stands on Captain Nelson's arm, her large, dark eyes soberly watchful as the cat opens red stripes on that broad, coal-black back.

The newspapers sent by Captain Nelson's father have made the rounds of the officers. They are conscientious about returning them or passing them on, and one day in the early part of August, I retrieve them again with the captain's correspondence.

He is ashore today with his lady friend in Savona. He hopes to find some rooms ashore for her where he could rest more comfortably. I support that. For all Signora Correglia's ministrations, he still looks and sounds unwell.

I sort the communications the way he prefers them and pick up the newspapers to put them in his locker. He has long since returned my knife. It is back in its accustomed place in my boot, although it took me some time to get used to having it there again.

As I open the locker, I glance at the topmost newspaper. Someone has left it folded open to an inner page, and with growing horror I see a familiar name.

ELEANOR BUCCLEUCH, *my wife, with no just cause of complaint, hath eloped from my bed and board. She is thirty years of age; of stature, five feet and three inches. She has light brown hair and grey eyes. She may be representing herself as a man. Whosoever can provide information leading to her return to me shall receive a* REWARD *of* FIVE GUINEAS.

It is hoped that Masters of ships and others shall be careful not to carry off or secrete said ELEANOR. *If she returns to her husband's household, all offenses shall be forgiven.*
RICHARD BUCCLEUCH
Morden, Surrey
15 June 1795

I feel dizzy. Why, after more than two years, is he looking for me now? What could have changed? I know he is vindictive, but I had begun to hope that he had forgotten me; that he had moved on.

It occurs to me with dismay that he may want to marry again but cannot unless he can prove that I am dead. God forbid that he should marry some other poor woman!

I will stay alive just to spite him, so help me.

Feeling like a thief, I remove this page of newspaper and fold it into my waistcoat. No one will see this one again, but I know this will not be the only advertisement that Richard has placed. There will be others.

I go down to where my pack is stowed and take the miniature out of the toe of my old stocking. In its place, I put the newspaper advertisement.

Captain Nelson returns the following day without Signora Correglia. He sits regarding his growing piles of correspondence unenthusiastically.

'Were you successful in finding rooms ashore, Captain?' I ask.

'No,' he says. He coughs painfully. 'There was nothing suitable. Too mean; too hot; too expensive.' He gets up to pour a glass of water. 'My dear friend the Signora has gone to Genoa to visit her mother. There is an action I intend to take soon, and she cannot be here for that.'

He does not invite comment, and I don't offer any.

'I need you to read for me today. My eyes are very bad.' He takes a small bottle out of his coat. 'An apothecary in Savona recommended I try this. May I ask you to make it up for me?'

I take the bottle and handwritten instructions. *Goulard's Extract of Lead*, reads the label.

Dilute one-half drachm in one-half cup of clear water and one-half teaspoon of brandy.

I carefully prepare the solution according to the instructions. Captain Nelson bathes his eyes with it, then sits at the table with his eyes closed for a few minutes.

'Is it helping?'

'I would like to say so, but I cannot tell; not yet.' He sighs heavily. 'My unhappy constitution is bearing me down. There is no other person in the Mediterranean who expends himself as I do. My exertions exceed my strength.'

There is perhaps some validity in that statement, but it is ungenerous toward some of his colleagues, who also work very hard. 'Mr Reynolds recommended you do less, sir,' I remind him.

'How could I do less?' he retorts. 'Who will do it, if I do not?'

Perhaps they would not do it to the level of perfection that you do, but it would get done. But his question was rhetorical; he isn't looking for an answer. And while there are plenty of men in the Royal Navy who do their jobs admirably, there is only one Horatio Nelson.

'Sir, may I ask a favour of you?'

'Of course, Mr Buckley; if it is within my power to grant it.'

I take a small package out of my coat. My brother's name, Arthur Anson, and his address in London are written on the front. It is time to send the miniature back to Arthur.

'Will you post this for me, sir, with your official letters? It is imperative that it reach its destination, and I do not trust that it will, should I send it myself.'

He opens his good eye and peers at the package. 'I can hardly see it,' he says plaintively. 'Arthur Anson. You are sending your sister's portrait miniature to him?'

I have the lie ready this time. 'He was... my sister was betrothed to him, sir. He bade me keep the miniature; he said it brought him too much pain. But I promised that I would send it to him in three years' time, and if he found it was no longer dear to him, he could return it.'

Captain Nelson takes the little package and tucks it into his own coat. 'I will see that it gets done, Mr Buckley.'

Now I can only pray that it makes it back to England.

Chapter Eighteen

A few days later, Nelson sends his boats stealthily into Alassio.

The manner in which the French have taken over neutral harbours, essentially rendering their neutrality void, has been stuck in Captain Nelson's throat like a fishbone for weeks. He has decided unilaterally that if the French abuse the neutrality of the ports, then the laws of neutrality will be suspended.

There are eight merchant vessels at anchor in the harbour at Alassio, and Nelson's nine boats mean to cut them out.

Commanded by Lieutenant Andrews and Lieutenant Spicer, our boats slip silently into the harbour under cover of darkness. We catch the merchant ships unawares, and by one o'clock all eight vessels have been successfully boarded. We are unable to tow them all out, however. French gunboats appear, alerted to the operation in the harbour, and our boats come under fire. We have to relinquish the prizes and would have lost them all had not the *Mutine* arrived to cover us. We manage to secure one prize out of the eight.

Captain Nelson is not discouraged. He begins planning another attempt.

The sight in his right eye is practically gone, and the left one has become so fatigued from his heavy correspondence load that it also is painful. His lady friend is still in Genoa, and Nelson intends that she should stay there until he makes his point to the French (and, indirectly, to the Genoese).

Mr Lepee and I try to prop him up, in addition to our other work.

'I was with him back in the Leeward Islands,' Mr Lepee tells me, 'and it was the same story. He had his teeth into those ships that were violating the Navigation Laws, and he wouldn't let go. Wore hisself down to a skeleton, practically. He got fevers, and megrims that almost blinded him and made him as sick as a dog, and damn me if he didn't work through them. When he finally married Mrs Nisbet and sailed for England, there was times I was afraid he wouldn't live through the passage.'

'When was this, Mr Lepee?'

He thinks. 'Would have been 1784 or '85, to sometime in 1787, I guess,' he says.

I am puzzled. 'What was his rank then?'

'Oh, he was a post-captain. Had been since 1780, I think.'

'How old *is* he, Mr Lepee? He doesn't look old enough to have been a post-captain for fifteen years. Not unless he made post at the age of fifteen.'

'I don't exactly know, Mr Buckley, but I reckon he's about thirty-five.'

'I am actually thirty-six, Frank. I will be thirty-seven on 29 September,' Captain Nelson says, coming in from the quarterdeck.

'Well, I wasn't too far off then, was I, sir?' The steward picks up the tray on which he had brought our dinner. 'Sit down and eat something, Captain. You're starting to look all-in.'

This is diplomatic on Mr Lepee's part. Truthfully, the captain has been looking all-in for days now, but he has his teeth into these 'neutral' ports and refuses to let go. Mr Lepee leaves with his tray as Captain Nelson sinks into a chair.

'Were you taking bets on whether I would live to see thirty-seven?' he asks wearily.

'Of course not. Although your odds would be better if you would stop working so hard.'

'As soon as I manage to take some of those deceitful merchant vessels out from under their French masters' noses, then I shall take a rest,' he assents.

But he doesn't get a chance to capture any more merchant ships before his body rebels.

I am sifting through the mountains of papers that he needs to contend with when he gets back from his meeting with Mr Drake, the British minister and liaison to the Austrian army. Mr Drake is a genuine diplomatic liaison, not the sham of a messenger-boy that I was in Corsica.

I did not expect him yet. He'd told me he intended to return around the start of the first dog-watch, and it is only a little past noon. But as soon as he walks into the cabin, I can see that he is very ill.

He is pale, his eyes look glazed, and his skin is clammy. 'I had to cut short the meeting with Drake and De Vins,' he says. He reaches for the back of a chair to pull it out and sit down, but his coordination is off, and he nearly falls. I am just fast enough to catch him.

'I am very unwell today.' He sags against me.

'Let me help you to bed, sir.'

I help him out of his coat. I can feel the heat radiating

off him, but he is shivering. He fumbles with the buttons on his waistcoat, but his hands are shaking, and he gives up.

'I'll do it, Captain.'

I end up having to undress him as he sits bowed in a chair. He tries to help but cannot work the buttons on his knee bands or the clasp of his neck stock.

I remember, in Gibraltar, a man in our regiment falling ill from dehydration at review. He looked similar to the way the captain looks now. 'Can you drink something, sir, or do you think it will make you vomit?' I ask.

'Best not,' he murmurs.

Frank Lepee opens the door and stalks into the cabin. 'There you are,' he scolds. 'I told you to wait for me.'

'I am not... in the habit... of being told what to do... by you, Frank,' he says, his teeth chattering.

'Put him to bed; I'll go for Mr Reynolds,' I say in an undertone to Mr Lepee.

Mr Reynolds follows me at a trot when I tell him the captain is ill. When we get to the cabin, Mr Lepee is standing by the captain's berth with his arms folded, his expression a mix of concern and exasperation.

'How many times have we been through this, Captain?' he asks.

Despite the August heat, Captain Nelson is shivering under two blankets. He doesn't answer Mr Lepee.

The surgeon examines the captain, checking the rate of his pulse and listening to his chest, assessing the colouring of the membranes in his mouth. 'Get a glass of water and a tablespoon,' he instructs no one in particular. Frank Lepee leaves to get them.

'You are exhausted,' Mr Reynolds tells Captain Nelson. 'You cannot keep up this pace; your body is telling you so. If you do not rest, your body will force you to rest. If you keep resisting it, you will likely go home in a leaguer.' He takes the glass of water and the tablespoon from Mr Lepee.

'I'm going to give you water from a tablespoon. I want you to drink no more than a tablespoon at a time, so that your stomach doesn't reject it.'

Captain Nelson obediently swallows the water from the tablespoon. He doesn't reply to the surgeon. Either he is conserving his energy, or he feels too ill to argue.

'Give him another spoonful of water every two to three minutes, for up to an hour,' Mr Reynolds tells us. 'No more than that, and no more frequently. Have you a watch?'

'I do,' I offer.

'I shall check on him again this evening, but if he needs me before then, send someone. In an hour or so give him a drink of orange whey; he may drink as much as he will take. He must have a light supper this evening, broth or coddled egg, something easily digestible.' He speaks softly. 'Keep him quiet. A day or two of rest, in bed, with no work, ought to see him through. But ideally, he needs more than that, and if he will not take it, there is not much that I can do.'

The surgeon leaves the cabin. Frank Lepee looks at me.

'Will you stay with him? Right now the captain and I will annoy one another.'

I nod.

'Thank you,' he says, and follows the surgeon out.

'Captain?' I ask gently.

'I don't know how I'm supposed to rest if you're meant to wake me every two minutes to make me swallow a tablespoon of water,' Captain Nelson mutters.

'I imagine if you can take a few more spoonfuls, then you'll be alright to sleep for a while,' I suggest.

'I am so tired that I don't know if I *can* sleep. When I close my eyes, I feel though if I am falling through space. Or that the ship is spinning in circles like a dog chasing her tail,' he says irritably. He coughs, and it racks his entire body.

I pour water into the spoon and help him swallow it.

'This is going to put me farther behind in my work,' he murmurs.

'Shh. You are not to talk about work. You are not even to think about work.'

'The Coalition is disintegrating. Every day... counts...'

'Sir, if you do not hush, I shall get Mr Lepee back in here to annoy you.'

He awards me a weak smile.

'I will do what I can to keep you from falling behind. But for the rest of the day and night, you are not to speak a word about it.'

'Bless you, Mr Buckley,' he says, closing his eyes.

Captain Nelson remains in bed for the rest of the day, overnight, and for part of the next day, but by afternoon he demands his writing box. He sits up in his berth, writing letters in a shaky script.

I am doing what I can to help, as promised. My hand aches at the end of the day from scribbling drafts while he dictates, then re-writing them in a clear hand for his signature.

I have fielded multiple worried questions from Mr Drake, Mr Trevor and Mr Jackson from Turin, and General De Vins. There is thinly veiled desperation in these communications. If Captain Nelson cannot continue, they will have to have a new squadron commander, and they do not appear to have great faith in Admiral Hotham.

When the captain is well enough to get up, the first thing he does is to go aboard Admiral Hotham's flagship, which is passing by Vado Bay, and request a meeting between the admiral and the Austrian general. Frank Lepee, as his coxswain, goes aboard with Captain Nelson, to whisk him back again should he start feeling ill.

'Hotham's in no better shape,' Mr Lepee tells me. 'Captain says he's waiting for permission to go home. 'Is hand shakes so much that he can hardly pick up a pen.'

I wonder if they will promote Admiral Goodall, or Admiral Parker, to Commander-in-Chief. Nelson doesn't think so.

'If only we had Lord Hood back,' he says, almost wistfully. His journey to the flagship has been disappointing. The admiral refused to meet with the army men and ministers from Austria and Sardinia-Piedmont.

'It might have helped,' Captain Nelson says wearily. 'Sardinia-Piedmont and Austria don't trust one another, and both think the navy isn't doing enough to support them.'

Shades of Corsica again. The captain looks dangerously tired. 'Maybe you could rest for a while, sir, before we start on the correspondence?'

'I will make you a bargain, Mr Buckley. I shall lie in my berth and dictate to you. If I happen to fall asleep, you need not wake me.'

Not quite the solution I had been hoping for, but I accept it.

'Before we begin on that, Mr Buckley: I am promoting Mr Withers to mate. I shall need a new clerk. He cannot perform his new office and continue to keep my books.'

'Whom do you intend to make clerk, Captain?'

'I was hoping you would accept the position, Mr Buckley. You are already doing almost everything but, and I know that you are conscientious and precise. You have proved it daily since Corsica.'

I accept without reflection. It hardly matters to me whether I am a soldier, a marine, or a clerk. More importantly, I owe the captain more than I can ever repay, even were it in my power to do so. He wants his commodore's pendant, and it doesn't arrive. If this was something I could accomplish, I would shed my own blood to do it.

Towards the end of the month, Captain Nelson orchestrates another attack on Alassio. This one is as audacious as the French presence is transparent. Nelson's ships attack at ten o'clock in the morning.

Whereas during the night operation earlier in the month I was in one of the boats that did the cutting out, this time I am on the quarterdeck with Captain Nelson.

He sends a declaration ashore: that the French have made an enemy coast of the ports on the Riviera. He demands the surrender of the French warship *La Resolve*.

Lieutenant Andrews and his boarding party take command of the French vessel, cut her cable, and bring her out. Nelson has not yet recovered his full strength and characteristic energy, but this sight causes him to beam with pride and satisfaction. But then, things stop proceeding as planned.

HMS *Ariadne* runs aground, and our boats must re-float her, using her anchor and capstan. During the delay, the merchant ships get further inshore and call for reinforcements; when our boats return, they are greeted by defending French troops on the shore.

Captain Nelson is unconcerned, and orders the ships' artillery to beat back the French defenders.

I am watching him carefully. His actions are modulated, and his voice is almost conversational, in contrast to the animated way he usually paces, and the quick way he gives orders during an action. But it is apparent to me that he feels more lively than he has in days. The spark in his eyes has returned.

We manage to bring out all the supply ships save one, which runs aground and wrecks on the shore. We could not prevent all the cargo from being unloaded, but Captain Nelson has demonstrated *his* resolve.

Captain Fremantle has been equally successful at Languelia, on the western end of Vado Bay. He takes a French gunboat and both the merchantmen she'd been protecting.

Captain Nelson is satisfied, but the operation is not without consequences. Midshipman Hoste fell into the coal hole on one of the prizes and broke his leg, and the captain is adamant that he will visit him and see about his well-being before addressing the other, more major, repercussion.

Which is, of course, the indignation at the captain's act of aggression in a 'neutral' port. 'The Genoese will complain; let them,' he says. 'They are equally complicit in violating the neutrality of Alassio by letting the French control the port.'

The activity of the day does not seem to have taken a great toll on him, but I'll reserve judgment for tomorrow. I feel as though we are walking on eggshells.

The statement made at Alassio wins Captain Nelson approbation from all the British ministers on the coast, as well as from Admiral Hotham. If it has not managed to get the captain his commodore's pendant, it does embolden him for more sorties of this nature.

The information flows fast and furious, far more so than the progress of the Austrian army. General De Vins seems cut from a similar cloth to General D'Aubant. Nelson and Mr Drake are beginning to conclude that the Austrian general has no real desire to assist the allies. They suspect that the Austrian government is only involved in the conflict for the British subsidies to which their participation entitles them.

I drop into my hammock like a stone every night, and occasionally I do not see it at all. More than once I have slept on the floor in the captain's dining room. Nelson himself is so focused on the situation in Italy, and his health is precarious enough, that I don't think he notices where I sleep, or if I sleep at all.

'We are in danger of losing the Mediterranean,' he mutters ominously. Admiral Hotham has reduced the captain's squadron in anticipation of the arrival of Neapolitan ships to replace them. Captain Nelson's scouring of the Italian Riviera has merely caused the mercenaries to relocate, and now they are disrupting British shipping from the island of Capraia. Meanwhile, Nelson is left with only one frigate and a sloop.

Captain Nelson's proposal for an amphibious operation goes nowhere. De Vins is unenthused ('When is he ever enthusiastic?' Nelson asks me sardonically). Admiral Hotham doesn't have the ships to provide; he even refuses the captain's request for two store ships for the purpose. Nelson's health wavers daily, and he is exhausted and depressed.

The reappearance of Signora Correglia for a brief period in September gives him a lift, and despite the awkwardness of having her aboard, I am happy to see Captain Nelson revive somewhat. It isn't long enough, however, and soon she is back ashore in Leghorn. Nelson's squadron is almost completely disbanded, and he is dejected by his obvious demotion in Admiral Hotham's concerns.

The weather does not aid Nelson's efforts to keep supplies from reaching the French either. Deprived of ships, he cannot cover all the ports on the coast, and the autumn gales are blowing what ships he has off their positions. In October, Admiral Hotham reassigns him to guarding Toulon.

'I have been relegated to near-uselessness,' he complains, coughing.

'You have not been unsuccessful,' I suggest, but he isn't mollified.

'Not successful enough,' he says. But he approaches his assignment outside Toulon with the same thoroughness with which he does everything else, and he takes a number of prizes before we are recalled to Vado Bay at the end of the month.

Chapter Nineteen

We are inundated with mail at Vado. The mail was prevented from reaching us outside Toulon; we were never where the cruisers expected us to be, and the weather usually drove them back to St Fiorenzo.

I am wading through this mountain of mail, in advance of Captain Nelson's attention to it, when I come across a letter written in a familiar hand.

Any mail that arrives for the captain that appears to be of a personal nature gets set aside unopened. I think that there is no chance that this letter can be construed as 'business', but I don't think it could be interpreted as personal, either. Captain Nelson has never met my brother.

I break the seal with trepidation.

Arthur's letter is an appeal for information. *'If I might presume to inquire how you obtained the miniature of my sister, and how the address on it came to be written in her hand, I would be highly indebted to you, sir.'*

I cannot let Captain Nelson see this letter. I go out onto the stern-gallery, intending to throw it into the sea. But I find I cannot. Arthur's handwriting is the first reminder of my former life that I have seen since I walked out of my home more than two years ago. It is too precious to me to destroy it.

I fold it into a small square and slip it inside my coat. *Forgive me, Captain. Under any other circumstance, I would not even consider such a trespass.*

So often mail to and from the fleet gets delayed or lost. It may be months before Arthur writes again. Who knows what might happen in that time? But I remember the reason that I sent the miniature to Arthur in the first place. I have to reply.

The captain returns to the cabin while I am on the gallery. 'What are you doing out here?' he asks. 'It's too cold to be taking the air.'

It is not as cold as it might be, but I remember what he told me the first time I saw the great cabin. *'I feel the damp and cold profoundly.'* I return to the cabin and shut the door to the gallery.

'Trying to keep myself awake,' I tell him.

'I keep meaning to try to find more convenient accommodations for you,' he says. 'It has not escaped my attention that you often sleep on the floor. You are invaluable to me; I don't wish to have to try to replace you. You are entitled to the clerk's cabin, you know.'

I had not felt justified in displacing Mr Withers from the clerk's cabin. The mate's accommodation seemed to me like a distinct demotion, although Mr Withers told me he did not mind at all. I thought the captain was unaware of this, but I ought to know that very little escapes his notice. 'Perhaps I will reconsider,' I reply.

'I need to write to Admiral Hotham again,' he informs me. 'Another convoy of supply ships got into Alassio while we were engaged with that Genoese merchantman. There must be one hundred of them sitting in Alassio now, thumbing their noses at me! If the admiral will allow me three line-of-battle ships and eight or ten frigates, we can replay

our performance in Alassio and capture all of them together.
See if we don't!'

It is not until after supper that I manage to set pen to
paper on my own behalf.

*'Arthur, do not search for me. One day I shall explain. I love
you.* — *Nell'*

Nelson's latest request for ships goes unheeded, because
Hotham has struck his flag and gone home. I read this letter
aloud to him, and I see Captain Nelson visibly sag. He is again
considering seriously the possibility of going home himself.
To make matters worse, Admiral Parker is appointed interim
Commander-in-Chief. Nelson would have preferred Goodall,
and indeed, Admiral Goodall is slighted and refuses to serve
under Parker. Goodall bids goodbye to Captain Nelson and
quits the fleet, leaving the captain feeling abandoned and
neglected.

In the midst of this, the French overrun the Austrian army.

Nelson has done all he could for the Austrians with his
decimated resources, but it was ultimately doomed to failure.
For all his conscientiousness, Captain Nelson could not light
a fire under the Austrian army. The French attack their inland
flank, where Nelson's ships cannot assist the Austrians. It all
happens so fast that Vado and Savona fall within three days of
one another, and the French capture two of our watering parties. Lieutenant Noble, Mr Withers, Midshipman Newman,
and eleven sailors and marines are taken captive, among them
George-Augustus Josephs.

Captain Nelson sits at the table with his head in his hands.
'I had expected it to happen,' he tells me glumly, 'but that
doesn't make it any easier to bear.'

What makes it even harder to bear is the sheaf of accusations from the new Austrian commander, impugning Captain Nelson's support as inadequate. These ignite the captain's indignation and rekindle some of his fire while he writes rebuttals to each charge, but it cannot last. The British ministers all rally to his defence, and even the Austrian government appears not to take the charges seriously. It is merely subterfuge, to deflect the blame from the army itself. Nelson's energy ebbs as quickly as it had built.

'I have fagged as hard as I could, Mr Buckley. I am tired, I am far from well, and I am unappreciated. I don't care to be made a scapegoat. I would not be missed if I was to go home to people who care about me,' he complains.

'I would miss you,' I say quietly.

'I will make certain that you are taken care of,' he replies, but that is of little consolation to me.

November is cheerless. With Mr Lepee, I plot to revive the captain's spirits. On an evening in late November, we initiate a covert operation. I secure the services of Mr Wilson the master, Lieutenants Andrews and Spicer, and Midshipmen Hoste, Weatherhead, and Nisbet to assemble all the officers of the wardroom. Mr Lepee prepares some of the captain's favourite dishes, and we host a surprise dinner in observance of Captain Nelson's birthday. It was weeks ago, but it seems a good premise on which to have a celebration.

The captain is expecting a private meal in his cabin, and I must keep him occupied whilst Frank prepares the wardroom and the mids assemble the players. Keeping him at his desk might ordinarily be no easy task; he will often jump up to attend something elsewhere as the mood strikes him.

But I have set aside a number of items 'urgently' requiring a response. If he chastises me for letting things escape my attention, I am prepared to bear it.

When it is past the normal hour for supper and Mr Lepee has shown no signs of appearing, it is time to spring the trap. Captain Nelson might just as easily have worked through the mealtime without remarking it, but I do not intend to allow it.

'Come sir, it's time for supper. Thank you for attending to these things; I apologise for letting them slip.'

'It is highly unlike you, Mr Buckley,' he says, but there is no heart in his rebuke. 'Perhaps you need a rest as much as I.'

I go to the door and look through. Mr Lepee indicates that everything is in readiness and disappears back down the companion ladder. 'Captain, will you come here for a moment, sir?'

'Whatever for? And where is our supper, anyway?'

Midshipman Weatherhead is waiting. 'Captain, sir; Mr Reynolds asks if you will attend him and Midshipman Hoste in the wardroom.' Weatherhead doesn't make any particular inference, but the name of one of the captain's favourite midshipman combined with that of the surgeon is prime bait for the trap.

When he sees the smiling faces around the table, he is momentarily nonplussed. Josiah Nisbet leads the company in a round of 'For He's a Jolly Good Fellow', and Captain Nelson looks at me and Frank Lepee for an explanation.

'It is in celebration of you living to see thirty-seven, sir,' I inform him. 'No doubt the entire ship would wish to be here to toast your good health for another year, but we can barely fit this many people in the wardroom.'

'The two of you deserve to be disciplined,' he says sternly, but then he breaks into one of his rare smiles.

'Come, sir, sit down and let us drink your health,' Lieutenant Andrews entreats him.

Mid-way through the festive dinner, Mr Lepee catches my eye and smiles. I return it covertly. It appears we have been relatively successful in making Captain Nelson aware of how deeply he actually is appreciated. At least, '*so say all of us*'.

The new Commander-in-Chief in the Mediterranean is Sir John Jervis. Nelson has limited acquaintance with the man, though they have mutual friends. Nevertheless, his only acknowledgement is to write to Admiral Jervis commending *Agamemnon* to his service, and to request a chance to defend his actions, should Jervis feel the necessity of answering the Austrian general's complaint.

The captain is glum again. He is battling another heavy cold, and his work recently has consisted of little more than making sure that no British merchant ships try to shelter in any of the ports on the Italian Riviera, now they are in hostile hands.

He is seated at the table writing personal letters whilst I review the account books. I hear him break open another seal; a moment later, he makes a dismissive noise.

'What has that to do with me?' he mutters, and sneezes.

'What is that, sir?'

'This letter,' he says, waving a single sheet of paper. 'Man thinks that I have stolen his wife, or something.'

I had hoped there wasn't a Signor Correglia, I think. But when Captain Nelson passes me the letter and I see the writing upon it, my vision blurs.

Written in my husband's neat, clerical hand, I read:

Captain Horatio Nelson
His Majesty's Ship Agamemnon of the Mediterranean
Fleet

Dear Sir,
    *I have been given reason to believe that you may
have information pertaining to the whereabouts of my
wife, Eleanor. If that be the case, I request that you relay
it to me without delay, that I may arrange to have her
returned to me.*
Your humble servant,
Richard Buccleuch

I read the letter twice, whilst I try to compose my face in a disinterested expression. 'Have you any knowledge of the lady, sir?'

'I can honestly say that I have never heard of her.' He takes the letter back from me and reads it again. 'What a high-handed fellow. If she ran off, I can't say that I blame her. I haven't the first idea why this man should think I would know where she was.'

I bend my face over the accounts in the slop book.

'He seems inclined to blame her for leaving, but I can't think why any woman would want to leave a *decent* man.' He tosses the letter aside. 'Still, a man of that sort can always find a stick with which to beat his dog.' He opens the next letter and sets it on the table to read it, propping his head in his hand.

'Do you… do you want me to reply to him, Captain?'

'Hm? Oh, yes… please tell him I have never met his wife.'

I intend to do no such thing, but I cannot have Captain Nelson correspond with Richard Buccleuch.

———

I had hoped that perhaps the Admiralty would award Captain Nelson his commodore's pendant by Christmas, but it is not forthcoming. The captain presides bleary-eyed and sneezing over a Christmas meal with his officers and goes to bed early. He is determined that he will quit the Mediterranean at the first available opportunity.

On Christmas Eve, he calls me into his cabin and presents me with a large parcel. 'I have been too distracted by other things recently; I should have given this to you when I made you my clerk,' he says, as I unwrap the paper.

Inside is a civilian coat, of the same rich blue that the officers wear, but without any adornment. The cloth is superfine, and the lining is navy shalloon. Underneath is a waistcoat of buff cassimere.

'Sir… Captain, it is too much. This is a gentleman's coat.'

'It is necessary. You were beginning to resemble Lord Hood's "ratty little soldier". I hope it suits you. I had the tailor use Josiah as a model.'

He has me remove the sailor's jacket that I have worn since I stopped serving as a marine. He helps me don the new waistcoat and then the coat. They fit beautifully.

'Well, that was luck,' he says. He examines the effect and looks suddenly rueful.

'What is wrong, sir?'

He sneezes. 'I should have thought to have them make you new breeches, too,' he observes with regret.

I now sleep in the tiny clerk's cabin. Despite the luxury of a private bed place, and my magnificent new coat and waistcoat, tonight I lie awake, preoccupied. I didn't expect any of this, and I know better than to consider it my due. But even as I berate myself for it, I can't help feeling dejected. Soon Captain Nelson will quit the Mediterranean, and all of this will be gone. I will be alone and adrift once more.

———

It is Admiral Jervis who changes Captain Nelson's mind.

The two do not meet until the middle of January, but it would seem that the admiral has already heard praise for Nelson from all quarters. He takes a look at the drooping, dejected officer and decides that he likes him. And suddenly things start looking up.

Captain Nelson finds in Admiral Jervis a man with a work ethic similar to that of Lord Hood, and consequently, Nelson's own. Jervis sees a highly capable officer with a quick mind and an inexhaustible amount of initiative. The two men understand each other. Jervis is amenable to all the suggestions that Hotham and Parker would not even entertain.

Despite the fact that the war is not going well, Captain Nelson's wounded pride begins to heal, and the work begins to feed the furnace of his passion again. Finally, in April, thanks to the intervention of Admiral Jervis, the captain receives his commodore's broad pendant. The spring has returned to his step, and the spark to his eyes. I could not be happier for him had he been my brother, rather than my captain.

———

I am waiting for him in his cabin, his correspondence and logs carefully sorted for his attention, but he hasn't arrived. I can hear activity above on the poop, and eventually curiosity gets the better of me. Leaving the paperwork, I go to discover what it is that I am hearing.

Commodore Nelson and Mr Withers, stripped of their coats, are practicing with swords on the poop. As I watch, the two of them feint, thrust, parry, advance, and retreat, back and forth across the deck. Their carefully controlled movements are almost like a dance, but this is a lethal dance. One single reckless or clumsy move...

Mr Withers advances on the captain, and Nelson blocks the thrust with a lightning-fast stroke of his weapon, but it appears to put him off balance. Mr Withers hesitates for less than an instant, but in that fraction of a second Commodore Nelson regains his equilibrium. The mate is perhaps just a hair too slow raising his sword again, and Nelson spies the error. Grinning wolfishly, he disarms Mr Withers with a flash of his blade. The sword clatters to the deck as Nelson grabs the mate's sword arm in his left hand and draws his weapon back for the thrust. I gasp; but the commodore raises his sword to his shoulder, smiling, and the two men clasp hands.

Nelson retrieves his coat from the signal locker and approaches the companion ladder where I am waiting. 'I suppose I must be a bit late,' he remarks, a little breathlessly. 'You have never come looking for me before.'

'I have never watched you practice before,' I reply, following him back to the quarterdeck and the great cabin. 'You are... very good.' This accolade sounds lame to my ears, but 'magnificent', the word that came to mind, does not seem appropriate.

Commodore Nelson puts his sword away. He pours water from the ewer into his washbasin and splashes his face, then scrubs it with a towel. 'It is more challenging now that I have only one good eye,' he says. 'But I tell my opponents not to go easy on me. The French obviously will not.'

He tosses the towel on the washstand and takes his seat at the table. 'So, Mr Buckley; where shall we begin?'

I have now been with Nelson for two years. His promotion to commodore has yet to be confirmed by the Admiralty, but he has made a friend of Lord Spencer. If the First Lord's 'cousin of some sort' has approached him about the ugly incident last year, Lord Spencer has not mentioned it to Nelson.

Whilst Commodore Nelson is daily becoming more convinced that his Riviera squadron can no longer contribute significantly to the war, which has moved inland, Admiral Jervis insists he cannot do without the captain's presence on the coast. Nelson is still highly active in intercepting transports and supply vessels bound for the French, and at the end of May, he scores a magnificent prize.

The convoy he captures is loaded with materiel for the French lines, and in addition, it contains valuable intelligence that will give the allies a marked advantage. It is a significant feather in his cap, and the captain basks in the glory of the moment.

I am growing concerned about him again, however. He is still full of the enthusiasm that Jervis' attention rekindled and has completely dropped his plans for going home. But more and more frequently, I notice that he looks peaked, and some days his energy is not equal to that wellspring of enthusiasm. It has made him calmer and given him an aura of maturity that I am slowly growing accustomed to, but a part of me longs for the return of that tireless young man who bounded up and down the steep slopes of Corsica.

It is some early hour of the middle watch when I wake with all my senses alert. Something feels different.

I listen hard. Beyond the regular noises of the ship at night, I hear something that sounds like gasping, then a wheezing breath. The sound is in the commodores's cabin.

I am out of my cot in a flash. 'Commodore? Sir?' I call in a low voice. I tap on the door of the cabin. 'Sir, are you there?'

'Come in, Mr Buckley,' he says breathlessly. His voice sounds strained.

The curtains are drawn over the stern lights, and the room is dark. 'May I light a candle, sir?' I ask urgently.

'Aye, you may.' His breathing is shallow.

I get the candle lit and turn to look at Nelson.

He is sitting slumped on the side of his berth, one hand pressed to the centre of his breast. Even in the warm glow of the candle, he looks pale.

'Are you in pain, sir? Do you need me to get the surgeon?'

'I cannot take a full breath,' he gasps. 'It is as though there is an iron band bound around my breast, and I cannot get it loose.'

Frank Lepee taps on the door. I did not get it latched in my haste to light the candle. Frank sleeps on the orlop, nearby the captain's storeroom, so I cannot think why he might be awake and here at this time of night, but I am extremely glad to see him. He looks in, then quickly enters and latches the door behind him.

'What's the matter? Are you ill, sir?'

'It…' he wheezes. 'It will cease by itself in a few minutes, I think.'

'You think?' Mr Lepee repeats. 'What makes you think so?'

The commodore gives him as indignant a look as he is capable of. 'Because this is not the first time… it has happened.'

'I'm going for the surgeon,' Frank announces, and he is gone before Commodore Nelson can protest.

'Sir, if I set your pillow behind you like this, do you think you can recline against it? There, that's good. ...Try to relax, sir. You are panicking. If this makes it worse, you can sit up again.'

He glares at me. 'I have... never... panicked in my life.'

He closes his eyes. I pick up his free hand and stroke it, the way I stroked my father's hand during his last illness. Gradually, Commodore Nelson's breathing gets deeper and slows down, and his gasping ceases. When Mr Lepee returns with Mr Reynolds, the commodore's breaths sound almost normal again.

Mr Reynolds asks Commodore Nelson to describe the attack. He takes the commodore's pulse and listens to his chest. 'You told Mr Lepee this has happened before.'

'Two or three times,' the commodore admits wearily. 'The attacks have not lasted this long before.'

'I want to see you tomorrow, when I can do a more thorough examination,' Mr Reynolds says gravely. 'Has this ever happened during the day?'

Commodore Nelson shakes his head.

'Has it ever happened more than once in a single night?'

'No. I think I shall be able to sleep soundly now.'

'Just to err on the side of caution, I would prefer if someone slept here in your cabin with you for the rest of the night, Commodore.'

Frank Lepee and I look at one another. 'I'll do it,' I say. 'Let me get my blanket. If you want to stay nearby, you can use my berth.'

'If it does happen again, wake me,' Frank says in an undertone. 'You can stay with him, and I'll go back for the surgeon.'

I nod wordlessly. Mr Reynolds and Mr Lepee leave the cabin, and I follow just long enough to grab a blanket out of my cot.

I set my blanket on the floor where my palliasse once lay. Before I extinguish the candle, I go to check on him one last time.

He is sleeping now, his breathing slow and regular. One arm lies limply on top of the coverlet, and I feel compelled to pick it up gently and put it underneath. I put out the candle and lie down, listening to his rhythmic breath. An undefined sense of worry gnaws at the edges of my consciousness, and it is some time before I sleep again.

Mr Reynolds looks unhappy.

'I cannot tell you what is causing it,' he says severely, 'but you are in danger of provoking another illness like the one you had last August. You need to rest, Commodore. Preferably at home, in England. If *Agamemnon* is going home, you should go with her.'

Commodore Nelson regards him with a stubborn expression. 'I am fine this morning,' he insists.

'At least let the fleet physician examine you. Possibly he will have a better idea of what is ailing you. But you know my opinion. You are exhausted. If you do not take better care of yourself, your body is going to betray you.'

I glance at Frank Lepee, who is standing behind Commodore Nelson by the stern lights with his arms folded. Frank has seen the commodore through serious illness more than once. He looks impatient.

'Very well, Mr Reynolds. I shall see the fleet physician. And I shall request some time to go to Pisa, to the baths there. That should set me up again, I should think.'

The surgeon isn't entirely satisfied, but he acquiesces. 'I am at your service, Commodore.'

Mr Reynolds leaves, and Commodore Nelson looks at me and Mr Lepee.

'What are the two of you staring at? I know you both have work to do. Please attend to it, and do not *hover*.'

Frank Lepee mutters as we leave the cabin. He is not well himself. For the past year he has been experiencing seizures, and they are getting worse. When he is well, he is as efficient as ever, but more and more often now, the seizures are accompanied by changes in his mood. Sometimes he is almost despondent and cannot work. At other times, he is irritable and impatient. When both Frank and the commodore are irritable, the atmosphere in the commodore's cabin is tense. Nelson suspects him of drinking, as a way of attempting to cope with his illness. I have not seen it, but the commodore has known him far longer than I.

'Obstinate, arrogant, mulish... he'll end up flat on his back again, and we will be the ones who have to nurse him. I have done it before, and I daresay I will do it again, but damn me if I will enjoy it.'

'If that happens, I will do it,' I console Mr Lepee. 'I do not mind, and he has less of a history with me. He does not get as impatient with me.'

'He will, before too long,' Mr Lepee grumbles ominously. But he accepts my offer.

Chapter Twenty

Agamemnon is going home. She is thoroughly rotten and will not remain seaworthy much longer. Although Commodore Nelson had first entertained the idea of going home with her over eighteen months ago, he no longer wants to leave the Mediterranean. Admiral Jervis is searching for another ship for him, but it requires another captain going home, and no one seems interested in leaving just now.

'Perhaps it would not be so bad,' Commodore Nelson tells me, as if trying to convince himself. 'This is just not the proper time! If I was to leave now, I might find my career becalmed indefinitely. And if I must strike my pendant, my promotion to commodore will not be confirmed. No, I cannot go now. As much as I hate to leave her, *Agamemnon* must go without me.' But the first of Admiral Jervis' negotiations fall through, and Commodore Nelson begins to prepare gloomily to quit the Mediterranean.

'What will you do, Mr Buckley?' he asks me. 'I shall do whatever I can to secure a new position for you; you could clerk for any one of us, now. If you improved your languages and cultivated some connexions, you might even become a flag officer's secretary one day.'

'I have not thought about it, sir. Maybe I will just go back to being a soldier.'

'Your skills are wasted as a common soldier,' he grumbles. 'If I had any expectation that I would be back in command shortly, I would take you with me. But I expect that they will pay *Agamemnon* off; her needs are too extensive. And so I do not know when I will get another ship.' He sighs. 'I am sorry to lose you.'

I cannot disguise my feelings. 'I am sorry to see you go, Commodore,' I tell him sadly. 'It has been a privilege to serve you, sir.' Not only that, but he rescued me from my worst nightmare, and my gratitude is boundless.

I will miss him. So many times I warned myself not to grow fond of him, because eventually he would leave, and I did not want to miss him. I didn't heed myself. But I am somewhat consoled by the fact that he will finally have a chance to rest. He has seen the fleet physician, but he has not gone to Pisa, and I still worry about his health.

In the end, *Agamemnon* quits the Mediterranean without Nelson. He will take over command of HMS *Captain*, a seventy-four-gun ship of the line.

Almost a third of the men who refer to themselves proudly as 'Agamemnons' choose to go with him, and I spend hours writing tickets for their transfers.

'It will be much the same, only on a different ship,' he tells me. 'We shall have plenty to do to make the crew of *Captain* equal to that of *Agamemnon*. And she has a greater complement of men, having ten more guns, so you will have more records to keep track of.' He stops. 'That is, I have presumed that you will come with me,' he says awkwardly, 'but I realise that I never asked you. Do you want to come with me to *Captain?*'

'I would be honoured, sir.'

He looks relieved. 'Ah. Very good. I am pleased to hear it, Mr Buckley.'

When Captain Smith takes over command of *Agamemnon* to sail her to England, Nelson's departing crew give him a stirring send-off. The cheers do not cease as his barge rows him out to *Captain,* not until he is almost out of earshot.

He looks at me, sitting opposite him in the barge beside a parting gift from the officers staying with *Agamemnon,* a rundlet of Madeira wine. He is glowing with pride, gratitude, and approbation, and his eyes are wet.

'She was my glory,' he says softly. 'The finest ship in the Mediterranean. Possibly in all the fleet. We accomplished great things together.'

'You have more great things in store, sir,' I reply quietly. 'I am sure of it.'

'Before that can happen,' he says, looking up at her hull as we come up alongside *Captain,* 'we have work to do.'

Captain's crew is not as professional as that of *Agamemnon,* but the men who came to her with Commodore Nelson will change that. Some of his best officers and seamen have made the transfer with him, and they get immediately to business. Nelson has not been aboard for more than a week before we are bound for Genoa again, and things are no less tense. The French are advancing into Italy.

Commodore Nelson spent some time ashore in Bastia, and he looks refreshed, if still not completely well. I am glad to see it. My relationship with the commodore has changed once again, and I shall now see less of him than I did before. I do not want to worry about him.

For one thing, now that he is a commodore, he has an official secretary. Mr Castang is efficient and business-like, and apart from handing over the initial audits of the account books to him, I have had no dealings with him at all.

Commodore Nelson seems uncharacteristically apologetic when he tells me about Mr Castang. 'You've served me excellently in the past, but now the position is official... I must have a professional secretary. I want you to continue as my clerk. If you will.'

He also has a new steward. Mr Lepee was no longer able to perform the duties that the commodore required. His health had deteriorated rapidly, and his drinking became the final straw; it was that which made Nelson lose patience with him.

It remains a mystery to me. Frank would more and more frequently slur his words, and his movements were uncoordinated, yet I never saw him drinking excessively, not smelt liquor on his breath. Nelson has released him to the surgeon in Leghorn, with a post waiting for him on HMS *Zealous* when he recovers. I had grown to like Frank, and I hope that the time ashore will be beneficial to him. He had become so erratic in the last weeks; it was distressing to see him struggle with the seizures, his mood, and his episodes of drunkenness, if indeed that is what they were.

The new steward is Tom Allen, a Norfolk man like Commodore Nelson, promoted from his role as the captain's senior servant. Nelson appears happy enough with him, as they have been together since coming to the Mediterranean; although, despite his irritation, I think the commodore was ultimately sorry to let Frank go. 'It was too melancholy watching him suffer,' he admits to me, and that is the last he says about the matter.

I have enough to do, yet I feel strangely rudderless without the commodore's reliance on me. It is almost as if my sense of relevance has diminished with my change in responsibility.

It has also made me aware that I have no mates anymore. I had thought, after Jack Mackay died, that I wanted this; never to get close to anyone again. For more than two years, my life has revolved almost exclusively around Commodore Nelson. I am not sure what to do with myself.

Secretary Castang has the private cabin, and I now share a space in the orlop with Tom Allen and another senior servant, James Lenstock. With this transfer to *Captain,* I have severed the final ties to my service as a rifleman and a marine. My transition is complete. I have become an idler.

In Genoa, the situation is no better. Nelson is incensed by Consul Brame's failure to defend his ships against Genoese allegations that they have been harassing neutral shipping. Brame referred the allegations back to the British foreign secretary without offering Commodore Nelson an opportunity to rebut the charges. Though the man's actions were prompted by ineptitude rather than malice, to Nelson's eye the damage is the same. I am not privy to his anger, but I know the cadence of his rant, and I can hear it from the space in the lobby where I work on the accounts.

I am standing on the gangway in the evening twilight when Tom Allen tracks me down. 'I need your help with something.'

'What is that?'

'The commodore tore his dress coat ashore this afternoon. I don't think I can do anything with it, but he said that you might.'

'I'll take a look at it,' I tell Mr Allen noncommittally, but something inside my chest leaps at the chance to be of service again.

The right sleeve of the commodore's coat is ripped for a length of nearly two inches next to the lower seam, just above the gold lace on his wrist. The sleeve lining is ripped as well.

'How did he manage to do this?' I ask Mr Allen.

'Says he caught it on something as he was leaving the consul's house, and he was so angry he just yanked it away. I'd say it made him even angrier when it tore.'

'I can imagine. Let me see what I can do. I hope he doesn't want it back by morning.'

'He has other coats.'

'Good. I'll work on this.'

There isn't a lot that I can do with it tonight. The sun has gone down, and lanterns get doused at the beginning of the first watch. But I go to bed feeling happier than I have for days. Commodore Nelson still needs me for something.

I learn from Tom Allen that Nelson is directing his anger and his energy into formulating replies to the charges, which he indignantly denounces as exaggerations and lies. I know him well enough after two years to be certain that he considers these accusations assaults on his own character, and he cannot be at peace until he answers them.

Whilst we are engulfed in this political maelstrom, Napoleon's troops march on Leghorn.

I am leaving the commodore's cabin, having delivered the audits for his log, when the ship suddenly explodes into action. Mr Thomas, the master, sees the question on my face and answers it before I have a chance to speak.

'Captain Fremantle is evacuating Leghorn. We're on our way there as fast as we can sail. The damned French are on the doorstep.'

'As fast as we can sail' doesn't feel fast enough. Even with a third of her crew members, *Captain* is no *Agamemnon*. When we arrive in Leghorn, we find that the redoubtable Captain Fremantle has affected the entire evacuation. *Captain* is in time to cover the last ships leaving the harbour.

I no longer have the privilege of knowing Commodore Nelson's plans. I can guess, based upon what I know of him, but I am no longer on the inside. I return to the space that I share with Tom Allen and resume working on the repair to the commodore's coat.

I have seen him, of course. He still comes on deck multiple times a day and speaks with Lieutenant Berry, Mr Thomas, or the officer of the watch. I have seen him have a relaxed conversation with Lieutenant Pierson of the marines and have witnessed him sharing a cheerful jest with one of his seamen. Twice he has passed me and said, 'Good day, Mr Buckley,' with a nod; the second time, he seemed poised to say more, but his attention was drawn away by a shout from the foretop.

I know that he has personally met with every commissioned officer and every warrant officer on the ship, because that is how he works. But I realise, with a sense of disappointment in myself, that I miss being in his confidence.

This has been a complicated repair. I have had to take the sleeve off the coat and open the seam in order to work on the tear from the inside. I put a sturdy patch on the tear in the lining, then went to work carefully closing the rent in the sleeve itself. I am satisfied with the repair; no one will be able to see it unless they look closely, and since it is on the underside of the sleeve, it's unlikely anyone would.

I am now reattaching the sleeve and its lining, and the coat will be finished.

If I can predict the commodore's next step, we will be blockading Leghorn for an indefinite period.

It is nearing the end of the second dog-watch when I bring the mended coat back to the commodore's cabin. Mr Allen told me just to leave it in the commodore's bed place and he would take care of it. I tap on the door as I was accustomed to doing on *Agamemnon*, but I do not expect an answer. At this time of the day, Commodore Nelson is on deck.

Except that he's not. I am startled when I turn and see him in the dusky light of the compartment, stretched out on his cot, fully dressed, from the bullion on his shoulders to the buckles on his shoes. For a fragment of a second, in my mind I see my father laid out in his coffin, and I irrationally think that the commodore is dead.

Of course he is not dead, the reasonable voice in my head reproaches me. But rather than turn around and leave the cabin as I ought, I approach his cot to reassure myself that he is breathing.

His chest rises and falls regularly, and one hand rests lightly on his stomach. I have seen him asleep many times, but this evening something looks different. It is just past the summer solstice, and even though the light here comes only from the gun ports, I can see him clearly.

In the past, his face in sleep had regained its boyish aspect; now, sleep can no longer erase the lines created by more than two years of care, pain, and illness. I instinctively want to smooth those lines away with the tips of my fingers. But he is no longer the youthful captain that I met on the mole in

St Fiorenzo over two years ago. He is Commodore Nelson now. He has outgrown me.

With this melancholy thought, I am about to leave when he opens his eyes. 'Mr Buckley,' he says, as casually as if he had expected to see me in his cabin when he awoke.

'I brought back your coat, sir, but before I left, I wanted to make sure you were alright. I did not expect you to be here.'

'I am perfectly alright. I had a headache, but it appears to be gone.' He sits up and swings his legs over the side of the cot. 'Let me see what you have done with my coat.'

I pick up the coat and give it to him. He examines the repair and says admiringly, 'Remarkable. You are a magician. I can hardly tell where it was torn.'

'Thank you, sir.' His praise is gratifying. I realise that I don't remember the last time someone had given me praise. I hadn't known that I missed it.

'It has been too long since we have had an opportunity to talk. Let's go into the great cabin; no one is looking for me at the moment. Tell me if you are happy with your new position.'

'It is fine, sir. If anything, I think I am a little bored. You used to keep me far busier.'

'I did. You were doing the clerk's job as well as a good deal of what Mr Castang does now. And some of Frank's work, as well. You deserve a rest.'

I hesitate. 'To tell you the truth, Commodore, I miss working for you, sir; I had worked two years for you, and I enjoyed it. I have no complaints, sir; please don't think that I do. It is just that the adjustment has been more difficult than I'd expected.'

He is solemn. 'I miss you as well, Mr Buckley. You and Frank knew my mind. I had become accustomed to that.'

'Sir, if I may make a confession; and I beg your pardon if this sounds inappropriate.'

He looks suddenly uncomfortable, although I can't think why. But he gives me permission.

'I find I had become used to knowing what was happening on the ship and in the squadron, and to some extent with the admiral and the fleet, and what to expect. Although I realise it really was none of my business, sir.'

His face transforms into an expression of recognition. 'You miss having your finger on the pulse,' he discerns. 'Mr Buckley, I knew there had to be a reason why you seemed to understand me so well. We have that in common.'

'I am aware, sir, that it was presumptuous of me. I am a nobody. The workings of the fleet are not my business,' I say again.

Commodore Nelson frowns. 'You have been discreet and professional, and I have never once considered the business of the ship or the fleet to be something you were not entitled to know. I have, over the last two years, received orders that no one was to know about save myself, but that is the only information that I have judged inappropriate to discuss with you; only because I could not discuss it with anyone, not because you were unworthy of the intelligence.' He leans back in his chair with a pensive look on his face.

'Thank you, Commodore. I appreciate your trust, sir.'

'Have you given any more thought to my suggestion that you become a midshipman? I would very gladly appoint you as soon as a place becomes available.'

Oh, wouldn't that be a fine thing: if one day they discovered that one of their 'young gentlemen' is not a 'gentleman' at all. 'Thank you, sir, but I do not see myself as an officer.'

He looks disgruntled. 'I think you would make a very fine officer, Mr Buckley. You have the right qualities, apart from being too self-effacing. But assertiveness and confidence can be taught, sir.'

'I will think about it,' I concede.

'Well, that is the best I can do,' he says, more to himself than to me, it seems. He steeples his fingers under his nose and we sit in silence for a long moment.

'Would you be willing to attend me in the evenings after supper?' he asks abruptly. 'Unless I have urgent business, I give Mr Castang the evenings for his own use.'

Again, I am aware of that unfamiliar leap in my breast. 'Sir, it would be a privilege.' I do not want to betray the depth of my pleasure at this offer, but I cannot entirely conceal it. I feel a smile spread across my face.

He answers with a smile of his own. He does not smile often, and when he does it restores a bit of his boyishness. My heart warms to him all over again.

'Excellent!' he exclaims. 'Mr Buckley, I profess that I love you the way I would love a son of my own. It will be a pleasure to have your company for part of the day again.'

'It will be a pleasure for me, too, sir.'

Suddenly tomorrow looks brighter than it did an hour ago.

I have slung my hammock in preparation for bed when Commodore Nelson sends for me from his cabin. He has a book that Captain Sawyer of HMS *Blanche* has asked to borrow.

'Would you mind packaging this up to send to him?' Nelson requests, presenting me with a copy of Josephus. 'He asked to borrow it some time ago and I have not remembered.' I assure him that I will see to it, and he bids me goodnight.

When I return to my hammock, there is a lump in the bottom, and I wonder who has put something in my hammock. I look in and find one of the ship's cats curled up there, regarding me balefully.

'What are you doing there? Shoo.' The cat blinks at me and shows no inclination to shoo.

I put the commodore's book in my trunk and address the issue of this cat.

It is a grey tabby-cat with mackerel-sky sides and a white-neckcloth breast, and paws that look as though the tips have been dipped in white paint. It is missing one eye.

'Hey there, One-Eyed Jack. Get out of my bed.' I poke the cat in its underbelly through the canvas of the hammock. It shifts position and stays put.

I try tipping the hammock over to dislodge the cat. It uses its claws and hangs fast.

I would have to be out of my mind to try picking up a ship's cat, unless I was willing to part with one of *my* eyes. I unsling the hammock and dump the cat on the floor. It stalks off with dignity, as though it had not been the loser in this standoff.

When Tom Allen comes to sling his hammock, I tell him about my encounter with the cat. He laughs.

'I'll have t' keep my eye out for that one. Usurper of hammocks, eh?'

In the middle of the night, I feel my hammock sway and wonder vaguely if there is a storm blowing up heavy seas. Then I feel a warm weight on my chest. I open my eyes and find myself face to face with One-Eyed Jack. His single eye glows with what reflected light there is in the space.

I try not to flinch. Has he come back to get revenge for dumping him out of my hammock?

His foreclaws knead my sternum: in, out, in, out. Then he turns around and curls up on my middle. He is purring.

Damned thing. It is as though he is saying, 'Ha: *I* win'.

The cat is gone in the morning. I imagine that he cannot have stayed for very long, but I wasn't aware of his departure. It was not entirely comfortable having a warm, furry body sitting on me on a warm night in late June, though I suppose it wasn't ideal for the cat, either. I think he was just proving a point, and I'm unlikely to see him again.

When I present myself at the commodore's cabin after supper, I find him in banyan and slippers, resting in an armchair. Unlike the great cabin on *Agamemnon,* this one now boasts two armchairs and a desk, as well as a table and chairs. I don't know when Commodore Nelson obtained these things, but they are more physical evidence of his promotion.

'Come and sit down, Mr Buckley. I hope that I am not required anymore today and can relax for the rest of the evening. It has been a very long day,' he confesses.

'What would you like me to do for you, sir?'

'I had hoped that you would read to me. My eyes are particularly bad tonight.'

'Of course, Commodore. Have you put any of the drops in your eyes?'

'Mr Allen did it for me just before you got here. They should begin to help soon, I hope.' He gives me a woebegone look. 'I suppose this is what I can expect to contend with for the rest of my life.'

'I hope not, sir,' I say earnestly. 'Perhaps when the war is over and they have a chance to rest and heal, there will be improvement.'

'I do not believe this war will be over anytime soon, Mr Buckley. But we British may soon be forced out of the Mediterranean, the way things are going.'

He doesn't elaborate, and I do not feel like pursuing the evidence behind that statement. 'Where are the documents you wanted me to read to you, sir?' I ask instead.

'Documents? Spare me any more documents! There is a book on my desk. Read that to me.'

The book is William Shakespeare's *A Midsummer Night's Dream*. 'A loan from Captain Fremantle,' Nelson explains. 'He loaned it to me some months ago, and now he would like it back to entertain a young lady evacuee from Leghorn. I asked him to give me a few days to finish it, so... I had better start it.'

As I am leaving in the evening, Commodore Nelson says to me, 'I hope you will join me for breakfast in the morning. There will be some others of the ship's officers, all of whom I suppose you know.'

'Thank you, sir; I would be honoured.'

'Don't bother about being honoured, Mr Buckley. Just show up and eat.'

In the middle of the night, I am awakened by a sense of something altered. My first inclination is to listen for the sound of the commodore's breathing, but that is not what woke me. At my hip is a soft, warm lump. Its claws go in and out, in and out, as it purrs. One-Eyed Jack is back.

The commodore's breakfast table is as generous on *Captain* as it was on *Agamemnon*. His guests this morning, besides myself, are Mr Thomas, the master; First Lieutenant Berry, who is acting as Commodore Nelson's flag captain; Mr Williams, the purser; and a young midshipman so reserved that I can barely hear his mumbled greeting. Commodore Nelson seats this boy beside him and speaks to him conspiratorially from time to time. I remember my first breakfast with Nelson and experience a pang of recognition. *He did the same with me.*

I am seated between Mr Williams and Mr Thomas. 'So, now that you've been aboard her for a while, how do you like *Captain?*' Mr Thomas asks me.

'She's a fine ship, sir,' I reply, mindful of the fact that *Captain* is Mr Thomas' ship, and he would be loyal to her if she was completely crank, sailed like a haystack, and constantly drifted to leeward. 'I have had a strange experience the last two nights, however.'

There is a lull in the conversation just as I make this statement, and suddenly I seem to have everyone's attention.

'Seen a ghost, have you?' asks Mr Williams, and even the retiring midshipman looks up expectantly.

'Not a ghost;' I say with a smile, 'it's a cat. Or perhaps it's a ghost cat, although it seems solid enough. For the past two nights it has invaded my hammock for a part of the night, but it is always gone by morning.'

'Would this cat happen to have only one eye?' asks Mr Williams.

'It would.'

'Well, I'll be. It's Tommy's cat,' says Mr Thomas.

'"Tommy's cat"?' I ask.

'Oh, yes; now here's a story,' says the master. 'That cat was one of a litter of kittens a year or two back. I figure there's still one or two of his brethren around somewhere, but they aren't social the way that one was.

'When that cat was not much bigger than a handful, he got into it with a rat, and the rat got the better end of the encounter. The cat was lucky to get out of it with no more than a damaged eye. It might have died anyway, but for this younker from the Marine Society. Thomas Sykes, his name was. I don't know where he came across the little beggar, but he took it upon himself to nurse the thing. Carried it around in his shirt and even convinced Mr Eshelby to stitch up its empty eye socket. That cat wouldn't have anything to do with anyone else, but it loved Tommy.'

'I take it Tommy isn't aboard any longer.'

'Tommy was killed in the engagement with *Ça Ira* and *Censeur* last year,' Mr Williams says quietly.

'The cat would show up where Tommy used to sleep and cry piteously every night for a while, and maybe some of the sailors did take it for a ghost,' the master continues. 'Then it must have realised that Tommy wasn't coming back, and we didn't see it around anymore. It had completely slipped my memory.'

'Did it have a name?' I ask curiously.

'Who names a ship's cat? As far as I know, it didn't. Are you going to give it one? Seeing as how it seems to have adopted you.'

'I guess I already have,' I admit. 'I called it "One-Eyed Jack". Like the gunner in the song. Although I must confess that when I opened my eyes and found the thing staring me in the face in the middle of the night, I was half-convinced it had come to take one of mine.'

'Don't you let the ratings hear you say that, or they'll believe it,' warns Mr Williams.

'"*Mind your back, it's One-Eyed Jack*",' Lieutenant Berry chortles. 'Who knows; it might be good for discipline,' he jokes.

'It is more likely to be bad for the cat,' Nelson contributes. 'I cannot abide cats, but I would hate to see anything happen to Mr Buckley's new friend.'

'What have you against cats, sir?' asks the midshipman hesitantly.

'I have nothing against them,' the commodore says, 'but if I am in a room with one for very long, my eyes begin to water. If neither I nor the cat leave the room at that point, then very shortly I will start to sneeze. When I say I can't abide them, that is what I mean; not that I don't like them,' he explains to the mid.

'Oh, yes sir; I see,' the boy says. He seems relieved to know that the commodore does not dislike cats. I wonder if this lad would like to have my cat. But then, One-Eyed Jack isn't really *my* cat, is he? It is probably more accurate to describe me as *his person*. It really appears that I have no say in the matter.

Chapter Twenty-One

With the blockade of Leghorn firmly established, *Captain* quits the region to return to Corsica at the end of June. There is little we can do here any longer, but the commodore is undaunted. Anything that can be done will be done, and more besides, if he has anything to say about it.

We have finished *A Midsummer Night's Dream,* and tonight we are sitting in companionable silence reading newspapers that recently arrived from England. He has not asked me to read them aloud tonight. 'My eyes are fine tonight,' he informs me. 'I would like to read for a bit, and then perhaps you will let me beat you at chess.'

We discovered when I was confined to his cabin on *Agamemnon* that he can beat me easily at chess, but he amuses himself by finding ways to make me think I might win before he trounces me. It is starting to improve my game, but only slightly; we don't play often enough for it to be remarkably effective.

'Here, isn't this that man who sent me a letter last winter; the one who thought I knew something about his wife?' Nelson hands me his newspaper. 'It appears he is still looking for her.'

Half-way down the page, on the far-right column, is the advertisement.

ELEANOR BUCCLEUCH: *All is forgiven. A critical illness requires that you come home before it is too late. Do not neglect us; your family's future depends on it. Your loving husband,* RICHARD.

'Seems he has changed his tune a bit, doesn't it?' Commodore Nelson comments.

I feel paralysed, and I have to force myself to take a careful breath in order to keep from gasping. Is this true, or a trap? Richard was once capable of kindness, even occasional gentleness, before he grew disappointed, sullen, and angry. The only family I have left, apart from Richard and my father's eldest sister in Devon, is Arthur. Could Arthur be truly ill, or is Richard using Arthur as bait?

I try to arrange my features in some semblance of mild interest before I give back the newspaper. 'I believe it is the same person, sir. I wonder what the story is?'

Nelson beats me resoundingly at chess tonight.

In the morning after breakfast, I take pen and paper and write another letter.

I had not intended to do this, not for years; perhaps not ever. I had hoped to fade from memory, even from my beloved brother's memory. But I must know if it is true.

Arthur knew nothing about the disintegration of my relationship with Richard. He knew, of course, about the still-birth of our first child. He knew about the first miscarriage. He did not know about the other two; I saw no point in telling him. And by the end, Arthur had too many sorrows of his own for me to even consider going to him for protection.

My brother had a bright and beautiful family: a son and

a daughter, and he and his wife were expecting a third child when smallpox struck.

Arthur lost both his children, his unborn child, and very nearly his wife. He was the only one of the family unaffected by the illness. Largely due to my father's progressive ideas, Arthur and I had been inoculated against the disease as children, and Arthur could not forgive his oversight of not having had his own children inoculated. It had not occurred to him that Anne might never have received an inoculation, either. She was desperately ill for weeks, and Arthur was devastated. He blamed himself. I was unable to provide any kind of support to them; my own emotional state was by that time too precarious.

When I left, I am sure that he was perplexed and even hurt, but by then it was too late to tell him.

I cannot send this letter by way of the commodore. I do not want Nelson to hear another word about the matter. It will have to go from Corsica.

I do not have the advertisement from the paper before me, but its words are burned into my brain.

Dearest Brother,

I read last night in the Norwich newspaper an advertisement placed by Richard. It inferred that some-one in the family was critically ill and requested I come home 'before it is too late'.

Arthur, if this be true, please tell me, and I will come home. If it is not, you must understand that I cannot return to Surrey. I cannot explain just now, but someday I shall. I promise.

Write to me in care of Edmund Buckley, HMS Cap-tain. He will ensure that the message gets to me.

Always, your loving Sister, Nell.

I feel that I am writing my own arrest warrant. I am aware that the newspaper is already weeks old, and by the time this letter reaches London it *will* be too late, if what the advertisement implies is true. But I cannot sit by and do nothing.

And I am sure that Richard knows it.

The next threat to the British presence in the Mediterranean is by way of Elba. Intelligence infers that Napoleon will try to establish troops on Elba, uncomfortably close to Corsica. We thwarted the French in their last attempt to retake Corsica, but Buonaparte is as undaunted as Nelson. The British are desperate to get men to Elba first.

Diplomacy has not convinced the governor of Elba to allow us to put soldiers on the island, so we have decided to make it a *fait accompli* by landing troops first and making up with the governor later. British diplomats are certain it will be successful, and Commodore Nelson is leading the assault.

The commodore is confident and animated as he plans the operation, and when his officers attend him in his cabin to learn their roles, Nelson is again very much the young commander I came to know in Corsica. His enthusiasm is contagious, and I think admiringly that it is as great a contributor to the ultimate success of the plan as is the plan itself.

And it is successful; if the operation hit any snags, I do not hear about it. When *Captain* leaves the harbour at Porto Ferraio, Commodore Nelson is quietly satisfied.

I must wait for him this evening after supper, because he is on deck, as is his habit. He comes into the cabin and asks me to help me with his coat, then dons his banyan and settles in his armchair, his favourite place to relax.

'I am weary tonight,' he confesses with a sigh. 'I have left Tom Allen in Porto Ferraio to try and obtain some things that need replenishing,' he goes on. 'I would like you to take his place. It should only be for a week, or two at most, until we come back.'

'Me, sir?' I am astonished by this pronouncement.

'Of course. Why not you, Mr Buckley?'

'I just… certainly, sir, you have servants who are more qualified.'

'Perhaps; but I want you,' he says, with a trace of peevishness. 'Do you not want to be my temporary steward?'

'I do, sir,' I reply uncertainly. 'But I am sure that I am unequal to preparing your meals. I can cook, sir, but not to the standards to which you are accustomed.'

'I do not intend to entertain, Mr Buckley. You know that when I do not have guests at my table, my tastes run to plain food. I am sure you can accommodate me.'

I bury my reservations. 'In that case, sir, I would be happy to accept your offer,' I say, with as much conviction as I can muster. 'But if we left Mr Allen in Porto Ferraio, what did you do for supper tonight?'

'I relied on the generosity of the wardroom,' he says. 'Lieutenant Berry has offered me a standing invitation. But to dine there every day would be exhausting both to their stores and to my reserves of conversation. I shall keep it as a last resort.'

I find myself hoping that my cooking does not make him want to re-prioritise.

'In respect to that, their wine has made me bleary. I felt compelled to have a second glass, but now I have the beginning of a headache, so perhaps I will go to bed.'

'Yessir. Breakfast at your usual time, sir?'

'Yes, Mr Buckley.'

'What would you like me to prepare?'

'Coffee first. Then porridge and a slice of cold ham will suffice. You can cook porridge, Mr Buckley?'

'Yessir, I can manage porridge.'

He smiles quietly. 'I knew you could,' he says.

I am awake at the beginning of the morning watch, agonising over porridge.

Ned, you blockhead, how many times in your life have you made porridge? You even know what he likes to put on it, so do stop worrying about it.

I listen to James Lenstock snore blissfully, but I cannot fall asleep again. Eventually, I get up and unsling my hammock, then take it out to the rails to stow it.

There is a warm drizzle falling, and the sky is beginning to get light. Although we have now passed the summer solstice, the sun still rises early and sets late.

I feel something brush against my leg and look down at One-Eyed Jack. The cat is proprietorial about me. He doesn't always make an appearance at night, but he finds ways to let me know that I belong to him. The morning he left a decapitated mouse in my hammock as a gift, James Lenstock had roared with laughter.

'Good morning, Mr Buckley.' Commodore Nelson is descending from the poop. 'You are up early. Not worried about the porridge, I hope.'

'No sir, of course not,' I start to say, and then I laugh. 'You know me far too well, sir. Yes, I awoke early, thinking about porridge.'

He looks at One-Eyed Jack, who is sitting at my feet like a dog. 'Is this your cat?'

'I don't think he's my cat, sir. I think he has decided that I'm his person.'

Nelson bends over and looks at the cat, which stares unblinkingly back. 'Hah. A cat may look at a king,' he comments wryly.

'And that one would, sir. You are up early yourself.'

The commodore straightens up. 'He's a handsome cat,' he remarks. 'You know that I often walk on the poop when I am having difficulty sleeping. So I might as well admit it; I couldn't sleep.'

'Was it something on your mind, sir?'

'There is always something on my mind, Mr Buckley. But no; I think it was the wine. It was not bad wine, but it did not agree with me.'

'Do you need some rhubarb, Commodore?'

'I think exercise and fresh air has helped. The rhubarb will not be necessary.'

'That's good, sir. How long have you been out here, then?'

'I think that I gave up on sleep in the early part of the middle watch. So perhaps a couple of hours.'

A passing shower punctuates the drizzle. 'I know it is still early, but would you like me to bring you your coffee now?'

'I would; thank you. But take your time. I am going to wash and shave before I drink it, so if you bring it in half an hour, that will be fine.'

He goes back into his cabin, and I make my way to the pantry where his table service and foodstuffs are stored. He is being very accommodating with me, but perhaps he is always this way with someone new to their role. Then again, I have observed the way he speaks to his favourite midshipmen, and it is similar. With them, he has infinite patience. He even tolerated a remarkable amount of familiarity from

Frank Lepee, although Frank was careful to keep it within the privacy of the captain's cabin until he started getting very ill.

I have the advantage of having eaten at his table often enough to know how strong he prefers his coffee, and how he likes his food prepared. *That's why he chose you, Ned. He doesn't have to train you. And he trusts you. Is that so surprising?*

When I bring in the tray with his coffee, he is seated at his desk, a towel across his shoulders to protect his clothes from his damp hair, which is loose and fanned out down his back. He is writing and does not acknowledge me as I pour the coffee and prepare it the way I have seen him do countless times.

He sips from the cup. 'Perfect,' he announces. 'My instincts were correct about you, Mr Buckley.'

'It is only a cup of coffee, Commodore. Perhaps you should reserve judgment until you actually taste some food I have prepared.'

'If you say so.' He returns to the letter he is writing.

As I prepare to leave, he stops me with a word.

'Bring a serving for yourself, Mr Buckley, so I do not have to eat alone.'

I eat breakfast with him. It is not terribly different from when I shared his cabin a year ago, except this time I prepared the food before we ate it.

'This appears to me to be a satisfactory arrangement,' Nelson decides. 'When you prepare my meals, I expect you will eat with me as well.'

'Very good, sir.' I look at the remaining food in front of him. 'Did I get the texture wrong?'

'No, the porridge is fine. Stop worrying. I just haven't much appetite this morning. Lingering effect of the heartburn, probably. Will you brush my hair and re-bind it, please?'

I find his brush and ribbon. His hair has dried from its rain-wet state this morning, but when I stroke the brush through his hair, it smells like rain and sea spray. He sighs heavily.

'Are you alright, sir? Perhaps a dose of rhubarb after all?'

'It isn't that, Mr Buckley. I am just tired. Last night's poor rest is telling on me, I suppose. The strokes of the hairbrush seem about to send me to sleep.'

His fair hair is shot through with silver threads. *When did that happen?* I tie his queue back up with the ribbon.

I remove the breakfast dishes and am gone before Mr Castang arrives to begin work.

———————

At close to noon, Mr Castang tracks me down outside the purser's storeroom.

'Commodore Nelson requested that I tell you he won't require a mid-day meal. He is sleeping.'

My brow furrows at this information. 'Thank you, Mr Castang. …Might I ask you; did he seem alright to you?'

The secretary pauses before he answers. 'In demeanour, he seemed the same as usual, but I thought he looked pale and tired. He said that he did not sleep well last night.'

'He told me as much. I just worry about him. He pushes himself too hard.'

Mr Castang nods. 'I have not been with him long, but I can see that. I'll see if I can persuade him to rest more often. As it is, he has told me that he'll send for me this afternoon if he wants me, but not to be concerned if he does not.'

'Thank you, Mr Castang.'

'He said to tell you that you may prepare whatever you'd like for yourself.'

I'm not sure what to make of this preferential treatment. 'That's kind of him, but I'll eat with the other servants the way I usually do.' I am uncomfortable with the idea that anyone might think that I occupy some sort of special place in the commodore's affections. 'Did he have any other instructions for me?'

'Only that you come to his cabin at four o'clock to get directions for supper.'

'Very well; I shall.'

Mr Castang takes his leave, and I stand for a moment, clutching the purser's audits to my chest, vaguely disquieted. I'm beginning to understand what might have made Frank Lepee so frustrated in his final year with Commodore Nelson.

I tap on the inner door of the commodore's bed place at four o'clock, resolved that I will sound him out and persuade him to see Mr Eshelby, if necessary. I do not want to see him go through another episode like the one last August.

My tap receives no response, so I crack open the door and put my head around it. 'Sir? Commodore?'

'Come, Mr Buckley,' he replies in a low voice.

He is lying in his cot, but when I enter, he sits up and plants his feet on the floor. He rests his elbows on his knees and runs his hands through his hair, making it stand out like wings. I remember first seeing him do this two years ago in Corsica, when the sailor lost his hand. It strikes me as a gesture of defeat.

'Did you sleep well, sir?'

'I dozed, Mr Buckley. I was not able to sleep as soundly as I had hoped.'

'Are you certain you are well, Commodore?'

He makes a noncommittal noise. 'I am not completely certain. It is nothing that I can identify; I just feel puny in body and distracted in mind. I thought sleep would set me up again, but I did not sleep.'

'What can I do, sir? Shall I tell Mr Eshelby that you would like to see him?'

'He will tell me to rest, and I am attempting to do that already. No, I don't think it is necessary.'

'Would you try some warm, sweet milk then?'

'I will try it, Mr Buckley,' he says wearily, probably more to get me to stop pestering him than because he wants it.

When I bring the milk, he has relocated to his armchair, but he does not look comfortable. However, he sips the milk dutifully without complaining.

'Did you intend to tell me what to prepare for supper, Commodore?'

'I did, but I do not feel like eating. I think that this may suffice.'

'Perhaps you would let me make you a plate of things that you can eat or not, as the mood strikes you.'

'If you like. Just make sure that it consists of things that you like, so that you may eat whatever I do not.' He presses a hand to his temple. 'My headache has returned,' he observes. He returns the empty glass to me and shuts his eyes.

He does not look restful. There is a furrow between his eyebrows and a tension to his body that bespeaks discomfort, probably the headache.

'May I get anything else for you, sir?' I try one last time.

'Nothing at the moment, thank you,' he murmurs.

I put together a plate of things that I hope may tempt him, mindful of the fact that anything he does not eat I will have to consume myself or return it to his stores. I set it down on the table in his cabin and pick up his coat, which needs brushing. One of the buttons on the right pocket flap is slightly loose as well.

'Clothing is not one of Tom's strengths, though he is getting better at it,' Nelson comments quietly from his chair.

'I thought you were sleeping, sir.'

'If I was, it was not deeply.' He looks at the single plate of food. 'Where is yours?'

'You told me that I should eat whatever you do not. I would be delighted if you were to eat all of that, but forgive me if I think it unlikely, sir.'

'I believe you know me quite as well as I know you, Mr Buckley,' he says.

'I will work on your coat this evening when you have gone to bed, sir.' I don't press him on the issue of the food. Indeed, I know very well that he will not force himself to eat when he is not hungry. 'May I get you something for your headache?'

'If I had any idea what was causing it, I might know how to treat it. Maybe I will try a few drops of ether. I cannot eat while my head is throbbing.'

'I will get it,' I say quietly.

I decant the ether into his palm. At something of a loss as to what to do next, I retrieve the commodore's housewife and go to work reattaching his loose button.

'Remind me why you did not want to become a midshipman,' Commodore Nelson says softly. 'You are too good to spend the rest of your life as a soldier; or sewing on buttons and keeping account books.'

I sigh. 'I did not tell you. It is chiefly because I am abysmal at mathematics.'

'Perhaps I should have asked you before I put you in charge of my books,' he says dryly. 'Although I have yet to find that you have made any errors.'

'I can balance an account book, sir, but advanced calculations, like those required for navigation, escape me. The numbers will not stay organised in my head,' I confess. *One hardly needs trigonometry to balance the household accounts,* Nell might have said; and did, on occasion.

'Do you not elevate when you aim field artillery?' he asks. 'If you can do that, you can navigate.'

'Perhaps, sir. I will consider it.'

'I believe you said that last time,' he grumbles. 'If you are finished with my coat, I will go on deck, and I shall address my supper when I come back. I have not spoken to my officers since this morning, and I hope the air will clear my head a little.'

I tie off the thread. 'Do you want to wait for me to brush it, sir?'

'Do it later.'

He stands, then immediately collapses back into the armchair, an expression of bewilderment on his face. 'It must be worse than I thought,' he murmurs in dismay.

I toss his coat on the table and dash to his side. 'What happened?'

'My legs would not support me.'

'Do you feel faint, or dizzy…?'

'I experienced a moment of weakness and vertigo. It appears to be gone.'

'Sir, will you allow me to check your forehead for fever?'

'Fine, fine.'

I lay the inside of my wrist against his temple, the way my mother did when Arthur and I were children. His skin feels unusually warm, but not alarmingly so.

'Would you open a window?' he asks.

'They are open, Commodore.'

'Oh. Why is my head so foggy, then? It feels unbearably warm in here.'

It is admittedly warm; but it is July, and no warmer than it was five minutes ago. My heart seems to miss a beat. This feels bad.

'It will undoubtedly get cooler once the sun sets. Let me help you back to bed, sir.'

'Perhaps you had better.'

He leans heavily on my arm. It is harder than I anticipated, getting the commodore back to his cot. He is slight, but he is taller than I by about three inches, and heavier than I expected. He really appears to have almost no strength in his limbs. I am thankful I did not drop him.

'I must get my stock off. Please. And my waistcoat.'

'Yes, of course, sir. Don't worry; let me do it.'

Without his neck stock and waistcoat, he sinks back against his pillows. When he had difficulty breathing in the middle of the night, Mr Reynolds suggested that he try sleeping with his head and chest elevated, so Frank Lepee found a bolster and another pillow for him in Leghorn.

'Do you want the bolster, too?' It is at the foot of his cot.

'Yes. Help me put it behind myself.'

'Does it feel as if the girth around your breast is back, sir?'

He shakes his head. 'This is different. Then, I cannot catch my breath; now, the air feels close and heavy, as if I am breathing through smoke... or fog.' He coughs.

'Rest, sir. Close your eyes. I'm going to get a cool cloth for your forehead.'

I go to the door of the commodore's dining room. James Lenstock is there, and I remember that he was supposed to help with the commodore's supper tonight. He raises his hands, as if to say, 'What happened'?

'He's not well. Will you find Mr Eshelby? Quickly.'

Chapter Twenty-Two

James is gone in an instant.

I wet a towel from the ewer at Commodore Nelson's washstand. 'Here, sir; perhaps this will make you feel a bit cooler.'

He sneezes. 'I... get me a glass of water. Please.'

'Of course.'

In the short time that it takes for Mr Lenstock to come back with Mr Eshelby, Nelson has gone from perspiring to shivering.

I am holding his hand, rubbing it in what I hope is a reassuring gesture. Mr Eshelby calmly asks us each to recount what happened, and when the commodore started feeling unwell. He examines Nelson, listens to his breathing, and tries to gauge the extent of his fever. He frowns.

'I do not think it is measles...' he begins.

'I have already had measles,' Nelson tells him.

'Good,' Mr Eshelby says. 'Not to say it is ever good to have measles, but it is much better not to have them aboard ship,' he explains conversationally. 'And since you have already had them, you are very unlikely ever to have them again.

'However, I cannot tell what it is that is making you ill. I am not inclined to bleed you or blister you if I am not convinced that it will help, and I am not convinced. You are not a plethoric person, Commodore, and I don't care to do something that might cause more harm than good.'

'It is immaterial to me how you proceed, sir, as long as whatever it is proves effective,' Nelson murmurs. 'But I am no great fan of being bled and blistered, so I am unlikely to complain in that regard.'

Mr Eshelby smiles encouragingly. 'Some people insist upon it, whether or not it is likely to help. I suggest that you sleep as best you can; drink water, or milk, or weak tea, but no wine or spirits; and eat a light meal if you are hungry, but do not force yourself to eat if you are not. If you find that you are in great discomfort, send for me again. I shall come and see you in the morning, regardless of whether you send for me tonight.' He indicates me and James Lenstock. 'Will one of these gentlemen be nearby?'

'We shall both be, sir,' I supply.

'Good,' the surgeon says. 'Try to make him comfortable and monitor his fever. Beyond that, there is very little to do at this point but let him rest.'

'Yessir.'

'Call on me if you need me.'

Mr Eshelby leaves, and Mr Lenstock addresses Commodore Nelson.

'Do you want Mr Buckley and me to stay here in the cabin with you, sir; or would you prefer to call us if you need us?'

The commodore doesn't open his eyes. 'I can see no reason why both of you should stay here. One of you will do,' he says tiredly.

'I'll stay,' I tell Mr Lenstock in an undertone. 'But I may wake you if he needs the seat of ease; he's not strong, and I can barely support him.'

He nods. 'I expect you're a better nurse than me, Ned; I'm clumsy with things like this. But I can pick him up and carry him in my arms if I have to. Just call me.'

I go back to the commodore's berth. He has gone from shivering to perspiring again, and has cast off the coverlet.

'What can I do to make you more comfortable, sir?' I ask gently.

'Help me take off my shirt. And my stockings.'

Nell baulks. I resolutely push her back into the past and help him slip the shirt over his head.

His torso is narrow, but the muscles of his chest and shoulders look as if they had been sculpted from alabaster. There are a few fair, soft hairs where his muscles meet in the centre of his chest. I am distracted by the sight of them, and I must force myself to look away.

I never saw Richard without his shirt.

I smooth out the sheet and coverlet and rearrange the bolster and pillows. 'Lie back, sir. I'll take care of your stockings.'

He coughs again. It's a thin cough, not like the one he often gets with a heavy cold, but it is worrisome that Mr Eshelby does not know what's causing it, nor the weakness and fever. I gently unbutton the knee bands of his breeches and ease the stockings down his long, thin calves. Again, the muscle is sharply defined beneath his skin. It fascinates me. Fortunately, his eyes are closed, and he cannot see me staring at his calves.

I pull the sheet up over his chest and leave the coverlet within reach at his waist. 'Is that better?'

'Aye,' he sighs. 'Is that glass of water somewhere?'

'Here, sir.'

He sips from the glass. 'Thank you, Mr Buckley,' he says quietly. 'I think I shall try to sleep now.'

'That's good, sir. If you need anything, I will be right here.'
I take a seat in his chair and scowl at the floor.

I had never seen Richard without his shirt, but I have seen other soldiers and sailors shirtless any number of times. I cannot understand my reaction to Commodore Nelson's bare chest. True, I have never looked at a man's chest so closely before. Dudley and Roger had not even taken off their waistcoats. But surely one man's body is very much like another's.

And why should I find his calves compelling? Certainly they are shapely, but they are the same shape with stockings on. And the ratings walk around bare-legged much of the time, so it isn't that.

I find the commodore's body attractive.

The realisation unnerves me.

He sneezes and causes me to look up. He is shivering violently again.

I pull the coverlet back up over his shoulders. Poor man, this swinging from one extreme to the other has to be terribly uncomfortable. At least with the intermittent fever, he only had to contend with one at a time.

'Would you like another blanket, Commodore?' I ask softly.

'Yes,' he says through clenched teeth. 'Thank you.'

They are folded into a trunk and sprinkled with lavender to keep away moths. I shake one out and lay it over him.

He mumbles a brief word of thanks, and I am about to go back to finish with his coat when he pushes himself up on one arm. 'Get Berry. I need to speak to him.' He collapses back against his pillows.

'Right away, sir.'

Mr Lenstock looks up when I step out of the cabin. 'He wants to see Lieutenant Berry.'

'I'll get him.' He rises. 'Is there anything else?'

'James, can you make tea?'

'What kind of question is that, Ned? Of course I can make tea. I can't guarantee that it's *good* tea, but I can make it.'

'Would you bring a pot? I hope to get him to drink a cup.'

'Should I do this before or after I speak to the lieutenant?'

'After.'

He turns to leave.

'James.' He stops and looks at me. 'Thank you. I don't mean to sound as if I'm ordering you about. I am aware that I'm only his *temporary* steward. I'm just worried about him.'

'I understand. I am too. And Ned... I'll let you know if I feel that you're ordering me about.'

By the time Lieutenant Berry arrives, the commodore has thrown off all the bedclothes again, his face and torso oily with perspiration. He blots his temples with a damp handkerchief.

I move a chair for the lieutenant next to Nelson's cot.

'Sir. I was told you were unwell. What is it?'

'Damned if I know, Berry. I am burning one minute and freezing the next. I ache everywhere, and I am as weak as an infant. I can hardly tell what is wrong with me, and unfortunately neither can Mr Eshelby.'

'I hope you will be well again tomorrow.'

'That would be a blessing. Until then, you must take command.'

'Yes, sir. Is there anything else I can do for you, Commodore?'

He coughs. 'This may be the one time in my life that I hope that we do not encounter the French. But if we do, Berry, engage 'em.'

'Absolutely, sir.'

Lieutenant Berry edges through the door past Mr Lenstock, who comes into the cabin with a tray laden with tea things.

'I could not remember how he takes it, precisely... so I brought anything I could think of,' he says in a low voice. 'I am embarrassed to admit I usually only carry the tray; I don't pay much attention to what's on it.'

'Thank you,' I whisper in reply.

He sets it on the table. 'Call me if you need me. I'm just outside.'

I prepare a cup of tea and take it to Commodore Nelson. He regards me with tired eyes.

'Will you have some tea, sir? Perhaps it will help.'

'If you insist, Mr Buckley.'

We set up the pillows so he can rest against them to drink his tea. It seems to take him a long time to lift the cup, sip, and set it down again. Normally his movements are brisk and deliberate; I presume he is conserving his energy.

'You didn't brew this tea,' he says flatly.

'Nosir; Mr Lenstock did.'

'He did not steep it long enough.'

'I think he was in a bit of a hurry, Commodore.'

He motions for me to take the cup, then sneezes again. 'Ah, my poor head,' he groans.

'Did the ether help earlier? I will get the bottle for you again if you wish, sir.'

He gestures for the tea again. 'I don't believe it was particularly effective. I'll own that I was somewhat distracted, though.'

I hesitate, then ask the question anyway. 'You seemed a bit disoriented. I hope that has gone away...?'

'It seems to come and go.'

'I wish you had told that to Mr Eshelby.'

'You may tell him if you think it is important,' he says impatiently. 'I hope that I shall be able to sleep, and that will put it right again.' He finishes his tea and hands me the cup again. 'I do not want any more.' His eyes drift closed.

He is starting to shiver again. I pull the bedclothes back up around him. 'Is that alright, sir?'

'It will do,' he whispers. 'I feel dreadful, Mr Buckley.'

I don't know what to tell him. 'I hope it will be over soon, Commodore. Try to sleep.'

The commodore drifts into an uneasy sleep, and over the next hour the episodes of shivering cease. His temperature seems to rise, though, and I take up position in the chair next to his cot, regularly dampening a cloth laid across his brow with cool water. I can't tell if it helps any.

James Lenstock taps on the door and stands in the doorway.

'I am going to sleep just outside, Ned. Wake me if he needs anything.'

I nod.

'Any improvement…?' he asks quietly.

I lead him into the great cabin. 'He isn't shivering anymore. I don't know if it's an improvement,' I tell him softly, glancing back at the commodore's bed place.

Mr Lenstock shakes his head. 'I wish I had a better idea what to do. I feel thoroughly useless.' He leaves and shuts the door behind him.

Commodore Nelson wakes coughing. 'Water,' he requests hoarsely.

I hold the glass while he sips from it. 'My throat feels as if someone has used a holystone on it,' he mutters.

'Would you perhaps like to try a warm gargle, sir?'

His eyes look unfocused. 'What...? Oh. No, not right now.' He pinches the bridge of his nose between his thumb and first finger and winces. 'I am sorry; I feel... very odd.'

'It's alright, sir.'

He is drifting back to sleep. 'Thank you, Mr...' He doesn't finish the sentence.

I leave the inner door to his bed place open while I doze in one of the armchairs. It isn't uncomfortable, but in this situation, I would not sleep soundly in a feather bed. The commodore's fever seems to be holding steady, which is better than having it go soaring; but I wish it would reach the crisis, so that he can sleep more restfully. As it is, he tosses fitfully, and I have untangled his bedclothes twice.

I hear the watch change over at four AM. It will begin to grow light soon. We have left a lantern burning all night, and I go to the stern-gallery and look out. I'd kept the curtains open to allow fresh air to circulate in the cabin—not that there was a great deal to be had. The breeze is so light that we are nearly becalmed. Once the sun rises, I shall have to decide whether to close the curtains against it and still whatever breeze there is.

Nelson mutters and rocks his head on the pillow as if seeking a cooler spot. I cannot tell if he is awake or not. I lift his head gently and turn the pillow over, then re-wet the cloth and lay it over his forehead again, stroking his damp hair back from his face. I haven't spoken during this operation, but now he asks almost inaudibly, 'Who is there?'

'It's Buckley, sir,' I answer quietly.

'Mother? ...Mother, don't leave me.'

'Shh. It's alright, Commodore,' I murmur awkwardly. 'I won't leave.'

His eyelids flutter open for a moment, but he doesn't appear to see me. He seems to be in a sort of waking dream. 'I need you,' he whispers plaintively to the darkness.

'I'm here,' I say, taking his hand. It is heavy and solid and somehow reassuring, when everything else seems so insubstantial. 'Rest. I will stay right here.'

He sighs and seems to relax; at least, he doesn't speak again.

I sit beside him, holding his hand, as the sky begins to lighten.

The next time he opens his eyes and asks for water, the cabin is fully light. I help him drink, then ask him, 'Do you want me to close the curtains in the great cabin, sir?'

He looks at me. 'Who are you?' he asks vaguely.

I take a breath. 'Buckley, sir. Ned Buckley,' I say reassuringly, although I feel anything but calm.

'Ned. Oh yes; Ned. Did you ask me something?'

'I asked if you would like me to close the curtains.'

'Close half of them, if you would. If you close them all it will become too warm in here.' He closes his eyes. 'Thank you, Ned. You're a good lad.'

When I recount this to Mr Eshelby, he frowns. 'How long would you estimate he has been disoriented?' he asks.

'He told me last night that it comes and goes, but I first noticed it just after he had tried to get up from his chair and could not. He asked me to open the windows, but they were all open already.'

Mr Eshelby strokes his lip and looks concerned. 'His fever is not inordinately high. It is high enough, mind, but I would not expect confusion under such a condition. Has he eaten or drunk anything?'

I shake my head. 'Nosir, he has eaten nothing. I have tried to make sure he is drinking enough, but he won't take much. A few swallows of water now and then is all.'

Standing by the table with the remains of our various offerings, James Lenstock looks perturbed.

The surgeon approaches the commodore's cot and puts a hand on Commodore Nelson's arm. 'Commodore? Wake up, sir.'

Nelson opens his eyes and blinks.

'Good morning,' says Mr Eshelby. 'Do you know me, sir?'

'You are the surgeon,' the commodore replies slowly. 'Have you discovered what is wrong with me?'

'Not entirely. How do you feel?'

'Miserable. Half-drowned. My throat is raw, my head aches, and I have no strength in my limbs.' He sneezes.

'Were you able to sleep last night?'

'I think I did. I'm having trouble remembering. My damned head is so foggy I can't think straight.'

'Did you dream at all, sir?'

'Not that I recall. What has that to do with anything?' Commodore Nelson asks irritably.

'I'm trying to determine why your head might feel foggy, Commodore.' Mr Eshelby measures the commodore's pulse. He listens to his chest and examines his throat.

'Well sir, you have no rash and no lesions on your throat, the absence of which are good news. I will mix up an ano-dyne preparation for you, and if you take it with hot, sweet tea it should help your throat. Use honey, rather than sugar. It would probably not hurt you to have a light meal of soup or jelly, as well.'

Nelson shakes his head. 'Mr... Lenstock.' He coughs.

'Yessir?' James Lenstock steps forward.

'Next time, steep the tea longer.'

James' mouth twitches. 'Would you like me to brew some now, sir?'

'If you would.'

Mr Eshelby departs with James Lenstock. 'I'll bring you the medicine directly, Commodore. Just rest.'

The commodore sighs. He looks at me. 'Ned.'

'Sir?'

'My faithful Ned.' His eyelids droop. 'I am so dreadfully fagged.'

'It will get better, sir; I am sure.'

He raises a hand in a gesture of resignation, then lets it fall heavily back on the mattress.

'Let me prepare something for you to eat, Commodore.'

'I do not want anything just yet, Mr…' he searches for the word. 'What is your last name, Ned?'

'Buckley, sir,' I say gently.

'Ah, just so. I shall have some tea and the surgeon's medicine, but I don't care to eat anything just now. I am sorry,' he says quietly. 'I should be able to remember your name. I cannot seem to hold on to thoughts and… and *sort* them properly. As long as I am in this condition, Mr Berry must command.'

'I'll tell him, sir. Would you like to speak to him?'

'Not now. I shall speak to him later.'

'Very good, sir.' I smooth the coverlet over him. 'Can I do anything for you? Are you comfortable?'

'I am decidedly *uncomfortable*, but there is nothing you can do about it.'

'If you think of anything that will help, tell me.'

Providentially, Mr Eshelby's anodyne and Mr Lenstock's tea arrive simultaneously. 'You'd better show me how to prepare it,' James tells me. 'Because I suspect I shall need to know.'

'He does not typically use honey in his tea,' I say. 'But apart from that, you should add milk until it is about this colour…'

I have to rouse the commodore to take the medicine and the tea. He tastes his tea and looks at James Lenstock. 'That's better,' he says.

'Thank you, sir.'

As he prepares to leave, James says to me, 'I brought a second cup. You should drink some. I'll only have to pour it out, otherwise. And you didn't have breakfast. Look, I'll stay with him at midday so that you can eat.'

'Thank you,' I say, as he slips out.

'What were the two of you discussing in low voices?' Commodore Nelson asks me when I turn back to his berth.

'Meals and such. Nothing pressing, sir.'

'I've something you could do for me,' he offers. 'If you will.'

'Of course, sir.'

'I've a pain here, like a sore muscle, or a stitch.' He indicates his breastbone, where I was distracted by the soft, sparse hairs when I helped him remove his shirt. 'It pains me when I inhale. If you rub there, it might ease it.'

I rearrange the bedcovers carefully and place my fingers hesitantly over the spot he indicated. 'Here, sir?'

He nods.

I press my fingertips gently against his flesh. The hair brushes my fingers as I make gentle circles. 'Is this the correct pressure, Commodore?'

'Yes; good.' He closes his eyes and sinks into his pillows. 'Thank you, Ned.'

I concentrate on keeping a steady pressure, because if I were to lift my fingers, my right hand would shake the way the left is currently shaking. I have never touched a man so intimately. Richard's tastes did not run to tenderness.

I feel him relax under my touch. His breathing deepens and I am sure that he is asleep, but I am hesitant to remove my hand for fear of waking him. Slowly, I reduce the pressure and the motion until my hand is resting lightly on his breast. A few minutes later, I lift it carefully and cover him again with the bedclothes.

I pour myself a cup of tea from the cooling pot, but I am too rattled to drink it. Instead, I shut myself in the quarter-gallery and bite the heel of my hand until the pain cuts sharply through my disordered thoughts.

Christ, Ned; you cannot. You cannot feel for him, not like this. It is every kind of improper thing you can think of. He is your commander, he is married… you have renounced womanly things. You absolutely cannot feel tenderness for him. It will destroy everything.

I try to think of something else. Images float through my mind. Jack breathing his last breath in my arms. *No, not that.* My brother's face, sorrowful and bewildered. *No.* Handsome Lieutenant Berry.

Oh—Lieutenant Berry. I told Commodore Nelson I would get a message to Lieutenant Berry.

I let myself out of the quarter-gallery and go to the commodore's bedside again.

'I will be right back, sir, and I shall ask Mr Lenstock to stay with you until I return,' I say softly.

He makes no indication of having heard me, but I had not expected that he would.

'Stay with him for a few minutes,' I request of James Lenstock. 'I need to convey a message to Lieutenant Berry. He's asleep… he seems more peaceful than he was last night, so maybe he's getting better.'

The air on deck seems fresher, even though there is hardly enough breeze to stir the topsails. The officer of the watch directs me to the lieutenant's cabin, where he is recording something in his log.

'I am sorry, sir; Commodore Nelson asked me to inform you that you are to remain in command. Until further notice, I guess... I should have told you sooner, but I have been distracted.'

Lieutenant Berry puts down his pen. 'I heard as much from Mr Eshelby this morning, actually. Is he no better?'

'Perhaps a little. He is sleeping more restfully than he did last night.'

'Well, pray that it will be so. Does he want to speak to me?'

'I asked him, sir. He inferred that he might want to see you this afternoon.'

'Thank you, Mr Buckley.'

My own head feels a little giddy in the sunlight and air of the quarterdeck. I'm reluctant to return to the commodore's cabin, but I do.

Mr Lenstock meets me at the door. 'Come to the stern-gallery with me,' he says in a low voice.

I glance at Commodore Nelson, but he appears to be sleeping as before. I follow Mr Lenstock onto the stern-gallery.

'He woke while you were gone. He didn't seem to know who I was. He asked for you, but he couldn't remember your last name.'

'Is it getting worse, James?'

'Can't tell. He knew me this morning, though.'

'The lucidness seems to come and go.'

'That's what you said. He did not seem confused; he knew *where* he was. He was just... vague.'

'I hope that is just a product of feeling ill. I know he's normally sharp, but he's very wretched. When he begins to feel better, he will probably be himself again.'

'I hope you're right, Ned. It makes me uneasy that he seems not to know who we are.'

'It makes me uneasy, too. I was just trying not to say so.'

He gives me a wry look before leaving the cabin.

I resume my seat by the commodore's bed.

The sleepless night is beginning to tell on me; I feel desperately tired. I pick up Nelson's hand again and smooth the back of it with my thumb. I'm not quite sure who I'm soothing: him, or me.

He opens his eyes briefly and looks at me, then closes them again. 'Mr Buckley.'

'Sir.'

He opens his eyes again and examines me, as if to make sure I am who I claim to be. 'Mr Eshelby asked me if I dreamt. I have remembered a dream that I had; if it is important to him, you may relay it.' He manages to look mildly annoyed. 'I tried to tell you earlier, but you were not here.'

'I took your message to Lieutenant Berry. What was your dream, Commodore?'

He looks at me through drowsy eyes. 'I thought I was back at school. I was dreadfully ill and very low, and I wanted to go home.'

'Could they not have sent you home, sir?' I remember Papa going to collect Arthur from school when he had whooping cough.

There is a long pause, and I think that he has fallen asleep again, but then he says, 'There was no one at home to receive me. My mother was dead, and my father spent the winters in Bath for his health. I suppose there was a nurse for my younger brothers and sisters, but she could hardly have travelled to Norwich to retrieve me. It matters not.' There is another silence before he speaks again.

'I got better...' he concludes, before drifting into sleep once more.

The air in the cabin is hot and close. I need to open the curtains, to try to get some more air in here. I shall, in just a minute...

I wake to a rapping on the cabin door. It takes me a second to figure out where I am. There is a cramp in my chest from sleeping twisted in the chair. *It is so hot.* I had meant to open the curtains. I get up and go into the great cabin.

Lieutenant Berry opens the door and looks in. 'I apologise, Mr Buckley,' he says quietly. 'When no one answered my knock, I thought I ought to check to see if the commodore was alright.'

'Please, sir. I'm the one who should apologise. I'm afraid I fell asleep.'

He steps into the room. 'I said that I would come and visit him this afternoon, but there's a storm coming. I shall have to delay it.'

'Come in, and tell him. He was awake just a moment ago. I'm sure he will want to know. Take the chair.'

The falling barometer makes my head pound. That, and the sultry air, signal a storm even to a landsman like me. I walk to the stern lights intending to open the curtains, but the ship seems to lurch underneath me. I reach out for the sill to steady myself, but I miss, and the floor comes rushing up at me.

———————————

It is hot, so hot.

I am lying on a bed in a dark room. Even the moonlight spilling through the windows is white hot, like a glowing steel blade. I do not know this room, but I know the bed. It is my husband's bed, with its tall corner posts and tester.

Somewhere a child is crying, but I am too weary to get up and go to it.

The latch rattles, and I whimper. I do not want to see Richard now. I do not want to see Richard ever again.

The door opens, and he steps into the room. He pads across the floor in the darkness, and I feel his hands at my throat, undoing my stock, unfastening the throat button of my shirt.

NO! I struggle against him and manage to get one arm free. I rake my hand down the side of his face, opening a furrow in his cheek with my fingers. I think that I hear Captain Spencer's angry snarl.

He rears back and staggers away from the bed. In the sharp moonlight I can see that his torso and legs are bare. His face comes into the light, and now I can see his features clearly.

It is Commodore Nelson, his expression hurt and bewildered.

I am falling, falling from a great height. I hit the surface of the ocean, but I do not sink. I float on the surface of the sea, cold wavelets lapping over me, watching as the British fleet sails away from the Mediterranean in the starlight, leaving me behind.

Jack Mackay sits on a rock, carving. It is not an animal this time; it is a full-rigged ship. 'Her name is Commodore,*' he tells me. 'But she sails the heavens instead of the sea.' He holds her up, and I can see the stars through her rigging.*

Then there is nothing at all.

Chapter Twenty-Three

I try to open my eyes, but my lids are as heavy as a window with a broken sash weight. They will not stay up.

Someone is coughing nearby. My mind drifts on a tide of disjointed impressions. Heat... darkness... curtains. Ships... a ship that sails the heavens. *Commodore*... Commodore!

My eyes fly open again, and I try to get up. I do not know where I am. This is not my hammock, nor am I in the great cabin.

'Well, there yeh are,' says a voice. 'Easy, younker; yeh don't need t' go anywhere jest now.' A large paw pushes me back against my pillow.

A man in a grubby apron assesses me critically. I realise that I am in the sick berth, and this man must be the loblolly boy. Although this particular person hasn't been a boy in many years.

He puts a cup to my lips. It contains vinegar whey. I take the cup from his hand and gulp from it, but he gently takes it away.

''Ere, yeh can't drink it like that. Yeh'll puke it back up again. Slow down.'

'I know,' I admit. 'I didn't know I was so thirsty.'

'Stands t' reason. Yeh en't drunk much since yeh got 'ere, and the fever 'll make a person dry as the Barbary Coast.' He lets me sip again from the cup.

I wipe my mouth on my sleeve. 'How long have I been here?'

''S been about two days, I guess, since Lieutenant Berry brung yeh here. Carried yeh in like a sack o' corn.' He turns to go.

'Wait! Please... Commodore Nelson, is he...?'

The loblolly boy comes limping back to stand next to my cot. His legs appear to be of two different lengths. ''E's mendin', I unnerstand. I en't seen him meself, but Mr Eshelby's been lookin' arfter 'im. Fever's been tearin' through the ship. There's five other men wi' it on t' other side o' that curtain, but surgeon said t' keep yeh apart from 'em, 'cause they got the cough, and you didn't.

'Dunno what it is,' he goes on. 'Seems like it affects people differntly. Some folks get a cough and runny nose wi' it, and others, like you, jest get the fever. It en't killed anyone... yet; but it's made some of 'em pretty sick fer awhile. Mr Eshelby thinks it come from Elba.'

Something else comes slamming back into my consciousness. I look down at myself.

My waistcoat and neck stock are missing, and my throat button is undone, but I am still wearing my shirt and breeches. 'Did you undress me?'

He chuckles. 'I tried to, lad, but yeh wouldn't let me. Fought like a lion, yeh did. I figgered that if yeh wanted t' keep your clothes s' bad, I'd let yeh. By the way, yeh kept callin' me Richards. Me name's Roberts, son, not Richards.'

I say a silent prayer of thanksgiving that Roberts didn't care to press the issue. Another man might have.

The panic that had dragged me into full consciousness is ebbing, and I struggle to keep my eyes open.

''S alright, son. Yeh can go back t' sleep. We'll keep our eye on things fer yeh.'

I take him at his word.

———————

I am in the sick berth for another full day and a half. 'Let me try to do it myself' becomes my stock phrase, and they are perfectly happy to allow me. They have enough other men to worry about.

This is the closest I have come to having my deception revealed since that awful night on the quarterdeck. The sooner I can get out of the sick berth, the more easily I will breathe again.

———————

When I am finally allowed to leave, Roberts kindly sees me off.

'Come back an' see me from time t' time, young sir,' he says affectionately. 'You're a plucky lad. I like yeh.'

'I like you, too,' I tell him. 'And I would be happy to come back and see you.'

The walk from the foreward part of the ship to the stern suddenly seems like a long way. I had no trouble getting around in the sick berth, but the one hundred and fifty feet fore to aft feel like a mile. I try not to let anyone on the quarterdeck see me wobble.

James Lenstock looks pleased to see me. 'You're back! But are you sure you're alright? You aren't going to go keel over again, are you?' He pulls out a chair for me.

'I'm alright.' But I'm happy to take the chair. 'It just seems farther to the stern than I remembered.'

'Well, I am incredibly glad to see you. I've had to become a steward by the seat of my pants this week. He's been very patient with me, but I can't tell you how many things I did wrong.'

'How is he, James?'

'He's just well enough to be irritable about the things he can't do yet,' James says wryly. 'But seriously; he's been out of bed since yesterday. It never got much worse than it was that second day, but it took a long time for him to begin to improve. Mr Castang got the fever, too, so he hasn't been able to do any work at all, and I think that's bothering him as much as anything.'

I tap on the door to the great cabin. 'Come!' Commodore Nelson snaps from inside.

He is seated at his desk with his back to me, pen in hand. He is completely dressed except for his coat and shoes; he wears his banyan and carpet slippers instead.

'Have you come to check up on me again already, Eshelby?' he asks, without looking up. 'I told you I would behave myself. I begin to believe that you do not trust me.' He puts down the pen and turns in his chair.

'Ned!' He shoves back the chair and embraces me.

This is the second time that he has surprised me with an unexpected gesture of affection. But although it was unanticipated, it does not appear to be out of character. Moreover, it makes me feel better.

'What a relief it is to have you back,' he says, releasing me. 'Mr Eshelby forbade me from coming to see you. But he said that your recovery was faster than mine, so I took him at his word. I didn't really have a choice,' he adds wryly.

His movements are brisk again, and he is alert, but his eyes are still tired, and his voice is slightly hoarse. 'Come and sit,' he orders me. 'I have been told to conserve my energy. I thought this thing had nearly done for me a few days ago.' He takes one of the armchairs and motions for me to take the other.

'I suppose I was in some sort of delirium. I could not think clearly. It was very disagreeable; I would begin to say something and not be able to finish the sentence.' He frowns. 'I do not mind bodily infirmities so much, but it bothers me greatly when I cannot think. Tell me, Ned, did I say or do anything odd…?'

Apart from calling me Ned? The only time in the past when he has used my first name was when he asked Seaman Washington to identify me. It feels too familiar somehow, but I don't dislike it. It will simply take some getting used to.

'Nosir. You just seemed very tired.' I decide not to tell him that he asked for his mother. 'Having now had it myself, I understand why.'

'A good portion of the ship seems to have caught it, but thankfully, most men seem to be able to continue to work. It is only a handful of us who got the worst of it, apparently.'

'Mr Lenstock told me that Mr Castang has caught it, too.'

He sighs. 'Yes, he did. Although I understand that his case is not too serious. Mr Eshelby says he simply does not want to risk my being re-infected, so I have been unable to get any work done,' he grumbles.

'I believe it is for the best, sir. Mr Allen will be back soon, and Mr Castang will be well, and everything will return to normal.'

He gives me a resigned look. 'You are undoubtably right. I am just impatient, and it makes me snap at poor Mr Lenstock. He has been forced to deal with me alone since you were taken ill, and I am sure it has not been easy. As you have already learnt, I am not a good patient.'

'Well sir, you are welcome to snap at me for a change, if you wish to give Mr Lenstock a break.'

'Tomorrow, Mr Buckley,' he says with satisfaction. 'I will snap at you tomorrow.'

Tom Allen returns at the end of the week, bearing a number of delicacies and nice things for the commodore's table, in addition to more pedestrian items like coffee, soft flour, and new stockings and handkerchiefs.

'I leave for a week, and everything goes to the devil?' he says to me and James Lenstock. 'I was not aware that I was so indispensable,' he prods us mildly.

'Had you been here, it might have been you who ended up in the sick berth, rather than Ned,' James says.

'I imagine the commodore would have been happy to have you here to share his misery,' I offer.

'Yes, I expect he got tired of looking at my ugly mug all the time,' James continues in the same vein.

'Alright, I get it; you don't have to gang up on me. I'm glad that everyone seems to be recovering. I'm not sorry that I missed it. Here.' He tosses a small cloth bag at each of us.

'Dates!' James exclaims, opening the bag. 'Forget that I ragged you, Tom Allen. All is forgiven.'

Mr Allen looks at me. 'I held nothing against you, Mr Allen,' I say. 'But thank you for thinking of us. It is a generous gift.'

'Spent my hard-earned pay on the two of you,' he says grudgingly. Then he grins. 'And it was a pleasure.'

We return to the Gulf of Genoa to find that Consul Brame has suffered a stroke, rendering him largely ineffective.

'He was hardly effective before, so what has changed?' Nelson mutters. But it throws up one more barrier to diplomacy that he must work around.

In August, we learn that Spain has signed a treaty with the French. The Spaniards, who were once our allies, are now our enemies.

'Their seamanship is no better than that of the French,' the commodore tells me. If it makes him uneasy, he doesn't show it, but the combined Franco-Spanish fleet now gravely outnumbers the British ships in the Mediterranean.

Anticipating a fleet action outside of Toulon, Admiral Jervis orders Commodore Nelson to transfer his pendant to a frigate and send *Captain* to Toulon without him. I don't know how long Nelson contemplated before disregarding this order; I doubt it was very long. He leaves his squadron on the coast and sails with *Captain* to Toulon, but as it is, there is no engagement.

I do not hear whether Jervis reprimands him. If he does, Commodore Nelson never speaks of it. He throws himself back into patrolling the coast, characteristically issuing passports to the Tuscan fisherman allowing them to pass the British blockade in order to sustain their livelihoods. He also embarks on a grand plan with Viceroy Elliot to retake Leghorn from the French. But as it must rely upon the co-operation of the Austrian army, the plan ultimately goes nowhere.

Amidst all of this, on 11 August Nelson is finally confirmed as a Commodore of the Red, First Class. With great personal satisfaction, he negotiates for Captain Ralph Willett Miller to become his official flag captain. Lieutenant Berry is to remain his first lieutenant. He shares a glass with me during our regular time together in the evening, but he is too busy to contemplate a celebration.

I have become invested in his success; I share his discontent or satisfaction. Perhaps it was a foregone conclusion, but it is one more step up the promotion ladder. Considering the amount of energy he throws into his work, unless he crosses the wrong person, how can he fail?

———————

With September's arrival, things get even thornier. Genoa finally breaks her cosmetic neutrality, placing an embargo on all British goods. Most of these goods belong to the British fleet, and Nelson jumps in with both feet to attempt to get them back, applying first to the Genoese senate, and then to the secretary of state. When he receives no reply, the commodore goes personally to negotiate with Secretary of State Castiglione. He requests and is granted an audience with the doge. But despite his relentless efforts, he makes no progress. The senate will not budge.

———————

On 11 September, we begin the day with the discovery that three men and a boat disappeared from *Captain* during the night. Lieutenant Berry puts together a search party to attempt to apprehend them, whilst the miserable lieutenant under whose watch they escaped stands looking stricken, anticipating his dressing-down.

Men run all the time; this is hardly an unusual event. The commodore once told me he thought that given the chance, men would desert from heaven to hell just for a change of scenery.

It is also routine to search other ships in the harbour to get deserters back. Men will frequently desert to a merchantman, but joining a merchant ship does not protect them from being reclaimed by the navy. I do not know if it was the lieutenant's intention to search the merchantmen at the mole, but as our boats approach a French bombard, one of the Genoese shore batteries opens fire on Lieutenant Berry's party.

This is—ostensibly—a neutral harbour, and our boats have done nothing that could remotely be considered aggressive. We have been aware for months, though, that the French are the ones controlling the Genoese guns, and this literal shot across the bow opens the door for hostile engagement.

The commotion brings Commodore Nelson from his cabin, followed by Mr Castang.

Lieutenant Berry coolly proceeds to board the bombard, but instead of searching her for our deserters, he ejects her crew, cuts her cable, and brings her out as *Captain's* prize.

'If they were so quick to defend her before we made our intentions clear,' Commodore Nelson observes, 'then she must have cargo that they do not want to lose. Prepare our guns, but hold your fire. I want to see how this is going to go.'

Onboard HMS *L'Eclair* the guns are being prepared as well, and the commodore signals her to engage first, as a handful of French privateers come out to try to reclaim the bombard. They quickly take cover from *L'Eclair's* fire, and *Captain* spits three warning shots at the batteries. For the next hour the shore batteries hurl shot at *Captain;* she sits sedately as the missiles fly all around her, not firing a shot in reply. None of the shot makes contact; it sails over us, or falls short, or flies wide. Still, I suspect I am not the only person who flinches at a couple of close calls. One such shot sends a spout of water onto our deck, soaking a seaman who shakes his fist at the battery.

With the Genoese guns still booming, Commodore Nelson retreats to his cabin and drafts a statement to Consul Brame, laying out the events of the morning and asserting the British position. He intends to make an offer to the Genoese; if they will formally apologise for insulting His

Britannic Majesty by allowing the French to control the port, Nelson will turn over his French prize to Genoa.

He instructs Lieutenant Compton to take the statement directly to Consul Brame, whom he exhorts to go immediately to the secretary of state. Nelson returns to his cabin, but I remain on deck, watching as the lieutenant and his men evade a pair of French gunboats. They make the landing, but once there, they are confronted by a mob of angry French seamen and Jacobins, and there are no Genoese guards in sight.

I cannot take my eyes off the landing. If Lieutenant Compton or his men are injured or killed by an irrational mob, what happens then? We certainly did not get up this morning intending to fight a pitched battle, but I have no doubt that if anything happens to the lieutenant and his party, Nelson will show no more restraint.

I do not hear Commodore Nelson come back on deck. He apparently is standing behind me when we hear the report of a pistol on the landing, and as I jump in alarm, I end up in his arms.

'Damn me, what was that?' he exclaims, setting me on my feet again and glaring over the rail.

'Lieutenant Compton and his men are in trouble. A mob got to them before the guards. It looks as if the guards are there now, but they cannot reach our men.'

Nelson swears softly. 'This is getting out of hand.' He summons the signal lieutenant. 'Signal to *L'Eclair* and the prize to move out of range of the batteries,' he tells the lieutenant tersely.

The Genoese guards have finally reached our landing party, and it appears that Lieutenant Compton was able to get away. The guards beat off the mob and disperse them, but in the process a French sailor falls and doesn't get up again. We can hear the muskets firing and see the smoke.

The guards take our men under their protection, but one man appears to be injured.

I continue to watch, appalled, as gangs of people bent on violence begin to gather on the shore. The crews of the French privateers swarm out of their ships, threatening the British merchantmen at the mole, and there is a tense and ugly standoff until Genoese soldiers board our merchant ships and repel the privateers.

By early afternoon, with the guns still firing, Nelson has received no response to his overture. He sends a second parley boat into Genoa, to no avail. Lieutenant Pierson returns, having been retained in the guards' room, with nothing to show for his mission but the information that Genoa will reply to Commodore Nelson's statement formally. They have closed the port to British shipping.

I hear later that the French accused the Genoese of intentionally missing *Captain* with the shot from the batteries. Even so, it hardly redeems the Genoese for firing on Lieutenant Berry in the first place.

The French have apparently demanded that Genoa choose between France and Britain, and the French are the less predictable factor in the equation. Castiglione sides with the French and confiscates all British property.

'The French told Castiglione that we attacked them unprovoked, and that I fabricated the deserters to disguise my intent,' Nelson tells me in disgust. 'And Castiglione swallowed it.'

Castiglione is a coward, but it is not hard to see why he might believe the French minister's lies. Nelson has cut ships out of Genoese harbours before in order to make a point. This, however, is the first time it has blown up in his face.

He has been writing furiously to Drake and Brame, trying to defend his position, and his confidence has been shaken, which concerns me more than a little. I have known him to be depressed and dejected, but never before have I seen him uncertain.

There is no help for it. The Genoese have shut down all diplomatic communication. Three dismal days after the incident, the commodore sails from Genoa, having to leave behind Lieutenant Compton, his jolly boat, and four impounded British ships at the mole.

Nelson refuses to be defeated. He has the unqualified support of Viceroy Elliot and Sir John Jervis, but Jervis advises him to exercise a level of diplomacy with the Genoese whilst Brame is attempting to effect the release of British citizens and property.

This approach only goes so far with Commodore Nelson. He leaves Genoese shipping alone, but he has a bigger prize in his sights. Within the space of four days, he plans, assaults, and captures the Genoese island of Capraia, without waiting for approval from Admiral Jervis. Viceroy Elliot gives him authorisation and commits his troops to the action. Nelson is doggedly determined, quietly belligerent. By 18 September, Capraia is in British hands.

I have not spent any time with him for several days, so when he requests my attendance, I am surprised to find him sitting at his desk with his head in his hands, a picture of dejection.

'Sir, is there anything the matter?'

He looks up. 'Nothing that anyone can remedy, Mr Buckley.'

I wait.

'The three deserters gave themselves up to Consul Brame and have asked him to intercede with the navy for leniency for them.'

I consider this. 'I do not believe that the fate of three deserters would make you so low,' I tell him quietly.

After a moment, he says, 'Captain Sawyer of the *Blanche* frigate is to be court-martialled for interfering with his men. I have had to suspend him from duty and arrest his officers.'

I did not expect this. I am speechless. 'When you say "interfering" …'

'I did not believe it at first. I thought—perhaps I hoped—that it was baseless. I would like to think that the accusations are not true. But I trust that Captain Cockburn would not have brought it to me if it did not merit investigation.'

He has been speaking softly, with his eyes fixed on the floor. Now he looks at me again.

'It makes me ill, Ned. His officers had apparently tried to bring the matter before me, but he blocked them.'

He sighs heavily. 'I know not whether to be revolted or melancholy. I liked him. I cannot believe that I did not know that this was going on in my squadron.'

I am momentarily silent, digesting this information. 'How could you have known, sir?' I ask gently. 'It is something he would have hidden from you at all costs. If indeed he… is guilty of such a thing.'

'I will not sit on his court-martial board. I hope they will find fairly.' He massages his brow with his thumb and three fingers.

He looks exhausted and defeated, and it makes my heart ache. 'Perhaps it will help to beat me at chess tonight, Commodore? If you can make up your mind to take Capraia and accomplish it practically overnight, you should be able to clean the board with me in just a few moves.'

He rewards me with a reluctant grin. 'That *was* rather good, wasn't it?' he says.

Nelson's triumph doesn't last. One week after taking possession of Capraia, I arrive after supper to find him sitting at his desk in the darkening cabin. It is nearing the end of September, and the sun is almost gone.

'Sir, shall I light a lantern?'

'Go ahead, Mr Buckley,' he says quietly.

I use the candle from his desk and light the lanterns, then return the candle. 'Is it Captain Sawyer's court-martial worrying you, sir?'

'No.' He hands me a sheet of paper. 'I expected that this was coming. But I had hoped it would not be so soon.'

It is an order from London, forwarded from Admiral Jervis. We are to evacuate Corsica and leave the Mediterranean.

Whilst *Captain* is refitting in Corsica, Commodore Nelson sails to Genoa on HMS *Diadem* to attempt to use Capraia as a means to getting the embargo lifted. It may be *Captain's* last chance before Gibraltar to get the work done that she needs, and Nelson is determined to follow through against Genoa before they learn of our imminent departure.

I sit outside the sick berth with Roberts, who has asked me to teach him to read.

'What makes you want to learn?' I ask him.

'Well, I ne'er did b'fore... me son, and me daughter, they were th' educated uns. They learnt to read and write and figure some at school. Their mam and me, well, we done alright wi' out.

'I was a top man, b'fore I broke me leg in three places. Tha's why this un's shorter than t'other, and me foot turns in like this. I din't need t' read to work on the yards; and now I'm a loblolly boy, I keep ever'thin' I need t' know 'bout the patients in me 'ead. But I'd like to read me wife's letters meself, instead o' 'avin' t' ask some other tar to read 'em to me.'

'Do you keep your wife's letters, Roberts?'

'Aye sir; every one.'

'Well then, let's begin with them.'

The letters are written in a graceless script, but they are perfectly legible. We begin by picking out individual characters and writing them in sequence.

''Magine the look on me dear Polly's face when I reads 'er own letters to 'er when I comes 'ome!' he says.

'Who writes your wife's letters, if she doesn't do it herself?'

He smiles broadly. He is missing two teeth on the left side of his jaw, but it doesn't detract from his smile. 'This is me daughrter Annabel's writin'. Me son used t' write for me.'

'How old is your son?' I ask idly, watching him copy a letter 'e.'

'Well sir, I reckon 'e'd be 'bout your age, if 'e was still alive.'

I am mortified. 'I am so sorry, Roberts. It never occurred to me that he might not still be living.'

'It's alright, younker,' he says kindly. 'I still miss 'im, but we're all goin' t' die one day. 'E were a sailor, like his Da. I was right proud of 'im. 'E drowned, few years back.'

This happens fairly regularly; I wonder why sailors do not learn to swim. Roberts supplies the answer before I even think to ask.

'If nob'dy comes t' get yeh, it's better t' die fast than by degrees.'

What a dismal thought.

Nelson's attempt to negotiate with Genoa is unsuccessful. By mid-October he returns to Bastia, with the French hot on his heels.

On 15 October he re-hoists his flag in *Captain*. By the morning of 20 October, working like lightning, he, Viceroy Elliott, and Lt. General de Burgh have completed a successful evacuation of the island of Corsica. The British ships sail away in the gathering dawn as the French invasion army tries frantically and unsuccessfully to clear the spiked guns in the defence towers.

Once again, I watch Corsica recede from view, only today I am on the quarterdeck instead of in the mizzen top. The melancholy sensation, however, is almost exactly the same.

Chapter Twenty-Four

Gibraltar in December.

We had only just arrived here when the decision was made to station the fleet off Portugal. The troops on Elba are to be transferred to Lisbon.

Jervis has sent Nelson back to Elba in the frigate *Minerve* to oversee the removal of the army. A seventy-four is too slow for this kind of work.

I have far more latitude ashore now than I ever did as a marine, if there were actually anything I wished to do ashore. I have money to spend, but no real desire to buy anything. I already have new shirts, stockings, and handkerchiefs, and two whole suits of small-clothes. I have replaced my worn-out boots with a pair of low-heeled shoes. I look like a gentleman. If I were to run into Will Fowler or Billy Baxter on the street, neither of them would recognise me. Not that I would expect to; I don't know where they ended up after Corsica.

I want nothing for myself, but I do want to purchase some gifts for Christmas, so on 20 December I go ashore in a contingent of sailors for twenty-four hours. I arrange for a room in a respectable inn some distance from the harbour and leave my bag in the room, then go in search of presents.

For Tom Allen, who brought us dates from Porto Fer-raio, I buy some good-quality pipe tobacco. Tom's pipe is his guilty pleasure, and he often retreats to the galley in the evening to smoke. He will smoke any tobacco he can get, and judging from the scent of it, some of it must be pretty awful.

For James Lenstock, who likes such things, I find an elegant silk neck cloth. The commodore has taken James with him to Elba, to have him gain more experience in the role of steward. Dressing the part will give him confidence, and I know that it will appeal to his vanity.

It is harder to shop for Commodore Nelson. I spend a good part of the day looking at watch chains and sleeve buttons, shoe buckles, silk handkerchiefs, gold pencils and pocketbooks. All these things seem far too personal to be a gift from a subordinate, and the commodore doesn't wear fancy baubles. Perhaps the gold epaulettes and lace on his coat are shiny enough to suit him.

I end up finally in a stationer and bookseller's shop. He does not need more writing paper or quills, and although they offer a selection of fine inkwells, I would prefer not to give him a gift that alludes to work.

On one table is a display of works published this year. I cannot see the commodore relaxing with *Observations on Mr Paine's Pamphlet Entitled the Decline and Fall of the English System of Finance,* or *A Letter from The Right Honourable Edmund Burke to a Noble Lord, on the Attacks made upon him and his pension.*

The shopkeeper asks if I would like a recommendation. 'I am looking for something diverting,' I tell him. 'To be read of an evening for recreation.'

'Well, this has been popular,' he suggests, picking up a volume bound in chocolate-coloured leather, 'if a little sensational. It is a ghost story, in two volumes.'

I take the slim book from him. *Bungay Castle*, by Mrs Bonhôte. I wonder if it will be anything like Shakespeare's *Macbeth*. The title doesn't inspire me; it sounds like the name of a merchantman with a penchant for wandering away from its convoy. But perhaps it is something different enough that it will interest him. If not, he can always lend it out.

I purchase the two volumes, along with a small pamphlet of Goethe's poem 'Prometheus,' in German with an English translation. Impulsively, I also buy a copy of *The Castle of Otranto*, by Horace Walpole, for Roberts. I remember reading it many years ago, curled in my father's big chair in front of the fire, in his library on a wet autumn afternoon.

Sailors are superstitious people, and on one hand, to Roberts, the curse of the castle of Otranto might seem utterly believable. But the concerns of its characters are so removed from the realities of life on a warship, that I think it will amount to nothing more than a fanciful story. We will work on reading it together, but ultimately the book will be Roberts' own, to do whatever he likes with it. I doubt that he has ever owned a book before. Why own a thing you cannot use?

I return to my room and put my purchases in my bag, then take the pamphlet of Goethe with me to go in search of supper.

There is a chophouse attached to a tavern that Jack Mackay and I used to frequent when we were here. They serve good, stodgy English food: beef and mutton, potatoes and ale, stout savoury puddings. I know that I will not be able to finish an entire plate, but I will enjoy intensely what I do eat.

Jack is always present in the back of my mind here in Gibraltar. We had drawn no conclusions at the time about what lay ahead of us, but we were unafraid of the future.

I do not regret it; not really. But the pretty streets and squares of neatly-shuttered houses seem less enchanting than they were three years ago.

It is beginning to get late, and it is already quite dark when I get to the chophouse; both the dining room and the tavern are full. I am lucky to get a tiny table in a corner where I can eat my supper and read.

'Prometheus' is an indictment of the Almighty. Rejected, Prometheus comes to reject in turn the idea that God's heart is moved with compassion for humankind.

It is both compelling and troubling.

One cannot look at the consequences of war without wondering where God's compassion figures into it. I could not read about the atrocities in France without thinking that God has turned His back on that nation. Now the French army is advancing like a disease throughout the Mediterranean, and threatens England, as well. The French have tried to recruit Englishmen with republican propaganda, hoping to gain a foothold in Great Britain. Thankfully, their agents were discovered, and the republican Committees of Correspondence dissolved. But they will certainly try again. The Admiralty knows that the new Directory in Paris desperately wants French boots on English soil.

I was very close to becoming Prometheus at one point, after my life with Richard became unbearable. It was Nelson's quiet, undemonstrative faith that pulled me back. Some devout believers are zealous in their conviction, and their very vocal insistence seemed only to increase my sense of isolation. Nelson never insisted on my participation. He invited me into his devotions but left me alone beyond that. It was as if he knew that faith was something that I had to re-encounter on my own.

Lost in thought, my meal paid for, I leave the dining room to head back to the inn.

It is later than I thought. There are few people on the streets, most folks having finished their meals and gone home, and the drinkers are firmly established in their drinking holes. The weather has been dirty this month, and although tonight is clear, no one is inclined to be out.

I am not immediately conscious of the footsteps behind me, but suddenly the hair on the back of my neck rises. *Beware.*

I try to assess the manner of the man by the sound of his steps. He is not stealthy, but neither is he staggering. If he has been drinking, he is not incapacitated. I quicken my pace a little, and my follower adjusts his accordingly.

I was foolish not to stay alert. A slight, solitary man dressed like a gentleman is an easy target. I have never considered carrying a stick; I thought it looked like an affectation. But now I wish that I did.

The footsteps behind me get closer, and I break into a run.

I am lighter than the man behind me; I can tell by the pounding of his feet. If he has been drinking, and I suspect that he has, then I can probably outrun him. I run flat out, and I can tell that I am opening a greater distance between us. It begins to appear that I will escape from my pursuer.

Then I make a mistake.

I turn into a lane that leads in the direction of the inn, my feet flying. But it is not the street I thought it was; it is little more than an alley between two rows of buildings. At the end of it is a tiny yard, enclosed on three sides by stone and stucco walls. There is a barred gate in one of them, but it is locked.

I look frantically around, but there is nothing to use as a weapon. There are not even any of the ubiquitous piles of refuse that often collect in alleyways. There is only a small, tidy stack of crates and casks next to the gate. Just my luck to have chosen a well-ordered alley.

I hear my pursuer's feet slow, his heavy breath grow calmer. He takes his time; he knows he has me trapped.

'Well, well. Look at the fine gentleman,' drawls a familiar voice. The moon is not yet up, but as he emerges into the yard there is enough starlight to make out his face. It is Captain Spencer.

Chapter Twenty-Five

He swaggers as he crosses the yard. Fear shrivels my belly, but I resolve not to cower in front of this man. As he nears me, he casually pulls a long, wicked-looking knife from beneath his coat. He looks me scornfully up and down.

'Where's yours?' he asks mockingly. 'I saw you sitting there in the chophouse,' he continues. 'All superior and aloof, with your face in a book. It was the perfect opportunity to teach you a lesson, now that you don't have your champion here to protect you. Tell me; do you let him fuck you, Ned Buckley?'

I do not know whether he intends to insult me, anger me, or intimidate me, but he is not successful. If anything, the coarseness of this statement gives me courage. It is the kind of thing a bully says, not a gentleman.

'Do not malign him, Captain. He doesn't share your filthy appetites,' I say, surprised by the coldness of my voice. I may die here in this alley, but I won't be a victim. Not ever again.

'Oho. Brave words, Edmund. Or should I call you *Eleanor?*'

I am stunned, and it must show on my face, because he smiles meanly.

'Oh yes, I put it together when I read your husband's notice in the London papers. I thought that there was something puzzling about you, but I couldn't put my finger on it.' He lets go a sarcastic laugh. 'Literally. When I saw the advertisement, I knew. *When I grabbed your cock, I couldn't feel your balls.*

'I thought about how satisfying it would be to turn you in and send you home in disgrace. I wrote to Richard Buccleuch and told him what I knew.' His voice regains its cool, proper tone, as if he is having a polite conversation with me. 'I've already spent the five guineas, and I thought that would be satisfactory, along with knowing that you were miserable, back where you belonged. But this will be a far, far more *delicious* revenge.'

He is close enough now that I can smell the liquor on his breath; liquor overlying something that smells like decay. It is sickening. I try to move away from him and feel the wall at my back. Despite my '*brave words*', Spencer is larger, stronger, and *crazier* than I am.

'He doesn't really want you back, you know. He would be just as happy if you were dead, and the impediment to his future removed.'

He lays the blade of the knife against my cheek. 'Do not shout, or I will cut out your tongue.'

With his free hand, he undoes his breeches buttons. 'It matters not to me that you are actually a woman. I shall enjoy you both ways. Then I will cut your throat and throw you in the harbour for your dear commodore to find. Although maybe I will carve up your face first, so that you know what it feels like.'

He grabs my hair and strikes my head sharply against the stones of the wall behind me, and an explosion of light and pain drops me to my knees.

His large hand grabs my jaw. He puts his lips against my ear, whispers like a snake slithering through dry grass. 'You humiliated me. If you had only cooperated, when I asked nicely. I would have been a gentleman.' He raps my head against the wall a second time, and the pain makes my vision blur with tears. I go limp, hoping he won't beat me unconscious. If I lose consciousness, I'm dead.

His hand is working in his breeches, and I hear him groan. But instead of tearing at my clothing, he rears back. The groan has become a choking sound. He reaches for his throat with both hands, and the knife thumps in the dirt of the yard somewhere on my left. My brain tells me to find the knife, but my body will not move.

I think Spencer must be suffering an apoplexy, but as my streaming vision clears, I can just see the broad forearm wrapped around his throat.

I watch in horror as he struggles for what seems like an eternity, but which in reality is probably no more than a minute. His assailant draws him gradually back into the blackness of the alley. Finally his body goes slack.

The shadowy figure picks up Captain Spencer and throws him over one shoulder. Before he disappears back down the alley, I hear a quiet voice, accented with the soft cadence of the West Indies.

'Now he gon' to pay for my stripes. You nevah seen me.'

I stagger to my feet and am sick beside the tidy stack of crates.

I do not remember how I got back to the inn, but thankfully I manage to make it up the stairs to my room without encountering anyone else.

I wet a towel with water from the ewer at the washstand and press it to the throbbing knot on the back of my head.

The towel comes away bloody. Gritting my teeth, I clean the wound until the worst of the blood is gone, then fold one of my handkerchiefs over it. I have to tie it up with the new neckcloth that I bought for James Lenstock. It is a shame to ruin it, but I can buy another in the morning. I may be able to soak and press this one and make it serviceable again, but it is no longer suitable as a gift.

I have lost my hat, and the pamphlet of 'Prometheus'.

My mouth tastes foul, and I almost wish I had some brandy, but the idea of drinking it makes my stomach lurch.

I lie down on the bed and lay my head gingerly on the pillow, willing the room to stop moving. I don't know if it does; the darkness covers me and then I know nothing at all.

I wake later in the morning than I am accustomed to doing. I should still have enough time to go back to the shop before the ship's boat comes; I cannot stomach the thought of breakfast.

I unbind the handkerchief from my head and fold it and the neckcloth into the corner of my bag, and very carefully brush my hair and retie it with a ribbon. I cannot stand to do anything else to it. My head still aches with a vengeance, and the skin around the wound feels stretched tight as a drumhead.

The shopkeeper looks alarmed when I enter. 'Sir, are you quite alright?'

'I am well enough. I was set upon by thieves last night. I was not carrying my purse, but they took the neckcloth that I bought yesterday. I was hoping to buy another.'

He tuts, 'It can be dangerous in some parts of town, especially near the waterfront, after dark, sir. Men get deeply in drink, and then they do unspeakable things.'

You have no idea how unspeakable. 'Thank you; I am aware of it. I am employed by the Royal Navy, and I have seen first-hand what drink will do to a man,' I tell him, trying to put him off before he begins giving me unwanted advice. 'I was simply unlucky last night.'

He tries to sell me a new hat, but putting a hat on my head is something I simply cannot contemplate right now. I leave the shop with a replacement neckcloth for Mr Lenstock and make my way slowly down to the harbour. Moving too quickly makes me dizzy; I would not be able to run right now if I saw the boat leaving without me, but as it is, I am early.

Captain's crew members are beginning to congregate, a few of them looking decidedly the worse for wear. There is one man being supported by his shipmate who looks worse than I do. One of his eyes is swollen shut, and I am no expert, but I am fairly certain that his nose is broken. His right hand is bound up in a grubby rag. I wonder what prompted the fight to which these injuries attest.

I have never understood the need that some men feel to drink, gamble, and whore until they are sick, broke, and sore. Even my brother Arthur came home drunk occasionally, but if he ever visited prostitutes, he was too discreet to let on, and I am almost certain he did not gamble.

It is beginning to rain gently, and I find a seat under the eaves of the harbour master's office and close my eyes. This makes the sensation of vertigo worse, so I open them again just as there is a shout from the pier. There is something in the water.

A sailor grabs a boat hook and runs down the pier, where he joins three other men. One of them points to the pilings that support the pier, and the man with the boat hook fishes until he snags something. All of them reach down to haul it onto the pier.

It is a body. A body in a red coat.

The harbour master comes out of his office and walks down the pier, but I can tell by his unhurried pace that he is certain the man at the end of the pier is already dead. The sailor takes the body's shoulders, and another man takes its knees, and they carry it back to the harbour master's office. Someone has covered the corpse's face with a handkerchief.

A wave of emotions crashes over me, and the undertow threatens to pull me under. I am sick with apprehension, relief, horror, and remorse, and I have to keep a tight rein on myself to keep my entire body from shaking.

The sailor comes out of the harbour master's office and sits down beside me. I can see by the ribbon on his hat that he is from *Captain*. He shakes his head.

'Allus a bad business, when the sea spits 'em up again.'

I am not sure the sea ever swallowed this one. 'What happened, do you think?' My voice is thin.

'Reckon 'e went fer a piss an' fell in. 'Is britches was undone.'

I shut my eyes with a moan. When I open them again, the sailor is peering at me.

'Looks like you could use a lit'l 'air o' the dog, young sir,' he suggests.

'That is most decidedly *not* what I need,' I say emphatically.

He grins. 'Well, tha's good, 'cause I ain't got any t' give ye. But if ye was t' get a whiff o' that feller's breath over there, I 'magine it'd do ye jest as well.'

I follow his hand and see a man who is so drunk that he is barely conscious, being deposited on the ground by his mate. I can practically smell the liquor on him from here.

I realise that I will have to take the boat back with this man and my stomach heaves. I lean away from my companion and retch, but nothing comes up but a string of sour saliva.

The sailor pats my back awkwardly. 'I'll let ye alone, younker. The boat'll be 'ere soon.'

Mr Eshelby examines the wound on the back of my head. 'It does not need to be stitched,' he decides, 'but I imagine it still smarts quite a bit.'

'Yes, it does.'

He nods. 'Were you sick?'

I admit this, too. He has me describe the vertigo to him. He takes a cloth and moistens it with spirits of wine. 'This is going to sting,' he warns. He cleans the wound gently. He was right. It feels as if my hair is on fire. 'They cut your face as well?'

I was not aware of this. When he picks up a mirror and shows me a small slice on my cheekbone, I say, 'Yes, there was a knife involved. But I did not realise that it had cut me.'

'This will heal without leaving a mark, I should expect. The ladies will still be able to appreciate your beauty.' He rubs it gently with the spirits of wine and a new, thin line of blood appears. 'I will cover it with a plaster. That should be sufficient.

'I would like you to stay here for a while so that we can observe you,' he informs me. 'I suspect that you have suffered a bit of bruising to your brain, but it does not appear to be critical. However, I want to keep you here until tomorrow morning.'

Roberts regards me glumly. 'Yeh should never walk alone down by the docks at night, Mr Buckley,' he admonishes me. 'I wouldn' 'ave let me own son do that, an' 'e were a good sight larger'n you.'

I do not tell him that I was nowhere near the docks. 'I was an idiot,' I agree.

'I reckon yeh'll never do it again,' he says severely. 'I'd hate t' lose yeh, younker.' He guides me to a cot and gives me a clumsy hug before leaving to clean up the things that Mr Eshelby used to patch me up.

I rest my head on my uninjured right cheek and hide the tears that want to escape from beneath my eyelids.

Two days later I stand at the back of the church in Gibraltar, listening to the burial service for Raleigh Spencer, Captain of Marines. I try to pray, but instead find myself hoping only that God does not condemn me for hating a man at his own funeral service.

Tom Allen's face lights up when he opens my gift. 'This smells heavenly,' he exclaims. 'I can't wait to taste it. Thank you, Ned.'

'Happy Christmas, Tom. Don't smoke it all in one go.'

He snorts. 'I intend to make it last. I'll smoke my regular tobacco for three days before I will let myself have some of this. Self-discipline is good for a man.'

He has given me some fine silk velvet hair ribbons. One of them is my habitual black, but another is a deep, rich blue, and the third is the colour of evergreens.

'If you ever want to find a girl, Ned, you need to put yourself out there a bit more.'

'Who says I'm looking for a girl, Tom?' I retort.

'You should. You live like a monk, for godsake. Find someone to keep you warm at night besides that cat.'

Roberts turns the book over carefully in his hands and reverently opens the cover. I cannot read his face.

'I thought that we could read it together, but it is yours to keep,' I say quietly.

He looks up. His expression is bewildered. ''Tis a fine book, Mr Buckley. I've ne'er owned sech a thing b'fore. I 'ope I don' ruin it.'

He caresses the leather binding, blue with a tooled design on the cover. 'I 'ave nothin' for you, sir,' he continues softly.

'You have given me your friendship. That is a gift I value greatly.'

He impulsively reaches out and enfolds me in his large arms. When he lets me go, his eyes are wet.

'You're a treasure, lad. I'll enjoy learnin' t' read this wi' yeh. The first book in the Robertses' library! Yeh might jest make a gennelman out o' me!'

Chapter Twenty-Six

In January, the fleet sets out for the coast of Lisbon. Commodore Nelson has not returned from Elba.

The winter has been severe. We have lost four ships, two of them permanently. HMS *Zealous* was forced onto a reef during a howling gale, and poor *Courageux* was torn from her mooring and broken to pieces on the Barbary Coast, losing all but one-hundred and thirty of her crew. More recently, HMS *Bombay Castle* was wrecked in Tagus Bay, and three others— *Culloden, Gibraltar,* and *St George*— were grounded but eventually re-floated.

Captain Miller has taken over the lobby for his cabin. The great cabin stands silent and empty, waiting for the commodore to return.

Roberts has turned out to be a quick learner, with a sharp mind. Once he knows a word, he does not forget it. He takes pride in his progress and is enthusiastic about each new assignment. It makes him a rewarding pupil.

'Do any of your mates give you a hard time about studying?' I ask him.

'They might think about it, but they wouldn' dare. They knows 'at if they end up flat on their backs in th' sick berth, they'll be at me mercy,' he says humorously.

When we begin *The Castle of Otranto,* and I read the preface to him, he asks me pressing questions about the origins of the characters in the story, and if one might be able to find the castle somewhere near Naples. Naples seems to Roberts like the kind of exotic place where it might be. He seems disappointed when I say that I do not know.

He is sceptical when we discuss the author's claim of 'realism' in regard to the first part of the story. 'I en't never 'eard o' a man gettin' crushed by a giant 'elmet. Th' main truck, mebbe; but not a 'elmet. Does he 'spect me to b'lieve that some giant knight is sittin' on a cloud somewheres, chucking armour at people?' he asks indignantly.

He makes me smile. *Take that, Lord Walpole.*

Despite his zeal, the progress is sometimes slow going. I had forgotten, having read the book so long ago, that Horace Walpole's syntax can be rather high-handed. More than once Roberts has read a sentence perfectly but has had no idea what it means. 'I dunno any people as talks like that,' he tells me.

'I am not sure that I do either,' I assure him. 'I have never made the acquaintance of any earls.'

'This feller's an earl? God 'elp the gov'nment,' he says dryly.

Today, to take a break from things gothic, I have copied out Prince Hal's St Crispin's Day speech from *Henry V* for Roberts. 'It is written in metre,' I tell him, 'which is why the text breaks in the middle of the sentence. Just read it as you would prose, pausing only at the commas and stopping at the periods.' It is a challenging assignment, but given his tolerance for Walpole, Shakespeare should not be impossible.

He is to read the piece through on his own first, and when he is ready, he will read it aloud to me.

It is a fine winter afternoon, and we are on the fo'c's'le between the belfry and the galley flue. The sun is warm, and the breeze is mild. Even poor Jack Mackay would have appreciated a day like this. I gaze out over the sea and let my mind wander.

When I turn my eyes back to Roberts, he is looking at me soberly.

'Have you finished it?' I ask. He shakes his head. 'Then have you a question?'

'Why do yeh look so unhappy, lad?'

I am taken aback. 'Do I?'

He gives a slight nod of his head. 'I seen it before, when yeh was alone an' thought no'un was lookin'. Did yeh lose someone? A lover?'

I catch myself unconsciously stroking the finger of my hand where my wedding band once resided, until I sold the hateful thing. I stop it immediately. 'I have never had a lover, Roberts.'

'I en't one t' tell yeh what t' do, younker, but mebbe yeh should think about leavin' the sea and findin' a pretty young thing like yoursel' t' be 'appy wi'. 'Fore yeh gets old an' ugly like me.'

'I do not think that you are ugly,' I respond.

'Thankfully me Polly don't either,' he says, with the smile that reveals his two missing teeth. 'An' even if I does get uglier b'fore I makes it home, I'll be able t' read to 'er arfter supper. She'll like that,' he says with satisfaction.

It is the second week of February, and Jervis is cruising off Cape St Vincent, lying in wait for the Spaniards.

They are out there, he says.

There is a thick fog in the night, and the fleet sticks close together, signal guns booming hollowly throughout the dark hours. As the morning lightens and the fog begins to thin, the message passes through the fleet that there is an unknown ship on the horizon, and we wait anxiously to know her identity. Is this the harbinger of the battle that Jervis is waiting for?

The ship gets closer, and eventually the red broad pendant can be seen flying at the masthead. It is *La Minerve*. Commodore Nelson has returned.

The ship's company stands at attention as the commodore is piped aboard, and his broad pendant is run up the mast. Now *Captain* is ready for the fight. With her commodore returned, nothing can stand in her way.

Nelson is swept immediately into the preparations for battle, but before he closets himself with his officers, he calls to me, 'I expect to see you this evening, Mr Buckley!'

Tom Allen, James Lenstock, and I are kept busy enough that we do not have time to ask James about his time in Elba. It will wait.

Commodore Nelson greets me with one of his rare smiles when I arrive at the great cabin after supper. He really has quite a nice smile, and I wonder why he doesn't smile more often. He looks relaxed and happy.

'Mr Buckley—Ned—come and sit with me. I presume that it was you and Mr Allen who kept my cabin prepared for me?'

'Yessir. Not knowing when you would return, we looked after it daily.'

'Help me remove my coat, if you would.' He turns so that I can take the coat by the collar and ease it off his shoulders, then slip the sleeves down his arms. His banyan is folded over his desk chair; not his old woollen one, but a new one of deep green silk faille. He slides his arms into the sleeves and sighs contentedly.

'I do not think that we will encounter the Spanish fleet until tomorrow,' he informs me. 'They were some distance west of here last night.'

'How do you know that, sir?' I ask, as we each take one of the armchairs.

'Because we sailed through them.'

He is enjoying the look on my face. '*You sailed through them?*'

'We got pushed west off the coast by a levanter, and in the middle of the night last night, in heavy fog, we found ourselves in the midst of a strange fleet. The signals were not recognisable, and eventually we discerned that the voices were Spanish. Originally, I thought we might have come upon a convoy bound for the West Indies, or perhaps a detached squadron.

'We stayed very, very quiet, and in time we managed to extricate ourselves. It was not until I spoke to Jervis this morning that I realised that we had fallen in with their main battle fleet.

'They outnumber us by a good deal, but Captain Hardy, who spent time as their prisoner, tells me that their ships are grossly under-manned, and their seamanship is no match for ours.' His eyes glow in anticipation of the fight. 'Who can say what will happen tomorrow, Mr Buckley, but tonight we are together as old friends.' He gets up from his chair and goes to a mahogany cabinet, from which he removes two glasses and a bottle of claret.

'It is very good to see you again,' he says, as he pours us each a glass. 'Mr Lenstock has improved immensely as a steward, but I have an affection for you fostered by three shared years of fagging that he cannot replace.'

'What happened on Elba, sir?' I take the proffered glass.

He raises his glass. 'The King.'

'The King,' I respond, and we drink.

'That used to be a bumper toast with me,' he says, setting the glass down on the arm of his chair. 'Now I fear I am grown too old, and my digestion will not tolerate it.

'Elba,' he says, 'was not successful. De Burgh would not remove from Elba without orders from his masters, and none was forthcoming. Even when I showed him Jervis' orders, he still would not commit. Eventually I left him there with only his little army and Captain Fremantle in charge of a tiny squadron.'

Some of the contentment leaves his face. 'I pray that nothing happens to bring them to grief. I do not like to leave my friends unprotected.'

'I am sorry that it was not a success, sir. You were gone for so many weeks that we had begun to grow a little anxious about you.'

'It was not entirely disagreeable,' he amends. 'There were theatre performances, and dinners with the General and the Viceroy, and it was pleasant to be amongst friends for Christmas. They appreciate me there, unlike some.'

'I...,' I begin, but he cuts me off.

'I know that you appreciate me, and Jervis does, and Trevor and Drake; I am not without friends. But I fear that our war is ending, and I shall be back on the beach on half pay, possibly for the rest of my life,' he says bitterly. 'After four years of hard service I shall have nothing to show for it.' He takes a swallow of wine. 'Will you come and visit me and my dear wife, Ned, when we are back in England? I must look for a home of our own; we have been living in my father's rectory. Although I fear that I will not be able to afford much. A little cottage would suffice.'

My spirits fall at this speech. I sip my own wine, buying time. 'Of course, I would be honoured to visit you wherever you are, sir.' *Only, not in England. I am afraid to go back to England.*

'Oh,' he says suddenly, 'I meant to ask you...' He gets out of his chair again and goes to his desk, where he retrieves a plain paper package tied with string. 'Do you know what this is?'

'I do,' I tell him. 'I put it there. It is your Christmas present.'

He comes back to the armchair, holding the package. 'I am ashamed to say that I did not get a gift for you,' he says quietly.

'You have given me more than enough over the years, sir,' I say, equally subdued. I try to revive his earlier good spirits. 'And I was not expecting a valentine.'

'Damn me; yes. Tomorrow is St Valentine's Day. How the weeks have fled.' He unties the string and opens the paper. '*Bungay Castle,*' he reads on the flyleaf. 'Ah; Mrs Fremantle was talking about this.'

'*Mrs Fremantle?*'

'Captain Fremantle married Miss Wynne in Naples,' Nelson informs me.

'I wish them every happiness,' I say, still dumbfounded. I would never have believed that Captain Fremantle would marry at all.

He smiles ironically. 'I can see by your face that you know our Captain Fremantle. I quite forgot that you were on *Tartar* before I met you. He appears to be utterly devoted to her.'

'Well, may God bless them both,' I say, and I mean it.

He turns the books over in his hands.

'I do not know if you will like it, sir, but I thought it would be more relaxing than reading an analysis of an analysis of the success of England's financial system, or Mr Burke whining about his reputation and his pension. The shopkeeper recommended it; based on its title, I probably would not have picked it up.'

'Why is that?' he asks.

'You will find this fanciful, I am sure, but I thought it sounded like the name of a lumbering merchant vessel that keeps wandering away from its convoy and has to be constantly retrieved.'

He laughs. *God, it's good to hear him laugh.* 'I have known a few of those. I would not be at all surprised to recall that one of them was called *Bungay Castle*. But it is an actual place, in Suffolk. If you was to triangulate south from Norwich and Yarmouth, you would run into it.'

'Have you been there, then?'

'No, why would I? I just happen to know where it is.' He sets down the books. 'Thank you, Ned. I shall look forward to reading them together of an evening, for as long as we are still together.' He refills both our glasses.

'What have you been doing while I was away on Elba?'

'Apart from maintaining the books, nothing very much. I have been teaching Roberts to read.'

'Who is Roberts?' he questions, sipping the wine.

'He is the loblolly boy.'

Nelson looks bemused. 'Why are you teaching the loblolly boy to read?'

'Because he asked me to. He is extremely intelligent. I suspect that the only reason he never learnt to read is because he never had the opportunity.'

'Hah. What are you reading together?'

'*The Castle of Otranto* and *Henry V.*'

He blinks. 'What is wrong with "Oranges and Lemons", or "The grand old Duke of York, he had ten thousand men"?'

'What fifty-something-year-old man would want to read nursery rhymes?' I respond.

'He is fifty years old?'

'Well, I do not know, actually; I have never asked him. But he appears to be approximately the same age my father would have been, if my father were still alive.'

The commodore's mouth quirks. 'How long have you been teaching him?'

'Since September, I guess. We did not start out with Horace Walpole or Shakespeare. We started by teaching him to read his wife's letters. He can read quite well now, except he sometimes has difficulty comprehending Lord Walpole.'

'*I* have had difficulty comprehending Lord Walpole,' Nelson remarks dryly.

I do not understand this remark. 'Do you mean the book?'

'No, I mean the man himself. He is a relation on my mother's side. I am named for Horatio Walpole, the son of Baron Walpole of Wolterton, who was a sponsor at my baptism. He was a cousin to Horace, Lord Walpole, Earl of Orford, who wrote that book.'

It is my turn to goggle. 'Of course, there is no reason that I might have known that, but I had no idea that you had such patrons, sir.'

'Any interest that I had of the Walpoles, I suppose I used up long ago. Horace Walpole must be in his eighties by now,' he says dismissively. 'And of course, for most of his life he was not the Earl of Orford, only the youngest son of the former Prime Minister. But I am amused that you are using his book to teach reading. You are an exceptional lad, Mr Buckley.'

He frowns. 'But I think that you are thinner than you were when last I saw you, and you are too pale. Perhaps you spend too much time with books, between the account books and your tutoring.'

'I am well, sir. I simply have not had much appetite since December, and I suppose it shows.'

'What happened in December?' he asks. Suddenly he does not look as relaxed as before.

If I do not tell him, he will find out from Mr Eshelby. I should not have spoken so thoughtlessly.

'I was attacked in an alley in Gibraltar, sir.'

'Good God, Ned; were you badly hurt?!'

'Not badly. I suffered a wound to the back of my head and had vertigo for a day or two.'

'What were you doing in an alley? Surely you know that the waterfront is dangerous at night,' he admonishes me.

'I was not near the waterfront,' I reply defensively. I have heard this once too often. 'I was going back to my room from a chophouse where I had gone to supper. It is a respectable place, sir. They serve plain, homely English food.'

'I think I know it. But a man alone can be easy prey to footpads. You must be more careful.'

The wine is heating my brain. 'It was not footpads, Commodore. I was targeted. He followed me from the dining room, and when I realised it and ran, he chased me. I made a wrong turn. That is how I ended up in an alley.'

'Did you know this man? If he is a member of this crew, I will ensure that he is punished.'

'I knew him, sir.' The words are gall in my mouth. 'He has never been a member of *this* crew.' I take a gulp of wine to wash the bitterness away. 'It was Captain Spencer.'

Nelson looks aghast. 'Tell me what happened,' he says quietly.

I had had no intention of telling him this tonight, nor, perhaps, of ever telling him at all. But now his mouth is set, and his eyes are steely. He is adamant, and he will get it from me.

'I had not seen him in the dining room, sir. I had brought a pamphlet of poetry with me to read, and I was thinking about it when I left, so I was not immediately aware that he was following me. He had been drinking, and I had not drunk any more than a glass of ale, so I might have gotten away; but I misjudged the lane and turned too soon. It was not the street I had thought, and it ended in a blind yard.'

I pause, but Nelson doesn't speak. 'He had a knife, and I had nothing. Not a stick, not even a rock. He backed me up against the wall, telling me everything that he intended to do to me. I had not known that he hated me so much.

'He said that if I shouted, he would cut out my tongue. Then he told me that when he was done with me, he would cut my throat and throw me in the harbour, but that before he did, he intended to carve up my face *so I would know what it feels like*. He grabbed me by my hair and hit my head sharply against the stones of the wall.'

I stop and take another swallow of wine. My hand is shaking, but there is nothing I can do about it. Even if I cared to.

'The pain blinded me and made me fall to my knees, and he grabbed my jaw. He struck my head against the wall again, to subdue me so I could not fight, I suppose. I was afraid I would black out, and I was afraid that if I did, that would be the end of me.

'My vision was blurred with pain and tears, so I could not see what happened next. All of a sudden, he made a choking sound, and I heard the knife hit the ground somewhere nearby. I thought that he was ill, but when my vision began to clear, I could see only enough to tell that someone had his arm around Captain Spencer's throat and was throttling him. This person dragged Captain Spencer back down the alley in the dark and left me alone there. The following morning he was found in the harbour. I saw them pull his corpse out of the water.'

'What did you do after he was gone?' His voice is expressionless, his eyes appalled.

I expel air from my nose in a derisive puff. 'I vomited. And then, somehow, I found my way back to the inn. I did not see anyone, and if anyone saw me, they were too horrified to say anything.'

'Do you know who it was who came to your assistance in the alley?'

'There was no moon, and it was very dark. I could not see the person.' This is not exactly what he asked, but he lets it go.

Commodore Nelson pours himself another glass of wine and offers me the bottle, but I decline. My head already feels swimmy. 'No sir; thank you.'

'I should not have any more myself, but I shall anyway. I suppose I have already murdered sleep.' He takes a generous swallow, then puts down the glass. He rests his elbows on his knees, running both hands through his hair.

'I am so very sorry, Ned. I thought that I had dealt wisely with this man. I thought that I had protected you. I failed.'

'There is no way to know what drink and bitterness will do to a man, sir. For all I know, he was angry about other things, and I was simply a convenient object for all his rage.' *I know a thing or two about this already.*

'But it was you that he hurt.' His face betrays self-reproach.

'Do not let it trouble you, sir. Mr Eshelby examined me and pronounced me in no danger, and Roberts looked after me until I was fit to go back to work.'

'I suppose I must meet this Roberts and thank him for his attention to my friend.'

'He claims to have become somewhat attached to me.'

He frowns. 'I profess to being rather attached to you too, Mr Buckley,' he says tersely. 'Come here; let me see.'

I respond as ordered. Nelson stands and cups his hand gently against the back of my head. 'Was it here that he hurt you?'

It does not hurt any longer, but I will remember the sensation for the rest of my life. I close my eyes and nod.

I can feel the stirring of air on my face as he breathes. I open my eyes and they meet his, wounded eyes full of concern and compassion. His hand is still cradling my head and his mouth is very close to mine, and it occurs to me that he means to kiss me. And I want him to. I want it like I have never wanted anything before.

Suddenly he jerks away his hand as if bitten and backs away, stumbling over his desk chair and nearly falling. I step back reflexively in the other direction, my hands rising defensively before I can stop them.

'What am I doing?' he breathes, his eyes wide. I stand miserably, paralysed, as he shucks off his banyan and struggles with his coat.

'I am sorry—I do not—I did not mean—I must check with the watch. We… You should get some sleep. Who can say what we will encounter in the morning? We must be prepared. Good night, Mr Buckley; I will see you at the beginning of the morning watch.' He is out the door and gone, one arm still struggling with his sleeve.

I am numb. How could everything have gone so wrong, so quickly?

I pick up his elegant dressing gown from the floor and fold it carefully lengthwise before laying it on his armchair. I retrieve my hammock from the rails and sling it. James Lenstock is already snoring, and Tom Allen's hammock is slung, but he is not there. If he has finished his work, he is probably enjoying his pipe before bed.

I lie in my hammock for the remaining hours of the middle watch, staring at the deck beams above my head, One-Eyed Jack flexing his claws contentedly against my leg.

Chapter Twenty-Seven

All is dark and close at four AM. Fog has again gathered around us like a blanket, but it just as effectively cloaks the Spanish fleet, wherever they are. We can hear their signal guns, but sound carries weirdly through the fog, and it is difficult to discern their position.

Commodore Nelson peers out over the water through a night glass, speaking in low tones to Captain Miller and Mr Castang. The atmosphere on *Captain* is subdued, but the air is charged with electric current, and I can feel it building like the presage to a violent storm. At last report, the Spaniards were fifteen miles to windward.

Our fleet is tightly aligned into parallel divisions, sailing towards destiny, confident in our abilities. This is why we are here, after all. Some of us will die this day, but that does not bear thinking about.

As the sky brightens, the Spanish are visible ahead. The mist begins to clear, and we get a fragmented picture as they slip in and out of pockets of fog. If we can see them, then by now they are aware of us. According to our ships in the van, they are about eight miles to windward.

Gradually the entire picture takes shape. By the time they are fully visible, we have counted twenty-five ships of the line, with attendant cruisers. Some of them are… enormous.

Their flagship, *Santissima Trinidad,* is a monster of four decks and somewhere in the neighbourhood of one hundred and thirty guns. In addition, the Spaniards have six three-decked first-rates, each of them larger than our own flagship, *Victory,* carrying around one hundred and twelve guns apiece. They tower like mountains in the dispersing mist.

We have fifteen ships of the line.

I hear the echo of the old top man on *Agamemnon* in my mind. *Things are about to get very warm.*

I risk a glance at Commodore Nelson. He is studying the Spaniards intensely.

They are crossing before us on the opposite tack, and it is apparent that they are in disarray. They have broken into two groups, and the smaller group in the van, now to leeward of us, consists of only a few ships of the line and a handful of merchantmen. The rest of the fleet lags them by almost seven miles, and several of them are riding abreast of each other, making it impossible for them to fire their broadsides.

Nelson's expression does not change, but he nods infinitesimally and inclines his head to Captain Miller, murmuring something. Miller nods in agreement.

Ten minutes after we have taken the Spaniards' measure, as six bells strike, Admiral Jervis flies the signal to form a single line of battle ahead and behind *Victory.* We are going to intercept the main division of the Spanish fleet, where the towering first-rates loom.

The commodore addresses me for the first time. 'Stay close, Mr Buckley. I may need you.' He turns his attention back to the Spanish fleet.

He has not said what he thinks he may need me to do. Haul broken bodies down to the cockpit, perhaps.

I wish I had my rifle.

At eleven thirty, we run up our colours. It must have already been clear to the Spanish what our intention was; now there can be no doubt. We are prepared to attack.

Captain is in the rear of the line, undoubtedly not where Nelson would prefer to be, but there will obviously be plenty of Spaniards for everyone.

We sail directly for the break in the Spanish line.

This appears to throw them into further disorder. Their commander tries to order them to change tacks, but three of them apparently miss the signal and keep sailing to leeward, trailing the division of merchant vessels. This reduces the main fleet to seventeen capital ships. Suddenly the numbers do not seem so daunting.

Their remaining ships complete the turn, but they do so in unsightly clumps. They have yet to form a line of battle.

The commodore's lip twitches. He appears as cool as a spring morning as he paces a precise line forward and aft, but I can feel the energy sparking through him; he is the mainspring of a gunlock at full cock.

Culloden, captained by Commodore Nelson's friend Thomas Troubridge, is at the head of the van. When Jervis gives the signal to engage, *Culloden,* by that point directly in the gap between the two Spanish divisions, opens fire magnificently, unleashing both her broadsides. Her guns maul the windward division and open the door for the rest of the British fleet.

Captain engages at approximately noon, and as what passes for the Spanish line sails past at a distance of about four or five cables, her guns thunder for the next three quarters of an hour. The Spanish receive far more fire than they return, but *Captain* does not emerge unscathed. Still, the commodore is hot to go after them.

Victory is flying a signal for each ship to tack in succession as she reaches the front of the line, to go in pursuit of the windward division, and the first four ships in the van have already made the turn. But as the rest of the fleet waits to reach the front of the line, the distance between us and the Spaniards grows. Then the Spanish commander signals for his fleet to close with our rear.

Not all of his ships respond, but enough of them heed the signal. Nelson and Miller converse tersely, and now the commodore's agitation is apparent. 'Let it be on my head,' he says firmly.

Captain Miller nods in acknowledgment. He steps away from the commodore. 'Prepare to come about!' he orders.

As *Captain* wears out of line and stands for the Spanish fleet, I watch Commodore Nelson, the man who has been my captain, my protector, my teacher, my commander, and until last night, my friend.

His entire being is a study in fierce, grim determination. What he has just done may be the end of his career; and I know, as well as I know anything, that he examined that consideration and discarded it.

He has disregarded a direct order from the commander-in-chief, and he is leaving the line of battle without authorisation. If he lives to see the end of this battle, the navy may have his head. There will be no half-pay, no modest home of his own, no future commands. It is all or nothing.

After three years with him, I know his convictions, and they are unshakable. I have seen him disobey with impunity orders that he thought were wrong-headed, and I have seen him act without any orders at all. I am not sure impunity will protect him now. I pray that Providence will.

By engaging the rear of the Spanish division, Nelson has foiled any attempt by their commander to double the British line. Now he goes directly for the heart of the Spanish command. Blithely passing the surrounding ships, *Captain* heads straight for *Santissima Trinidad.*

It is not a question of David and Goliath. This is far more evocative of a mouse and an elephant.

Captain's guns seem to fire in all directions at once. In addition to the enormous Spanish flagship, she engages two other first-rates.

'Very warm', indeed. This cannot last.

We are not unsupported for long. Captain Troubridge's *Culloden* joins us astern. Now there are two British mice, and they are fierce. Between us, we manage to deflect the course of the Spanish away from the British rear.

Still, *Captain* is being broken to pieces, and *Culloden* is enduring almost equal damage. The rest of the British fleet has caught up and entered the fray, but there is no respite for the two ships that began the engagement.

I no longer know how long we have been caught in this hell. *Captain*'s rigging is gone. She cannot manoeuvre; she can only pound her enemies until her powder and shot runs out. And she is losing men at an alarming rate.

I have watched perhaps two dozen men fall; I have helped desperately wounded men down the companion ladder, and I have shut the eyes of a boy who died gazing sightlessly at the broken masthead. I hope that he saw angels there, and not the carnage that the rest of us see.

When the gun captain of the nearest larboard nine-pounder falls with a musket ball through his throat, I step into his place without asking leave of the commodore. If either or both of us survive this, we can reconcile then.

Initially, our rhythm is ragged, but it improves quickly. I have never before fired a gun so close to an opponent. Only twenty yards away, I can see the faces of the men on the Spanish ship; they look like demons from the outer darkness. I suppose that I must, too. I forget about distance, and demons, and men, and just serve the gun.

Sponge, load, ram. Unstop the touch hole. Prick the cartridge. Prime the pan. Bruise the priming. Secure the powder. Stop the touch hole. Run out your gun. Unstop the touch hole. Fire!

The loader fails to appear immediately with the next ball, and as I turn from the gun to look for him, I see something strike Commodore Nelson in the stomach, knocking him off his feet. Captain Miller catches the commodore in his arms and lowers him to the deck.

I do not make a conscious decision to leave my gun; I only know that if Nelson is wounded, I must go to him. But as I thrust the linstock at the nearest gunner, something rips into my shoulder and breast with the razor-sharp claws of a lion, knocking me to the deck. I lie there stunned, watching my own blood run across the boards past my eyes.

Hot, murky air, thick with the odour of metal. Someone moaning, and the guns are still thundering. How did I get here? My whole left side is in agony.

Someone picks me up and carries me a short distance and lays me on a hard surface. They are cutting away my coat. A hand lifts my left arm, and the entire world explodes in red light, followed by blackness.

A heavy paw strokes my hair, murmuring something I cannot understand. I think I know this person, but I cannot name him. I drift.

'Lass, wake up. C'mon, love.'

I try to force my eyes open. I see light, and a knee of the bulwark. My eyes close again. Something does not make sense.

'There now, tha's good. Try again.'

Roberts. I open my eyes once more and look into the kind face which looks gently back.

''Ello, me dear. I'm sorry t' wake yeh, but ye're goin' t' be goin' on a lit'le trip.'

'Are they... are they throwing me out, Roberts?'

'Nah. There's jest some'un who wants yeh somewheres else.' He is tucking a blanket tightly around me, his big hands as gentle as a mother's.

'I'm so sorry,' I whisper.

'What for, darlin'?'

'For deceiving you.' It is so hard to form the words. 'Forgive me.'

'Nothin' t' forgive. I 'spect yeh had your reasons. It don't change our friendship, yeh being a lass.'

He lifts my head and holds a cup to my lips. 'This journey is like t' be a lit'le uncomf'tble. Drink this down. It'll help.'

I obediently swallow the liquid in the cup.

'Come back and see me, lass. I'll be hurt if yeh don't.' Roberts and another sailor lower my cot and prepare to transport me... somewhere. Roberts is right; it is more than a little uncomfortable, but then whatever he gave me to drink begins to take effect and I drift away again.

'…opium. I don't know if she will be lucid.'

A familiar voice murmurs something indistinct.

'Are you quite certain you should be up, sir? Let me get a chair for you.'

I hear footsteps receding. A hand grasps mine; a thumb strokes my palm.

I open my eyes, and I am looking at deck beams again. 'Hello, Ned.'

I turn my face to the right and look into the tired eyes of Commodore Nelson.

He looks ill, but he is indisputably alive. 'Thank God,' I whisper. 'I saw you get struck on the quarterdeck, but before I could go to you…' My tongue feels heavy and uncooperative. 'I was so afraid… I thought you were dead.'

'Do not worry about me. I am injured, but it will heal,' he says quietly. 'I did not know that you had been wounded until this morning. I am afraid that I had lost track of you.

'I was unable to come to you, so I arranged to have you brought to me. We are on *Irresistible*. I hope that it was not an uncomfortable journey.'

'Slept through it,' I manage, with an attempt at a smile. 'Are you… will you…' I stop and try again. 'Are you still a commodore?'

'We will talk about all this in future, when we are both feeling better. But yes, I am still a commodore.' His tired face glows as if lit from within. 'I have finally won a great victory! My happy moment has arrived. I may be in pain, Ned, but I am in my glory.' He squeezes my hand gently. 'But I suppose your name is not really Ned, is it? Or were you called Edwina…?'

I shake my head. 'Nell. My family called me Nell, but my name is Eleanor.'

'Eleanor. Not… the woman whose husband wrote to me?'

I nod unhappily.

'I will be damned,' he says in amazement.

'I am sorry, sir. I did not like to deceive you. But it was… necessary.'

'Do not explain now. There is time.' He moves uncomfortably on his chair and pain flickers across his features.

I had not noticed until now that he is not completely dressed. His dressing gown is unbelted, and he is wearing his shirt loose over his breeches.

'Does Tom Allen know that you are walking around undressed like that?'

'Mr Allen was against my coming here, but I told him that I would make his life very difficult if he opposed me.' He smiles wryly. 'When I was struck—I think it was a piece of a block that hit me—it appears to have injured my bowels. My belly is too sore and swollen for me to dress properly, so he and everyone else will just have to accommodate me for a few days.'

I look down the length of my body. Someone has folded the blanket back to my waist, and I am wearing one of my own shirts, but the left sleeve is empty. I remember Captain Clark and my breath catches in my throat.

'Sir, did they—do I still have my left arm?'

'Yes; Mr Eshelby saved your arm, he thinks. Something sliced your shoulder all the way to the bone and dislocated the joint, and they removed multiple splinters from your arm and breast, I am told. But he believes he managed to get all the debris. As long as the wounds do not become infected, he thinks you will regain the full use of your arm. At the moment, it is bound to your body, to keep it stable.'

This seems like a lot of information to process. I want to keep him here, but it is becoming hard to stay awake.

'I will leave you now for a while,' he says gently. 'I told Mr Allen that if I was not back in half an hour, he was within his rights to come looking for me. And I have work to finish. Do you remember I once told you that I would get my accolades if I had to write them myself...?'

'Yes, I do; very well, sir.'

'Well, this time I am writing them myself,' he says, with the flicker of a grin. He stands stiffly and takes up my hand again, then leans carefully over my cot and kisses my forehead. 'Rest, Nell.' He frowns. 'May I call you Nell?'

Yes. Yes... say my name. I want to hear you say it again. I nod. 'Please,' I say.

'Rest, and I will see you again soon.' He limps haltingly away, and I close my eyes, trying to imprint the sensation of his lips in my memory.

Chapter Twenty-Eight

I am surprised the following morning to see George-Augustus Josephs come into the sick berth, a bandage wrapped rakishly over his left ear and around the circumference of his head.

'You're famous,' Joe tells me.

'Infamous, more likely,' I reply. Then the implication of his words hits me like a mallet. 'Don't let people talk about me, Joe. I can't allow someone to know where I am. Please, please tell them not to let it get out!'

'If that's what you want, we'll bury it in th' silence of th' grave. You've earned a lorta respect, Ned. Here, do you still want me ter call you Ned?'

'You might as well. It has been my name for the past four years, and it works just as well as the one I had before.'

'We never once'd thourght you might be a woman, Ned; we just thourght you was a parti'cl'arly spindly boy. You fooled all of us.'

'I didn't intend to fool anyone, Joe, I just had to get away from my life,' I say tiredly. I have to steer us away from this subject. 'Tell me about how the battle ended.'

'You sure you en't too tired? I don't want ter wear you out.'

'I have nothing to do but lie here. I think I can manage to listen.'

He parks himself on a three-legged stool. 'Well, it might have ended a whole lot diffr'ntly, I can tell you. *Captain*'s rigging was all shot away, and she hardly had a mast standing; all her shrouds and stays were gone, so I don't even know what was keeping what was left of her up there. And that damn Spaniard was still firing into us. I think I lost my entire mess, God rest 'em,' he says grimly.

'It looked like we were gonner have ter fall back or be taken. But the commodore weren't having none of it. He told Captain Miller ter run us in ter that Spaniard, and he called for boarders.

'He divided us up into two parties, and then when the captain had pooped her with what was left of our bowsprit, harf of us boarded the Spaniard from the bowsprit under command of Lieutenant Berry. Commodore Nelson led the rest of us on ter her quarter-galleries by jumping from our cathead.'

'Commodore Nelson led the boarding party?' I am astounded. The man I saw yesterday afternoon was in such pain that he could only walk with difficulty, but the day before he was jumping from catheads?

'That he did. We broke a wind'r in ter the great cabin, but the door ter the quarterdeck was locked. We had to bust through it, while they was firin' pistols at us from the other side of the door.

'Lieutenant Berry's boarding party had already taken the poop, and it was the work of only a few minutes t' get 'em ter yield once we had 'em caught between our two parties—but what a few minutes! You never seen anything like it. A Spanish sailor tried ter take off my head with a cutlass, but I dodged 'im. Cut off a good part of my ear, though.' He touches his bandage gingerly.

'The commodore took that whole ship as neat as you please, but he weren't done yet. Y'see, there was this big

Spanish first-rate, *San Josef,* fouled with her on the other side, and her marines were shooting down on us from her stern-gallery. We were all set ter return fire, but then the commodore did something even more outrageous. He called over ter *Captain* for more men, and when he had another boarding party assembled, he threw himself at *San Josef's* main chains like one of them capuchin monkeys I seen once in Naples. He hauled himself up on the deck of that first-rater, and the rest of us foll'rd. That one didn't put up much of a fight. We had hardly got aboard her when they told us they surrendered.

'So *San Josef* struck to the commodore, too. He took both those ships, both of 'em bigger than *Captain,* by using the *San Nicolas* ter board the *San Josef.* They're calling it "Nelson's Patent-Bridge for Boarding First-Rates"!

'I was ter have been part of the prize crew on *San Josef,* but then I had ter go and faint from losing too much blood. I'm not really sure how I got here, why they didn't just leave me on the Spaniard. Maybe they meant ter send me back ter *Captain,* but somebody got confused.' He grins. I don't think I've ever seen Joe grin before. 'It's a story fer the ages, in't it?'

'If I did not know that you are a terrible story-teller, Joe, I would think you had made the whole thing up.'

He smiles even larger and begins to rub his ear, then jerks his hand away.

'Blast it, I keep doing that. My mother's gonner have hysterics when she finds out I've gone and lost part of my ear. Surgeon told me just grow my hair longer and no one will know. Maybe I ourght ter get the other one cut down ter match it. My wife always said my ears was too big.'

'You have a wife, Joe?'

'Wife and little daughrter. They live with my parents, God help 'em. My wife and daughrter, that is, not my parents.'

'You never said,' I admonish him.

'What's ter say? I've never even seen the baby, she was born arfter I left for the war.'

He goes, and I fall asleep with fantastic images of Commodore Nelson, leaping across chasms of ocean from a precarious perch on the cathead, playing in my head.

I receive a letter from Roberts, written painstakingly with a pen and ink on good paper.

> *Dearest Lass,*
>
> *This is the first letter that I has ever wrote. I hope that I has done well. I tried to remmember ever thing you ~~teach taw~~ t a u g h t me.*
>
> *I am right proud of you. I feel like I has lost a son. but I hope that I has gained a d a u g h ter.*
> *Your humble Sirvnt,*
> *John Roberts*

It is a masterful letter. It is a shame that I have stained it in two spots with tears.

I hope to see Commodore Nelson again, but my next visitor is Captain Miller.

'I could scarce believe it when Mr Eshelby told me,' he says. 'I saw you work that leeward gun like you had been drilling with them all along.' He looks regretful. 'You have done a very fine job, but I'm afraid I have had to appoint someone else to the position of clerk. I am sorry.'

'I understand, Captain. I shall not be with the navy much longer.'

He does not contradict me, but I do not expect him to. For officers to tolerate a member of the ship's company who is not acknowledged to be a woman is one thing, but an *acknowledged* woman cannot serve on one of His Majesty's ships. Nor in His Majesty's army. My military career is over.

'I came to see Commodore Nelson, but I wanted to stop and see you, too, in part to thank you for your rather remarkable service.'

I do not think that my service is more remarkable for having been performed by a woman, but rather because they did not know that I *was* a woman for so long. 'How is he?' I ask, my thoughts on Commodore Nelson.

'He has been rather ill, but he is mending. When he was struck, I was afraid for a moment that we had lost him. Whatever hit him left a huge bruise on my thigh, and it didn't even touch me. But he recovered himself and went right on.' The captain seems slightly awed as he recounts this.

'One of my former messmates told me about the commodore leading the boarding parties.'

'He told me he wanted to lead one of them, and I acquiesced. I had no idea the athletics he was prepared to perform in the process. He is the toast of the entire fleet.'

'He will keep his rank, then,' I say, relieved.

'More than that. There is talk that he will be made an admiral.'

'That is good, since he deports himself like one already,' I say. I am utterly delighted for him, but my reserves of strength are running out.

Captain Miller laughs. 'You spoke it, but I think that the rest of us have thought it. He deserves it.' He picks up a deep, lidded rush basket from the floor and says, 'Before I leave; I have brought you something that you left behind on *Captain*.'

I cannot think of anything that I might have left on *Captain*. I know that someone brought my trunk, but I have not opened it to see if everything is inside. I can scarcely sit up without everything tilting.

Captain Miller lifts the lid from the basket and looks inside, then removes the lid entirely and tips the basket so that I can see what it contains.

One-Eyed Jack blinks at me reproachfully, then jumps from Captain Miller's custody into my cot. He pats my bandaged arm twice with his paw, then settles on my belly, his one eye fixed pointedly on my face.

'He was roaming the quarterdeck at night, crying to be let into the lobby, looking for you. I suppose it was the only part of the ship he could not gain access to. I had to bring him; it was self-preservation as much as anything. I also was afraid that one of the other men might throw him over the side.'

'I am sorry if he disturbed your sleep. I have heard him cry, and it can be blood-curdling.'

On my stomach, One-Eyed Jack purrs as if he is completely incapable of such wickedness.

My left side throbs, from my fingers to my shoulder to my head, and back down again to my toes. My arm and shoulder and breast feel hot and tight, as if the sun is burning my skin. I am so terribly tired.

The cat butts my free hand with his head, demanding to be petted, but I cannot find the energy to lift my hand.

Someone gives me opium, and I go spiralling down into blessed darkness.

———————————

I am in the foretop with Jack Mackay. 'No one gets seasick up here,' he tells me with a beautiful smile.

Below, the sea sparkles like the royal court; brilliant spangles on turquoise water. I look behind me for the quarterdeck, but I cannot see it through the main course. Is Commodore Nelson there?

'Don't look back, Nell,' Jack says. 'Look for what lies ahead.'

He takes my hand.

Chapter Twenty-Nine

Why does it hurt again…?

Gauzy, tattered threads of a dream disperse like mist on a late summer morning. I try to hold on to them—*Jack, do not go…!* But it is no use; I am back in the sick berth, and my shoulder pulses with pain to the rhythm of my heartbeat.

When I make the decision to open my eyes, the first thing I see is the loblolly boy sitting at a table, rolling bandages. I cannot remember his name, if I have ever known it. This loblolly boy is actually a boy; probably not more than fifteen or sixteen.

I want to get his attention, but my muddled head cannot think how to do it.

One-Eyed Jack has no pretensions to politeness. He stands up from the foot of my cot and stretches, then launches himself to the floor with a yowl.

The boy looks up. 'Welcome back, miss,' he says.

'Did I go somewhere?' I croak.

'Well, as to that, I dunno,' he says. 'But you weren't here, exactly.' He offers me water. It feels like silk on my throat.

I look down at myself and realise with a jolt that I am naked under the sheet. 'What happened to my clothes?'

'Surgeon said to take 'em off you. Your fever went so high that we thought we was losing you. He were trying to cool you down.' He looks at me with an awestruck expression. 'The commodore even come and sat with you for part of the night, holding your hand.'

Did I have clothes on at that point? I cannot give voice to this thought.

'He like to have stayed the whole night, but your cat come in, and it made him sneeze. He asked us to move it to somewheres else, but it wouldn't let us catch it. Sat there giving the commodore the evil eye. He tried to stay longer, but every time he sneezed his injury hurt him something fierce.'

'I suppose I should consider myself honoured; being fought over by a cat and a commodore.' *Damn your eyes— erm—eye, One-Eyed Jack. You won again.*

'You're the first one ever, s'far as I know,' he says.

The wife of one of the marines brings me a shift and helps me dress. She is very young, and pregnant. Her body is all soft arcs; as opposed to mine, which is nothing but sharp angles.

'Did you undress me, too?'

'Yes, miss; I and one of the officers' wives.'

I am relieved. Undoubtedly Roberts and the surgeons saw me unclothed, but the idea of that does not bother me as much. Roberts is not sixteen.

'When is your baby due?' I ask, trying to be polite, despite the aching of my arm.

'In about two months, the surgeon tells me. Our first.' She smooths her gown over the curve of her belly. 'I'm a little worried about giving birth at sea, but my husband says not to worry; he's known of plenty of babies born at sea.'

'I am sure they will take good care of you. Thank you for the loan of your shift. I'm sorry; I should have asked you... what is your name?'

'I'm Abby. I can't wear this shift anymore; I've gained too much weight. You may keep it. Do you have children, miss?'

'No.' It is the easiest answer.

She hesitates. 'May I ask you, miss, what it was like to be thought a man…?'

'It was… complicated.' I am too tired to try to explain. 'If you will come back and talk to me again, I shall try to tell you about what it was like to be a man; I am too sleepy right now,' I say apologetically. 'It has been a long time since I have had a conversation with a woman,' I add. 'I would like it if you would come again.'

She shyly agrees.

I watch as the surgeon's mate examines my wounds. This is the first time that I have paid any attention to what he is doing, so it is my first time seeing the ruins of my left arm and breast.

The wound in my shoulder is just below the joint. It starts on the front face of my arm and wraps around towards my back; I cannot see where it ends. It looks as if someone has cut off my arm and stitched it back on again.

There are also a number of smaller wounds in the flesh of my arm and below my collarbone. They are not as long, but they are no less ugly.

'Those are where the surgeon removed splinters,' the mate tells me. 'He had to open the wound farther with a scalpel to make sure he got all the fragments out. Puncture wounds are dangerous. But as long as they don't become infected, you should be alright.'

'How would I know if they become infected?' I ask quietly.

'You would know; believe me.'

My left breast has a suture almost an inch and a half long, just above the areola.

'I do not know if you will be able to nurse a child, should you have children. Deep scar tissue like this does not stretch easily.'

I do not say that this is no longer a concern. My breasts are so flat now as to be practically non-existent.

The loblolly boy, whose name, I have learned, is Nate, informs me that the commodore has requested to see me in his cabin. 'Surgeon says you may go, miss, if you'll let me walk you down there.'

I look at myself. I am wearing nothing other than Abby's shift. 'I cannot go to the commodore's cabin like this.' I am suddenly mortified at the idea of walking the length of the gun deck, in view of the entire crew.

'He thought of that, miss, and he sent this for you to wear.'

It is his old banyan, the rich colour of old port. Nate helps me put it on. It is a couple of inches too long for me, but it encircles me like woollen armour, making me feel inexplicably safe. I breathe in the scent of him. I did not realise that Nelson had a particular scent, but it is indisputably his: a hint of lavender and something vaguely citrus-y… bergamot, perhaps.

Nate brushes out my hair and ties it with one of Tom Allen's velvet ribbons. 'There; you look right pretty, miss.'

I doubt it. But he is trying to be kind.

We walk slowly down the gun deck to the stern. I am terribly self-conscious, but no one pays us any mind. It is a relief.

At the door to the great cabin the sentry tells me that I am expected, but I tap hesitantly on the door nonetheless. Ned would have gone right in, but Nell can no more walk into a gentleman's room unannounced than she can fly.

'Come,' his voice commands.

Nate has already abandoned me, so I have nowhere to go but in.

I feel apprehensive. I have not been alone with him since the disastrous night before the battle. What can we say to each other now?

He looks up when I enter. He is seated in a low chair, a book open on his lap, in his dressing gown and carpet slippers. His shirt is still worn loose, but he seems far more properly dressed than I. I do not even have slippers; my feet are as bare as a street urchin's.

'Come; sit down, Nell. Thank you from coming to see me.' He motions to an identical chair, positioned so that two people can have a comfortable conversation. 'I apologise for not rising. Getting in and out of my chair is still most uncomfortable, so I am trying to limit the number of times that I do it.'

I position myself carefully in the other chair. 'Thank you for lending me your banyan, sir. My own clothes… I do not even know how to put them on using only one arm.'

'You may use it for as long as you like. I shall arrange to get you proper ladies' rig. I do not trust myself to know what to buy, but I know someone who will.'

He closes the book and searches my face, looking for… what? Some trace of the person he thought he knew?

'I am so relieved to see you,' he says. 'They informed me that you were very ill, and I tried to stay with you for a time, but your cat does not appear to like me.'

'I do not believe he actually likes anyone, sir. Except for me, for some reason. Thank you for… for coming to see me. I am very sorry that he made you sneeze.'

He makes a wry face. 'I have endured worse. But I could not stay, and it made me dreadfully anxious for you. I am sorry that I had to ask you to come here, but under the circumstances, I could not go there.'

'It is alright, sir. I do not mind.' *How could I tell him that I would go to the moon for him?*

'Nell, I…' he hesitates. 'I don't know how to address you. You said that I might call you Nell, but I am not sure…'

'If "Nell" is too familiar, you may call me Miss Anson. It was my name before I married; I may reclaim it for my use. But… I would be pleased if you would call me Nell.'

'Anson. So Arthur Anson is…?'

'My brother.'

'And that portrait miniature; it was not your sister. It was you, wasn't it?'

I nod reluctantly. 'Arthur had it commissioned as a wedding gift for my husband when Richard and I married. Richard did not deserve to keep it. It meant nothing to him. I had always intended to send it back to Arthur one day, so that he would know that I was still alive, but only when I was sure that Richard was no longer looking for me.

'But Richard placed an advertisement in the London papers, offering a reward for information that would lead to my being returned to him. I saw it in the newspapers that your father sent to you. The only reason I could think that he would do so was because he wanted to remarry, but he would have to prove that I was dead first. I could not allow him to do to another woman the things that he had done to me. So I sent the miniature to Arthur.'

I watch the sunlight reflected off the waves dancing on the forward bulkhead. 'But Captain Spencer saw the advertisement, too. And he made the connexion. Because, he told me, "when he'd grabbed my cock, he couldn't feel my balls".' I should blush at using such language with the commodore, but it no longer seems to matter. 'He wrote to Richard and told him where to find me.

'Captain Spencer told me this on the night that he assaulted me in Gibraltar. I expect that soon you will get another letter from Richard, demanding that you turn me over to him. But I will no longer be here by then, and you do not have to know where I have gone.'

He is shaking his head. 'No. I failed to protect you from Spencer, but I can help you disappear where your husband will not find you, if that is what you want. But what did he do to you? Why did he mistreat you so badly that you felt you had to run away from him?'

'I suppose he was angry at me, sir. He was disappointed and angry, and he blamed me because he could not have what he wanted. So he punished me for it.

'He never struck me, sir; that was not his way. He used his sex, and his scorn. He forced me to do things that I hated, and I grew to hate him as a result.'

'What was it that he wanted so badly that he thought you prevented him from having?' he asks quietly.

'A child. I never gave him an heir. He considered that he had certainly done *his* part, so the fault must lie with me.'

He is silent for a long moment, then he says carefully, 'I have known men who have used other people as targets for their resentment.' He pauses, and I can see his mind working, remembering what I told him after Captain Spencer's assault aboard *Agamemnon*.

'Sadly, we are both aware that there are men who indulge in unnatural sexual appetites. I am sure that if these things were the case with your husband, it was very disagreeable for you, but…' His voice betrays discomfort with this topic. '…are you certain that it was deliberate cruelty?'

Something inside me gives way, like a broken dike. Anger flows from the breach, the way it did so long ago when my mother died. 'I know exactly when it became deliberate cruelty,' I say. My voice is low and as sharp as a blade. 'It was when it progressed from being "very disagreeable" to rape and buggery. It was when he offered me to his two best friends. "Why pay a prostitute when I have a girl right here that you can use for free? You don't have to worry, you can't get any bastards on her; oh, and she's clean, too".'

My voice is filled with loathing; for them, and for myself. 'I don't understand why he gave me to them, if it was not to punish me; nor why they accepted, since they had nothing but contempt for me. Tell me; *is it incredibly erotic to swive your best friend's wife?*'

He does not speak, nor move. Silence descends like a cloud bank, smothering everything, drawing all the air from the room.

I cannot look at him. He is appalled. I have certainly crossed a line with this abhorrent question. I have implied that he understands why a man would do such a thing, and in the most offensive language possible. I have all but called him a blackguard like my husband. I set my jaw, fix my eyes on the floor, and wait for him to tell me to get out.

He gets up from his chair, slowly and painfully. But rather than going to the door to ask the sentry to escort me back to the sick berth, he goes down stiffly on one knee in front of my chair. He reaches out carefully, like a man reaching for the bridle of a spooked horse, and gently lifts my chin with two fingers.

'Look at me,' he commands. His eyes search mine out and hold them. *'It is not your fault.'*

Tears well in my eyes and spill over. He gathers me to him and draws my head against his breast, and he holds me there, not speaking. I can hear his heart beating in his breast, like the comforting tick of my father's watch.

'I am so sorry,' I say after a moment. 'I have stained your beautiful silk.'

'Silk be damned,' he says. 'Mr Allen can take care of the silk.' He speaks quietly, and I can feel his words whisper in my hair. 'I thought Ned Buckley was an exceptionally fine lad, but Nell Anson is an even more remarkable woman. How can I tell you how deeply sorry I am, that you have been so grievously treated—repeatedly—by evil men? But listen to me,' he says gently. 'You are a strong, spirited, and brave woman. You are not a victim. Your husband may not have valued you, but to another man you will be a pearl of great price. You are correct; he did not deserve you.'

He releases me and braces himself on the arm of my chair. 'I need to sit again,' he murmurs apologetically. 'My belly is becoming exceedingly painful.' He levers himself carefully upright and moves stiffly to his berth, where he retrieves a pillow and rests it against the back of his chair. He sinks against the pillow with a soft groan.

'I know that you are aware that my wife and I have no children of our own,' he says softly. 'I have always suspected that the problem lies with me, since Josiah is her son by her first husband.' He is silent for a moment. 'You may yet be able to have a child with a someone else, one who will love and honour you the way you deserve to be loved and honoured,' he offers.

Meant to be encouraging; his words fill me with despair. *Will I ever find another man for whom I could be a wife?* 'You are very kind, sir, and your words mean more to me than I can possibly tell you.' My voice hardly rises above a whisper, as if it doesn't want to be overheard. 'But I will never be a prize. I am barren. I know this because I have conceived; four times. But I cannot anymore.'

His eyes are sorrowful. I have seen sadness in them far more often than I have seen them merry. I wonder why that is.

'What happened to your children?' he asks gently.

'Our first was stillborn. He might have lived, if…' I shake my head. *There is no point in finishing this thought. It will change nothing.* 'The other three were born far too early. Miscarriages, each one earlier than the last. After the final one, my monthly courses stopped completely. My womb can no longer sustain life.'

This recitation no longer pains me. After the anger and despair, the only thing left is resignation. I look at my hand, lying motionless in my lap: a flightless bird. Like my babies, who never grew up to take wing.

'Nell.'

I look up.

'Despite what your husband taught you to believe, a man does not require a child to love his wife.'

I study his face; so kind, and so dear to me. 'She must miss you terribly,' I comment.

I think he actually blushes. 'I do not know when we will see one another again, but patience is one of her great virtues.' He winces and presses a hand against his belly.

'Are you in great discomfort, sir?'

'It has been worse. The day after I spoke to you in the sick berth, I was so ill I could not get out of bed. But the swelling has been easing a bit every day, and I expect that in a few days' time I will even be able to wear a waistcoat again, with all that that entails.' He offers me a crooked smile. 'I had no idea how many things one uses one's stomach muscles to do.'

'How many things…?'

'All of them.' He runs a hand through his hair. 'You are very stoic. I am sure you must have pain, but you do not show it.'

'Actually, I am counting the minutes until the beginning of the first watch, when I shall be allowed to have opium again,' I confess.

'Ah, I wish that I could help,' he says with feeling. 'I know what it is like.' He picks up a bell, which I had not noticed lying on the low table between us, and gives it a shake.

'It makes me feel a bit like a gouty old magistrate when I do that,' he comments, as James Lenstock opens the cabin door.

'Yessir, commodore?'

'Tea please, Mr Lenstock. And make sure you steep it sufficiently. You are slipping back into your old habits.'

'Yessir. Hello, Ne… erm, Mist… Miss…?'

'You can still call me Ned, James. For Edwina,' I tell him.

'Do you not want people to know your proper name?' Nelson asks me after James Lenstock leaves.

'Nosir, I don't think that I do. Although I told you my name, I do not want to leave any sort of trail for Richard to follow. So I think I will continue to be Ned to everyone else until I leave the Royal Navy.'

'May I ask you something?'

I nod.

'Why did you choose the army?' he asks. 'After what you had suffered at the hands of men, why hide yourself amongst them?'

'I thought no one would think to look for me there. It seemed an obvious solution; they needed soldiers for the war, and I already knew how to shoot. It was simply a matter of learning the drill. Initially, it was nothing more a way to sustain myself until someone shot and killed me. I did not expect to survive so long.'

I look at myself, clad in a woman's shift and a man's banyan. 'I am hardly a woman any longer, but I cannot be a man. What does that make me, I wonder?'

'I do not understand.' He rests his elbows on the arms of his chair and leans forward. 'Even if you can no longer bear children…'

I close my eyes. My arm is throbbing. 'I have no womanly graces left,' I explain. 'I have seen things no woman is supposed to see. I have lived intimately amongst men for four years. I have watched them make water in front of me and listened to them pleasure themselves at night. I have shot at them, and I have undoubtedly killed some of them. I have watched men die. I have held the corpse of my best friend in my arms. How can I go back to the drawing room and the dining table, and be a gracious hostess and a dutiful wife? I would be a lie, a counterfeit. What man could tolerate that?'

We are both silent as James Lenstock brings in a tray of tea and sets it on the table. I watch him pour the commodore's tea and add the correct amount of milk, then pour a second cup for me. 'May I bring you anything else, sir?'

Nelson shakes his head. 'Thank you, Mr Lenstock, that will be all.'

The commodore rises with a grimace and retrieves a bottle of brandy from his trunk, and moving stiffly, pours a measure into each of our teacups. He places the brandy on the table before lowering himself carefully back into his chair.

'Drink,' he orders mildly.

I must twist myself in my chair to reach for my cup with my right hand, and my left side protests more stridently. He watches me clench my jaw and says, 'Stop, Nell.'

He puts down his own cup and gets up again, picking up my tea from the table and handing it to me.

'I was thoughtless,' he says, as I balance the saucer on my knee. 'I am sorry.

'The two of us must look fit for nothing more than a pair of beds at Greenwich Hospital,' he remarks, settling himself back into his chair with his own expression of pain. He takes a swallow of his tea and fixes me with his gaze.

'Do you remember the day we met, when I told you what I intended you to do for me? You looked at me in utter disbelief. I could tell that you thought me completely mad. What I told you that day still holds true, my dear. *Confidence works wonders.*'

Chapter Thirty

The silence this time is comfortable, as we sip the brandy-laced tea. The warmth of it somehow soothes the fire in my arm and shoulder a bit.

'Might I ask you to do something for me?' he asks after a few minutes.

'Of course.'

'Would you get that other pillow from my cot?'

I turn carefully to set my tea on the table and rise cautiously. I have far less difficulty moving than he does, but the pulsing pain makes me feel light-headed.

I collect the pillow and bring it to him. 'Where would you like it, sir?'

'On the floor, by my foot. It is for you to sit on,' he explains. 'If you will indulge me.'

I have some doubts, but I arrange myself carefully on the pillow. The low armchair puts my shoulder higher than his knee, and it makes me aware of how difficult it must be for him to get in and out of this chair. But this is not his cabin, and these are the chairs that are here.

'Now, if you will just rest yourself against my knee, like that…' He lays his hand on the crown of my head. 'I want you to concentrate on my hand. Pay attention to its weight, its temperature, and the feel of it on your hair.'

He begins to stroke my hair, slowly and very lightly. He must feel me tense, because he tells me, 'Do not worry; I promise I shall not do anything to threaten you. Relax and just focus on the sensation of my hand.'

I try to do as he directs. It is soothing. My father used to stroke my hair like this when I was a child; it has been many years since someone has touched me in this way. It reminds me once again that Richard was never inclined to tenderness.

His voice is quiet. 'I learnt this in the West Indies. "Counter-irritation," the doctors called it. The woman who nursed me did not hold with the "irritation" part. "You have more than enough irritation to be getting on with," she told me. "Focus on something pleasant, and it will be much more effective".'

'You have spoken of this woman in Jamaica before. You implied that she saved your life.'

'I fully believe it. When I was brought back to Port Royal, I was beyond anything that the naval hospital could do for me. My commander had me lodged with Cuba Cornwallis. She brought me through the worst of it. I don't imagine that I do this as well as she could, but I doubt anyone else can. She could put me to sleep when my head was splitting and my stomach was griping, just by rubbing my back.'

'What happened that made you so ill, sir?'

'I can only guess. We were sent on an expedition up the San Juan river in Nicaragua, to take possession of a fort there and open a passage to the Pacific Ocean. We made it as far as the fort and we took it successfully, but then I received an order from the admiral recalling me to Port Royal. The captain of a larger frigate had died, and I was to take over his command.

'I was already unwell by then. I was never well in port in the Indies, the intermittent fever troubled me; and this had begun with the agues and fever again, but it progressed into something much worse. One of our native guides had me convinced that I had poisoned myself by drinking water contaminated by the fruit from a manchineel tree. It may have been an ordinary flux, or the Yellow Jack. Or possibly all of these combined. But by the time I reached Jamaica again, I was more dead than alive.'

His hand continues its slow, hypnotic rhythm. 'My orders had been only to ensure the arrival of the army and their materiel and wait off the coast for their return. But the idea of sitting on my ship for weeks on end, waiting… I turned my command over to my first lieutenant and pitched in with the army commanders.

'It is perhaps just as well that I did. The fever came to the ships, too; and men were dying there on the coast just as quickly as they died in the jungle. I have always believed that if I had stayed with my ship, I would have been one of them.'

The pulsing pain in my shoulder seems to have calmed a little. I feel peaceful for the first time in… months. 'What happened to the expedition?' I ask quietly.

'It failed. I was much too ill to follow its progress; but it never made it to Lake Nicaragua.

'I had days when it seemed that I would be able to return to work, but then I would sink back into the fever again. I never got well enough to take effective command of the *Janus*, and eventually I had to return to England. The doctors had determined that I would never recover in the West Indies.'

I remember something that Frank Lepee had told me about Nelson's time in the West Indies. 'How old were you at this time, sir?'

'Let me think. I was made post in 1779, and *Hinchenbroke* was my first command as a post-captain. So I would have been twenty-one.'

His hand has stopped moving, and rests lightly on my head like a benediction. 'So young,' I murmur, 'and already reinterpreting orders.'

He exhales with an ironic huff. 'I learnt early; it has served me well enough, I suppose.'

'This time, at least,' I concur.

'Since you have asked a familiar question, may I ask one next?'

'I believe I owe it to you,' I assent.

'When I met you, you told me you were twenty. I had no reason to doubt you, but unless you were married at sixteen…'

'I am sorry to have deceived you. I am thirty-three. But I hope you can understand…'

'I understand. You do not have to defend it.' He brushes away a lock of hair from my face that has come loose from its ribbon. 'I suppose that I should tell you why I asked you to come here,' he says heavily. 'Apart from wanting to see for myself that you were recovering.'

The tone of his voice indicates that the intimate part of this interview is over. There is business we must discuss. Presumably, it concerns what to do with me. I pick myself up from the pillow and offer it to him, but he shakes his head, and I return it to his cot before taking my chair again.

'In a few days' time, the fleet will leave Lagos Bay. I plan to return to *Captain* at that point. Do you wish to come with me, or would you prefer to stay here?'

'If you do not mind, sir, I would like to go with you.'

'I do not mind. Wherever you are, I need to arrange a berth for you. But the greater issue is where you will go when you leave the fleet. Have you thought what you will do when you are "on the beach"? I now understand that you cannot go back to England, and you cannot stay in the Royal Navy. Would you consider the refuge of a convent?'

I shake my head unequivocally. 'I could not live in a convent, sir; I am sorry. I would go mad with the solitude. And I would not be able to live with myself, knowing myself to be a hypocrite. When I attended Captain Spencer's burial service in Gibraltar, I could not pray for him. I was ashamed: that I was glad he was dead, and that I wished that Richard was being buried with him.'

He looks at me strangely; I cannot interpret it. 'God does not blame the victim, Nell,' he says gently. He shakes his head. 'I did not think it was suitable, but I had to ask.

'I considered applying for a pension for you, but even if it was successful—and there is no guarantee—it would take far too long. And I am afraid that it would make the kind of attention that you are trying to avoid inevitable.'

'I had not let myself think about what I would do if I survived the war, but I was not expecting to live out the rest of my life on half-pay, sir.'

'Nor do I think that you should hire yourself out as a mercenary,' he says, half-humorously. 'But you have other skills which can serve you well. I have seen your talent with a needle, and your record-keeping is impeccable. You have also been an excellent body-servant, although I would rather see you employ one than be one yourself... but nevertheless.' He stops short for a minute, a distant look in his eyes. 'That day you shaved me... had I but known...'

I blush. 'I could not stand to see you cut yourself, sir; but then I spent the next fifteen minutes terrified that I would cut you instead.'

'Here is my proposal,' he says slowly. 'I will help you find a situation ashore. I am uncomfortable with the idea of trying to establish you in Lisbon or Naples, and Cadiz is now out of the question... the future is too uncertain, and I do not need another friend in harm's way. I hope, however, that you will be safe in Gibraltar. It is British soil, and defensible.

'I am going to keep Ned Buckley on the books as a widow's man. That will provide you with a small amount of income, although it will not be much.'

'A "widow's man," sir?'

'A widow's man is a fictitious seaman who is kept on the books to provide support for the widow of a man killed at sea, beyond whatever pay he has due him. It is intended to keep a family from ending up in the workhouse when their income stops, hopefully until they can find another means of support. Gilbert Godfroy was a widow's man.'

I saw this name on *Agamemnon*'s books when I was Nelson's clerk, but it would never have occurred to me to think that he was not an actual person. One day not long before Nelson transferred command to *Captain*, I came across his name in an entry in the surgeon's log: *D; f*. It indicated that the man had died of fever. When I ask him about this, Nelson explains:

'It is not exactly a secret practice, but it is decidedly unauthorised. A widow's man might transfer from one ship to another with a commander, but it is better to either leave him to the ship's new officer, or kill him off and establish another. As *Agamemnon* would be paid off when she reached England, it was a convenient time to do for Gilbert Godfroy. The pay accrued against his name would be removed to another account, if there was no beneficiary.'

'To think that I kept your books for months and never knew anything about that,' I say.

'Going forward, I will list Ned Buckley in the logs as one of my allotted servants; he will transfer with me if I change vessels. But it will only work for as long as I am in command, so we must make haste to find you a livelihood.'

'Captain Miller said that there is talk of making you an admiral.'

His smile is slow, but it touches his entire face. He is positively radiant. 'An admiral can be made redundant more quickly than a commodore, and certainly more-so than a captain,' he tells me. 'But it is the culmination of a dream I have had all my life.'

Three days later I sit in the captain's barge with Commodore Nelson as we are rowed back across Lagos Bay to where *Captain* rests at anchor. Like the two of us, *Captain* is much improved, but she is not completely whole yet.

I can now move my left arm well enough to put it through a sleeve. It is not easy, and very uncomfortable, but now that it is no longer bandaged to my torso I can dress more like a fully functional person, and less like an invalid. I still must carry it in a sling across my body, but it is a relief to wear clothes. Having worn men's clothes for so long, I am not sure about this gown, however.

The 'rig' that Commodore Nelson has provided for me is of a high-waisted style, with fitted sleeves and a rose-coloured ribbon under my bosom, in a pale-sprigged cotton muslin that is almost too thin for the end of February, even in Portugal. 'It is a style that is very popular in Naples now, I am told,' he informs me in a note accompanying the clothes.

Popular perhaps, but I have had to open the seam of the left sleeve to fit it over my dressings, and tie it closed with ribbons. Nate-the-loblolly-boy has proved himself quite handy with a needle.

I was also provided with a pair of short stays, but I cannot wear them because of the bandages. It is not as if I need them;

there is nothing for them to contain. But I feel nearly as undressed as I did when wearing only a shift. I was more fully clothed in Nelson's old banyan. Thankfully, some thoughtful person included a soft rose-coloured shawl.

The commodore is fully turned out in his undress coat and impeccable white small-clothes, and he looks magnificent. He moves almost as briskly as he normally would, but I see him press his hand briefly against his side as he steps from the boarding ladder into the stern of the barge. They might have lowered him into the boat as they did me, but he would not hear of it. As for me, I could not negotiate the boarding ladder with only one arm.

At my feet in their new flat slippers is the rush basket, from which occasional rumblings can be heard. One-Eyed Jack is indignant about being confined to its depths, but he allowed me to put him in it and close the lid without subjecting me to the need for more sutures. I wondered briefly how Captain Miller got him in there the first time.

We have not seen nor spoken to one another since the interview in *Irresistible*'s great cabin, and for a moment we sit side by side, neither of us speaking. When we do, we both begin at once.

'How are you…'

'I hope you are…'

He smiles. 'You speak first.'

'You are looking very much restored, sir. I am pleased to see it.'

'I think that I am almost as good as new again. As long as I don't do anything too strenuous, I am nearly free from pain.'

'So no more throwing yourself into the enemy's main chains,' I suggest.

'Heard about that, did you?'

'I did. Just after I heard about how you jumped from the cathead onto the *San Nicolas's* quarter-gallery. One would almost think you could fly.'

'Perhaps I could, for a moment. I have been subsequently grounded, I am afraid. I have got my wings clipped.'

'You will fly again. I am sure of it.' *But I will not be here to see it,* I think sadly.

'I do hope you are improving as quickly,' he says solicitously. 'The colour of the shawl suits you. When I saw the gown, I was not sure... but it looks lovely on you.'

'Thank you, sir. I feel a bit like I am wearing my nightclothes,' I confess in an undertone.

'I thought that I would find it odd to see you in a gown,' he admits. 'But it does not look odd at all.'

'Would you find it as easy to adapt to Tom Allen in a gown?' I say lightly.

'Mr Allen? With his noxious pipe? I think he would look better in yellow.'

He looks at my astonished face and laughs.

Chapter Thirty-One

The day is blowing and wet, and the sea is choppy, and I feel like a proper idiot in my cotton gown. I wish I were wearing my good swanskin breeches and wool coat. But my coat was destroyed by whatever nearly took my arm; and ladies do not wear breeches.

The launch bumps against the pier in almost the same place where they pulled Captain Spencer's body out of the water in December, and I shudder. The coxswain, thinking that I am cold, says as he steadies the boat for me, 'Here, you'll be able to get warm soon; he'll take you to a nice tearoom, miss,' then he hands me up to Commodore Nelson.

'You look nearly as damp as I am,' he says. 'Thank God it is not cold, too.'

He takes my arm and escorts me to the harbour master's office, where he retrieves an umbrella, then walks with me to a pleasant, pretty room where he orders tea and sandwiches.

'I did not know about this place,' I tell him, looking around at the cloth-covered tables and boxes of flowers that adorn the windows.

'I would not have expected you to,' he says. 'It is where officers bring their ladies.'

On such a wet and gloomy day as this, there are few tables occupied, but I see that he is right. The tables that do have people seated at them each contain a single couple, bent low over their meals, speaking in conspiratorial murmurs.

'It is perfect for our purpose, and they serve excellent tea,' he continues.

Unceremoniously, he takes my left hand in its sling in his, and gently slides a ring onto my finger. It is delicately filigreed silver, with a faceted, pale rose-coloured stone.

'You are now *Mrs* Eleanor Anson,' he tells me.

I look at the ring. It is not showy and expensive like the ring that Richard gave me; the ring that I sold at the earliest opportunity. But I immediately like it more. It is understated and elegant in its simplicity.

'What is the stone?' I ask him.

'I asked the jeweller, but I forget what he called it. I chose it because I liked how it looked, not because it was particularly fashionable. The stone reminded me of your shawl.'

'I like it, too,' I assure him. He seems stiff and slightly awkward, and I wonder what is coming next.

What comes next happens to be the tea, and a plate of sandwiches. I pour his cup and add just the right amount of milk. It has become almost second-nature to me.

'Nell,' he says, 'you do not have to do that.'

'How many more opportunities do you think I will get?' I try to say lightly, but the truth behind this question makes my heart sore.

He clears his throat, sips his tea, and clears his throat again.

'I have found rooms for you. They are only two, but it has a private garden, and the owner is an elderly woman who is delighted to have a respectable officer's wife renting them. She apparently does not see much better than I do, but the ring seemed like a necessary accessory. She has no objection to cats, so One-Eyed Jack is welcome. Captain Miller is afraid that if you leave him on board, someone will drown him to silence him. I shall take you there after we eat.'

He still looks uncomfortable. 'I told her that you were the wife of one of my officers, but I suspect that she thinks this is a fiction. I believe she thinks you are my mistress.'

No fool this one, then. She knows the kinds of fictions naval officers spin. 'It does not matter to me what she believes, as long as she does not abuse me for it.'

Now he looks sheepish. 'I don't anticipate that she will. It is said that she was once the mistress of an admiral.' He rubs his breast unconsciously. 'And not just any admiral, but the commander-in-chief.'

'It sounds perfect,' I say.

The apartment *is* perfect. It is just off a well-travelled street, in a quiet square. Compared to its neighbours, the house is tiny.

'The landlady lives upstairs,' he says, as he unlocks the house door.

There is a front room and a bedchamber, both modestly furnished but clean and neat. The bedchamber has a door of glass panes flanked by two full-height windows that look out into the garden, allowing light and air into the room. 'I thought that this was particularly nice,' Nelson comments. 'There is a drapery here, so that you can draw it across at night if the weather is chill. If you open both windows and the door, all three at once, it is almost as if the room and the garden are one.'

I look out into the tiny garden. It is no wider than the house, but it is paved in a miniature labyrinth pattern, with ornamental trees and flowering plants in planter boxes. 'Mrs Bowling has a balcony up there,' he says, nodding above us with his head. 'She tells me that she likes to sit there of an evening, but she assures me that she will not use it to spy upon you.

'The rent is paid for the next eight weeks,' he continues. 'There is a woman whom I spoke to who runs a... well, a mantua-making shop is perhaps too grand a description for the shop, but it makes ladies' things. I told her of your skill with a needle, and your impeccable record-keeping. She is very interested to meet you, but I told her that it might be some weeks before you had the use of both your hands.'

'What did you tell her happened to me?' I will need to know what fictions I will have to maintain.

He rubs his breast again. 'The truth, essentially; that you were aboard one of the British ships during the recent battle and were injured. I did not tell her about the gun,' he adds. 'She thinks you were assisting the wounded.'

We return to the front room. The hearth is cold and will do double duty as a kitchen hearth and sitting room fire, but there is a pair of comfortable chairs that can be positioned in front of it, and the commodore pulls them together.

'The lease is in your name, not mine. I have told your landlady and your potential employer that your husband's name is Scott Anson, and that he is a British naval officer. I hope that it will not be necessary to go into any more detail than that. In time, you will receive an official letter informing you that Scott Anson is dead. Then you will be a respectable widow.' He looks anxiously around the room. 'I realise that it is a little spartan. I hope it is alright.'

'It is more than alright,' I assure him. 'I am delighted with it. Do not forget, sir, that I once carried everything I owned on my back and lived in a canvas tent with five other men.'

'I would like to forget that, actually,' he says. His brows knit, and he rubs his breast once more.

'Are you having pain there again?'

He seems surprised at himself. 'Not... no. I think it is indigestion, actually. I have been preoccupied and haven't really given it much notice.' He stifles a hiccough.

'Sir, you must tell Mr Allen and Mr Lenstock to look after you better, or I shall want to know why not.'

'Sometimes I think you sound just like Frank Lepee.'

'I learnt from him, after all. How is he...?'

'Not very well, I'm afraid. I am trying to make arrangements for him at Greenwich. I have not seen him, but I am told that he gets worse rather than better.'

'I am very sorry.'

He is silent, looking pensively into the empty hearth. After a moment he says, 'I shall take you to meet Miss St Clair next. She is the daughter of an army officer and is well-connected in Gibraltar. She is also the sole-proprietress of the dressmaking shop, and she is quite taken with the idea of having a partner to share the running of it.'

He looks at me now. 'I feel as though I am casting you adrift. You will be alone here in Gibraltar, at least initially. Miss St Clair will make sure that you are introduced to the proper people. And although I shall be back here infrequently... if at all... if you ever require my assistance, I implore you to write to me.'

'I will be alright, sir. One-Eyed Jack and I, we always land on our feet.'

He rises from his chair and straightens his coat, then takes the house key from his pocket and hands it to me. 'This one is for the street door, and this is the key to these rooms. It also locks the garden door. The apartment is yours to occupy as soon as you are ready. I presume that you will want time to say farewell to some of your shipmates...

simply tell me when you want them, and I shall have your things brought here.'

He clears his throat nervously again. 'I hope you will take the opportunity to purchase some things from Miss St Clair's shop. I have established a line of credit for you. You must have more than one gown; even I know this. I am informed it by my wife, who is not extravagant by any means; so if she suggests that you should have three or four, buy six.'

Chapter Thirty-Two

The rain falls gently and steadily on the lemon tree, the olive, and the damask roses. The air is cool for the end of May, but I have the window open so that the smell of the rain scents the room. It is early evening, but my work at the shop for the day is done. Nancy St Clair will mind the hours after supper.

It is a good partnership, and I am grateful for it. My wounds are almost completely healed, but the scars will never go away. Miss St Clair has taken this as a personal challenge. I will never be able to wear the daringly low bodices and sleeveless evening gowns that are becoming the height of fashion, but together she and I have created gowns of the same silhouette, incorporating chemisettes and fichus that disguise the scarred flesh on my left breast. A gauzy, draped shawl on my left shoulder hides the scars on my arm. It is not as if I attend evening entertainments often; I don't. But thanks to Nancy St Clair, I look quite respectable when I do.

Remarkably, my breasts have filled out again. They will never be large, but they are once again the same size that they were when I married Richard. 'Healthful food, rest, and moderate exercise are all you needed, my dear,' says Mrs Bowling. 'How your husband could have let you get into such a state, I will never know. Women should never go to sea. But he will be more than pleased to see you again, I am sure.' She gives me a wink that I pretend to ignore.

I have not seen Admiral Nelson since the day he brought me here. He is a Rear-Admiral of the Blue now, and as such I am sure he is even busier than he was as a commodore. I have received a few notes from him wishing me well, with vague promises that he will call on me the next time he is in Gibraltar. I have replied with the assurance that I will always welcome him, but I do not place much stock in these exchanges. We have moved on.

Still, I miss him every day.

It was more bitter than sweet to bid farewell to the men I have spent so many years with, but despite their good-natured acceptance of my changed status, our relationships can never be the same. Tom Allen and James Lenstock have both written to me, letters detailing something of what it is like to serve an admiral. I have assured them both that if they do not take good care of him, I shall have to put my breeches back on.

John Roberts writes to me regularly, each letter better than the last. In my last package, I sent him a copy of *Peregrine Pickle*. I am looking forward to hearing his comments about it.

One-Eyed Jack is stalking a dove in the garden. He has adapted seamlessly to life ashore. He comes and goes from the garden as he pleases, but somehow he always finds his way in through the window in the middle of the night to curl up by my side, his claws flexing against my belly. It is comforting. Despite Jack's difficult character, he is a loyal, if possessive, companion.

I watch as he pounces just a moment too late. The dove relocates to the olive tree and sits there wittering at him. I have discovered that he is not good at catching birds. Having only one eye must affect his depth perception. Perhaps rats are slower.

A stronger burst of rain patters on the garden tiles and shakes the leaves of the trees. Someone is tapping on the street door.

I have visitors even less frequently than I go to evening entertainments. The person I have seen most often here is the doctor who has been overseeing my recovery from my wounds. But I do not expect him tonight, and Mrs Bowling, of course, has her own key.

The visitor is a naval officer, water dripping from his hat. When he lifts his head, I see that it is Nelson.

'Good heavens! Admiral!'

'I almost thought I'd come here for naught,' he says. 'No one answered.'

'People rarely come to visit me, except the doctor, and Mrs Bowling usually answers the door even then. Come inside; the fire is almost out, but I will build it up again.'

I take his hat from him and shake the worst of the water from it. His coat is wet as well. 'Did you have no umbrella?'

'I did not expect to need one.'

'Let me take your coat, sir. I still have your old banyan; I shall get it.' I help him out of the damp coat and hang it by the hearth. 'I had meant to return this to you...' I say, getting the banyan from the wardrobe.

'Do you wear it?' I nod. 'Then by all means, keep it. I thought it looked nicer on you, anyway.'

He takes a seat in one of the chairs as I stir up the fire and put another stick of wood on it.

'How are you, Nell?' he asks quietly.

'I am well, sir. My injuries are almost completely healed. The scars are not pretty, but they are not important. I still have the use of my arm. I hope that you are well?'

'Well enough. It appears that when I was hurt at Cape St. Vincent, it tore something in my belly... I forget precisely what the fleet physician called it. I had a cough some weeks ago, and my belly swelled up again. They tell me that it forced a part of my bowel into the tear in my… whatever it is called. I can apparently expect that it will happen again from time to time. But it is not important, either.'

It is distressing to me that he has been ill. 'Oh, sir… is there anything I can do?'

'First of all, if you must call me "sir," then you must follow it with "Horatio".'

'Sir… Horatio? You have been knighted!'

'Knight Companion of the Order of the Bath.' There is the slow smile that I love so well.

'Oh… oh, I wish that I had known! I should have liked to celebrate with something, but all I have is a bottle of Madeira. The doctor told me that if I was to drink wine, it should be fortified wine,' I explain.

'I would be honoured to share a glass of Madeira with you to toast my investiture.'

I find the bottle and two cordial glasses in the pantry cupboard and pour a glass for each of us.

'The King,' he proposes.

'The King,' I respond. Today, he drains the glass.

'Now I must refill it,' I say, filling his glass to the brim again, 'because I have the next toast. Sir Horatio: long may he sail!'

Feeling reckless and just a little like Ned Buckley again, this time I drain my glass.

'Fill it again,' he requests. When I have refilled my glass, he says, 'To Nell, the prettiest man in the Royal Navy.' He drinks down his glass.

I am blushing and a little giddy. I rarely have more than a partial glass in the evening anymore. I resolve to sip conservatively from this point on. I do not want to embarrass myself.

'Sometimes, in the evening, I miss Ned Buckley,' he says. 'I have tried having stimulating conversations with the chaplain, but he and I simply do not share the same interests, and neither of us cares to debate theology at the end of the day. At least I can play chess with Mr Castang.'

'I hope you cannot beat him as easily as you used to beat me.'

'Oh, sometimes I do,' he says.

His glass is empty, and I refill it. There is but an inch left in the bottom of the bottle, but I do not intend to drink any more.

'Have you had supper, sir... Sir Horatio?' When he shakes his head, I say, 'Then you must let me offer you something.'

'I did not come here to eat your food and drink your wine, Nell.'

'May I remind you that it is *your* food and *your* wine, Admiral? You made it possible for me to have a home, and employment, and society. The least I can do is offer you bread and cheese.'

I slice bread and cheese and a bit of a cold joint. 'I hope this will suffice. I could always make you eggs, or porridge...'

'The last time you made me porridge, we both ended up with a dreadful fever. It was not the fault of the porridge, but I think I shall forgo it. This is quite enough.'

I sit across the table and watch him eat. He eats sparingly, as always.

'Tell me, how did things work out with the mantua shop?'

'Better than I could have hoped, sir. Miss St Clair and I work very well together, and we enjoy each other's company. Between the two of us the work is not at all tiresome, and we now have three sempstresses, so we can concentrate on fancy work. We have gained some new custom since I joined her, as well.' I stand and show him my gown.

'We designed this gown together. The challenge is always, in my case, to respect the current tastes but hide the wreckage of my arm and breast.'

He asks me to turn full circle. 'I am not very knowledge-able about ladies' fashions,' he says, 'but I like this. It is lovely. One would not suspect that there was anything amiss with your arm or your… breast.' He stumbles over this word, and when I turn to him again, he is blushing like a boy.

I remember attending him in his fever, the distraction of his breast, and the soft, fair hairs that grew there. Now I am suddenly shy as well. I look down at my slippers, searching for composure.

He stands up from the table. 'I did not intend…'

'No, please do not apologise,' I say softly.

'I came because we are targeting Spanish shipping outside the Gut, and it may be some time before I return to Gibraltar. I did not want to leave without seeing you again.'

'I am exceedingly glad that you came.'

He hesitates. 'Nell, I…'

I look up and meet his eyes. They are wide and sober and somehow bewildered, and immediately I am lost in them.

He does not take his eyes from mine as he reaches for my cheek and brushes it with the back of his hand. Then he kisses me.

His lips are soft and yielding and they ask permission, unlike my husband's, which were thin and aggressive and demanding. He stops, questioning.

'Again,' I breathe.

It is delicious, and more intoxicating than the wine we drank earlier. I have never in my life kissed a man earnestly in return, but I am kissing him, and I do not want it to end.

His hand cradles my head, and I feel the pins come loose; my hair cascades over his hand.

He slips my gown off of my left shoulder and traces the scar lightly with his fingers, then he kisses it tenderly. I have never felt anything so electrifying.

'May I see the rest?' he murmurs.

My bodice closes with a draw-cord; as I untie it, the gown slips down my arms, revealing the tops of my breasts above the cups of my short stays.

'Beautiful,' he whispers. He kisses the scar on my breast, and I think that I will melt.

'Take them off of me,' I tell him. The stays lace between my breasts with a ribbon, and I take his hand and lay it on the ribbon. He pulls it slowly and undoes the spiral lacing. I shiver, feeling reckless and afraid simultaneously. It is a similar feeling to the way I felt when I first came under fire in battle, and that makes it almost familiar.

When he lifts the stays from my body, I undo the buttons of my gown and it falls in a puddle of sheer cotton voile to the floor. I am clothed in nothing but my shift.

'Take off your shirt,' I implore him. 'Please.'

He slides his arms out of the banyan, and it drops to the floor to join my gown. He unfastens his stock and neckband, and the ruffle at his throat opens to reveal his collarbone. As I did once before, a lifetime ago, I unbutton his waistcoat and help him draw the shirt over his head.

I stroke the soft hairs on his breast with my index finger, and he shivers in turn. When I kiss them, he moans. His beautiful, sculpted breast rises and falls with his breathing, like a tide crashing and receding beneath his ribs.

I rest my head against his breast and listen to the pounding of his heart. I can feel his arousal against my belly, but unlike in the past, I do not want to run away. Instead, this evidence of his desire kindles a bewildering excitement within me.

I had never known that it could be like this. Every stroke of his fingers, every touch of his lips is like velvet. Every one of my senses is heightened to a degree I have never experienced before. Yet when he looks longingly at the door to the bedchamber, my heart flutters like a frightened bird. I want this. But I do not know if I can go through with it.

His lips find my nipple and I gasp at the way the sensation courses throughout my entire body.

I grasp his hand and take him to my bed.

I brace myself when we are both naked beneath the bedclothes. I have never before been completely naked with a man. And my body knows what happens next.

He strokes my hair, my cheek. 'Not yet,' he murmurs. 'You are brave, my darling girl.'

He kisses and caresses me; my arms, my breasts, my belly; until my body relaxes again. I trace his breast with my lips and warm his nipple with my breath.

I have never explored a man's body. It is an incredible adventure. I kiss his flat abdomen, his navel, and the line of fair hair that leads downward towards his sex. I hear his breath catch and speed up.

When he slips inside, it is as if he was designed to be there. My body does not resist him. He fits like a key in a lock.

He does not move right away, and when he does his strokes are deep and slow. I can feel him to the core of me. When he begins to move faster, my body matches his rhythm. It is as if we have ceased to be two people; the beating of our hearts and the pulse of our blood synchronised into a single organism.

An electric sensation begins somewhere near the back of my knees, growing and travelling upwards until it explodes in the centre of me. I cry aloud and feel him release, and the world is full of stars.

We sleep, and at some point, after it is dark, we wake and couple again. This time it is more urgent, and exciting in a different way. I respond to him the way *Agamemnon* responded to her helm. I will follow him anywhere.

Nelson sneezes, and I wake. He sneezes again, and I know immediately what is wrong. I reach for the candle and light it.

One-Eyed Jack sits squarely in the middle of Nelson's chest, looking him in the face. He reaches out with a paw and pats Nelson's cheek, and Nelson flinches.

'Sorry, Jack, old boy.' I scoop the cat off the admiral and toss him out the window, then latch it. He will be in high dudgeon tomorrow, but he will just have to forgive me. Or find another person to terrorise. 'This time, *I* win.'

I slip back beneath the bedclothes against his warm body. 'I'm sorry,' I say, 'now he will probably sit outside under the window and howl.'

'I can ignore him,' Nelson says, giving me a sleepy kiss.

We wake in the morning before the sky begins to lighten and come together one last time. It is different yet again, more tender and almost melancholy, but no less wonderful for it. Afterwards, we lie nested together as the darkness fades away.

'On the night before Cape St Vincent, when I came so close to kissing you, I was terrified that I was becoming something that I didn't understand, compelled to do something that I deplored. I had believed that I could never be so unprincipled and criminal as to approach a lad for…

personal gratification. So when I experienced the desire to kiss you—a young man whom I knew had been assaulted in just such a way—I was disgusted and afraid of myself,' Nelson tells me, as we watch the garden taking shape in the morning sunlight. One-Eyed Jack is nowhere to be seen; I imagine he is sulking somewhere.

'When I was told that you were not a young man, but a young woman, I was so relieved and conflicted that I had to shut myself in the quarter-gallery to be sick. It did not help my injury any," he adds dryly.

'I am sorry,' I say softly.

'I knew when I saw you again that my desire had not changed. It had simply been validated. That is why I stayed away for so many weeks. If I could simply have gone away… but I could not.'

I rest my temple against his breast, hearing again the comforting beat of his heart. 'I was afraid that our friendship had been destroyed that night. I thought that you were afraid of *me*, and I did not know if I could bear it. If that was to be the case, I did not care if a cannonball took off my head. I had expected it for years, anyway.'

He sighs; his breath feathers my hair. 'I wish that I could stay just one more day. It seems like such a brief resolution, after so many years… But the fleet is leaving today, and I must go with them.'

I make a breakfast of bread soaked in eggs and milk and cooked in a skillet; we both agree that porridge is bad luck. I grate a nutmeg and some brown sugar over the top and serve it with coffee. I know well how he takes his coffee.

After breakfast he returns his banyan to me. 'Keep it. I have the other, and knowing that it is here will give me an excuse to return, perhaps.'

'I hope you will never feel that you need an excuse.'

He puts on his coat and picks up his hat, then sets it on the table again. He puts his hands on my shoulders, the way he did when I was Ned.

'Goodbye, Eleanor Anson. My Nell.'

'Goodbye, Admiral. Sir Horatio.'

He shakes his head. 'Just Horatio.' He kisses me one last time.

Epilogue

The church bells are ringing... ringing. Ringing for victory; for Victory. *For the victorious dead.*

'Mother! Mother, the fleet is in the bay—you can see the ships! If you come with me, I will show you; you can see HMS Victory! *The governor says that there is to be a grand celebration! Mother... Why are you crying?'*

'I am crying for someone who has died, Ned.'

'Don't weep, Mother. The prayer book tells us not to be sorry, as men without hope, for them that sleep in God.'

'Precocious child, come here. Let me hold you for a moment, if you are not too big for such things.'

He embraces me, his thin arms around my waist, his soft, unruly hair, so like his father's, against my breast. My son. 'How old are you now?'

'You know this, Mother. I was born on St Valentine's Day, 1798. I am seven.'

'Then you are old enough to understand: I am not crying because I am sorry for the man who has died, Ned. I am crying because I loved him, and I am sorry for myself.'

'Was he on one of the ships?'

'Yes, my love.'

'Did he know my father?'

'Yes; he knew your father very well.'

'*Did I ever meet him?*'

'*No, Edmund Nelson Anson, my beloved boy. He never knew about you.*'

ENDNOTES

On 24 July 1797, approximately eight weeks after the close of this story, Rear-Admiral Sir Horatio Nelson lost his right arm in the siege of Santa Cruz de Tenerife and was sent home to England. He would not return to the Mediterranean until April 1798, when he pursued the French fleet to Aboukir Bay and defeated them at the momentous Battle of the Nile, on 1 August 1798. He suffered a severe head injury in the battle and convalesced in Naples at the home of Sir William Hamilton and his wife Emma, Lady Hamilton. It was the beginning of a relationship that has defined Lord Nelson ever since.

Stylistically I have retained some eighteenth-century grammatical quirks, which may have appeared incorrect. However, for instance, some people (and Lord Nelson in particular) did say, 'if you was', rather than, 'if you were'. And Nelson consistently referred to his stepson Josiah Nisbet as his son-in-law, which was not uncommon in this period. If you think about it, it makes sense: a stepson is your son by marriage, thereby 'in-law'.

I hope that readers have not been offended by attitudes expressed in the book towards Black people and people of homosexual orientation. I feel compelled to defend my characters a little; I've grown fond of them over the course of our journey together. I have tried to be true to the prevalent attitudes of the period as much as possible, and the characters' opinions reflect that. They do not reflect my own beliefs or opinions. I do think it rather unfair to judge people who lived more than two hundred years ago by standards that it has taken us—sadly—over two hundred years to develop, and I apologise if *that* gives offense to anyone. I hope we have become more enlightened.

I have found little evidence of malice or malignant discrimination toward Black sailors in the Royal Navy of the time. There is apparently little evidence to be had. The Royal Navy was far more likely to record a recruit's nationality; almost never did they record his race. Men of all nationalities and races, from Lascars to Americans, served as ratings in the Royal Navy; and evidence suggests that they were all treated more or less equally on the basis of their skill and character. Another sailor might have as much cause to dislike an Irishman indiscriminately as a Black man. And we won't even touch on the French. Some Frenchmen served in the Royal Navy during this period, but they were considered unreliable. (I wonder why.)

Homosexual behaviour was far more subject to suspicion than race, for a host of reasons that still hold true in some societies today. Without going into all the reasons it was considered abhorrent, I will observe that in the Royal Navy what was particularly condemned was men in authority using their position to force subordinates to provide them with sexual gratification. In a characteristic injustice of the age, however, ratings convicted of sodomy were far more likely to be hanged than an officer. An officer convicted was seldom hanged. He was booted ignominiously out of the service, never to return, and forfeited his rank and any entitlement to half-pay or pension. The trial of Captain Sawyer of the *Blanche* frigate in 1796 is a case in point.

Apologies to the men whose role as clerk Ned usurped for the purposes of this story. It is the nature of writing fiction around actual people that someone will have evidence to be able to say, 'It didn't happen like that.' And of course, they will be right.

There is no evidence at all that Horatio Nelson ever fathered a child with anyone other than Emma Hamilton. However, it is not impossible...

I also do not have any reason to believe that he was actually allergic to cats.

If this is your first encounter with Lord Nelson and you would like to know more, there are any number of excellent biographies that have been written about him. He was an extraordinary commander, and a fascinating man. I love him, in part, because he wore his decorations on his breast, and his heart on his sleeve.

I am indebted to the research of Peter Goodwin, Andrew Lambert, and N.A.M. Rodger for providing insight into the Royal Navy and its ships in the eighteenth century, to B.R. Burg on the subject of sexual misconduct and courts-martial, and to John Sugden and Carola Oman for their biographies of Nelson. And of course, to the words of Nelson himself. There are seven volumes of his letters and dispatches, and I have read every one.

A note on style, because this stuff does matter when you're a writer—not so much to a reader. We went back and forth numerous times regarding how to refer to ships' names in this work. Because my characters are not writing papers about ships, I tried to capture how people tend to *speak* about ships. And we speak differently about them if they are a ship we have a 'relationship' with, as opposed to a ship we've never 'met.'

In the end, I (nominally) used The 1805 Club's style guide, which, admittedly, is intended for *writing* about ships. But that will explain why I do not use the article when my characters discuss ships. I confess that having not been there, I don't actually know how people in the eighteenth century referred to ships when speaking of them, only how they wrote about them.

Many thanks to my marvellous editor, Jessica Ellis-Wilson, for her patience with my style choices, nautical terminology, antique words, and eighteenth-century grammar conventions; to my dear friend Rita Kogler Carver for her cover design concept; and to Geoff Hunt, P.P.R.S.M.A., for permission to use his painting of HMS *Agamemnon* on the cover. Also to everyone who read this work in progress and made inspired comments.

Special thanks are due to Graham Capel, of The Nelson Society, and Capt. John Rodgaard, USN, Ret., of The 1805 Club, who read my first attempt to write about Lord Nelson and allowed me to fail with dignity. Without your supportive words, I might never again have picked up my pen.

Finally, thank you to my boys, Jordan and Paul, who didn't laugh at me; and to Steve, who gave me the freedom to try my hand at writing.

Any errors are entirely my own.

Selected Glossary of Terms

I will refrain from getting too technical with these terms. If you would like a more comprehensive definition, I highly recommend *A Sea of Words,* by Dean King and John Hattendorf. They are Navy men and scholars of this period of naval history; I am merely an interpreter.

ague: The cold phase, with chills and shivering, that precedes a fever. Also a generic term for a malarial fever.

beakhead: The foremost part of the upper deck, forward of the forecastle (fo'c'sle). Where the latrines (heads) for ratings and marines were located.

bivouac: When a noun, it refers to a temporary camp without tents or shelters. When a verb, it is to bed down in a location without shelter.

boatswain/bosun: The officer responsible for the ship's rigging, sails, boats, and anchors. Also responsible for discipline.

cable: The rope to which the ship's anchor is attached. Also, a measurement of distance: in the Royal Navy, equal to 100 fathoms/one-tenth of a nautical mile/approximately 200 yards/185 meters.

carronade: A short-barrelled, short-range gun, capable of firing a heavy ball a relatively short distance.

cathead: A beam projecting from the ship's bow, used to raise and to hold the anchor away from the side of the ship.

Charleville: A French military firelock.

clodhopper: A landsman.

clyster: Enema.

companionway: A ladder leading between decks.

corvette: A ship-rigged vessel, smaller than a frigate but larger than a sloop-of-war.

crank: Unstable.

dismast: A ship that has lost her masts has been dismasted.

dolphin: Part of the cannon that was used to lift the gun onto or off its carriage, so called because they were once cast in the shape of dolphins.

(to) drift to leeward: A ship that is 'drifting to leeward' has failed to hold her course.

fag: To work to the point of exhaustion; exhausted.

fighting top: A platform constructed at the junction of the lower mast and the topmast, where sharpshooters were stationed.

frigate: A ship-rigged vessel with a single, covered gun deck carrying more than 20 guns.

holystone: A rectangular stone, about the size of a Bible, which was used with sand and salt water to scrub the deck.

housewife: Sewing kit.

howitzer: A field gun which could fire explosive shells (as opposed to inert projectiles).

knot: A measure of speed in nautical miles per hour.

(gold) lace: Woven bands of metallic thread used to decorate military uniforms.

larboard: The left-hand side of the ship, now called the *port* side.

leaguer: A cask for storing water, holding somewhere in the vicinity of 150 gallons.

leeward: Relative to a particular reference point, for example, an object, the direction downwind; sheltered from the wind.

linstock: A staff holding a lit match for the firing of cannon. When firing artillery that utilised a gun lock, the linstock was backup, in case the flint didn't spark.

main chains: The chains are where the lower shrouds of the mast are secured to the outer side of the ship. They are referred to by the name of the mast they're supporting, in this case, the mainmast.

(ship's) master: The officer responsible for navigation and sailing.

materiel: Military supplies and equipment.

megrim: Migraine headache.

mess: In a military context, a group of men who dined together. Also, a dining place, *e.g.,* the Midshipmen's mess

mole: A man-made pier or breakwater; also, the harbour thus created.

mortar: A piece of short field artillery which shot a shell, frequently used as a siege gun. It shot a higher trajectory than a long gun.

out-of-kelter: Not in the best condition.

picquet (piquet, picket): A man or group of men stationed ahead of, or on the perimeter of, a position, to act as lookout.

post-captain: An officer who has received a commission to command a post ship, *i.e.,* a ship of more than 20 guns.

QM/quartermaster: A military officer responsible for providing quarters (accommodations), supplies, clothing, and food. Also, a naval petty officer responsible for assisting with signals, navigation, and steering.

quarters/quarter bill/beat to quarters: Battle stations. The quarter-bill was the list of each crew member's assigned battle station. 'Beat to quarters' was the drum cadence that called the crew to battle stations. More commonly, accommodations.

ratings: Classification, by skill, of seamen not holding a warrant or commission, most notably Ordinary Seamen, Able Seamen, Petty Officers, Landsmen, and Boys.

ratlines: Component of the rigging: horizontal lines attached to the vertical shrouds, used as a ladder.

redoubt: A temporary fortification, often of earthworks.

(to) sail like a haystack: As best as I can determine, this referred to Thames hay barges, which sailed rather slowly.

sempstress: Seamstress.

shrouds: Standing rigging that supports the masts to larboard and starboard.

small-clothes: Essentially, underclothes. An eighteenth century man without coat or waistcoat was considered undressed. In that context, breeches could be considered small-clothes.

starboard: The right-hand side of the ship. The opposite of *larboard.*

stays: On a ship, stays support the masts fore and aft. On a female person, they support something else (although during the Regency period, some fashionable men wore them, too).

subaltern: An officer in the British army below the rank of captain.

tops'l/topsail: In a ship-rigged vessel, the sail between the course, and the topgallant.

truck: On a naval or garrison gun, trucks are the wheels of the gun carriage. In the ship's rigging, a truck allows flags to be run up the mast.

warrant officer: An officer who held a warrant, rather than a commission. Commissions were the purview of the Admiralty, while warrants were issued by the Navy Board. Warrant officers included the master, boatswain, purser, and medical officer.

watch/watch bill: A 24-hour period was divided into seven watches, five of which were four hours long, and two, the dog-watches, which were two hours long. The dog-watches served to rotate men through each watch; without them a man would stand the same watches every day. The watch bill listed the rotation of the men through the watches.

windward: Relative to a particular reference point, *e.g.,* an object, the direction from which the wind is blowing, upwind.